Praise for Ted Chiang

"Confirms that blending science and fine art at this length can produce touching works, tales as intimate as our own blood cells, with the structural strength of just-discovered industrial alloys."
—*The Seattle Times*

"Summarizing these stories does not do justice to Chiang's talent. . . . Chiang derides lazy thinking, weasels it out of its hiding place, and leaves it cowering." —*The Washington Post*

"Ted Chiang's stories mirror the process of scientific discovery: complex ideas emerge from the measured, methodical accumulation of information until epiphany strikes. . . . The best science fiction inspires awe for the natural properties of the universe; it renders the fundamentals of science poignant and affecting. Mr. Chiang's writing manages all of this." —*The Economist*

"Throughout all his work, though no more so than in 'Story of Your Life,' you can feel his months of removing sentences from his stories. Perhaps that he writes so little does something good for him, or maybe it's just that he doesn't write enough." —*The Millions*

"The stories range widely in time, subject and style but are united by a patient but ruthless fascination with the limits of knowledge."
—*Los Angeles Times*

TED CHIANG

Arrival

Ted Chiang was born in Port Jefferson, New York, and holds a degree in computer science. In 1989 he attended the Clarion Science Fiction and Fantasy Writers' Workshop. His fiction has won four Hugo, four Nebula, and four Locus Awards, and he is the recipient of the John W. Campbell Award for Best New Writer and the Theodore Sturgeon Memorial Award. His story "Story of Your Life" is the basis for the major motion picture *Arrival*. The book *Stories of Your Life and Others* has been translated into twenty-one languages. He lives near Seattle, Washington.

Arrival

Arrival

Ted Chiang

Originally published as *Stories of Your Life and Others*

VINTAGE BOOKS
A Division of Penguin Random House LLC
New York

FIRST VINTAGE BOOKS MOVIE TIE-IN EDITION, OCTOBER 2016

Copyright © 2002 by Ted Chiang

Vintage Books Movie Tie-In ISBN: 978-0-525-43367-5
eBook ISBN: 978-0-525-43368-2

www.vintagebooks.com

Printed in the United States of America
10   9   8   7   6   5

*In memory of
Brian Chiang
and
Jenna Felice.*

Contents

Arrival

Tower of Babylon

Were the tower to be laid down across the plain of Shinar, it would be two days' journey to walk from one end to the other. While the tower stands, it takes a full month and a half to climb from its base to its summit, if a man walks unburdened. But few men climb the tower with empty hands; the pace of most men is slowed by the cart of bricks that they pull behind them. Four months pass between the day a brick is loaded onto a cart, and the day it is taken off to form a part of the tower.

Hillalum had spent all his life in Elam, and knew Babylon only as a buyer of Elam's copper. The copper ingots were carried on boats that traveled down the Karun to the Lower Sea, headed for the Euphrates. Hillalum and the other miners traveled overland, alongside a merchant's caravan of loaded onagers. They walked along a dusty path leading down from the plateau, across the plains, to the green fields sectioned by canals and dikes.

None of them had seen the tower before. It became visible when they were still leagues away: a line as thin as a strand of flax, wavering in the shimmering air, rising up from the crust of mud that was Babylon itself. As they drew closer, the crust grew into the mighty city walls, but all they saw was the tower. When they did lower their gazes to the level of the river-plain, they saw the marks the tower had made outside the city: the Euphrates itself now flowed at the bottom of a wide, sunken bed, dug to provide clay for bricks. To the south of the city could be seen rows upon rows of kilns, no longer burning.

As they approached the city gates, the tower appeared more massive than anything Hillalum had ever imagined: a single column that must have been as large around as an entire temple, yet rising so high that it shrank into invisibility. All of them walked with their heads tilted back, squinting in the sun.

Hillalum's friend Nanni prodded him with an elbow, awestruck. "We're to climb that? To the top?"

"Going *up* to dig. It seems . . . unnatural."

The miners reached the central gate in the western wall, where another caravan was leaving. While they crowded forward into the narrow strip of shade provided by the wall, their foreman Beli shouted to the gatekeepers who stood atop the gate towers. "We are the miners summoned from the land of Elam."

The gatekeepers were delighted. One called back, "You are the ones who are to dig through the vault of heaven?"

"We are."

The entire city was celebrating. The festival had begun eight days ago, when the last of the bricks were sent on their way, and would last two more. Every day and night, the city rejoiced, danced, feasted.

Along with the brickmakers were the cart-pullers, men whose legs were roped with muscle from climbing the tower. Each morning a crew began its ascent; they climbed for four days, transferred their loads to the next crew of pullers, and returned to the city with empty carts on the fifth. A chain of such crews led all the way to the top of the tower, but only the bottommost celebrated with the city. For those who lived upon the tower, enough wine and meat had been sent up earlier to allow a feast to extend up the entire pillar.

In the evening, Hillalum and the other Elamite miners sat upon clay stools before a long table laden with food, one table among many laid out in the city square. The miners spoke with the pullers, asking about the tower.

Nanni said, "Someone told me that the bricklayers who work at the top of the tower wail and tear their hair when a brick is dropped, because it will take four months to replace, but no one takes notice when a man falls to his death. Is that true?"

One of the more talkative pullers, Lugatum, shook his head. "Oh no, that is only a story. There is a continuous caravan of bricks going up the tower; thousands of bricks reach the top each day. The loss of a single brick means nothing to the bricklayers." He leaned over to them. "However, there is something they value more than a man's life: a trowel."

"Why a trowel?"

"If a bricklayer drops his trowel, he can do no work until a new one is brought up. For months he cannot earn the food that he eats, so he must go into debt. The loss of a trowel is cause for much wailing. But if a man falls, and his trowel remains, men are secretly relieved. The next one to drop his trowel can pick up the extra one and continue working, without incurring debt."

Hillalum was appalled, and for a frantic moment he tried to count how many picks the miners had brought. Then he realized. "That cannot be true. Why not have spare trowels brought up? Their weight would be nothing against all the bricks that go up there. And surely the loss of a man means a serious delay, unless they have an extra man at the top who is skilled at bricklaying. Without such a man, they must wait for another one to climb from the bottom."

All of the pullers roared with laughter. "We cannot fool this one," Lugatum said with much amusement. He turned to Hillalum. "So you'll begin your climb once the festival is over?"

Hillalum drank from a bowl of beer. "Yes. I've heard that we'll be joined by miners from a western land, but I haven't seen them. Do you know of them?"

"Yes, they come from a land called Egypt, but they do not mine ore as you do. They quarry stone."

"We dig stone in Elam, too," said Nanni, his mouth full of pork.

"Not as they do. They cut granite."

"Granite?" Limestone and alabaster were quarried in Elam, but not granite. "Are you certain?"

"Merchants who have traveled to Egypt say that they have stone ziggurats and temples, built with limestone and granite, huge blocks of it. And they carve giant statues from granite."

"But granite is so difficult to work."

Lugatum shrugged. "Not for them. The royal architects believe such stoneworkers may be useful when you reach the vault of heaven."

Hillalum nodded. That could be true. Who knew for certain what they would need? "Have you seen them?"

"No, they are not here yet, but they are expected in a few days' time. They may not arrive before the festival ends, though; then you Elamites will ascend alone."

"You will accompany us, won't you?"

"Yes, but only for the first four days. Then we must turn back, while you lucky ones go on."

"Why do you think us lucky?"

"I long to make the climb to the top. I once pulled with the higher crews, and reached a height of twelve days' climb, but that is as high as I have ever gone. You will go far higher." Lugatum smiled ruefully. "I envy you, that you will touch the vault of heaven."

To touch the vault of heaven. To break it open with picks. Hillalum felt uneasy at the idea. "There is no cause for envy—" he began.

"Right," said Nanni. "When we are done, all men will touch the vault of heaven."

The next morning, Hillalum went to see the tower. He stood in the giant courtyard surrounding it. There was a temple off to one side that would have been impressive if seen by itself, but it stood unnoticed beside the tower.

He could sense the utter solidity of it. According to all the tales, the tower was constructed to have a mighty strength that no ziggurat possessed; it was made of baked brick all the way through, when ordinary ziggurats were mere sun-dried mud brick, having baked brick only for the facing. The bricks were set in a bitumen mortar, which soaked into the fired clay, forming a bond as strong as the bricks themselves.

The tower's base resembled the first two platforms of an ordinary ziggurat. There stood a giant square platform some two hundred cubits on a side and forty cubits high, with a triple staircase against its south face. Stacked upon that first platform was another level, a smaller platform reached only by the central stair. It was atop the second platform that the tower itself began.

It was sixty cubits on a side, and rose like a square pillar that bore the weight of heaven. Around it wound a gently inclined ramp, cut into the side, that banded the tower like the leather strip wrapped around the handle of a whip. No; upon looking again, Hillalum saw that there were two ramps, and they were intertwined. The outer edge of each ramp was studded with pillars, not thick but broad, to provide some shade behind them. In running his gaze up the tower, he saw alternating bands, ramp, brick, ramp, brick, until they could no longer be distinguished. And still the tower rose up and up, farther than the eye could see; Hillalum blinked, and squinted, and grew dizzy. He stumbled backwards a couple steps, and turned away with a shudder.

Hillalum thought of the story told to him in childhood, the tale following that of the Deluge. It told of how men had once again populated all the corners of the earth, inhabiting more lands than they ever had before. How men had sailed to the edges of the world, and seen the ocean falling away into the mist to join the black waters of the Abyss far below. How men had thus realized the extent of the earth, and felt it to be small, and desired to see what lay beyond its borders, all the rest of Yahweh's Creation. How they looked skyward, and wondered about Yahweh's dwelling place, above the reservoirs that contained the waters of heaven. And how, many centuries ago, there began the construction of the tower, a pillar to heaven, a stair that men might ascend to see the works of Yahweh, and that Yahweh might descend to see the works of men.

It had always seemed inspiring to Hillalum, a tale of thousands of men toiling ceaselessly, but with joy, for they worked to know Yahweh better. He had been excited when the Babylonians came to Elam looking for miners. Yet now that he stood at the base of the tower, his senses rebelled, insisting that nothing should stand so high. He didn't feel as if he were on the earth when he looked up along the tower.

Should he climb such a thing?

On the morning of the climb, the second platform was covered, edge to edge, with stout two-wheeled carts arranged in rows. Many were loaded with nothing but food of all sorts: sacks filled with barley, wheat, lentils, onions, dates, cucumbers, loaves of bread, dried fish. There were countless giant clay jars of water, date wine, beer, goat's milk, palm oil. Other carts were loaded with such goods as might be sold at a bazaar: bronze vessels, reed baskets, bolts of linen, wooden stools and tables. There was also a fattened ox and a goat that some priests were fitting with hoods so that they could not see to either side, and would not be afraid on the climb. They would be sacrificed when they reached the top.

Then there were the carts loaded with the miners' picks and hammers, and the makings for a small forge. Their foreman had also ordered a number of carts be loaded with wood and sheaves of reeds.

Lugatum stood next to a cart, securing the ropes that held the wood. Hillalum walked up to him. "From where did this wood come? I saw no forests after we left Elam."

"There is a forest of trees to the north, which was planted when the tower was begun. The cut timber is floated down the Euphrates."

"You planted an entire *forest*?"

"When they began the tower, the architects knew that far more wood would be needed to fuel the kilns than could be found on the plain, so they had a forest of trees planted. There are crews whose job is to provide water, and plant one new tree for each that is cut."

Hillalum was astonished. "And that provides all the wood needed?"

"Most of it. Many other forests in the north have been cut as well, and their wood brought down the river." He inspected the wheels of the cart, uncorked a leather bottle he carried, and poured a little oil between the wheel and axle.

Nanni walked over to them, staring at the streets of Babylon laid out before them. "I've never before been even this high, that I can look down upon a city."

"Nor have I," said Hillalum, but Lugatum simply laughed.

"Come along. All of the carts are ready."

Soon all the men were paired up and matched with a cart. The men stood between the cart's two pull rods, which had rope loops for pulling. The carts pulled by the miners were mixed in with those of the regular pullers, to ensure that they would keep the proper pace. Lugatum and another puller had the cart right behind that of Hillalum and Nanni.

"Remember," said Lugatum, "stay about ten cubits behind the cart in front of you. The man on the right does all the pulling when you turn corners, and you'll switch every hour."

Pullers were beginning to lead their carts up the ramp. Hillalum and Nanni bent down and slung the ropes of their cart over their opposite shoulders. They stood up together, raising the front end of the cart off the pavement.

"Now PULL," called Lugatum.

They leaned forward against the ropes, and the cart began rolling. Once it was moving, pulling seemed to be easy enough, and they wound their way around the platform. Then they reached the ramp, and they again had to lean deeply.

"This is a light wagon?" muttered Hillalum.

The ramp was wide enough for a single man to walk beside a cart if he had to pass. The surface was paved with brick, with two grooves worn deep by centuries of wheels. Above their heads, the ceiling rose in a corbeled vault, with the wide, square bricks arranged in overlapping layers until they met in the middle. The pillars on the right were broad enough to make the ramp seem a bit like a tunnel. If one didn't look off to the side, there was little sense of being on a tower.

"Do you sing when you mine?" asked Lugatum.

"When the stone is soft," said Nanni.

"Sing one of your mining songs, then."

The call went down to the other miners, and before long the entire crew was singing.

As the shadows shortened, they ascended higher and higher. Shaded from the sun, with only clear air surrounding them, it was much cooler than in the narrow alleys of a city at ground level, where the heat at midday could kill lizards as they scurried across the street. Looking out to the side, the miners could see the dark Euphrates, and the green fields stretching out for leagues, crossed by canals that glinted in the sunlight. The city of Babylon was an intricate pattern of closely set streets and buildings, dazzling with gypsum whitewash; less and less of it was visible, as it seemingly drew nearer the base of the tower.

Hillalum was again pulling on the right-hand rope, nearer the edge, when he heard some shouting from the upward ramp one level below. He thought of stopping and looking down the side, but he didn't wish to interrupt their pace, and he wouldn't be able to see the lower ramp clearly anyway. "What's happening down there?" he called to Lugatum behind him.

"One of your fellow miners fears the height. There is occasionally such a man among those who climb for the first time. Such a man embraces the floor, and cannot ascend further. Few feel it so soon, though."

Hillalum understood. "We know of a similar fear, among those who would be miners. Some men cannot bear to enter the mines, for fear that they will be buried."

"Really?" called Lugatum. "I had not heard of that. How do you feel yourself about the height?"

"I feel nothing." But he glanced at Nanni, and they both knew the truth.

"You feel nervousness in your palms, don't you?" whispered Nanni.

Hillalum rubbed his hands on the coarse fibers of the rope, and nodded.

"I felt it too, earlier, when I was closer to the edge."

"Perhaps we should go hooded, like the ox and the goat," muttered Hillalum jokingly.

"Do you think we too will fear the height, when we climb further?"

Hillalum considered. That one of their comrades should feel the fear so soon did not bode well. He shook it off; thousands climbed with no fear, and it would be foolish to let one miner's fear infect them all. "We are merely unaccustomed. We will have months to grow used to the height. By the time we reach the top of the tower, we will wish it were taller."

"No," said Nanni. "I don't think I'll wish to pull this any further." They both laughed.

In the evening they ate a meal of barley and onions and lentils, and slept inside narrow corridors that penetrated into the body of the tower. When they woke the next morning, the miners were scarcely able to walk, so sore were their legs. The pullers laughed, and gave them salve to rub into their muscles, and redistributed the load on the carts to reduce the miners' burden.

By now, looking down the side turned Hillalum's knees to water. A wind blew steadily at this height, and he anticipated that it would grow stronger as they climbed. He wondered if anyone had ever been blown off the tower in a moment of carelessness. And the fall; a man would have time to say a prayer before he hit the ground. Hillalum shuddered at the thought.

Aside from the soreness in the miners' legs, the second day was similar to the first. They were able to see much farther now, and the breadth of land visible was stunning; the deserts beyond the fields were visible, and caravans appeared to be little more than lines of insects. No other miner feared the height so greatly that he couldn't continue, and their ascent proceeded all day without incident.

On the third day, the miners' legs had not improved, and Hillalum felt like a crippled old man. Only on the fourth day did their legs feel better, and they were pulling their original loads again. Their climb continued until the evening, when they met the second crew of pullers leading empty carts rapidly along the downward ramp. The upward and downward ramps wound around each other without touching, but they were joined by the corridors through the tower's body. When the crews had intertwined thoroughly on the two ramps, they crossed over to exchange carts.

The miners were introduced to the pullers of the second crew, and they all talked and ate together that night. The next morning, the first crew readied the empty carts for their return to Babylon, and Lugatum bid farewell to Hillalum and Nanni.

"Take care of your cart. It has climbed the entire height of the tower, more times than any man."

"Do you envy the cart, too?" asked Nanni.

"No, because every time it reaches the top, it must come all the way back down. I could not bear to do that."

When the second crew stopped at the end of the day, the puller of the cart behind Hillalum and Nanni came over to show them something. His name was Kudda.

"You have never seen the sun set at this height. Come, look."

The puller went to the edge and sat down, his legs hanging over the side. He saw that they hesitated. "Come. You can lie down and peer over the edge, if you like." Hillalum did not wish to seem like a fearful child, but he could not bring himself to sit at a cliff face that stretched for thousands of cubits below his feet. He lay down on his belly, with only his head at the edge. Nanni joined him.

"When the sun is about to set, look down the side of the tower."

Hillalum glanced downward, and then quickly looked to the horizon. "What is different about the way the sun sets here?"

"Consider, when the sun sinks behind the peaks of the mountains to the west, it grows dark down on the plain of Shinar. Yet here, we are higher than the mountaintops, so we can still see the sun. The sun must descend further for us to see night."

Hillalum's jaw dropped as he understood. "The shadows of the mountains mark the beginning of night. Night falls on the earth before it does here."

Kudda nodded. "You can see night travel up the tower, from the ground up to the sky. It moves quickly, but you should be able to see it."

He watched the red globe of the sun for a minute, and then looked down and pointed. "Now!"

Hillalum and Nanni looked down. At the base of the immense pillar, tiny Babylon was in shadow. Then the darkness climbed the tower, like a canopy unfurling upward. It moved slowly enough that Hillalum felt he could count the moments passing, but then it grew faster as it approached, until it raced past them faster than he could blink, and they were in twilight.

Hillalum rolled over and looked up, in time to see darkness rapidly ascend the rest of the tower. Gradually, the sky grew dimmer as the sun sank beneath the edge of the world, far away.

"Quite a sight, is it not?" said Kudda.

Hillalum said nothing. For the first time, he knew night for what it was: the shadow of the earth itself, cast against the sky.

———

After climbing for two more days, Hillalum had grown more accustomed to the height. Though they were the better part of a league straight up, he could bear to stand at the edge of the ramp and look down the tower. He held on to one of the pillars at the edge, and cautiously leaned out to look upward. He noticed that the tower no longer looked like a smooth pillar.

He asked Kudda, "The tower seems to widen further up. How can that be?"

"Look more closely. There are wooden balconies reaching out from the sides. They are made of cypress, and suspended by ropes of flax."

Hillalum squinted. "Balconies? What are they for?"

"They have soil spread on them, so people may grow vegetables. At this height water is scarce, so onions are most commonly grown. Higher up, where there is more rain, you'll see beans."

Nanni asked, "How can there be rain above that does not also fall here?"

Kudda was surprised at him. "It dries in the air as it falls, of course."

"Oh, of course." Nanni shrugged.

By the end of the next day they reached the level of the balconies. They were flat platforms, dense with onions, supported by heavy ropes from the tower wall above, just below the next tier of balconies. On each level the interior of the tower had several narrow rooms inside, in which the families of the pullers lived. Women could be seen sitting in the doorways sewing tunics, or out in the gardens digging up bulbs. Children chased each other up and down the ramps, weaving amidst the pullers' carts, and running along the edge of the balconies without fear. The tower dwellers could easily pick out the miners, and they all smiled and waved.

When it came time for the evening meal, all the carts were set down and food and other goods were taken off to be used by the people here. The pullers greeted their families, and invited the miners to join them for the evening meal. Hillalum and Nanni ate with the family of Kudda, and they enjoyed a fine meal of dried fish, bread, date wine, and fruit.

Hillalum saw that this section of the tower formed a tiny kind of town, laid out in a line between two streets, the upward and downward ramps. There was a temple, in which the rituals for the festivals were performed; there were magistrates, who settled disputes; there were shops, which were stocked by the caravan. Of course, the town was inseparable from the caravan: neither could exist without the other. And yet any caravan was essentially a journey, a thing that began at one place and ended at another. This town was never intended as a permanent place, it was merely part of a centuries-long journey.

After dinner, he asked Kudda and his family, "Have any of you ever visited Babylon?"

Kudda's wife, Alitum, answered, "No, why would we? It's a long climb, and we have all we need here."

"You have no desire to actually walk on the earth?"

Kudda shrugged. "We live on the road to heaven; all the work that we do is to extend it further. When we leave the tower, we will take the upward ramp, not the downward."

As the miners ascended, in the course of time there came the day when the tower appeared to be the same when one looked upward or downward from the ramp's edge. Below, the tower's shaft shrank to nothing long before it seemed to reach the plain below. Likewise, the miners were still far from being able to see the top. All that was visible was a length of the tower. To look up or down was frightening, for the reassurance of continuity was gone; they were no longer part of the ground. The tower might have been a thread suspended in the air, unattached to either earth or to heaven.

There were moments during this section of the climb when Hillalum despaired, feeling displaced and estranged from the world; it was as if the earth had rejected him for his faithlessness, while heaven disdained to accept him. He wished Yahweh would give a sign, to let men know that their venture was approved; otherwise how could they stay in a place that offered so little welcome to the spirit?

The tower dwellers at this altitude felt no unease with their station; they always greeted the miners warmly and wished them luck with their task at the vault. They lived inside the damp mists of clouds, they saw storms from below and from above, they harvested crops from the air, and they never feared that this was an improper place for men to be. There were no divine assurances or encouragements to be had, but the people never knew a moment's doubt.

With the passage of the weeks, the sun and moon peaked lower and lower in their daily journeys. The moon flooded the south side of the tower with its silver radiance, glowing like the eye of Yahweh peering at them. Before long, they were at precisely the same level as the moon when it passed; they had reached the height of the first of the celestial bodies. They squinted at the moon's pitted face, marveled at its stately motion that scorned any support.

Then they approached the sun. It was the summer season, when the sun appears nearly overhead from Babylon, making it pass close by the tower at this height. No families lived in this section of the tower, nor were there any balconies, since the heat was enough to roast barley. The mortar between the tower's bricks was no longer bitumen, which would have softened and flowed, but clay, which had been virtually baked by the heat. As protection against the day temperatures, the pillars had been widened until they formed a nearly continuous wall, enclosing the ramp into a tunnel with only narrow slots admitting the whistling wind and blades of golden light.

The crews of pullers had been spaced regularly up to this point, but here an adjustment was necessary. They started out earlier and earlier each morning, to gain more darkness for when they pulled. When they were at the level of the sun, they traveled entirely at night. During the day, they tried to sleep, naked and sweating in the hot breeze. The miners worried that if they did manage to sleep, they would be baked to death before they awoke. But the pullers had made the journey many times, and never lost a man, and eventually they passed above the sun's level, where things were as they had been below.

Now the light of day shone *upward*, which seemed unnatural to the utmost. The balconies had planks removed from them so that the sunlight could shine through, with soil on the walkways that remained; the plants grew sideways and downward, bending over to catch the sun's rays.

Then they drew near the level of the stars, small fiery spheres spread on all sides. Hillalum had expected them to be spread more thickly, but even with the tiny stars invisible from the ground, they seemed to be thinly scattered. They were not all set at the same height, but instead occupied the next few leagues above. It was difficult to tell how far they were, since there was no indication of their size, but occasionally one would make a close approach, evidencing its astonishing speed. Hillalum realized that all the objects in the sky hurtled by with similar speed, in order to travel the world from edge to edge in a day's time.

During the day, the sky was a much paler blue than it appeared from the earth, a sign they were nearing the vault. When studying the sky, Hillalum was startled to see that there were stars visible during the day. They couldn't be seen from the earth amidst the glare of the sun, but from this altitude they were quite distinct.

One day Nanni came to him hurriedly and said, "A star has hit the tower!"

"What!" Hillalum looked around, panicked, feeling like he had been struck by a blow.

"No, not now. It was long ago, more than a century. One of the tower dwellers is telling the story; his grandfather was there."

They went inside the corridors, and saw several miners seated around a wizened old man. "—lodged itself in the bricks about half a league above here. You can still see the scar it left; it's like a giant pockmark."

"What happened to the star?"

"It burned and sizzled, and was too bright to look upon. Men considered prying it out, so that it might resume its course, but it was too hot to approach closely, and they dared not quench it. After weeks it cooled into a knotted mass of black heaven-metal, as large as a man could wrap his arms around."

"So large?" said Nanni, his voice full of awe. When stars fell to the earth of their own accord, small lumps of heaven-metal were sometimes found, tougher than the finest bronze. The metal could not be melted for casting, so it was worked by hammering when heated red; amulets were made from it.

"Indeed, no one had ever heard of a mass of this size found on the earth. Can you imagine the tools that could be made from it!"

"You did not try to hammer it into tools, did you?" asked Hillalum, horrified.

"Oh no. Men were frightened to touch it. Everyone descended from the tower, waiting for retribution from Yahweh for disturbing the workings of Creation. They waited for months, but no sign came. Eventually they returned, and pried out the star. It sits in a temple in the city below."

There was silence. Then one of the miners said, "I have never heard of this in the stories of the tower."

"It was a transgression, something not spoken of."

As they climbed higher up the tower, the sky grew lighter in color, until one morning Hillalum awoke and stood at the edge and yelled from shock: what had before seemed a pale sky now appeared to be a white ceiling stretched far above their heads. They were close enough now to perceive the vault of heaven, to see it as a solid carapace enclosing all the sky. All of the miners spoke in hushed tones, staring up like idiots, while the tower dwellers laughed at them.

As they continued to climb, they were startled at how *near* they actually were. The blankness of the vault's face had deceived them, making it undetectable until it appeared, abruptly, seeming just above their heads. Now instead of climbing into the sky, they climbed up to a featureless plain that stretched endlessly in all directions.

All of Hillalum's senses were disoriented by the sight of it. Sometimes when he looked at the vault, he felt as if the world had flipped around somehow, and if he lost his footing he would fall upward to meet it. When the vault did appear to rest above his head, it had an oppressive *weight*. The vault was a stratum as heavy as all the world, yet utterly without support, and he feared what he never had in the mines: that the ceiling would collapse upon him.

Too, there were moments when it appeared as if the vault were a vertical cliff face of unimaginable height rising before him, and the dim earth behind him was another like it, and the tower was a cable stretched taut between the two. Or worst of all, for an instant it seemed that there was no up and no down, and his body did not know which way it was drawn. It was like fearing the height, but much worse. Often he would wake from an unrestful sleep, to find himself sweating and his fingers cramped, trying to clutch the brick floor.

Nanni and many of the other miners were bleary-eyed too, though no one spoke of what disturbed their sleep. Their ascent grew slower, instead of faster as their foreman Beli had expected; the sight of the vault inspired unease rather than eagerness. The regular pullers became impatient with them. Hillalum wondered what sort of people were forged by living under such conditions; how did they escape madness? Did they grow accustomed to this? Would the children born under a solid sky scream if they saw the ground beneath their feet?

Perhaps men were not meant to live in such a place. If their own natures restrained them from approaching heaven too closely, then men should remain on the earth.

When they reached the summit of the tower, the disorientation faded, or perhaps they had grown immune. Here, standing upon the square platform of the top, the miners gazed upon the most awesome scene ever glimpsed by men: far below them lay a tapestry of soil and sea, veiled by mist, rolling out in all directions to the limit of the eye.

Just above them hung the roof of the world itself, the absolute upper demarcation of the sky, guaranteeing their vantage point as the highest possible. Here was as much of Creation as could be apprehended at once.

The priests led a prayer to Yahweh; they gave thanks that they were permitted to see so much, and begged forgiveness for their desire to see more.

And at the top, the bricks were laid. One could catch the rich, raw smell of tar, rising out of the heated cauldrons in which the lumps of bitumen were melted. It was the most earthy odor the miners had smelled in four months, and their nostrils were desperate to catch a whiff before it was whipped away by the wind. Here at the summit, where the ooze that had once seeped from the earth's cracks now grew solid to hold bricks in place, the earth was growing a limb into the sky.

Here worked the bricklayers, the men smeared with bitumen who mixed the mortar and deftly set the heavy bricks with absolute precision. More than anyone else, these men could not permit themselves to experience dizziness when they saw the vault, for the tower could not vary a finger's width from the vertical. They were nearing the end of their task, finally, and after four months of climbing, the miners were ready to begin theirs.

The Egyptians arrived shortly afterwards. They were dark of skin and slight of build, and had sparsely bearded chins. They had pulled carts filled with dolerite hammers, and bronze tools, and wooden wedges. Their foreman was named Senmut, and he conferred with Beli, the Elamites' foreman, on how they would penetrate the vault. The Egyptians built a forge with what they had brought, as did the Elamites, for recasting the bronze tools that would be blunted during the mining.

The vault itself remained just above a man's outstretched fingertips; it felt smooth and cool when one leapt up to touch it. It seemed to be made of fine-grained white granite, unmarred and utterly featureless. And therein lay the problem.

Long ago, Yahweh had released the Deluge, unleashing waters from both below and above; the waters of the Abyss had burst forth from the springs of the earth, and the waters of heaven had poured through the sluice gates in the vault. Now men saw the vault closely, but there were no sluice gates discernible. They squinted at the surface in all directions, but no openings, no windows, no seams interrupted the granite plain.

It seemed that their tower met the vault at a point between any reservoirs, which was fortunate indeed. If a sluice gate had been visible, they would have had to risk breaking it open and emptying the reservoir. That would mean rain for Shinar, out of season and heavier than the winter rains; it would cause flooding along the Euphrates. The rain would most likely end when the reservoir was emptied, but there was always the possibility that Yahweh would punish them and continue the rain until the tower fell and Babylon was dissolved into mud.

Even though there were no visible gates, a risk still existed. Perhaps the gates had no seams perceptible to mortal eyes, and a reservoir lay directly above them. Or perhaps the reservoirs were huge, so that even if the nearest sluice gates were many leagues away, a reservoir still lay above them.

There was much debate over how best to proceed.

"Surely Yahweh will not wash away the tower," argued Qurdusa, one of the bricklayers. "If the tower were sacrilege, Yahweh would have destroyed it earlier. Yet in all the centuries we've been working, we have never seen the slightest sign of Yahweh's displeasure. Yahweh will drain any reservoir before we penetrate it."

"If Yahweh looked upon this venture with such favor, there would already be a stairway ready-made for us in the vault," countered Eluti, an Elamite. "Yahweh will neither help or hinder us; if we penetrate a reservoir, we will face the onrush of its waters."

Hillalum could not keep his doubts silent at such a time. "And if the waters are endless?" he asked. "Yahweh may not punish us, but Yahweh may allow us to bring our judgment upon ourselves."

"Elamite," said Qurdusa, "even as a newcomer to the tower, you should know better than that. We labor for our love of Yahweh, we have done so for all our lives, and so have our fathers for generations back. Men as righteous as we could not be judged harshly."

"It is true that we work with the purest of aims, but that doesn't mean we have worked wisely. Did men truly choose the correct path when they opted to live their lives away from the soil from which they were shaped? Never has Yahweh said that the choice was proper. Now we stand ready to break open heaven, even when we know that water lies above us. If we are misguided, how can we be sure Yahweh will protect us from our own errors?"

"Hillalum advises caution, and I agree," said Beli. "We must ensure that we do not bring a second Deluge upon the world, nor even dangerous rains upon Shinar. I have conferred with Senmut of the Egyptians, and he has shown me designs which they have employed to seal the tombs of their kings. I believe their methods can provide us with safety when we begin digging."

The priests sacrificed the ox and the goat in a ceremony in which many sacred words were spoken and much incense was burned, and the miners began work.

Long before the miners reached the vault it had been obvious that simple digging with hammers and picks would be impractical: even if they were tunneling horizontally, they would make no more than two fingers' width of progress a day through granite, and tunneling upward would be far, far slower. Instead, they employed fire-setting.

With the wood they had brought, a bonfire was built below the chosen point of the vault, and fed steadily for a day. Before the heat of the flames, the stone cracked and spalled. After letting the fire burn out, the miners splashed water onto the stone to further the cracking. They could then break the stone into large pieces, which fell heavily onto the tower. In this manner they could progress the better part of a cubit for each day the fire burned.

The tunnel did not rise straight up, but at the angle a staircase takes, so that they could build a ramp of steps up from the tower to meet it. The fire-setting left the walls and floor smooth; the men built a frame of wooden steps underfoot, so that they would not slide back down. They used a platform of baked bricks to support the bonfire at the tunnel's end.

After the tunnel rose ten cubits into the vault, they leveled it out and widened it to form a room. After the miners had removed all the stone that had been weakened by the fire, the Egyptians began work. They used no fire in their quarrying. With only their dolerite balls and hammers, they began to build a sliding door of granite.

They first chipped away stone to cut an immense block of granite out of one wall. Hillalum and the other miners tried to help, but found it very difficult: one did not wear away the stone by grinding, but instead pounded chips off, using hammer blows of one strength alone, and lighter or heavier ones would not do.

After some weeks, the block was ready. It stood taller than a man, and was even wider than that. To free it from the floor, they cut slots around the base of the stone and pounded in dry wooden wedges. Then they pounded thinner wedges into the first wedges to split them, and poured water into the cracks so that the wood would swell. In a few hours, a crack traveled into the stone, and the block was freed.

At the rear of the room, on the right-hand side, the miners burned out a narrow upward-sloping corridor, and in the floor in front of the chamber entrance they dug a downward-sloping channel into the floor for a cubit. Thus there was a smooth continuous ramp that cut across the floor immediately in front of the entrance, and ended just to its left. On this ramp the Egyptians loaded the block of granite. They dragged and pushed the block up into the side corridor, where it just barely fit, and propped it in place with a stack of flat mud bricks braced against the bottom of the left wall, like a pillar lying on the ramp.

With the sliding stone to hold back the waters, it was safe for the miners to continue tunneling. If they broke into a reservoir and the waters of heaven began pouring down into the tunnel, they would break the bricks one by one, and the stone would slide down until it rested in the recess in the floor, utterly blocking the doorway. If the waters flooded in with such force that they washed men out of the tunnels, the mud bricks would gradually dissolve, and again the stone would slide down. The waters would be retained, and the miners could then begin a new tunnel in another direction, to avoid the reservoir.

The miners again used fire-setting to continue the tunnel, beginning at the far end of the room. To aid the circulation of air within the vault, ox hides were stretched on tall frames of wood, and placed obliquely on either side of the tunnel entrance at the top of the tower. Thus the steady wind that blew underneath the vault of heaven was guided upward into the tunnel; it kept the fire blazing, and it cleared the air after the fire was extinguished, so that the miners could dig without breathing smoke.

The Egyptians did not stop working once the sliding stone was in place. While the miners swung their picks at the tunnel's end, the Egyptians labored at the task of cutting a stair into the solid stone, to replace the wooden steps. This they did with the wooden wedges, and the blocks they removed from the sloping floor left steps in their place.

Thus the miners worked, extending the tunnel on and on. The tunnel always ascended, though it reversed direction regularly like a thread in a giant stitch, so that its general path was straight up. They built other sliding door rooms, so that only the uppermost segment of the tunnel would be flooded if they penetrated a reservoir. They cut channels in the vault's surface from which they hung walkways and platforms; starting from these platforms, well away from the tower, they dug side tunnels, which joined the main tunnel deep inside. The wind was guided through these to provide ventilation, clearing the smoke from deep inside the tunnel.

For years the labor continued. The pulling crews no longer

hauled bricks, but wood and water for the fire-setting. People came to inhabit those tunnels just inside the vault's surface, and on hanging platforms they grew downward-bending vegetables. The miners lived there at the border of heaven; some married, and raised children. Few ever set foot on the earth again.

With a wet cloth wrapped around his face, Hillalum climbed down from wooden steps onto stone, having just fed some more wood to the bonfire at the tunnel's end. The fire would continue for many hours, and he would wait in the lower tunnels, where the wind was not thick with smoke.

Then there was a distant sound of shattering, the sound of a mountain of stone being split through, and then a steadily growing roar. And then a torrent of water came rushing down the tunnel.

For a moment, Hillalum was frozen in horror. The water, shockingly cold, slammed into his legs, knocking him down. He rose to his feet, gasping for breath, leaning against the current, clutching at the steps.

They had hit a reservoir.

He had to descend below the highest sliding door, before it was closed. His legs wished to leap down the steps, but he knew he couldn't remain on his feet if he did, and being swept down by the raging current would likely batter him to death. Going as fast as he dared, he took the steps one by one.

He slipped several times, sliding down as many as a dozen steps each time; the stone steps scraped against his back, but he felt no pain. All the while he was certain the tunnel would collapse and crush him, or else the entire vault would split open, and the sky would gape beneath his feet, and he would fall down to earth amidst the heavenly rain. Yahweh's punishment had come, a second Deluge.

How much further until he reached the sliding stone? The tunnel seemed to stretch on and on, and the waters were pouring down even faster now. He was virtually running down the steps.

Suddenly he stumbled and splashed into shallow water. He had run down past the end of the stairs, and fallen into the room of the sliding stone, and there was water higher than his knees.

He stood up, and saw Damqiya and Ahuni, two fellow miners, just noticing him. They stood in front of the stone that already blocked the exit.

"No!" he cried.

"They closed it!" screamed Damqiya. "They did not wait!"

"Are there others coming?" shouted Ahuni, without hope. "We may be able to move the block."

"There are no others," answered Hillalum. "Can they push it from the other side?"

"They cannot hear us." Ahuni pounded the granite with a hammer, making not a sound against the din of the water.

Hillalum looked around the tiny room, only now noticing that an Egyptian floated facedown in the water.

"He died falling down the stairs," yelled Damqiya.

"Is there nothing we can do?"

Ahuni looked upward. "Yahweh, spare us."

The three of them stood in the rising water, praying desperately, but Hillalum knew it was in vain: his fate had come at last. Yahweh had not asked men to build the tower or to pierce the vault; the decision to build it belonged to men alone, and they would die in this endeavor just as they did in any of their earthbound tasks. Their righteousness could not save them from the consequences of their deeds.

The water reached their chests. "Let us ascend," shouted Hillalum.

They climbed the tunnel laboriously, against the onrush, as the water rose behind their heels. The few torches illuminating the tunnel had been extinguished, so they ascended in the dark, murmuring prayers that they couldn't hear. The wooden steps at the top of the tunnel had dislodged from their place, and were jammed farther down in the tunnel. They climbed past them, until they reached the smooth stone slope, and there they waited for the water to carry them higher.

They waited without words, their prayers exhausted. Hillalum imagined that he stood in the black gullet of Yahweh, as the mighty one drank deep of the waters of heaven, ready to swallow the sinners.

The water rose, and bore them up, until Hillalum could reach up with his hands and touch the ceiling. The giant fissure from which the waters gushed forth was right next to him. Only a tiny pocket of air remained. Hillalum shouted, "When this chamber is filled, we can swim heavenward."

He could not tell if they heard him. He gulped his last breath as the water reached the ceiling, and swam up into the fissure. He would die closer to heaven than any man had ever before.

The fissure extended for many cubits. As soon as Hillalum passed through, the stone stratum slipped from his fingers, and his flailing limbs touched nothing. For a moment he felt a current carrying him, but then he was no longer sure. With only blackness around him, he once again felt that horrible vertigo that he had experienced when first approaching the vault: he could not distinguish any directions, not even up or down. He pushed and kicked against the water, but did not know if he moved.

Helpless, he was perhaps floating in still water, perhaps swept furiously by a current; all he felt was numbing cold. Never did he see any light. Was there no surface to this reservoir that he might rise to?

Then he was slammed into stone again. His hands felt a fissure in the surface. Was he back where he had begun? He was being forced into it, and he had no strength to resist. He was drawn into the tunnel, and was rattled against its sides. It was incredibly deep, like the longest mine shaft: he felt as if his lungs would burst, but there was still no end to the passage. Finally his breath would not be held any longer, and it escaped from his lips. He was drowning, and the blackness around him entered his lungs.

But suddenly the walls opened out away from him. He was being carried along by a rushing stream of water; he felt air above the water! And then he felt no more.

———

Hillalum awoke with his face pressed against wet stone. He could see nothing, but he could feel water near his hands. He rolled over and groaned; his every limb ached, he was naked and much of his skin was scraped raw or wrinkled from wetness, but he breathed air.

Time passed, and finally he could stand. Water flowed rapidly about his ankles. Stepping in one direction, the water deepened. In the other, there was dry stone; shale, by the feel of it.

It was utterly dark, like a mine without torches. With torn fingertips he felt his way along the floor, until it rose up and became a wall. Slowly, like some blind creature, he crawled back and forth. He found the water's source, a large opening in the floor. He remembered! He had been spewed up from the reservoir through this hole. He continued crawling for what seemed to be hours; if he was in a cavern, it was immense.

He found a place where the floor rose in a slope. Was there a passage leading upward? Perhaps it could still take him to heaven.

Hillalum crawled, having no idea of how much time passed, not caring that he would never be able to retrace his steps, for he could not return whence he had come. He followed upward tunnels when he found them, downward ones when he had to. Though earlier he had swallowed more water than he would have thought possible, he began to feel thirst, and hunger.

And eventually he saw light, and raced to the outside.

The light made his eyes squeeze closed, and he fell to his knees, his fists clenched before his face. Was it the radiance of Yahweh? Could his eyes bear to see it? Minutes later he could open them, and he saw desert. He had emerged from a cave in the foothills of some mountains, and rocks and sand stretched to the horizon.

Was heaven just like the earth? Did Yahweh dwell in a place such as this? Or was this merely another realm within Yahweh's Creation, another earth above his own, while Yahweh dwelled still higher?

A sun lay near the mountaintops behind his back. Was it rising or falling? Were there days and nights here?

Hillalum squinted at the sandy landscape. A line moved along the horizon. Was it a caravan?

He ran to it, shouting with his parched throat until his need for breath stopped him. A figure at the end of the caravan saw him, and brought the entire line to a stop. Hillalum kept running.

The one who had seen him seemed to be man, not spirit, and was dressed like a desert-crosser. He had a waterskin ready. Hillalum drank as best he could, panting for breath.

Finally he returned it to the man, and gasped, "Where is this place?"

"Were you attacked by bandits? We are headed to Erech."

Hillalum stared. "You would deceive me!" he shouted. The man drew back, and watched him as if he were mad from the sun. Hillalum saw another man in the caravan walking over to investigate. "Erech is in Shinar!"

"Yes it is. Were you not travelling to Shinar?" The other man stood ready with his staff.

"I came from—I was in—" Hillalum stopped. "Do you know Babylon?"

"Oh, is that your destination? That is north of Erech. It is an easy journey between them."

"The tower. Have you heard of it?"

"Certainly, the pillar to heaven. It is said men at the top are tunneling through the vault of heaven."

Hillalum fell to the sand.

"Are you unwell?" The two caravan drivers mumbled to each other, and went off to confer with the others. Hillalum was not watching them.

He was in Shinar. He had returned to the earth. He had climbed above the reservoirs of heaven, and arrived back at the earth. Had Yahweh brought him to this place, to keep him from reaching further above? Yet Hillalum still hadn't seen any signs, any indication that Yahweh noticed him. He had not experienced any miracle that Yahweh had performed to place him here. As far as he could see, he had merely swum up from the vault and entered the cavern below.

Somehow, the vault of heaven lay beneath the earth. It was as if they lay against each other, though they were separated by many leagues. How could that be? How could such distant places touch? Hillalum's head hurt trying to think about it.

And then it came to him: *a seal cylinder.* When rolled upon a tablet of soft clay, the carved cylinder left an imprint that formed a picture. Two figures might appear at opposite ends of the tablet, though they stood side by side on the surface of the cylinder. All the world was as such a cylinder. Men imagined heaven and earth as being at the ends of a tablet, with sky and stars stretched between; yet the world was wrapped around in some fantastic way so that heaven and earth touched.

It was clear now why Yahweh had not struck down the tower, had not punished men for wishing to reach beyond the bounds set for them: for the longest journey would merely return them to the place whence they'd come. Centuries of their labor would not reveal to them any more of Creation than they already knew. Yet through their endeavor, men would glimpse the unimaginable artistry of Yahweh's work, in seeing how ingeniously the world had been constructed. By this construction, Yahweh's work was indicated, and Yahweh's work was concealed.

Thus would men know their place.

Hillalum rose to his feet, his legs unsteady from awe, and sought out the caravan drivers. He would go back to Babylon. Perhaps he would see Lugatum again. He would send word to those on the tower. He would tell them about the shape of the world.

Understand

A layer of ice; it feels rough against my face, but not cold. I've got nothing to hold on to; my gloves just keep sliding off it. I can see people on top, running around, but they can't do anything. I'm trying to pound the ice with my fists, but my arms move in slow motion, and my lungs must have burst, and my head's going fuzzy, and I feel like I'm dissolving—

I wake up, screaming. My heart's going like a jackhammer. Christ. I pull off my blankets and sit on the edge of the bed.

I couldn't remember that before. Before I only remembered falling through the ice; the doctor said my mind had suppressed the rest. Now I remember it, and it's the worst nightmare I've ever had.

I'm grabbing the down comforter with my fists, and I can feel myself trembling. I try to calm down, to breathe slowly, but sobs keep forcing their way out. It was so real I could *feel* it: feel what it was like to die.

I was in that water for nearly an hour; I was more vegetable than anything else by the time they brought me up. Am I recovered? It was the first time the hospital had ever tried their new drug on someone with so much brain damage. Did it work?

———

The same nightmare, again and again. After the third time, I know I'm not going to sleep again. I spend the remaining hours before dawn worrying. Is this the result? Am I losing my mind?

Tomorrow is my weekly checkup with the resident at the hospital. I hope he'll have some answers.

I drive into downtown Boston, and after half an hour Dr. Hooper can see me. I sit on a gurney in an examining room, behind a yellow curtain. Jutting out of the wall at waist height is a horizontal flatscreen, adjusted for tunnel vision so it appears blank from my angle. The doctor types at the keyboard, presumably calling up my file, and then starts examining me. As he's checking my pupils with a penlight, I tell him about my nightmares.

"Did you ever have any before the accident, Leon?" He gets out his little mallet and taps at my elbows, knees, and ankles.

"Never. Are these a side effect of the drug?"

"Not a side effect. The hormone K therapy regenerated a lot of damaged neurons, and that's an enormous change that your brain has to adjust to. The nightmares are probably just a sign of that."

"Is this permanent?"

"It's unlikely," he says. "Once your brain gets used to having all those pathways again, you'll be fine. Now touch your index finger to the tip of your nose, and then bring it to my finger here."

I do what he tells me. Next he has me tap each finger to my thumb, quickly. Then I have to walk a straight line, as if I'm taking a sobriety test. After that, he starts quizzing me.

"Name the parts of an ordinary shoe."

"There's the sole, the heel, the laces. Um, the holes that the laces go through are eyes, and then there's the tongue, underneath the laces . . ."

"Okay. Repeat this number: three nine one seven four—"

"—six two."

Dr. Hooper wasn't expecting that. "What?"

"Three nine one seven four six two. You used that number the first time you examined me, when I was still an inpatient. I guess it's a number you test patients with a lot."

"You weren't supposed to memorize it; it's meant to be a test of immediate recall."

"I didn't intentionally memorize it. I just happened to remember it."

"Do you remember the number from the second time I examined you?"

I pause for a moment. "Four zero eight one five nine two."

He's surprised. "Most people can't retain so many digits if they've only heard them once. Do you use mnemonic tricks?"

I shake my head. "No. I always keep phone numbers in the autodialer."

He goes to the terminal and taps at the numeric keypad. "Try this one." He reads a fourteen-digit number, and I repeat it back to him. "You think you can do it backwards?" I recite the digits in reverse order. He frowns, and starts typing something into my file.

I'm sitting in front of a terminal in one of the testing rooms in the psychiatric ward; it's the nearest place Dr. Hooper could get some intelligence tests. There's a small mirror set in one wall, probably with a video camera behind it. In case it's recording, I smile at it and wave briefly. I always do that to the hidden cameras in automatic cash machines.

Dr. Hooper comes in with a printout of my test results. "Well, Leon, you did . . . very well. On both tests you scored in the ninety-ninth percentile."

My jaw drops. "You're kidding."

"No, I'm not." He has trouble believing it himself. "Now that number doesn't indicate how many questions you got right; it means that relative to the general population—"

"I know what it means," I say absently. "I was in the seventieth percentile when they tested us in high school." Ninety-ninth percentile.

Inwardly, I'm trying to find some sign of this. What should it feel like?

He sits down on the table, still looking at the printout. "You never attended college, did you?"

I return my attention to him. "I did, but I left before graduating. My ideas of education didn't mesh with the professors."

"I see." He probably takes this to mean I flunked out. "Well, clearly you've improved tremendously. A little of that may have come about naturally as you grew older, but most of it must be a result of the hormone K therapy."

"This is one hell of a side effect."

"Well, don't get too excited. Test scores don't predict how well you can do things in the real world." I roll my eyes upward when Dr. Hooper isn't looking. Something amazing is going on, and all he can offer is a truism. "I'd like to follow up on this with some more tests. Can you come in tomorrow?"

I'm in the middle of retouching a holograph when the phone rings. I waver between the phone and the console, and reluctantly opt for the phone. I'd normally have the answering machine take any calls when I'm editing, but I need to let people know I'm working again. I lost a lot of business when I was in the hospital: one of the risks of being a free-lancer. I touch the phone and say, "Greco Holographics, Leon Greco speaking."

"Hey Leon, it's Jerry."

"Hi Jerry. What's up?" I'm still studying the image on the screen: it's a pair of helical gears, intermeshed. A trite metaphor for coopera-tive action, but that's what the customer wanted for his ad.

"You interested in seeing a movie tonight? Me and Sue and Tori were going to see *Metal Eyes*."

"Tonight? Oh, I can't. Tonight's the last performance of the one-woman show at the Hanning Playhouse." The surfaces of the gear teeth are scratched and oily-looking. I highlight each surface using the cursor, and type in the parameters to be adjusted.

"What's that?"

"It's called *Symplectic*. It's a monologue in verse." Now I adjust the lighting, to remove some of the shadows from where the teeth mesh. "Want to come along?"

"Is this some kind of Shakespearean soliloquy?"

Too much: with that lighting, the outer edges will be too bright. I specify an upper limit for the reflected light's intensity. "No, it's a stream-of-consciousness piece, and it alternates between four different meters; iambic's only one of them. All the critics called it a tour de force."

"I didn't know you were such a fan of poetry."

After checking all the numbers once more, I let the computer recalculate the interference pattern. "Normally, I'm not, but this one seemed really interesting. How's it sound to you?"

"Thanks, but I think we'll stick with the movie."

"Okay, you guys have fun. Maybe we can get together next week." We say good-bye and hang up, and I wait for the recalc to finish.

Suddenly it occurs to me what's just happened. I've never been able to do any serious editing while talking on the phone. But this time I had no trouble keeping my mind on both things at once.

Will the surprises never end? Once the nightmares were gone and I could relax, the first thing I noticed was the increase in my reading speed and comprehension. I was actually able to read the books on my shelves that I'd always meant to get around to, but never had the time; even the more difficult, technical material. Back in college, I'd accepted the fact that I couldn't study everything that interested me. It's exhilarating to discover that maybe I can; I was positively gleeful when I bought an armload of books the other day.

And now I find I can concentrate on two things at once; something I never would have predicted. I stand up at my desk and shout out loud, as if my favorite baseball team has just surprised me with a triple play. That's what it feels like.

The neurologist-in-chief, Dr. Shea, has taken over my case, presumably because he wants to take the credit. I scarcely know him, but he acts as if I've been his patient for years.

He's asked me into his office to have a talk. He interlaces his fingers and rests his elbows on his desk. "How do you feel about the increase in your intelligence?" he asks.

What an inane question. "I'm very pleased about it."

"Good," says Dr. Shea. "So far, we've found no adverse effects of the hormone K therapy. You don't require any further treatment for the brain damage from your accident." I nod. "However, we're conducting a study to learn more about the hormone's effect on intelligence. If you're willing, we'd like to give you a further injection of the hormone, and then monitor the results."

Suddenly he's got my attention; finally, something worth listening to. "I'd be willing to do that."

"You understand that this is purely for investigational purposes, not therapeutic. You may benefit from it with further gains in your intelligence, but this is not medically necessary for your health."

"I understand. I suppose I have to sign a consent form."

"Yes. We can also offer you some compensation for participating in this study." He names a figure, but I'm barely listening.

"That'll be fine." I'm imagining where this might lead, what it might mean for me, and a thrill runs through me.

"We'd also like you to sign a confidentiality agreement. Clearly this drug is enormously exciting, but we don't want any announcements to be made prematurely."

"Certainly, Dr. Shea. Has anyone been given additional injections before?"

"Of course; you're not going to be a guinea pig. I can assure you, there haven't been any harmful side effects."

"What sort of effects did they experience?"

"It's better if we don't plant suggestions in your mind: you might imagine you were experiencing the symptoms I mention."

Shea's very comfortable with the doctor-knows-best routine. I keep pushing. "Can you at least tell me how much their intelligence increased?"

"Every individual is different. You shouldn't base your expectations on what's happened to others."

I conceal my frustration. "Very well, Doctor."

If Shea doesn't want to tell me about hormone K, I can find out about it on my own. From my terminal at home I log on to the datanet. I access the FDA's public database, and start perusing their current INDs, the Investigational New Drug applications that must be approved before human trials can begin.

The application for hormone K was submitted by Sorensen Pharmaceutical, a company researching synthetic hormones that encourage neuron regeneration in the central nervous system. I skim the results of the drug tests on oxygen-deprived dogs, and then baboons: all the animals recovered completely. Toxicity was low, and long-term observation didn't reveal any adverse effects.

The results of cortical samples are provocative. The brain-damaged animals grew replacement neurons with many more dendrites, but the healthy recipients of the drug remained unchanged. The conclusion of the researchers: hormone K replaces only damaged neurons, not healthy ones. In the brain-damaged animals, the new dendrites seemed harmless: PET scans didn't reveal any change in brain metabolism, and the animals' performance on intelligence tests didn't change.

In their application for human clinical trials, the Sorensen researchers outlined protocols for testing the drug first on healthy subjects, and then on several types of patients: stroke victims, sufferers of Alzheimer's, and persons—like me—in a persistent vegetative state. I can't access the progress reports for those trials: even with patient anonymity, only participating doctors have clearance to examine those records.

The animal studies don't shed any light on the increased intelligence in humans. It's reasonable to assume that the effect on intelligence is proportional to the number of neurons replaced by the hormone, which in turn depends on the amount of initial damage. That means that the deep-coma patients would undergo the greatest improvements. Of course, I'd need to see the progress of the other patients to confirm this theory; that'll have to wait.

The next question: is there a plateau, or will additional dosages of the hormone cause further increases? I'll know the answer to that sooner than the doctors.

I'm not nervous; in fact, I feel quite relaxed. I'm just lying on my stomach, breathing very slowly. My back is numb; they gave me a local anesthetic, and then injected the hormone K intraspinally. An intravenous wouldn't work, since the hormone can't get past the blood-brain barrier. This is the first such injection I can recall having, though I'm told that I've received two before: the first while still in the coma, the second when I had regained consciousness but no cognitive ability.

More nightmares. They're not all actually violent, but they're the most bizarre, mind-blowing dreams I've ever had, often with nothing in them that I recognize. I often wake up screaming, flailing around in bed. But this time, I know they'll pass.

There are several psychologists at the hospital studying me now. It's interesting to see how they analyze my intelligence. One doctor perceives my skills in terms of components, such as acquisition, retention, performance, and transfer. Another looks at me from the angles of mathematical and logical reasoning, linguistic communication, and spatial visualization.

I'm reminded of my college days when I watch these specialists, each with a pet theory, each contorting the evidence to fit. I'm even less convinced by them now than I was back then; they still have nothing to teach me. None of their categorizations are fruitful in analyzing my performance, since—there's no point in denying it—I'm equally good at everything.

I could be studying a new class of equation, or the grammar of a foreign language, or the operation of an engine; in each case, everything fits together, all the elements cooperate beautifully. In each case, I don't have to consciously memorize rules, and then apply them mechanically. I just perceive how the system behaves as a whole, as an entity. Of course, I'm aware of all the details and individual steps, but they require so little concentration that they almost feel intuitive.

Penetrating computer security is really quite dull; I can see how it might attract those who can't resist a challenge to their cleverness, but it's not intellectually aesthetic at all. It's no different than tugging on the doors of a locked house until you find an improperly installed lock. A useful activity, but hardly interesting.

Getting into the FDA's private database was easy. I played with one of the hospital wall terminals, running the visitor information program, which displays maps and a staff directory. I broke out of the program to the system level, and wrote a decoy program to mimic the opening screen for logging on. Then I simply left the terminal alone; eventually one of my doctors came by to check one of her files. The decoy rejected her password, and then restored the true opening screen. The doctor tried logging on again, and was successful this time, but her password was left with my decoy.

Using the doctor's account, I had clearance to view the FDA patient-record database. In the Phase I trials, on healthy volunteers, the hormone had no effect. The ongoing Phase II clinical trials are a different matter. Here are weekly reports on eighty-two patients, each identified by a number, all treated with hormone K, most of them victims of a stroke or Alzheimer's, some of them coma cases. The latest reports confirm my prediction: those with greater brain damage display greater increases in intelligence. PET scans reveal heightened brain metabolism.

Why didn't the animal studies provide a precedent for this? I think the concept of critical mass provides an analogy. Animals fall below some critical mass in terms of synapses; their brains support only minimal abstraction, and gain nothing from additional synapses. Humans exceed that critical mass. Their brains support full self-awareness, and—as these records indicate—they use any new synapses to the fullest possible extent.

The most exciting records are those of the newly begun investigational studies, using a few of the patients who volunteered. Additional injections of the hormone do increase intelligence further, but again it depends on the degree of initial damage. The patients with minor strokes haven't even reached genius levels. Those with greater damage have gone further.

Of the patients originally in deep-coma states, I'm the only one thus far who's received a third injection. I've gained more new synapses than anyone previously studied; it's an open question as to how high my intelligence will go. I can feel my heart pounding when I think about it.

Playing with the doctors is becoming more and more tedious as the weeks go by. They treat me as if I were simply an idiot savant: a patient who exhibits certain signs of high intelligence, but still just a patient. As far as the neurologists are concerned, I'm just a source of PET scan images and an occasional vial of cerebrospinal fluid. The psychologists have the opportunity to gain some insight into my thinking through their interviews, but they can't shed their preconception of me as someone out of his depth, an ordinary man awarded gifts that he can't appreciate.

On the contrary, the doctors are the ones who don't appreciate what's happening. They're certain that real-world performance can't be enhanced by a drug, and that my ability exists only according to the artificial yardstick of intelligence tests, so they waste their time with those. But the yardstick is not only contrived, it's too short: my consistently perfect scores don't tell them anything, because they have no basis for comparison this far out on the bell curve.

Of course, the test scores merely capture a shadow of the real changes occurring. If only the doctors could feel what's going on in my head: how much I'm recognizing that I missed before, how many uses I can see for that information. Far from being a laboratory phenomenon, my intelligence is practical and effectual. With my near-total recall and my ability to correlate, I can assess a situation immediately, and choose the best course of action for my purposes; I'm never indecisive. Only theoretical topics pose a challenge.

No matter what I study, I can see patterns. I see the gestalt, the melody within the notes, in everything: mathematics and science, art and music, psychology and sociology. As I read the texts, I can think only that the authors are plodding along from one point to the next, groping for connections that they can't see. They're like a crowd of people unable to read music, peering at the score for a Bach sonata, trying to explain how one note leads to another.

As glorious as these patterns are, they also whet my appetite for more. There are other patterns waiting to be discovered, gestalts of another scale entirely. With respect to those, I'm blind myself; all my sonatas are just isolated data points by comparison. I have no idea what form such gestalts might assume, but that'll come in time. I want to find them, and comprehend them. I want this more than anything I've ever wanted before.

The visiting doctor's name is Clausen, and he doesn't behave like the other doctors. Judging by his manner, he's accustomed to wearing a mask of blandness with his patients, but he's a bit uncomfortable today. He affects an air of friendliness, but it isn't as fluent as the perfunctory noise that the other doctors make.

"The test works this way, Leon: you'll read some descriptions of various situations, each presenting a problem. After each one, I want you to tell me what you'd do to solve that problem."

I nod. "I've had this kind of test before."

"Fine, fine." He types a command, and the screen in front of me fills with text. I read the scenario: it's a problem in scheduling and prioritizing. It's realistic, which is unusual; scoring such a test is too arbitrary for most researchers' tastes. I wait before giving my answer, though Clausen is still surprised at my speed.

"That's very good, Leon." He hits a key on his computer. "Try this one."

We continue with more scenarios. As I'm reading the fourth one, Clausen is careful to display only professional detachment. My response to this problem is of special interest to him, but he doesn't want me to know. The scenario involves office politics and fierce competition for a promotion.

I realize who Clausen is: he's a government psychologist, perhaps military, probably part of the CIA's Office of Research and Development. This test is meant to gauge hormone K's potential for producing strategists. That's why he's uncomfortable with me: he's used to dealing with soldiers and government employees, subjects whose job is to follow orders.

It's likely that the CIA will wish to retain me as a subject for more tests; they may do the same with other patients, depending on their performance. After that, they'll get some volunteers from their ranks, starve their brains of oxygen, and treat them with hormone K. I certainly don't wish to become a CIA resource, but I've already demonstrated enough ability to arouse their interest. The best I can do is to downplay my skills and get this question wrong.

I offer a poor course of action as my answer, and Clausen is disappointed. Nonetheless, we press on. I take longer on the scenarios now, and give weaker responses. Sprinkled among the harmless questions are the critical ones: one about avoiding a hostile corporate takeover, another about mobilizing people to prevent the construction of a coal-burning plant. I miss each of these questions.

Clausen dismisses me when the test ends; he's already trying to formulate his recommendations. If I'd shown my true abilities, the CIA would recruit me immediately. My uneven performance will reduce their eagerness, but it won't change their minds; the potential returns are too great for them to ignore hormone K.

My situation has changed profoundly; when the CIA decides to retain me as a test subject, my consent will be purely optional. I must make plans.

It's four days later, and Shea is surprised. "You want to withdraw from the study?"

"Yes, effective immediately. I'm returning to work."

"If it's a matter of compensation, I'm sure we can—"

"No, money's not the problem. I've simply had enough of these tests."

"I know the tests become tiring after a while, but we're learning a great deal. And we appreciate your participation, Leon. It's not merely—"

"I know how much you're learning from these tests. It doesn't change my decision: I don't wish to continue."

Shea starts to speak again, but I cut him off. "I know that I'm still bound by the confidentiality agreement; if you'd like me to sign something confirming that, send it to me." I get up and head for the door. "Good-bye, Dr. Shea."

It's two days later when Shea calls.

"Leon, you have to come in for an examination. I've just been informed: adverse side effects have been found in patients treated with hormone K at another hospital."

He's lying; he'd never tell me that over the phone. "What sort of side effects?"

"Loss of vision. There's excessive growth of the optic nerve, followed by deterioration."

The CIA must have ordered this when they heard that I'd withdrawn from the study. Once I'm back in the hospital, Shea will declare me mentally incompetent, and confine me to their care. Then I'll be transferred to a government research institution.

I assume an expression of alarm. "I'll come down right away."

"Good." Shea is relieved that his delivery was convincing. "We can examine you as soon as you arrive."

I hang up and turn on my terminal to check the latest information in the FDA database. There's no mention of any adverse effects, on the optic nerve or anywhere else. I don't discount the possibility that such effects might arise in the future, but I'll discover them by myself.

It's time to leave Boston. I begin packing. I'll empty my bank accounts when I go. Selling the equipment in my studio would generate more cash, but most of it is too large to transport; I take only a few of the smallest pieces. After I've been working a couple of hours, the phone rings again: Shea wondering where I am. This time I let the machine pick it up.

"Leon, are you there? This is Dr. Shea. We've been expecting you for quite some time."

He'll try calling one more time, and then he'll send the orderlies in white suits, or perhaps the actual police, to pick me up.

Seven-thirty p.m. Shea is still in the hospital, waiting for news about me. I turn the ignition key and pull out of my parking spot across the street from the hospital. Any moment now, he'll notice the envelope I slipped under the door to his office. As soon as he opens it he'll realize that it's from me.

Greetings, Dr. Shea,
    I imagine you're looking for me.

A moment of surprise, but no more than a moment; he'll regain his composure, and alert security to search the building for me, and check all departing vehicles. Then he'll continue reading.

You can call off those burly orderlies who are waiting at my apartment; I don't want to waste their valuable time. You're probably determined to have the police issue an APB on me, though. Therefore, I've taken the liberty of inserting a virus in the DMV computer, that will substitute information whenever my license plate number is requested. Of course, you could give a description of my car, but you don't even know what it looks like, do you?

Leon

He'll call the police to have their programmers work on that virus. He'll conclude that I have a superiority complex, based on the arrogant tone of the note, the unnecessary risk taken in returning to the hospital to deliver it, and the pointless revelation of a virus which might otherwise have gone undetected.

Shea will be mistaken, though. Those actions are designed to make the police and CIA underestimate me, so I can rely on their not taking adequate precautions. After cleaning my virus from the DMV computer, the police programmers will assess my programming skills as good but not great, and then load the backups to retrieve my actual license number. This will activate a second virus, a far more sophisticated one. This one will modify both the backups and the active database. The police will be satisfied that they've got the correct license number, and spend their time chasing that wild goose.

My next goal is to get another ampule of hormone K. Doing so, unfortunately, will give the CIA an accurate idea of how capable I really am. If I hadn't sent that note, the police would discover my virus later, at a time when they'd know to take super-stringent precautions when eradicating it. In that case, I might never be able to remove my license number from their files.

Meanwhile, I've checked into a hotel, and am working out of the room's datanet terminal.

———

I've broken into the private database of the FDA. I've seen the addresses of the hormone K subjects, and the internal communications of the FDA. A clinical hold was instituted for hormone K: no further testing permitted until the hold is lifted. The CIA has insisted on capturing me and assessing my threat potential before the FDA goes any further.

The FDA has asked all the hospitals to return the remaining ampules by courier. I must get an ampule before this happens. The nearest patient is in Pittsburgh; I reserve a seat on a flight leaving early tomorrow morning. Then I check a map of Pittsburgh, and make a request to the Pennsylvania Courier company for a pickup at an investment firm in the downtown area. Finally I sign up for several hours of CPU time on a supercomputer.

I'm parked in a rental car around the corner from a skyscraper in Pittsburgh. In my jacket pocket is a small circuit board with a keypad. I'm looking down the street in the direction the courier will arrive from; half the pedestrians wear white air filter masks, but visibility is good.

I see it two intersections away; it's a late-model domestic van, Pennsylvania Courier painted on the side. It's not a high-security courier; the FDA isn't that worried about me. I get out of my car and begin walking toward the skyscraper. The van arrives shortly, parks, and the driver gets out. As soon as he's inside, I enter the vehicle.

It's just come from the hospital. The driver is on his way to the fortieth floor, expecting to pick up a package from an investment firm there. He won't be back for at least four minutes.

Welded to the floor of the van is a large locker, with double-layered steel walls and door. There is a polished plate on the door; the locker opens when the driver lays his palm against its surface. The plate also has a dataport in its side, used for programming it.

Last night I penetrated the service database for Lucas Security Systems, the company that sells handprint locks to Pennsylvania Courier. There I found an encrypted file containing the codes to override their locks.

I must admit that, while penetrating computer security remains generally unaesthetic, certain aspects of it are indirectly related to very interesting problems in mathematics. For example, a commonly used method of encryption normally requires years of supercomputer time to break. However, during one of my forays into number theory, I found a lovely technique for factoring extremely large numbers. With this technique, a supercomputer could break this encryption scheme in a matter of hours.

I pull the circuit board from my pocket and connect it to the dataport with a cable. I tap in a twelve-digit number, and the locker door swings open.

By the time I'm back in Boston with the ampule, the FDA has responded to the theft by removing all pertinent files from any computer accessible through the datanet: as expected.

With the ampule and my belongings, I drive to New York City.

The fastest way for me to make money is, oddly enough, gambling. Handicapping horse races is simple enough. Without attracting undue attention, I can accumulate a moderate sum, and then sustain myself with investments in the stock market.

I'm staying in a room in the cheapest apartment I could find near New York that has datanet outlets. I've arranged several false names under which to make my investments, and will change them regularly. I shall spend some time on Wall Street, so that I can identify high-yield, short-term opportunities from the body language of brokers. I won't go more than once a week; there are more significant matters to attend to, gestalts beckoning my attention.

As my mind develops, so does my control over my body. It is a misconception to think that during evolution humans sacrificed physical skill in exchange for intelligence: wielding one's body is a mental activity. While my strength hasn't increased, my coordination is now well above average; I'm even becoming ambidextrous. Moreover, my powers of concentration make biofeedback techniques very effective. After comparatively little practice, I am able to raise or lower my heart rate and blood pressure.

I write a program to perform a pattern match for photos of my face and search for occurrences of my name; I then incorporate it into a virus for scanning all public display files on the datanet. The CIA will have the national datanet news briefs display my picture and identify me as a dangerously insane escaped patient, perhaps a murderer. The virus will replace my photo with video static. I plant a similar virus in the FDA and CIA computers, to search for copies of my picture in any downloads to regional police. These viruses should be immune to anything that their programmers can come up with.

Undoubtedly Shea and the other doctors are in consultation with the psychologists of the CIA, guessing where I might have gone. My parents are dead, so the CIA is turning its attention to my friends, asking whether I've contacted them; they'll maintain surveillance on them in the event I do. A regrettable invasion of their privacy, but it isn't a pressing matter.

It's unlikely that the CIA will treat any of their agents with hormone K to locate me. As I myself demonstrate, a superintelligent person is too difficult to control. However, I'll keep track of the other patients, in case the government decides to recruit them.

The quotidian patterns of society are revealed without my making an effort. I walk down the street, watching people go about their business, and though not a word is spoken, the subtext is conspicuous. A young couple strolls by, the adoration of one bouncing off the tolerance of the other. Apprehension flickers and becomes steady as a businessman, fearful of his supervisor, begins to doubt a decision he made earlier today. A woman wears a mantle of simulated sophistication, but it slips when it brushes past the genuine article.

As always, the roles one plays become recognizable only with greater maturity. To me, these people seem like children on a playground; I'm amused by their earnestness, and embarassed to remember myself doing those same things. Their activities are appropriate for them, but I couldn't bear to participate now; when I became a man, I put away childish things. I will deal with the world of normal humans only as needed to support myself.

I acquire years of education each week, assembling ever-larger patterns. I view the tapestry of human knowledge from a broader perspective than anyone ever has before; I can fill gaps in the design where scholars never even noticed a lack, and enrich the texture in places that they felt were complete.

The natural sciences have the clearest patterns. Physics admits of a lovely unification, not just at the level of fundamental forces, but when considering its extent and implications. Classifications like "optics" or "thermodynamics" are just straitjackets, preventing physicists from seeing countless intersections. Even putting aside aesthetics, the practical applications that have been overlooked are legion; years ago engineers could have been artifically generating spherically symmetric gravity fields.

Having realized this, however, I won't build such a device, or any other. It would require many custom-built components, all difficult and time-consuming to procure. Furthermore, actually constructing the device wouldn't give me any particular satisfaction, since I already know it would work, and it wouldn't illuminate any new gestalts.

I'm writing part of an extended poem, as an experiment; after I've finished one canto, I'll be able to choose an approach for integrating the patterns within all the arts. I'm employing six modern and four ancient languages; they include most of the significant worldviews of human civilization. Each one provides different shades of meaning and poetic effects; some of the juxtapositions are delightful. Each line of the poem contains neologisms, born by extruding words through the declensions of another language. If I were to complete the entire piece, it could be thought of as *Finnegans Wake* multiplied by Pound's *Cantos*.

The CIA interrupts my work; they're baiting a trap for me. After two months of trying, they've accepted that they can't locate me by conventional methods, so they've turned to more drastic measures. The news services report that the girlfriend of a deranged murderer has been charged with aiding and abetting his escape. The name given is Connie Perritt, someone I was seeing last year. If it goes to trial, it's a foregone conclusion that she'll be sentenced to a lengthy prison term; the CIA is hoping that I won't allow that. They expect me to attempt a maneuver that will expose me to capture.

Connie's preliminary hearing is tomorrow. They'll ensure that she's released on bail, through a bondsman if necessary, to give me an opportunity to contact her. Then they'll saturate the area around her apartment with undercover agents to wait for me.

I begin editing the first image onscreen. These digital photos are so minimal compared to holos, but they serve the purpose. The photos, taken yesterday, show the exterior of Connie's apartment building, the street out front, and nearby intersections. I move the cursor across the screen, drawing small crosshairs in certain locations on the images. A window, with lights out but curtains open, in the building diagonally opposite. A street vendor two blocks from the rear of the building.

I mark six locations altogether. They indicate where CIA agents were waiting last night, when Connie went back to her apartment.

Having been cued by the videotapes of me in the hospital, they knew what to look for in all male or ambiguous passersby: the confident, level gait. Their expectations worked against them; I simply lengthened my stride, bobbed my head up and down a bit, reduced my arm motion. That and some atypical clothes were sufficient for them to ignore me as I walked through the area.

At the bottom of one photo I type the radio frequency used by the agents for communication, and an equation describing the scrambling algorithm employed. Once I've finished, I transmit the images to the Director of the CIA. The implication is clear: I could kill his undercover agents at any time, unless they withdraw.

To have them drop charges against Connie, and for a more permanent deterrent against the CIA's distractions, I shall have to do some more work.

Pattern recognition again, but this time it's of a mundane variety. Thousands of pages of reports, memos, correspondence; each one is a dot of color in a pointillist painting. I step back from this panorama, watching for lines and edges to emerge and create a pattern. The megabytes that I scanned constituted only a fraction of the complete records for the period I investigated, but they were enough.

What I've found is rather ordinary, far simpler than the plot of a spy novel. The Director of the CIA was aware of a terrorist group's plan to bomb the Washington, D.C., metro system. He let the bombing occur, in order to gain congressional approval for the use of extreme measures against that group. A congressman's son was among the casualties, and the CIA Director was given a free hand in handling the terrorists. While his plans aren't actually stated in CIA records, they're implied quite clearly. The relevant memos make only oblique references, and they float in a sea of innocuous documents; if an investigating committee were to read all of the records, the evidence would be drowned out by the noise. However, a distillation of the incriminating memos would certainly convince the press.

I send the list of memos to the Director of the CIA, with a note: *Don't bother me, and I won't bother you.* He'll realize that he has no alternative.

This little episode has reinforced my opinion of the affairs of the world; I could detect clandestine ploys everywhere if I kept informed about current events, but none of them would be interesting. I shall resume my studies.

Control over my body continues to grow. By now I could walk on hot coals or stick needles in my arm, if I were so inclined. However, my interest in Eastern meditation is limited to its application to physical control; no meditative trance I can attain is nearly as desirable to me as my mental state when I assemble gestalts out of elemental data.

I'm designing a new language. I've reached the limits of conventional languages, and now they frustrate my attempts to progress further. They lack the power to express concepts that I need, and even in their own domain, they're imprecise and unwieldy. They're hardly fit for speech, let alone thought.

Existing linguistic theory is useless; I'll reevaluate basic logic to determine the suitable atomic components for my language. This language will support a dialect coexpressive with all of mathematics, so that any equation I write will have a linguistic equivalent. However, mathematics will be only a small part of the language, not the whole; unlike Leibniz, I recognize symbolic logic's limits. Other dialects I have planned will be coexpressive with my notations for aesthetics and cognition. This will be a time-consuming project, but the end result will clarify my thoughts enormously. After I've translated all that I know into this language, the patterns I seek should become evident.

I pause in my work. Before I develop a notation for aesthetics, I must establish a vocabulary for all the emotions I can imagine.

I'm aware of many emotions beyond those of normal humans; I see how limited their affective range is. I don't deny the validity of the love and angst I once felt, but I do see them for what they were: like the infatuations and depressions of childhood, they were just the forerunners of what I experience now. My passions now are more multifaceted; as self-knowledge increases, all emotions become exponentially more complex. I must be able to describe them fully if I'm to even attempt the composing tasks ahead.

Of course, I actually experience far fewer emotions than I could; my development is limited by the intelligence of those around me, and the scant intercourse I permit myself with them. I'm reminded of the Confucian concept of *ren*: inadequately conveyed by "benevolence," that quality which is quintessentially human, which can only be cultivated through interaction with others, and which a solitary person cannot manifest. It's one of many such qualities. And here am I, with people, people everywhere, yet not a one to interact with. I'm only a fraction of what a complete individual with my intelligence could be.

I don't delude myself with either self-pity or conceit: I can evaluate my own psychological state with the utmost objectivity and consistency. I know precisely which emotional resources I have and which I lack, and how much value I place on each. I have no regrets.

My new language is taking shape. It is gestalt oriented, rendering it beautifully suited for thought, but impractical for writing or speech. It wouldn't be transcribed in the form of words arranged linearly, but as a giant ideogram, to be absorbed as a whole. Such an ideogram could convey, more deliberately than a picture, what a thousand words cannot. The intricacy of each ideogram would be commensurate with the amount of information contained; I amuse myself with the notion of a colossal ideogram that describes the entire universe.

The printed page is too clumsy and static for this language; the only serviceable media would be video or holo, displaying a time-evolving graphic image. Speaking this language would be out of the question, given the limited bandwidth of the human larynx.

My mind seethes with expletives from ancient and modern languages, and they taunt me with their crudeness, reminding me that my ideal language would offer terms with sufficient venom to express my present frustration.

I cannot complete my artificial language; it's too large a project for my present tools. Weeks of concentrated effort have yielded nothing usable. I've attempted to write it via bootstrapping, by employing the rudimentary language that I've already defined to rewrite the language and produce successively fuller versions. Yet each new version only highlights its own inadequacies, forcing me to expand my ultimate goal, condemning it to the status of a Holy Grail at the end of a divergent infinite regress. This is no better than trying to create it ex nihilo.

What about my fourth ampule? I can't remove it from my thoughts: every frustration I experience at my present plateau reminds me of the possibility for still greater heights.

Of course, there are significant risks. This injection might be the one that causes brain damage or insanity. Temptation by the Devil, perhaps, but temptation nonetheless. I find no reason to resist.

I'd have a margin of safety if I injected myself in a hospital, or, failing that, with someone standing by in my apartment. However, I imagine the injection will either be successful or else cause irreparable damage, so I forego those precautions.

I order equipment from a medical supply company, and assemble an apparatus for administering the spinal injection by myself. It may take days for the full effects to become evident, so I'll confine myself to my bedroom. It's possible that my reaction will be violent; I remove breakables from the room and attach loose straps to the bed. The neighbors will interpret anything they hear as an addict howling. I inject myself and wait.

My brain is on fire, my spine burns itself through my back, I feel near apoplexy. I am blind, deaf, insensate.

I hallucinate. Seen with such preternatural clarity and contrast that they must be illusory, unspeakable horrors loom all around me, scenes not of physical violence but of psychic mutilation.

Mental agony and orgasm. Terror and hysterical laughter.

For a brief moment, perception returns. I'm on the floor, hands clenched in my hair, some uprooted tufts lying around me. My clothes are soaked in sweat. I've bitten my tongue, and my throat is raw: from screaming, I surmise. Convulsions have left my body badly bruised, and a concussion is likely, given the contusions on the back of my head, but I feel nothing. Has it been hours or moments?

Then my vision clouds and the roar returns.

....

Critical mass.

....

Revelation.

I understand the mechanism of my own thinking. I know precisely how I know, and my understanding is recursive. I understand the infinite regress of this self-knowing, not by proceeding step by step endlessly, but by apprehending the *limit*. The nature of recursive cognition is clear to me. A new meaning of the term "self-aware."

Fiat logos. I know my mind in terms of a language more expressive than any I'd previously imagined. Like God creating order from chaos with an utterance, I make myself anew with this language. It is meta-self-descriptive and self-editing; not only can it describe thought, it can describe and modify its own operations as well, at all levels. What Godel would have given to see this language, where modifying a statement causes the entire grammar to be adjusted.

With this language, I can see how my mind is operating. I don't pretend to see my own neurons firing; such claims belong to John Lilly and his LSD experiments of the sixties. What I can do is perceive the gestalts; I see the mental structures forming, interacting. I see myself thinking, and I see the equations that describe my thinking, and I see myself comprehending the equations, and I see how the equations describe their being comprehended.

I know how they make up my thoughts.

These thoughts.

Initially I am overwhelmed by all this input, paralyzed with awareness of my self. It is hours before I can control the flood of self-describing information. I haven't filtered it away, nor pushed it into the background. It's become integrated into my mental processes, for use during my normal activities. It will be longer before I can take advantage of it, effortlessly and effectively, the way a dancer uses her kinesthetic knowledge.

All that I once knew theoretically about my mind, I now see detailed explicitly. The undercurrents of sex, aggression, and self-preservation, translated by the conditioning of my childhood, clash with and are sometimes disguised as rational thought. I recognize all the causes of my every mood, the motives behind my every decision.

What can I do with this knowledge? Much of what is conventionally described as "personality" is at my discretion; the higher-level aspects of my psyche define who I am now. I can send my mind into a variety of mental or emotional states, yet remain ever aware of the state and able to restore my original condition. Now that I understand the mechanisms that were operating when I attended to two tasks at once, I can divide my consciousness, simultaneously devoting almost full concentration and gestalt recognition abilities to two or more separate problems, meta-aware of all of them. What can't I do?

I know my body afresh, as if it were an amputee's stump suddenly replaced by a watchmaker's hand. Controlling my voluntary muscles is trivial; I have inhuman coordination. Skills that normally require thousands of repetitions to develop, I can learn in two or three. I find a video with a shot of a pianist's hands playing, and before long I can duplicate his finger movements without a keyboard in front of me. Selective contraction and relaxation of muscles improve my strength and flexibility. Muscular response time is thirty-five milliseconds, for conscious or reflex action. Learning acrobatics and martial arts would require little training.

I have somatic awareness of kidney function, nutrient absorption, glandular secretions. I am even conscious of the role that neurotransmitters play in my thoughts. This state of consciousness involves mental activity more intense than in any epinephrine-boosted stress situation; part of my mind is maintaining a condition that would kill a normal mind and body within minutes. As I adjust the programming of my mind, I experience the ebb and flow of all the substances that trigger my emotional reactions, boost my attention, or subtly shape my attitudes.

And then I look outward.

Blinding, joyous, fearful symmetry surrounds me. So much is incorporated within patterns now that the entire universe verges on resolving itself into a picture. I'm closing in on the ultimate gestalt: the context in which all knowledge fits and is illuminated, a mandala, the music of the spheres, *kosmos.*

I seek enlightenment, not spiritual but rational. I must go still further to reach it, but this time the goal will not be perpetually retreating from my fingertips. With my mind's language, the distance between myself and enlightenment is precisely calculable. I've sighted my final destination.

Now I must plan my next actions. First, there are the simple enhancements to self-preservation, starting with martial arts training. I will watch some tournaments to study possible attacks, though I will take only defensive action; I can move rapidly enough to avoid contact with even the fastest striking techniques. This will let me protect myself and disarm any street criminals, should I be assaulted. Meanwhile, I must eat copious amounts of food to meet my brain's nourishment requirements, even given increased efficiency in my metabolism. I shall also shave my scalp, to allow greater radiative cooling for the heightened blood flow to my head.

Then there is the primary goal: decoding those patterns. For further improvements to my mind, artificial enhancements are the only possibility. A direct computer-mind link, permitting mind downloading, is what I need, but I must create a new technology to implement it. Anything based on digital computation will be inadequate; what I have in mind requires nanoscale structures based on neural networks.

Once I have the basic ideas laid out, I set my mind to multiprocessing: one section of my mind deriving a branch of mathematics that reflects the networks' behavior; another developing a process for replicating the formation of neural pathways on a molecular scale in a self-repairing bioceramic medium; a third devising tactics for guiding private industrial R & D to produce what I'll need. I cannot waste time: I will introduce explosive theoretical and technical breakthroughs so that my new industry will hit the ground running.

I've gone into the outside world to reobserve society. The sign language of emotion I once knew has been replaced by a matrix of interrelated equations. Lines of force twist and elongate between people, objects, institutions, ideas. The individuals are tragically like marionettes, independently animate but bound by a web they choose not to see; they could resist if they wished, but so few of them do.

At the moment I'm sitting at a bar. Three stools to my right sits a man, familiar with this type of establishment, who looks around and notices a couple in a dark corner booth. He smiles, motions for the bartender to come over, and leans forward to speak confidentially about the couple. I don't need to listen to know what he's saying.

He's lying to the bartender, easily, extemporaneously. A compulsive liar, not out of a desire for a life more exciting than his own, but to revel in his facility for deceiving others. He knows the bartender is detached, merely affecting interest—which is true—but he knows the bartender is still fooled—which is also true.

My sensitivity to the body language of others has increased to the point that I can make these observations without sight or sound: I can smell the pheromones exuded by his skin. To an extent, my muscles can even detect the tension within his, perhaps by their electric field. These channels can't convey precise information, but the impressions I receive provide ample basis for extrapolation; they add texture to the web.

Normal humans may detect these emanations subliminally. I'll work on becoming more attuned to them; then perhaps I can try consciously controlling my own expressions.

I've developed abilities reminiscent of the mind-control schemes offered by tabloid advertisements. My control over my somatic emanations now lets me provoke precise reactions in others. With pheromones and muscle tension, I can cause another person to respond with anger, fear, sympathy, or sexual arousal. Certainly enough to win friends and influence people.

I can even induce a self-sustaining reaction in others. By associating a particular response with a sense of satisfaction, I can create a positive reinforcement loop, like biofeedback; the person's body will strengthen the reaction on its own. I'll use this on corporate presidents to create support for the industries I'll need.

I can no longer dream in any normal sense. I lack anything that would qualify as a subconscious, and I control all the maintenance functions performed by my brain, so normal REM sleep tasks are obsolete. There are moments when my grasp on my mind slips, but they cannot be called dreams. Meta-hallucinations, perhaps. Sheer torture. These are periods during which I'm detached: I understand how my mind generates the strange visions, but I'm paralyzed and unable to respond. I can scarcely identify what I see; images of bizarre transfinite self-references and modifications that even I find nonsensical.

My mind is taxing the resources of my brain. A biological structure of this size and complexity can just barely sustain a self-knowing psyche. But the self-knowing psyche is also self-regulating, to an extent. I give my mind full use of what's available, and restrain it from expanding beyond that. But it's difficult: I'm cramped inside a bamboo cage that doesn't let me sit down or stand up. If I try to relax, or try to extend myself fully, then agony, madness.

I'm hallucinating. I see my mind imagining possible configurations it could assume, and then collapsing. I witness my own delusions, my visions of what form my mind might take when I grasp the ultimate gestalts.

Will I achieve ultimate self-awareness? Could I discover the components that make up my own mental gestalts? Would I penetrate racial memory? Would I find innate knowledge of morality? I might determine whether mind could be spontaneously generated from matter, and understand what relates consciousness with the rest of the universe. I might see how to merge subject and object: the zero experience.

Or perhaps I'd find that the mind gestalt cannot be generated, and some sort of intervention is required. Perhaps I would see the soul, the ingredient of consciousness that surpasses physicality. Proof of God? I would behold the meaning, the true character of existence. I would be enlightened. It must be euphoric to experience . . .

My mind collapses back into a state of sanity. I must keep a tighter rein over my self. When I'm in control at the metaprogramming level, my mind is perfectly self-repairing; I could restore myself from states that resemble delusion or amnesia. But if I drift too far on the metaprogramming level, my mind might become an unstable structure, and then I would slide into a state beyond mere insanity. I will program my mind to forbid itself from moving beyond its own reprogramming range.

These hallucinations strengthen my resolve to create an artificial brain. Only with such a structure will I be able to actually perceive those gestalts, instead of merely dreaming about them. To achieve enlightenment, I'll need to exceed another critical mass in terms of neuronal analogs.

I open my eyes: it's two hours, twenty-eight minutes, and ten seconds since I closed my eyes to rest, though not to sleep. I rise from bed.

I request a listing of my stocks' performance on my terminal. I look down the flatscreen, and freeze.

The screen shouts at me. It tells me that there is another person with an enhanced mind.

Five of my investments have demonstrated losses; they're not precipitous, but large enough that I'd have detected them in the body language of the stockbrokers. Reading down the alphabetical list, the initial letters of the corporations whose stock values have dropped are: C, E, G, O, and R. Which, when rearranged, spell GRECO.

Someone is sending me a message.

There's someone else out there like me. There must have been another comatose patient who received a third injection of hormone K. He erased his file from the FDA database before I accessed it, and supplied false input to his doctors' accounts so that they wouldn't notice. He too stole another ampule of the hormone, contributing to the FDA's closing of their files, and with his whereabouts unknown to the authorities, he's reached my level.

He must have recognized me through the investment patterns of my false identities; he'd have to have been supercritical to do that. As an enhanced individual, he could have effected sudden and precise changes to trigger my losses, and attract my attention.

I check various data services for stock quotes; the entries on my listing are correct, so my counterpart didn't simply edit the values for my account alone. He altered the selling patterns of the stock of five unrelated corporations, for the sake of a word. It makes for quite a demonstration; I consider it no mean feat.

Presumably his treatment began before mine did, meaning that he is farther along than I, but by how much? I begin extrapolating his likely progress, and will incorporate new information as I acquire it.

The critical question: is he friend or foe? Was this merely a good-natured demonstration of his power, or an indication of his intent to ruin me? The amounts I lost were moderate; does this indicate concern for me, or for the corporations which he had to manipulate? Given all the harmless ways he could have attracted my attention, I must assume that he is to some degree hostile.

In which case, I am at risk, vulnerable to anything from another prank to a fatal attack. As a precaution, I will leave immediately. Obviously, if he were actively hostile, I'd be dead already. His sending a message means that he wishes us to play games. I'll have to place myself on equal terms with him: hide my location, determine his identity, and then attempt to communicate.

I pick a city at random: Memphis. I switch off the flatscreen, get dressed, pack a travel bag, and collect all the emergency cash in the apartment.

In a Memphis hotel, I begin working at the suite's datanet terminal. The first thing I do is reroute my activities through several dummy terminals; to an ordinary police trace, my queries will appear to originate from different terminals all over the state of Utah. A military intelligence facility might be able to track them to a terminal in Houston; continuing the trace to Memphis would try even me. An alarm program at the Houston terminal will alert me if someone has successfully traced me there.

How many clues to his identity has my twin erased? Lacking all FDA files, I'll begin with the files of courier services in various cities, looking for deliveries from the FDA to hospitals during the time of the hormone K study. Then a check of the hospital's brain-damage cases at that time, and I'll have a place to start.

Even if any of this information remains, it's of minor value. What will be crucial is an examination of the investment patterns, to find the traces of an enhanced mind. This will take time.

His name is Reynolds. He's originally from Phoenix, and his early progress closely parallels mine. He received his third injection six months and four days ago, giving him a head start over me of fifteen days. He didn't erase any of the obvious records. He waits for me to find him. I estimate that he's been supercritical for twelve days, twice as long as I've been.

I now see his hand in the investment patterns, but the task of locating Reynolds is Herculean. I examine usage logs across the datanet to identify the accounts he's penetrated. I have twelve lines open on my terminal. I'm using two single-hand keyboards and a throat mike, so I can work on three queries simultaneously. Most of my body is immobile; to prevent fatigue, I'm ensuring proper blood flow, regular muscle contraction and relaxation, and removal of lactic acid. While I absorb all the data I see, studying the melody within the notes, looking for the epicenter of a tremor in the web.

Hours pass. We both scan gigabytes of data, circling each other.

His location is Philadelphia. He waits for me to arrive.

I'm riding in a mud-splattered taxi to Reynolds's apartment.

Judging by the databases and agencies Reynolds has queried over the past months, his private research involves bioengineered micro-organisms for toxic waste disposal, inertial containment for practical fusion, and subliminal dissemination of information through societies of various structures. He plans to save the world, to protect it from itself. And his opinion of me is therefore unfavorable.

I've shown no interest in the affairs of the external world, and made no investigations for aiding the normals. Neither of us will be able to convert the other. I view the world as incidental to my aims, while he cannot allow someone with enhanced intelligence to work purely in self-interest. My plans for mind-computer links will have enormous repercussions for the world, provoking government or popular reactions that would interfere with his plans. As I am proverbially not part of the solution, I am part of the problem.

If we were members of a society of enhanced minds, the nature of human interaction would be of a different order. But in this society, we have unavoidably become juggernauts, by whose measure the actions of normals are inconsequential. Even if we were twelve thousand miles apart we couldn't ignore each other. A resolution is necessary.

Both of us have dispensed with several rounds of games. There are a thousand ways we could have attempted to kill the other, from painting neurotoxin-laced DMSO on a doorknob to ordering a surgical strike from a military killsat. We both could have swept the physical area and datanet for each of the myriad possibilities beforehand, and set more traps for each other's sweeps. But neither of us has done any of that, has felt a need to check for those things. A simple infinite regression of second-guessing and double-thinking has dismissed those. What will be decisive are those preparations that we could not predict.

The taxi stops; I pay the driver and walk up to the apartment building. The electric lock on the door opens for me. I take off my coat and climb four flights.

The door to Reynolds's apartment is also open. I walk down the entryway to the living room, hearing a hyperaccelerated polyphony from a digital synthesizer. Evidently it's his own work; the sounds are modulated in ways undetectable to normal hearing, and even I can't discern any pattern to them. An experiment in high-information-density music, perhaps.

There is a large swivel chair in the room, its back turned toward me. Reynolds is not visible, and he is restricting his somatic emanations to comatose levels. I imply my presence and my recognition of his identity.

<Reynolds.>

Acknowledgment. <Greco.>

The chair turns around smoothly, slowly. He smiles at me and shuts off the synthesizer at his side. Gratification. <A pleasure to meet you.>

To communicate, we are exchanging fragments from the somatic language of the normals: a shorthand version of the vernacular. Each phrase takes a tenth of a second. I give a suggestion of regret. <A shame it must be as enemies.>

Wistful agreement, then supposition. <Indeed. Imagine how we could change the world, acting in concert. Two enhanced minds; such an opportunity missed.>

True, acting cooperatively would produce achievements far out-stripping any we might attain individually. Any interaction would be incredibly fruitful: how satisfying it would be simply to have a discussion with someone who can match my speed, who can offer an idea that is new to me, who can hear the same melodies I do. He desires the same. It pains us both to think that one of us will not leave this room alive.

An offer. <Do you wish to share what we've learned in the past six months?>

He knows what my answer is.

We will speak aloud, since somatic language has no technical vocabulary. Reynolds says, quickly and quietly, five words. They are more pregnant with meaning than any stanza of poetry: each word provides a logical toehold I can mount after extracting everything implicit in the preceding ones. Together they encapsulate a revolutionary insight into sociology; using somatic language he indicates that it was among the first he ever achieved. I came to a similar realization, but formulated it differently. I immediately counter with seven words, four that summarize the distinctions between my insight and his, and three that describe a nonobvious result of the distinctions. He responds.

We continue. We are like two bards, each cueing the other to extemporize another stanza, jointly composing an epic poem of knowledge. Within moments we accelerate, talking over each other's words but hearing every nuance, until we are absorbing, concluding, and responding, continuously, simultaneously, synergistically.

Many minutes pass. I learn much from him, and he from me. It's exhilarating, to be suddenly awash in ideas whose implications would take me days to consider fully. But we're also gathering strategic information: I infer the extent of his unspoken knowledge, compare it with my own, and simulate his corresponding inferences. For there is always the awareness that this must come to an end; the formulation of our exchanges renders ideological differences luminously clear.

Reynolds hasn't witnessed the beauty that I have; he's stood before lovely insights, oblivious to them. The sole gestalt that inspires him is the one I ignored: that of the planetary society, of the biosphere. I am a lover of beauty, he of humanity. Each feels that the other has ignored great opportunities.

He has an unmentioned plan for establishing a global network of influence, to create world prosperity. To execute it, he'll employ a number of people, some of whom he'll give simple heightened intelligence, some meta-self-awareness; a few of them will pose threats to him. <Why assume such a risk for the sake of the normals?>

<Your indifference toward the normals would be justified if you were enlightened; your realm wouldn't intersect theirs. But as long as you and I can still comprehend their affairs, we can't ignore them.>

I can measure the distance between our respective moral stances precisely, see the stress between their incompatible radiating lines. What motivates him is not simply compassion or altruism, but something that entails both those things. On the other hand, I concentrate only on understanding the sublime. <What about the beauty visible from enlightenment? Doesn't it attract you?>

<You know what kind of structure would be required to hold an enlightened consciousness. I have no reason to wait the time it would take to establish the necessary industries.>

He considers intelligence to be a means, while I view it as an end in itself. Greater intelligence would be of little use to him. At his present level, he can find the best possible solution to any problem within the realm of human experience, and many beyond. All he'd require is sufficient time to implement his solution.

There's no point in further discussion. By mutual assent, we begin.

It's meaningless to speak of an element of surprise when we time our attacks; our awareness can't become more acute with forewarning. It's not affording a courtesy to each other when we agree to begin our battle, it's actualizing the inevitable.

In the models of each other that we've constructed from our inferences, there are gaps, lacunae: the internal psychological developments and discoveries that each has made. No echoes have radiated from those spaces, no strands have tied them to the world web, until now.

I begin.

I concentrate on initiating two reinforcing loops in him. One is very simple: it increases blood pressure rapidly and enormously. If it were to continue unchecked for over a second, this loop would raise his blood pressure to stroke levels—perhaps 400 over 300—and burst capillaries in his brain.

Reynolds detects it immediately. Though it's clear from our conversation that he never investigated the inducement of biofeedback loops in others, he recognizes what is happening. Once he does, he reduces his heart rate and dilates the blood vessels throughout his body.

But it is the other, subtler reinforcing loop that is my real attack. This is a weapon I've been developing ever since my search for Reynolds began. This loop causes his neurons to dramatically overproduce neurotransmitter antagonists, preventing impulses from crossing his synapses, shutting down brain activity. I've been radiating this loop at a much higher intensity than the other.

As Reynolds is parrying the ostensible attack, he experiences a slight weakening of his concentration, masked by the effects of the heightened blood pressure. A second later, his body begins to amplify the effect on its own. Reynolds is shocked to feel his thoughts blurring. He searches for the precise mechanism: he'll identify it soon, but he won't be able to scrutinize it for long.

Once his brain function has been reduced to the level of a normal, I should be able to manipulate his mind easily. Hypnotic techniques can make him regurgitate most of the information his enhanced mind possesses.

I inspect his somatic expressions, watching them betray his diminishing intelligence. The regression is unmistakable.

And then it stops.

Reynolds is in equilibrium. I'm stunned. He was able to break the reinforcing loop. He has stopped the most sophisticated offensive I could mount.

Next, he reverses the damage already done. Even starting with reduced capabilities, he can correct the balance of neurotransmitters. Within seconds, Reynolds is fully restored.

I too was transparent to him. During our conversation he deduced that I had investigated reinforcing loops, and as we communicated, he derived a general preventative without my detecting it. Then he observed the specifics of my particular attack while it was working, and learned how to reverse its effects. I am astonished at his discernment, his speed, his stealth.

He acknowledges my skill. <A very interesting technique; appropriate, given your self-absorption. I saw no indication when—> Abruptly he projects a different somatic signature, one that I recognize. He used it when he walked behind me at a grocery store, three days ago. The aisle was crowded; around me were an old woman, wheezing behind her air filter, and a thin teenager on an acid trip, wearing a liquid crystal shirt of shifting psychedelic patterns. Reynolds slipped behind me, his mind on the porn mag stands. His surveillance didn't inform him of my reinforcing loops, but it did permit a more detailed picture of my mind.

A possibility I anticipated. I reformulate my psyche, incorporating random elements for unpredictability. The equations of my mind now bear little resemblance to those of my normal consciousness, undermining any assumptions Reynolds may have made, and rendering ineffectual any psyche-specific weapons of his.

I project the equivalent of a smile.

Reynolds smiles back. <Have you ever considered—> Suddenly he projects only silence. He is about to speak, but I can't predict what. Then it comes, as a whisper: "self-destruct commands, Greco?"

As he says it, a lacuna in my reconstruction of him fills and overflows, the implications coloring all that I know about him. He means the Word: the sentence that, when uttered, would destroy the mind of the listener. Reynolds is claiming that the myth is true, that every mind has such a trigger built in; that for every person, there is a sentence that can reduce him to an idiot, a lunatic, a catatonic. And he is claiming he knows the one for me.

I immediately tune out all sensory input, directing it to an insulated buffer of short-term memory. Then I conceive a simulator of my own consciousness to receive the input and absorb it at reduced speed. As a metaprogrammer I will monitor the equations of the simulation indirectly. Only after the sensory information has been confirmed as safe will I actually receive it. If the simulator is destroyed, my consciousness should be isolated, and I'll retrace the individual steps leading to the crash and derive guidelines for reprogramming my psyche.

I get everything in place by the time Reynolds has finished saying my name; his next sentence could be the destruct command. I'm now receiving my sensory input with a one-hundred-and-twenty-millisecond time lag. I reexamine my analysis of the human mind, explicitly searching for evidence to verify his assertion.

Meanwhile I give my response lightly, casually. <Hit me with your best shot.>

<Don't worry; it's not on the tip of my tongue.>

My search produces something. I curse myself: there's a very subtle back door to a psyche's design, which I lacked the necessary mind-set to notice. Whereas my weapon was one born of introspection, his is something only a manipulator could originate.

Reynolds knows that I've built my defenses; is his trigger command designed to circumvent them? I continue deriving the nature of the trigger command's actions.

<What are you waiting for?> He's confident that additional time won't allow me to construct a defense.

<Try to guess.> So smug. Can he actually toy with me so easily?

I arrive at a theoretical description of a trigger's effects on normals. A single command can reduce any subcritical mind to a tabula rasa, but an undetermined degree of customization is needed for enhanced minds. The erasure has distinctive symptoms, which my simulator can alert me to, but those are symptoms of a process calculable by me. By definition the destruct command is that specific equation beyond my ability to imagine; would my metaprogrammer collapse while diagnosing the simulator's condition?

<Have you used the destruct command on normals?> I begin calculating what's needed to generate a customized destruct command.

<Once, as an experiment on a drug dealer. Afterward I concealed the evidence with a blow to the temple.>

It becomes obvious that the generation is a colossal task. Generating a trigger requires intimate knowledge of my mind; I extrapolate what he could have learned about me. It appears to be insufficient, given my reprogramming, but he may have techniques of observation unknown to me. I'm acutely aware of the advantage he's gained by studying the outside world.

<You will have to do this many times.>

His regret is evident. His plan can't be implemented without more deaths: those of normal humans, by strategic necessity, and those of a few enhanced assistants of his, whose temptation by greater heights would interfere. After using the command, Reynolds may reprogram them—or me—as savants, having focused intentions and restricted self-metaprogrammers. Such deaths are a necessary cost of his plan.

<I make no claims of being a saint.>

Merely a savior.

Normals might think him a tyrant, because they mistake him for one of them, and they've never trusted their own judgment. They can't fathom that Reynolds is equal to the task. His judgment is optimal in questions of their affairs, and their notions of greed and ambition do not apply to an enhanced mind.

In a histrionic gesture, Reynolds raises his hand, forefinger extended, as if to make a point. I don't have sufficient information to generate his destruct command, so for the moment I can only attend to defense. If I can survive his attack, I may have time to launch another one of my own.

With his finger upraised, he says, "Understand."

At first I don't. And then, horrifyingly, I do.

He didn't design the command to be spoken; it's not a sensory trigger at all. It's a memory trigger: the command is made out of a string of perceptions, individually harmless, that he planted in my brain like time bombs. The mental structures that were formed as a result of those memories are now resolving into a pattern, forming a gestalt that defines my dissolution. I'm intuiting the Word myself.

Immediately my mind is working faster than ever before. Against my will, a lethal realization is suggesting itself to me. I'm trying to halt the associations, but these memories can't be suppressed. The process occurs inexorably, as a consequence of my awareness, and like a man falling from a height, I'm forced to watch.

Milliseconds pass. My death passes before my eyes.

An image of the grocery store when Reynolds passed by. The psychedelic shirt the boy was wearing; Reynolds had programmed the display to implant a suggestion within me, ensuring that my "randomly" reprogrammed psyche remained receptive. Even then.

No time. All I can do is metaprogram myself over randomly, at a furious pace. An act of desperation, possibly crippling.

The strange modulated sounds that I heard when I first entered Reynolds's apartment. I absorbed the fatal insights before I had any defenses raised.

I tear apart my psyche, but still the conclusion grows clearer, the resolution sharper.

Myself, constructing the simulator. Designing those defense structures gave me the perspective needed to recognize the gestalt.

I concede his greater ingenuity. It bodes well for his endeavor. Pragmatism avails a savior far more than aestheticism.

I wonder what he intends to do after he's saved the world.

I comprehend the Word, and the means by which it operates, and so I dissolve.

Division by Zero

1

Dividing a number by zero doesn't produce an infinitely large number as an answer. The reason is that division is defined as the inverse of multiplication; if you divide by zero, and then multiply by zero, you should regain the number you started with. However, multiplying infinity by zero produces only zero, not any other number. There is nothing which can be multiplied by zero to produce a nonzero result; therefore, the result of a division by zero is literally "undefined."

1A

Renee was looking out the window when Mrs. Rivas approached.

"Leaving after only a week? Hardly a real stay at all. Lord knows I won't be leaving for a long time."

Renee forced a polite smile. "I'm sure it won't be long for you." Mrs. Rivas was the manipulator in the ward; everyone knew that her attempts were merely gestures, but the aides wearily paid attention to her lest she succeed accidentally.

"Ha. They wish I'd leave. You know what kind of liability they face if you die while you're on status?"

"Yes, I know."

"That's all they're worried about, you can tell. Always their liability—"

Renee tuned out and returned her attention to the window, watching a contrail extrude itself across the sky.

"Mrs. Norwood?" a nurse called. "Your husband's here."

Renee gave Mrs. Rivas another polite smile and left.

1B

Carl signed his name yet another time, and finally the nurses took away the forms for processing.

He remembered when he had brought Renee in to be admitted, and thought of all the stock questions at the first interview. He had answered them all stoically.

"Yes, she's a professor of mathematics. You can find her in *Who's Who*."

"No, I'm in biology."

And:

"I had left behind a box of slides that I needed."

"No, she couldn't have known."

And, just as expected:

"Yes, I have. It was about twenty years ago, when I was a grad student."

"No, I tried jumping."

"No, Renee and I didn't know each other then."

And on and on.

Now they were convinced that he was competent and supportive, and were ready to release Renee into an outpatient treatment program.

Looking back, Carl was surprised in an abstracted way. Except for one moment, there hadn't been any sense of déjà vu at any time during the entire ordeal. All the time he was dealing with the hospital, the doctors, the nurses: the only accompanying sensation was one of numbness, of sheer tedious rote.

2

There is a well-known "proof" that demonstrates that one equals two. It begins with some definitions: "Let a = 1; let b = 1." It ends with the conclusion "a = 2a," that is, one equals two. Hidden inconspicuously in the middle is a division by zero, and at that point the proof has stepped off the brink, making all rules null and void. Permitting division by zero allows one to prove not only that one and two are equal, but that any two numbers at all—real or imaginary, rational or irrational—are equal.

2A

As soon as she and Carl got home, Renee went to the desk in her study and began turning all the papers facedown, blindly sweeping them together into a pile; she winced whenever a corner of a page faced up during her shuffling. She considered burning the pages, but that would be merely symbolic now. She'd accomplish as much by simply never glancing at them.

The doctors would probably describe it as obsessive behavior. Renee frowned, reminded of the indignity of being a patient under such fools. She remembered being on suicide status, in the locked ward, under the supposedly round-the-clock observation of the aides. And the interviews with the doctors, who were so condescending, so obvious. She was no manipulator like Mrs. Rivas, but it really was easy. Simply say "I realize I'm not well yet, but I do feel better," and you'd be considered almost ready for release.

2B

Carl watched Renee from the doorway for a moment, before he passed down the hallway. He remembered the day, fully two decades past, when he himself had been released. His parents had picked him up, and on the trip back his mother had made some inane comment about how glad everyone would be to see him, and he was just barely able to restrain himself from shaking her arm off his shoulders.

He had done for Renee what he would have appreciated during his period under observation. He had come to visit every day, even though she refused to see him at first, so that he wouldn't be absent when she did want to see him. Sometimes they talked, and sometimes they simply walked around the grounds. He could find nothing wrong in what he did, and he knew that she appreciated it.

Yet, despite all his efforts, he felt no more than a sense of duty towards her.

3

In the *Principia Mathematica*, Bertrand Russell and Alfred Whitehead attempted to give a rigorous foundation to mathematics using formal logic as their basis. They began with what they considered to be axioms, and used those to derive theorems of increasing complexity. By page 362, they had established enough to prove "$1 + 1 = 2$."

3A

As a child of seven, while investigating the house of a relative, Renee had been spellbound at discovering the perfect squares in the smooth marble tiles of the floor. A single one, two rows of two, three rows of three, four rows of four: the tiles fit together in a *square*. Of course. No matter which side you looked at it from, it came out the same. And more than that, each square was bigger than the last by an *odd number of tiles*. It was an epiphany. The conclusion was necessary: it had a rightness to it, confirmed by the smooth, cool feel of the tiles. And the way the tiles were fitted together, with such incredibly fine lines where they met; she had shivered at the precision.

Later on there came other realizations, other achievements. The astonishing doctoral dissertation at twenty-three, the series of acclaimed papers; people compared her to Von Neumann, universities wooed her. She had never paid any of it much attention. What she did pay attention to was that same sense of rightness, possessed by every theorem she learned, as insistent as the tiles' physicality, and as exact as their fit.

3B

Carl felt that the person he was today was born after his attempt, when he met Laura. After being released from the hospital, he was in no mood to see anyone, but a friend of his had managed to introduce him to Laura. He had pushed her away initially, but she had known better. She had loved him while he was hurting, and let him go once he was healed. Through knowing her Carl had learned about empathy, and he was remade.

Laura had moved on after getting her own master's degree, while he stayed at the university for his doctorate in biology. He suffered various crises and heartbreaks later on in life, but never again despair.

Carl marveled when he thought about what kind of person she was. He hadn't spoken to her since grad school; what had her life been like over the years? He wondered whom else she had loved. Early on he had recognized what kind of love it was, and what kind it wasn't, and he valued it immensely.

4

In the early nineteenth century, mathematicians began exploring geometries that differed from Euclidean geometry; these alternate geometries produced results that seemed utterly absurd, but they didn't produce logical contradictions. It was later shown that these non-Euclidean geometries were consistent relative to Euclidean geometry: they were logically consistent, as long as one assumed that Euclidean geometry was consistent.

The proof of Euclidean geometry's consistency eluded mathematicians. By the end of the nineteenth century, the best that was achieved was a proof that Euclidean geometry was consistent as long as arithmetic was consistent.

4A

At the time, when it all began, Renee had thought it little more than an annoyance. She had walked down the hall and knocked on the open door of Peter Fabrisi's office. "Pete, got a minute?"

Fabrisi pushed his chair back from his desk. "Sure, Renee, what's up?"

Renee came in, knowing what his reaction would be. She had never asked anyone in the department for advice on a problem before; it had always been the reverse. No matter. "I was wondering if you could do me a favor. You remember what I was telling you about a couple weeks back, about the formalism I was developing?"

He nodded. "The one you were rewriting axiom systems with."

"Right. Well, a few days ago I started coming up with really ridiculous conclusions, and now my formalism is contradicting itself. Could you take a look at it?"

Fabrisi's expression was as expected. "You want—sure, I'd be glad to."

"Great. The examples on the first few pages are where the problem is; the rest is just for your reference." She handed Fabrisi a thin sheaf of papers. "I thought if I talked you through it, you'd just see the same things I do."

"You're probably right." Fabrisi looked at the first couple pages. "I don't know how long this'll take."

"No hurry. When you get a chance, just see whether any of my assumptions seem a little dubious, anything like that. I'll still be going at it, so I'll tell you if I come up with anything. Okay?"

Fabrisi smiled. "You're just going to come in this afternoon and tell me you've found the problem."

"I doubt it: this calls for a fresh eye."

He spread his hands. "I'll give it a shot."

"Thanks." It was unlikely that Fabrisi would fully grasp her formalism, but all she needed was someone who could check its more mechanical aspects.

4B

Carl had met Renee at a party given by a colleague of his. He had been taken with her face. Hers was a remarkably plain face, and it appeared quite somber most of the time, but during the party he saw her smile twice and frown once; at those moments, her entire countenance assumed the expression as if it had never known another. Carl had been caught by surprise: he could recognize a face that smiled regularly, or a face that frowned regularly, even if it were unlined. He was curious as to how her face had developed such a close familiarity with so many expressions, and yet normally revealed nothing.

It took a long time for him to understand Renee, to read her expressions. But it had definitely been worthwhile.

Now Carl sat in his easy chair in his study, a copy of the latest issue of *Marine Biology* in his lap, and listened to the sound of Renee crumpling paper in her study across the hall. She'd been working all evening, with audibly increasing frustration, though she'd been wearing her customary poker face when last he'd looked in.

He put the journal aside, got up from the chair, and walked over to the entrance of her study. She had a volume opened on her desk; the pages were filled with the usual hieroglyphic equations, interspersed with commentary in Russian.

She scanned some of the material, dismissed it with a barely perceptible frown, and slammed the volume closed. Carl heard her mutter the word "useless," and she returned the tome to the bookcase.

"You're gonna give yourself high blood pressure if you keep up like this," Carl jested.

"Don't patronize me."

Carl was startled. "I wasn't."

Renee turned to look at him and glared. "I know when I'm capable of working productively and when I'm not."

Chilled. "Then I won't bother you." He retreated.

"Thank you." She returned her attention to the bookshelves. Carl left, trying to decipher that glare.

5

At the Second International Congress of Mathematics in 1900, David Hilbert listed what he considered to be the twenty-three most important unsolved problems of mathematics. The second item on his list was a request for a proof of the consistency of arithmetic. Such a proof would ensure the consistency of a great deal of higher mathematics. What this proof had to guarantee was, in essence, that one could never prove one equals two. Few mathematicians regarded this as a matter of much import.

5A

Renee had known what Fabrisi would say before he opened his mouth.

"That was the damnedest thing I've ever seen. You know that toy for toddlers where you fit blocks with different cross sections into the differently shaped slots? Reading your formal system is like watching someone take one block and sliding it into every single hole on the board, and making it a perfect fit every time."

"So you can't find the error?"

He shook his head. "Not me. I've slipped into the same rut as you. I can only think about it one way."

Renee was no longer in a rut: she had come up with a totally different approach to the question, but it only confirmed the original contradiction. "Well, thanks for trying."

"You going to have someone else take a look at it?"

"Yes, I think I'll send it to Callahan over at Berkeley. We've been corresponding since the conference last spring."

Fabrisi nodded. "I was really impressed by his last paper. Let me know if he can find it: I'm curious."

Renee would have used a stronger word than "curious" for herself.

5B

Was Renee just frustrated with her work? Carl knew that she had never considered mathematics really difficult, just intellectually challenging. Could it be that for the first time she was running into problems that she could make no headway against? Or did mathematics work that way at all? Carl himself was strictly an experimentalist; he really didn't know how Renee made new math. It sounded silly, but perhaps she was running out of ideas?

Renee was too old to be suffering from the disillusionment of a child prodigy becoming an average adult. On the other hand, many mathematicians did their best work before the age of thirty, and she might be growing anxious over whether that statistic was catching up to her, albeit several years behind schedule.

It seemed unlikely. He gave a few other possibilities cursory consideration. Could she be growing cynical about academia? Dismayed that her research had become overspecialized? Or simply weary of her work?

Carl didn't believe that such anxieties were the cause of Renee's behavior; he could imagine the impressions that he would pick up if that were the case, and they didn't mesh with what he was receiving. Whatever was bothering Renee, it was something he couldn't fathom, and that disturbed him.

6

In 1931, Kurt Gödel demonstrated two theorems. The first one shows, in effect, that mathematics contains statements that may be true, but are inherently unprovable. Even a formal system as simple as arithmetic permits statements that are precise, meaningful, and seem certainly true, and yet cannot be proven true by formal means.

His second theorem shows that a claim of the consistency of arithmetic is just such a statement; it cannot be proven true by any means using the axioms of arithmetic. That is, arithmetic as a formal system cannot guarantee that it will not produce results such as "$1 = 2$"; such contradictions may never have been encountered, but it is impossible to prove that they never will be.

6A

Once again, he had come into her study. Renee looked up from her desk at Carl; he began resolutely, "Renee, it's obvious that—"

She cut him off. "You want to know what's bothering me? Okay, I'll tell you." Renee got out a blank sheet of paper and sat down at her desk. "Hang on; this'll take a minute." Carl opened his mouth again, but Renee waved him silent. She took a deep breath and began writing.

She drew a line down the center of the page, dividing it into two columns. At the head of one column she wrote the numeral "1" and for the other she wrote "2." Below them she rapidly scrawled out some symbols, and in the lines below those she expanded them into strings of other symbols. She gritted her teeth as she wrote: forming the characters felt like dragging her fingernails across a chalkboard.

About two-thirds of the way down the page, Renee began reducing the long strings of symbols into successively shorter strings. *And now for the masterstroke*, she thought. She realized she was pressing hard on the paper; she consciously relaxed her grip on the pencil. On the next line that she put down, the strings became identical. She wrote an emphatic "=" across the center line at the bottom of the page.

She handed the sheet to Carl. He looked at her, indicating incomprehension. "Look at the top." He did so. "Now look at the bottom."

He frowned. "I don't understand."

"I've discovered a formalism that lets you equate any number with any other number. That page there proves that one and two are equal. Pick any two numbers you like; I can prove those equal as well."

Carl seemed to be trying to remember something. "It's a division by zero, right?"

"No. There are no illegal operations, no poorly defined terms, no independent axioms that are implicitly assumed, nothing. The proof employs absolutely nothing that's forbidden."

Carl shook his head. "Wait a minute. Obviously one and two aren't the same."

"But formally they are: the proof's in your hand. Everything I've used is within what's accepted as absolutely indisputable."

"But you've got a contradiction here."

"That's right. Arithmetic as a formal system is inconsistent."

6B

"You can't find your mistake, is that what you mean?"

"*No*, you're not listening. You think I'm just frustrated because of something like that? There is no mistake in the proof."

"You're saying there's something wrong within what's accepted?"

"Exactly."

"Are you—" He stopped, but too late. She glared at him. Of course she was sure. He thought about what she was implying.

"Do you see?" asked Renee. "I've just disproved most of mathematics: it's all meaningless now."

She was getting agitated, almost distraught; Carl chose his words carefully. "How can you say that? Math still works. The scientific and economic worlds aren't suddenly going to collapse from this realization."

"That's because the mathematics they're using is just a gimmick. It's a mnemonic trick, like counting on your knuckles to figure out which months have thirty-one days."

"That's not the same."

"Why isn't it? Now mathematics has absolutely *nothing* to do with reality. Never mind concepts like imaginaries or infinitesimals. Now goddamn integer addition has nothing to do with counting on your fingers. One and one will always get you two on your fingers, but on paper I can give you an infinite number of answers, and they're all equally valid, which means they're all equally invalid. I can write the most elegant theorem you've ever seen, and it won't mean any more than a nonsense equation." She gave a bitter laugh. "The positivists used to say all mathematics is a tautology. They had it all wrong: it's a contradiction."

Carl tried a different approach. "Hold on. You just mentioned imaginary numbers. Why is this any worse than what went on with those? Mathematicians once believed they were meaningless, but now they're accepted as basic. This is the same situation."

"It's *not* the same. The solution there was to simply expand the context, and that won't do any good here. Imaginary numbers added something new to mathematics, but my formalism is redefining what's already there."

"But if you change the context, put it in a different light—"

She rolled her eyes. "No! This follows from the axioms as surely as addition does; there's no way around it. You can take my word for it."

7

In 1936, Gerhard Gentzen provided a proof of the consistency of arithmetic, but to do it he needed to use a controversial technique known as transfinite induction. This technique is not among the usual methods of proof, and it hardly seemed appropriate for guaranteeing the consistency of arithmetic. What Gentzen had done was prove the obvious by assuming the doubtful.

7A

Callahan had called from Berkeley, but could offer no rescue. He said he would continue to examine her work, but it seemed that she had hit upon something fundamental and disturbing. He wanted to know about her plans for publication of her formalism, because if it did contain an error that neither of them could find, others in the mathematics community would surely be able to.

Renee had barely been able to hear him speaking, and mumbled that she would get back to him. Lately she had been having difficulty talking to people, especially since the argument with Carl; the other members of the department had taken to avoiding her. Her concentration was gone, and last night she had had a nightmare about discovering a formalism that let her translate arbitrary concepts into mathematical expressions: then she had proven that life and death were equivalent.

That was something that frightened her: the possibility that she was losing her mind. She was certainly losing her clarity of thought, and that came pretty close.

What a ridiculous woman you are, she chided herself. Was Gödel suicidal after he demonstrated his incompleteness theorem?

But that was beautiful, numinous, one of the most elegant theorems Renee had ever seen.

Her own proof taunted her, ridiculed her. Like a brainteaser in a puzzle book, it said gotcha, you skipped right over the mistake, see if you can find where you screwed up; only to turn around and say, gotcha again.

She imagined Callahan would be pondering the implications that her discovery held for mathematics. So much of mathematics had no practical application; it existed solely as a formal theory, studied for its intellectual beauty. But that couldn't last; a self-contradictory theory was so pointless that most mathematicians would drop it in disgust.

What truly infuriated Renee was the way her own intuition had betrayed her. The damned theorem made sense; in its own perverted way, it *felt right*. She understood it, knew why it was true, believed it.

7B

Carl smiled when he thought of her birthday.

"I can't believe you! How could you possibly have known?" She had run down the stairs, holding a sweater in her hands.

Last summer they had been in Scotland on vacation, and in one store in Edinburgh there had been a sweater that Renee had been eyeing but didn't buy. He had ordered it, and placed it in her dresser drawer for her to find that morning.

"You're just so transparent," he had teased her. They both knew that wasn't true, but he liked to tell her that.

That was two months ago. A scant two months.

Now the situation called for a change of pace. Carl went into her study, and found Renee sitting in her chair, staring out the window. "Guess what I got for us."

She looked up. "What?"

"Reservations for the weekend. A suite at the Biltmore. We can relax and do absolutely nothing—"

"Please stop," Renee said. "I know what you're trying to do, Carl. You want us to do something pleasant and distracting to take my mind off this formalism. But it won't work. You don't know what kind of hold this has on me."

"Come on, come on." He tugged at her hands to get her off the chair, but she pulled away. Carl stood there for a moment, when suddenly she turned and locked eyes with him.

"You know I've been tempted to take barbiturates? I almost wish I were an idiot, so I wouldn't have to think about it."

He was taken aback. Uncertain of his bearings, he said, "Why won't you at least try to get away for a while? It couldn't hurt, and maybe it'll take your mind off this."

"It's not anything I can take my mind off of. You just don't understand."

"So explain it to me."

Renee exhaled and turned away to think for a moment. "It's like everything I see is shouting the contradiction at me," she said. "I'm equating numbers all the time now."

Carl was silent. Then, with sudden comprehension, he said, "Like the classical physicists facing quantum mechanics. As if a theory you've always believed has been superseded, and the new one makes no sense, but somehow all the evidence supports it."

"No, it's not like that at all." Her dismissal was almost contemptuous. "This has nothing to do with evidence; it's all a priori."

"How is that different? Isn't it just the evidence of your reasoning then?"

"Christ, are you joking? It's the difference between my measuring one and two to have the same value, and my intuiting it. I can't maintain the concept of distinct quantities in my mind anymore; they all feel the same to me."

"You don't mean that," he said. "No one could actually experience such a thing; it's like believing six impossible things before breakfast."

"How would you know what I can experience?"

"I'm trying to understand."

"Don't bother."

Carl's patience was gone. "All right then." He walked out of the room and canceled their reservations.

They scarcely spoke after that, talking only when necessary. It was three days later that Carl forgot the box of slides he needed, and drove back to the house, and found her note on the table.

Carl intuited two things in the moments following. The first came to him as he was racing through the house, wondering if she had gotten some cyanide from the chemistry department: it was the realization that, because he couldn't understand what had brought her to such an action, he couldn't feel anything for her.

The second intuition came to him as he was pounding on the bedroom door, yelling at her inside: he experienced déjà vu. It was the only time the situation would feel familiar, and yet it was grotesquely reversed. He remembered being on the other side of a locked door, on the roof of a building, hearing a friend pounding on the door and yelling for him not to do it. And as he stood there outside the bedroom door, he could hear her sobbing, on the floor paralyzed with shame, exactly the same as he had been when it was him on the other side.

8

Hilbert once said, "If mathematical thinking is defective, where are we to find truth and certitude?"

8A

Would her suicide attempt brand her for the rest of her life? Renee wondered. She aligned the corners of the papers on her desk. Would people henceforth regard her, perhaps unconsciously, as flighty or unstable? She had never asked Carl if he had ever felt such anxieties, perhaps because she never held his attempt against him. It had happened many years ago, and anyone seeing him now would immediately recognize him as a whole person.

But Renee could not say the same for herself. Right now she was unable to discuss mathematics intelligibly, and she was unsure whether she ever could again. Were her colleagues to see her now, they would simply say, She's lost the knack.

Finished at her desk, Renee left her study and walked into the living room. After her formalism circulated through the academic community, it would require an overhaul of established mathematical foundations, but it would affect only a few as it had her. Most would be like Fabrisi; they would follow the proof mechanically, and be convinced by it, but no more. The only persons who would feel it nearly as keenly as she had were those who could actually grasp the contradiction, who could intuit it. Callahan was one of those; she wondered how he was handling it as the days wore on.

Renee traced a curly pattern in the dust on an end table. Before, she might have idly parameterized the curve, examined some of its characteristics. Now there seemed no point. All of her visualizations simply collapsed.

She, like many, had always thought that mathematics did not derive its meaning from the universe, but rather imposed some meaning onto the universe. Physical entities were not greater or less than one another, not similar or dissimilar; they simply were, they existed. Mathematics was totally independent, but it virtually provided a semantic meaning for those entities, supplying categories and relationships. It didn't describe any intrinsic quality, merely a possible interpretation.

But no more. Mathematics was inconsistent once it was removed from physical entities, and a formal theory was nothing if not consistent. Math was *empirical*, no more than that, and it held no interest for her.

What would she turn to, now? Renee had known someone who gave up academia to sell handmade leather goods. She would have to take some time, regain her bearings. And that was just what Carl had been trying to help her do, throughout it all.

8b

Among Carl's friends were a pair of women who were each other's best friend, Marlene and Anne. Years ago, when Marlene had considered suicide, she hadn't turned to Anne for support: she had turned to Carl. He and Marlene had sat up all night on a few occasions, talking or sharing silence. Carl knew that Anne had always harbored a bit of envy for what he had shared with Marlene, that she had always wondered what advantage he held that allowed him to get so close to her. The answer was simple. It was the difference between sympathy and empathy.

Carl had offered comfort in similar situations more than once in his lifetime. He had been glad he could help, certainly, but more than that, it had felt right to sit in the other seat, and play the other part.

He had always had reason to consider compassion a basic part of his character, until now. He had valued that, felt that he was nothing if not empathic. But now he'd run up against something he'd never encountered before, and it rendered all his usual instincts null and void.

If someone had told him on Renee's birthday that he would feel this way in two months' time, he would have dismissed the idea instantly. Certainly such a thing could happen over years; Carl knew what time could do. But two months?

After six years of marriage, he had fallen out of love with her. Carl detested himself for the thought, but the fact was that she had changed, and now he neither understood her nor knew how to feel for her. Renee's intellectual and emotional lives were inextricably linked, so that the latter had moved beyond his reach.

His reflex reaction of forgiveness cut in, reasoning that you couldn't ask a person to remain supportive through any crisis. If a man's wife were suddenly afflicted with mental illness, it would be a sin for him to leave her, but a forgivable one. To stay would mean accepting a different kind of relationship, something which not everyone was cut out for, and Carl never condemned a person in such a situation. But there was always the unspoken question: What would I do? And his answer had always been, I would stay.

Hypocrite.

Worst of all, he had been there. He had been absorbed in his own pain, he had tried the endurance of others, and someone had nursed him through it all. His leaving Renee was inevitable, but it would be a sin he couldn't forgive.

9

Albert Einstein once said, "Insofar as the propositions of mathematics give an account of reality they are not certain; and insofar as they are certain they do not describe reality."

9A = 9B

Carl was in the kitchen, stringing snow pea pods for dinner, when Renee came in. "Can I talk to you for a minute?"

"Sure." They sat down at the table. She looked studiedly out the window: her habit when beginning a serious conversation. He suddenly dreaded what she was about to say. He hadn't planned to tell her that he was leaving until she'd fully recovered, after a couple of months. Now was too soon.

"I know it hasn't been obvious—"

No, he prayed, don't say it. Please don't.

"—but I'm really grateful to have you here with me."

Pierced, Carl closed his eyes, but thankfully Renee was still looking out the window. It was going to be so, so difficult.

She was still talking. "The things that have been going on in my head—" She paused. "It was like nothing I'd ever imagined. If it had been any normal kind of depression, I know you would have understood, and we could have handled it."

Carl nodded.

"But what happened, it was almost as if I were a theologian proving that there was no God. Not just fearing it, but knowing it for a fact. Does that sound absurd?"

"No."

"It's a feeling I can't convey to you. It was something that I believed deeply, implicitly, and it's not true, and I'm the one who demonstrated it."

He opened his mouth to say that he knew exactly what she meant, that he had felt the same things as she. But he stopped himself: for this was an empathy that separated rather than united them, and he couldn't tell her that.

Story of Your Life

Your father is about to ask me the question. This is the most important moment in our lives, and I want to pay attention, note every detail. Your dad and I have just come back from an evening out, dinner and a show; it's after midnight. We came out onto the patio to look at the full moon; then I told your dad I wanted to dance, so he humors me and now we're slow-dancing, a pair of thirtysomethings swaying back and forth in the moonlight like kids. I don't feel the night chill at all. And then your dad says, "Do you want to make a baby?"

Right now your dad and I have been married for about two years, living on Ellis Avenue; when we move out you'll still be too young to remember the house, but we'll show you pictures of it, tell you stories about it. I'd love to tell you the story of this evening, the night you're conceived, but the right time to do that would be when you're ready to have children of your own, and we'll never get that chance.

Telling it to you any earlier wouldn't do any good; for most of your life you won't sit still to hear such a romantic—you'd say sappy—story. I remember the scenario of your origin you'll suggest when you're twelve.

"The only reason you had me was so you could get a maid you wouldn't have to pay," you'll say bitterly, dragging the vacuum cleaner out of the closet.

"That's right," I'll say. "Thirteen years ago I knew the carpets would need vacuuming around now, and having a baby seemed to be the cheapest and easiest way to get the job done. Now kindly get on with it."

"If you weren't my mother, this would be illegal," you'll say, seething as you unwind the power cord and plug it into the wall outlet.

That will be in the house on Belmont Street. I'll live to see strangers occupy both houses: the one you're conceived in and the one you grow up in. Your dad and I will sell the first a couple years after your arrival. I'll sell the second shortly after your departure. By then Nelson and I will have moved into our farmhouse, and your dad will be living with what's-her-name.

I know how this story ends; I think about it a lot. I also think a lot about how it began, just a few years ago, when ships appeared in orbit and artifacts appeared in meadows. The government said next to nothing about them, while the tabloids said every possible thing.

And then I got a phone call, a request for a meeting.

I spotted them waiting in the hallway, outside my office. They made an odd couple; one wore a military uniform and a crewcut, and carried an aluminum briefcase. He seemed to be assessing his surroundings with a critical eye. The other one was easily identifiable as an academic: full beard and mustache, wearing corduroy. He was browsing through the overlapping sheets stapled to a bulletin board nearby.

"Colonel Weber, I presume?" I shook hands with the soldier. "Louise Banks."

"Dr. Banks. Thank you for taking the time to speak with us," he said.

"Not at all; any excuse to avoid the faculty meeting."

Colonel Weber indicated his companion. "This is Dr. Gary Donnelly, the physicist I mentioned when we spoke on the phone."

"Call me Gary," he said as we shook hands. "I'm anxious to hear what you have to say."

We entered my office. I moved a couple of stacks of books off the second guest chair, and we all sat down. "You said you wanted me to listen to a recording. I presume this has something to do with the aliens?"

"All I can offer is the recording," said Colonel Weber.

"Okay, let's hear it."

Colonel Weber took a tape machine out of his briefcase and pressed PLAY. The recording sounded vaguely like that of a wet dog shaking the water out of its fur.

"What do you make of that?" he asked.

I withheld my comparison to a wet dog. "What was the context in which this recording was made?"

"I'm not at liberty to say."

"It would help me interpret those sounds. Could you see the alien while it was speaking? Was it doing anything at the time?"

"The recording is all I can offer."

"You won't be giving anything away if you tell me that you've seen the aliens; the public's assumed you have."

Colonel Weber wasn't budging. "Do you have any opinion about its linguistic properties?" he asked.

"Well, it's clear that their vocal tract is substantially different from a human vocal tract. I assume that these aliens don't look like humans?"

The colonel was about to say something noncommittal when Gary Donnelly asked, "Can you make any guesses based on the tape?"

"Not really. It doesn't sound like they're using a larynx to make those sounds, but that doesn't tell me what they look like."

"Anything—is there anything else you can tell us?" asked Colonel Weber.

I could see he wasn't accustomed to consulting a civilian. "Only that establishing communications is going to be really difficult because of the difference in anatomy. They're almost certainly using sounds that the human vocal tract can't reproduce, and maybe sounds that the human ear can't distinguish."

"You mean infra- or ultrasonic frequencies?" asked Gary Donnelly.

"Not specifically. I just mean that the human auditory system isn't an absolute acoustic instrument; it's optimized to recognize the sounds that a human larynx makes. With an alien vocal system, all bets are off." I shrugged. "*Maybe* we'll be able to hear the difference between alien phonemes, given enough practice, but it's possible our ears simply can't recognize the distinctions they consider meaningful. In that case we'd need a sound spectrograph to know what an alien is saying."

Colonel Weber asked, "Suppose I gave you an hour's worth of recordings; how long would it take you to determine if we need this sound spectrograph or not?"

"I couldn't determine that with just a recording no matter how much time I had. I'd need to talk with the aliens directly."

The colonel shook his head. "Not possible."

I tried to break it to him gently. "That's your call, of course. But the only way to learn an unknown language is to interact with a native speaker, and by that I mean asking questions, holding a conversation, that sort of thing. Without that, it's simply not possible. So if you want to learn the aliens' language, someone with training in field linguistics—whether it's me or someone else—will have to talk with an alien. Recordings alone aren't sufficient."

Colonel Weber frowned. "You seem to be implying that no alien could have learned human languages by monitoring our broadcasts."

"I doubt it. They'd need instructional material specifically designed to teach human languages to nonhumans. Either that, or interaction with a human. If they had either of those, they could learn a lot from TV, but otherwise, they wouldn't have a starting point."

The colonel clearly found this interesting; evidently his philosophy was, the less the aliens knew, the better. Gary Donnelly read the colonel's expression too and rolled his eyes. I suppressed a smile.

Then Colonel Weber asked, "Suppose you were learning a new language by talking to its speakers; could you do it without teaching them English?"

"That would depend on how cooperative the native speakers were. They'd almost certainly pick up bits and pieces while I'm learning their language, but it wouldn't have to be much if they're willing to teach. On the other hand, if they'd rather learn English than teach us their language, that would make things far more difficult."

The colonel nodded. "I'll get back to you on this matter."

The request for that meeting was perhaps the second most momentous phone call in my life. The first, of course, will be the one from Mountain Rescue. At that point your dad and I will be speaking to each other maybe once a year, tops. After I get that phone call, though, the first thing I'll do will be to call your father.

He and I will drive out together to perform the identification, a long silent car ride. I remember the morgue, all tile and stainless steel, the hum of refrigeration and smell of antiseptic. An orderly will pull the sheet back to reveal your face. Your face will look wrong somehow, but I'll know it's you.

"Yes, that's her," I'll say. "She's mine."

You'll be twenty-five then.

The MP checked my badge, made a notation on his clipboard, and opened the gate; I drove the off-road vehicle into the encampment, a small village of tents pitched by the Army in a farmer's sun-scorched pasture. At the center of the encampment was one of the alien devices, nicknamed "looking glasses."

According to the briefings I'd attended, there were nine of these in the United States, one hundred and twelve in the world. The looking glasses acted as two-way communication devices, presumably with the ships in orbit. No one knew why the aliens wouldn't talk to us in person; fear of cooties, maybe. A team of scientists, including a physicist and a linguist, was assigned to each looking glass; Gary Donnelly and I were on this one.

Gary was waiting for me in the parking area. We navigated a circular maze of concrete barricades until we reached the large tent that covered the looking glass itself. In front of the tent was an equipment cart loaded with goodies borrowed from the school's phonology lab; I had sent it ahead for inspection by the Army.

Also outside the tent were three tripod-mounted video cameras whose lenses peered, through windows in the fabric wall, into the main room. Everything Gary and I did would be reviewed by countless others, including military intelligence. In addition we would each send daily reports, of which mine had to include estimates on how much English I thought the aliens could understand.

Gary held open the tent flap and gestured for me to enter. "Step right up," he said, circus barker-style. "Marvel at creatures the likes of which have never been seen on God's green earth."

"And all for one slim dime," I murmured, walking through the door. At the moment the looking glass was inactive, resembling a semicircular mirror over ten feet high and twenty feet across. On the brown grass in front of the looking glass, an arc of white spray paint outlined the activation area. Currently the area contained only a table, two folding chairs, and a power strip with a cord leading to a generator outside. The buzz of fluorescent lamps, hung from poles along the edge of the room, commingled with the buzz of flies in the sweltering heat.

Gary and I looked at each other, and then began pushing the cart of equipment up to the table. As we crossed the paint line, the looking glass appeared to grow transparent; it was as if someone was slowly raising the illumination behind tinted glass. The illusion of depth was uncanny; I felt I could walk right into it. Once the looking glass was fully lit it resembled a life-size diorama of a semicircular room. The room contained a few large objects that might have been furniture, but no aliens. There was a door in the curved rear wall.

We busied ourselves connecting everything together: microphone, sound spectrograph, portable computer, and speaker. As we worked, I frequently glanced at the looking glass, anticipating the aliens' arrival. Even so I jumped when one of them entered.

It looked like a barrel suspended at the intersection of seven limbs. It was radially symmetric, and any of its limbs could serve as an arm or a leg. The one in front of me was walking around on four legs, three non-adjacent arms curled up at its sides. Gary called them "heptapods."

I'd been shown videotapes, but I still gawked. Its limbs had no distinct joints; anatomists guessed they might be supported by vertebral columns. Whatever their underlying structure, the heptapod's limbs conspired to move it in a disconcertingly fluid manner. Its "torso" rode atop the rippling limbs as smoothly as a hovercraft.

Seven lidless eyes ringed the top of the heptapod's body. It walked back to the doorway from which it entered, made a brief sputtering sound, and returned to the center of the room followed by another heptapod; at no point did it ever turn around. Eerie, but logical; with eyes on all sides, any direction might as well be "forward."

Gary had been watching my reaction. "Ready?" he asked.

I took a deep breath. "Ready enough." I'd done plenty of fieldwork before, in the Amazon, but it had always been a bilingual procedure: either my informants knew some Portuguese, which I could use, or I'd previously gotten an intro to their language from the local missionaries. This would be my first attempt at conducting a true monolingual discovery procedure. It was straightforward enough in theory, though.

I walked up to the looking glass and a heptapod on the other side did the same. The image was so real that my skin crawled. I could see the texture of its gray skin, like corduroy ridges arranged in whorls and loops. There was no smell at all from the looking glass, which somehow made the situation stranger.

I pointed to myself and said slowly, "Human." Then I pointed to Gary. "Human." Then I pointed at each heptapod and said, "What are you?"

No reaction. I tried again, and then again.

One of the heptapods pointed to itself with one limb, the four terminal digits pressed together. That was lucky. In some cultures a person pointed with his chin; if the heptapod hadn't used one of its limbs, I wouldn't have known what gesture to look for. I heard a brief fluttering sound, and saw a puckered orifice at the top of its body vibrate; it was talking. Then it pointed to its companion and fluttered again.

I went back to my computer; on its screen were two virtually identical spectrographs representing the fluttering sounds. I marked a sample for playback. I pointed to myself and said "Human" again, and did the same with Gary. Then I pointed to the heptapod, and played back the flutter on the speaker.

The heptapod fluttered some more. The second half of the spectrograph for this utterance looked like a repetition: call the previous utterances [flutter1], then this one was [flutter2flutter1].

I pointed at something that might have been a heptapod chair. "What is that?"

The heptapod paused, and then pointed at the "chair" and talked some more. The spectrograph for this differed distinctly from that of the earlier sounds: [flutter3]. Once again, I pointed to the "chair" while playing back [flutter3].

The heptapod replied; judging by the spectrograph, it looked like [flutter3flutter2]. Optimistic interpretation: the heptapod was confirming my utterances as correct, which implied compatibility between heptapod and human patterns of discourse. Pessimistic interpretation: it had a nagging cough.

At my computer I delimited certain sections of the spectrograph and typed in a tentative gloss for each: "heptapod" for [flutter1], "yes" for [flutter2], and "chair" for [flutter3]. Then I typed "Language: Heptapod A" as a heading for all the utterances.

Gary watched what I was typing. "What's the 'A' for?"

"It just distinguishes this language from any other ones the heptapods might use," I said. He nodded.

"Now let's try something, just for laughs." I pointed at each heptapod and tried to mimic the sound of [flutter1], "heptapod." After a long pause, the first heptapod said something and then the second one said something else, neither of whose spectrographs resembled anything said before. I couldn't tell if they were speaking to each other or to me since they had no faces to turn. I tried pronouncing [flutter1] again, but there was no reaction.

"Not even close," I grumbled.

"I'm impressed you can make sounds like that at all," said Gary.

"You should hear my moose call. Sends them running."

I tried again a few more times, but neither heptapod responded with anything I could recognize. Only when I replayed the recording of the heptapod's pronunciation did I get a confirmation; the heptapod replied with [flutter2], "yes."

"So we're stuck with using recordings?" asked Gary.

I nodded. "At least temporarily."

"So now what?"

"Now we make sure it hasn't actually been saying 'aren't they cute' or 'look what they're doing now.' Then we see if we can identify any of these words when that other heptapod pronounces them." I gestured for him to have a seat. "Get comfortable; this'll take a while."

In 1770, Captain Cook's ship *Endeavour* ran aground on the coast of Queensland, Australia. While some of his men made repairs, Cook led an exploration party and met the aboriginal people. One of the sailors pointed to the animals that hopped around with their young riding in pouches, and asked an aborigine what they were called. The aborigine replied, "Kanguru." From then on Cook and his sailors referred to the animals by this word. It wasn't until later that they learned it meant "What did you say?"

I tell that story in my introductory course every year. It's almost certainly untrue, and I explain that afterwards, but it's a classic anecdote. Of course, the anecdotes my undergraduates will really want to hear are ones featuring the heptapods; for the rest of my teaching career, that'll be the reason many of them sign up for my courses. So I'll show them the old videotapes of my sessions at the looking glass, and the sessions that the other linguists conducted; the tapes are instructive, and they'll be useful if we're ever visited by aliens again, but they don't generate many good anecdotes.

When it comes to language-learning anecdotes, my favorite source is child language acquisition. I remember one afternoon when you are five years old, after you have come home from kindergarten. You'll be coloring with your crayons while I grade papers.

"Mom," you'll say, using the carefully casual tone reserved for requesting a favor, "can I ask you something?"

"Sure, sweetie. Go ahead."

"Can I be, um, honored?"

I'll look up from the paper I'm grading. "What do you mean?"

"At school Sharon said she got to be honored."

"Really? Did she tell you what for?"

"It was when her big sister got married. She said only one person could be, um, honored, and she was it."

"Ah, I see. You mean Sharon was maid of honor?"

"Yeah, that's it. Can I be made of honor?"

Gary and I entered the prefab building containing the center of operations for the looking-glass site. Inside it looked like they were planning an invasion, or perhaps an evacuation: crewcut soldiers worked around a large map of the area, or sat in front of burly electronic gear while speaking into headsets. We were shown into Colonel Weber's office, a room in the back that was cool from air conditioning.

We briefed the colonel on our first day's results. "Doesn't sound like you got very far," he said.

"I have an idea as to how we can make faster progress," I said. "But you'll have to approve the use of more equipment."

"What more do you need?"

"A digital camera, and a big video screen." I showed him a drawing of the setup I imagined. "I want to try conducting the discovery procedure using writing; I'd display words on the screen, and use the camera to record the words they write. I'm hoping the heptapods will do the same."

Weber looked at the drawing dubiously. "What would be the advantage of that?"

"So far I've been proceeding the way I would with speakers of an unwritten language. Then it occurred to me that the heptapods must have writing, too."

"So?"

"If the heptapods have a mechanical way of producing writing, then their writing ought to be very regular, very consistent. That would make it easier for us to identify graphemes instead of phonemes. It's like picking out the letters in a printed sentence instead of trying to hear them when the sentence is spoken aloud."

"I take your point," he admitted. "And how would you respond to them? Show them the words they displayed to you?"

"Basically. And if they put spaces between words, any sentences we write would be a lot more intelligible than any spoken sentence we might splice together from recordings."

He leaned back in his chair. "You know we want to show as little of our technology as possible."

"I understand, but we're using machines as intermediaries already. If we can get them to use writing, I believe progress will go much faster than if we're restricted to the sound spectrographs."

The colonel turned to Gary. "Your opinion?"

"It sounds like a good idea to me. I'm curious whether the heptapods might have difficulty reading our monitors. Their looking glasses are based on a completely different technology than our video screens. As far as we can tell, they don't use pixels or scan lines, and they don't refresh on a frame-by-frame basis."

"You think the scan lines on our video screens might render them unreadable to the heptapods?"

"It's possible," said Gary. "We'll just have to try it and see."

Weber considered it. For me it wasn't even a question, but from his point of view it was a difficult decision; like a soldier, though, he made it quickly. "Request granted. Talk to the sergeant outside about bringing in what you need. Have it ready for tomorrow."

I remember one day during the summer when you're sixteen. For once, the person waiting for her date to arrive is me. Of course, you'll be waiting around too, curious to see what he looks like. You'll have a friend of yours, a blond girl with the unlikely name of Roxie, hanging out with you, giggling.

"You may feel the urge to make comments about him," I'll say, checking myself in the hallway mirror. "Just restrain yourselves until we leave."

"Don't worry, Mom," you'll say. "We'll do it so that he won't know. Roxie, you ask me what I think the weather will be like tonight. Then I'll say what I think of Mom's date."

"Right," Roxie will say.

"No, you most definitely will not," I'll say.

"Relax, Mom. He'll never know; we do this all the time."

"What a comfort that is."

A little later on, Nelson will arrive to pick me up. I'll do the introductions, and we'll all engage in a little small talk on the front porch. Nelson is ruggedly handsome, to your evident approval. Just as we're about to leave, Roxie will say to you casually, "So what do you think the weather will be like tonight?"

"I think it's going to be really hot," you'll answer.

Roxie will nod in agreement. Nelson will say, "Really? I thought they said it was going to be cool."

"I have a sixth sense about these things," you'll say. Your face will give nothing away. "I get the feeling it's going to be a scorcher. Good thing you're dressed for it, Mom."

I'll glare at you, and say good night.

As I lead Nelson toward his car, he'll ask me, amused, "I'm missing something here, aren't I?"

"A private joke," I'll mutter. "Don't ask me to explain it."

At our next session at the looking glass, we repeated the procedure we had performed before, this time displaying a printed word on our computer screen at the same time we spoke: showing HUMAN while saying "Human," and so forth. Eventually, the heptapods understood what we wanted, and set up a flat circular screen mounted on a small pedestal. One heptapod spoke, and then inserted a limb into a large socket in the pedestal; a doodle of script, vaguely cursive, popped onto the screen.

We soon settled into a routine, and I compiled two parallel corpora: one of spoken utterances, one of writing samples. Based on first impressions, their writing appeared to be logographic, which was disappointing; I'd been hoping for an alphabetic script to help us learn their speech. Their logograms might include some phonetic information, but finding it would be a lot harder than with an alphabetic script.

By getting up close to the looking glass, I was able to point to various heptapod body parts, such as limbs, digits, and eyes, and elicit terms for each. It turned out that they had an orifice on the underside of their body, lined with articulated bony ridges: probably used for eating, while the one at the top was for respiration and speech. There were no other conspicuous orifices; perhaps their mouth was their anus too. Those sorts of questions would have to wait.

I also tried asking our two informants for terms for addressing each individually; personal names, if they had such things. Their answers were of course unpronounceable, so for Gary's and my purposes, I dubbed them Flapper and Raspberry. I hoped I'd be able to tell them apart.

The next day I conferred with Gary before we entered the looking-glass tent. "I'll need your help with this session," I told him.

"Sure. What do you want me to do?"

"We need to elicit some verbs, and it's easiest with third-person forms. Would you act out a few verbs while I type the written form on the computer? If we're lucky, the heptapods will figure out what we're doing and do the same. I've brought a bunch of props for you to use."

"No problem," said Gary, cracking his knuckles. "Ready when you are."

We began with some simple intransitive verbs: walking, jumping, speaking, writing. Gary demonstrated each one with a charming lack of self-consciousness; the presence of the video cameras didn't inhibit him at all. For the first few actions he performed, I asked the heptapods, "What do you call that?" Before long, the heptapods caught on to what we were trying to do; Raspberry began mimicking Gary, or at least performing the equivalent heptapod action, while Flapper worked their computer, displaying a written description and pronouncing it aloud.

In the spectrographs of their spoken utterances, I could recognize their word I had glossed as "heptapod." The rest of each utterance was presumably the verb phrase; it looked like they had analogs of nouns and verbs, thank goodness.

In their writing, however, things weren't as clear-cut. For each action, they had displayed a single logogram instead of two separate ones. At first I thought they had written something like "walks," with the subject implied. But why would Flapper say "the heptapod walks" while writing "walks," instead of maintaining parallelism? Then I noticed that some of the logograms looked like the logogram for "heptapod" with some extra strokes added to one side or another. Perhaps their verbs could be written as affixes to a noun. If so, why was Flapper writing the noun in some instances but not in others?

I decided to try a transitive verb; substituting object words might clarify things. Among the props I'd brought were an apple and a slice of bread. "Okay," I said to Gary, "show them the food, and then eat some. First the apple, then the bread."

Gary pointed at the Golden Delicious and then he took a bite out of it, while I displayed the "what do you call that?" expression. Then we repeated it with the slice of whole wheat.

Raspberry left the room and returned with some kind of giant nut or gourd and a gelatinous ellipsoid. Raspberry pointed at the gourd while Flapper said a word and displayed a logogram. Then Raspberry brought the gourd down between its legs, a crunching sound resulted, and the gourd reemerged minus a bite; there were corn-like kernels beneath the shell. Flapper talked and displayed a large logogram on their screen. The sound spectrograph for "gourd" changed when it was used in the sentence; possibly a case marker. The logogram was odd: after some study, I could identify graphic elements that resembled the individual logograms for "heptapod" and "gourd." They looked as if they had been melted together, with several extra strokes in the mix that presumably meant "eat." Was it a multi-word ligature?

Next we got spoken and written names for the gelatin egg, and descriptions of the act of eating it. The sound spectrograph for "heptapod eats gelatin egg" was analyzable; "gelatin egg" bore a case marker, as expected, though the sentence's word order differed from last time. The written form, another large logogram, was another matter. This time it took much longer for me to recognize anything in it; not only were the individual logograms melted together again, it looked as if the one for "heptapod" was laid on its back, while on top of it the logogram for "gelatin egg" was standing on its head.

"Uh-oh." I took another look at the writing for the simple noun-verb examples, the ones that had seemed inconsistent before. Now I realized all of them actually did contain the logogram for "heptapod"; some were rotated and distorted by being combined with the various verbs, so I hadn't recognized them at first. "You guys have got to be kidding," I muttered.

"What's wrong?" asked Gary.

"Their script isn't word divided; a sentence is written by joining the logograms for the constituent words. They join the logograms by rotating and modifying them. Take a look." I showed him how the logograms were rotated.

"So they can read a word with equal ease no matter how it's rotated," Gary said. He turned to look at the heptapods, impressed. "I wonder if it's a consequence of their bodies' radial symmetry: their bodies have no 'forward' direction, so maybe their writing doesn't either. Highly neat."

I couldn't believe it; I was working with someone who modified the word "neat" with "highly." "It certainly is interesting," I said, "but it also means there's no easy way for us to write our own sentences in their language. We can't simply cut their sentences into individual words and recombine them; we'll have to learn the rules of their script before we can write anything legible. It's the same continuity problem we'd have had splicing together speech fragments, except applied to writing."

I looked at Flapper and Raspberry in the looking glass, who were waiting for us to continue, and sighed. "You aren't going to make this easy for us, are you?"

To be fair, the heptapods were completely cooperative. In the days that followed, they readily taught us their language without requiring us to teach them any more English. Colonel Weber and his cohorts pondered the implications of that, while I and the linguists at the other looking glasses met via videoconferencing to share what we had learned about the heptapod language. The videoconferencing made for an incongruous working environment: our video screens were primitive compared to the heptapods' looking glasses, so that my colleagues seemed more remote than the aliens. The familiar was far away, while the bizarre was close at hand.

It would be a while before we'd be ready to ask the heptapods why they had come, or to discuss physics well enough to ask them about their technology. For the time being, we worked on the basics: phonemics/graphemics, vocabulary, syntax. The heptapods at every looking glass were using the same language, so we were able to pool our data and coordinate our efforts.

Our biggest source of confusion was the heptapods' "writing." It didn't appear to be writing at all; it looked more like a bunch of intricate graphic designs. The logograms weren't arranged in rows, or a spiral, or any linear fashion. Instead, Flapper or Raspberry would write a sentence by sticking together as many logograms as needed into a giant conglomeration.

This form of writing was reminiscent of primitive sign systems, which required a reader to know a message's context in order to understand it. Such systems were considered too limited for systematic recording of information. Yet it was unlikely that the heptapods developed their level of technology with only an oral tradition. That implied one of three possibilities: the first was that the heptapods had a true writing system, but they didn't want to use it in front of us; Colonel Weber would identify with that one. The second was that the heptapods hadn't originated the technology they were using; they were illiterates using someone else's technology. The third, and most interesting to me, was that the heptapods were using a nonlinear system of orthography that qualified as true writing.

I remember a conversation we'll have when you're in your junior year of high school. It'll be Sunday morning, and I'll be scrambling some eggs while you set the table for brunch. You'll laugh as you tell me about the party you went to last night.

"Oh man," you'll say, "they're not kidding when they say that body weight makes a difference. I didn't drink any more than the guys did, but I got so much *drunk*er."

I'll try to maintain a neutral, pleasant expression. I'll really try. Then you'll say, "Oh, come on, Mom."

"What?"

"You know you did the exact same things when you were my age."

I did nothing of the sort, but I know that if I were to admit that, you'd lose respect for me completely. "You know never to drive, or get into a car if—"

"God, of course I know that. Do you think I'm an idiot?"

"No, of course not."

What I'll think is that you are clearly, maddeningly not me. It will remind me, again, that you won't be a clone of me; you can be wonderful, a daily delight, but you won't be someone I could have created by myself.

The military had set up a trailer containing our offices at the looking-glass site. I saw Gary walking toward the trailer, and ran to catch up with him. "It's a semasiographic writing system," I said when I reached him.

"Excuse me?" said Gary.

"Here, let me show you." I directed Gary into my office. Once we were inside, I went to the chalkboard and drew a circle with a diagonal line bisecting it. "What does this mean?"

"'Not allowed'?"

"Right." Next I printed the words NOT ALLOWED on the chalkboard. "And so does this. But only one is a representation of speech."

Gary nodded. "Okay."

"Linguists describe writing like this"—I indicated the printed words—"as 'glottographic,' because it represents speech. Every human written language is in this category. However, this symbol"— I indicated the circle and diagonal line—"is 'semasiographic' writing, because it conveys meaning without reference to speech. There's no correspondence between its components and any particular sounds."

"And you think all of heptapod writing is like this?"

"From what I've seen so far, yes. It's not picture writing, it's far more complex. It has its own system of rules for constructing sentences, like a visual syntax that's unrelated to the syntax for their spoken language."

"A visual syntax? Can you show me an example?"

"Coming right up." I sat down at my desk and, using the computer, pulled up a frame from the recording of yesterday's conversation with Raspberry. I turned the monitor so he could see it. "In their spoken language, a noun has a case marker indicating whether it's a subject or object. In their written language, however, a noun is identified as subject or object based on the orientation of its logogram relative to that of the verb. Here, take a look." I pointed at one of the figures. "For instance, when 'heptapod' is integrated with 'hears' this way, with these strokes parallel, it means that the heptapod is doing the hearing." I showed him a different one. "When they're combined this way, with the strokes perpendicular, it means that the heptapod is being heard. This morphology applies to several verbs.

"Another example is the inflection system." I called up another frame from the recording. "In their written language, this logogram means roughly 'hear easily' or 'hear clearly.' See the elements it has in common with the logogram for 'hear'? You can still combine it with 'heptapod' in the same ways as before, to indicate that the heptapod can hear something clearly or that the heptapod is clearly heard. But what's really interesting is that the modulation of 'hear' into 'hear clearly' isn't a special case; you see the transformation they applied?"

Gary nodded, pointing. "It's like they express the idea of 'clearly' by changing the curve of those strokes in the middle."

"Right. That modulation is applicable to lots of verbs. The logogram for 'see' can be modulated in the same way to form 'see clearly,' and so can the logogram for 'read' and others. And changing the curve of those strokes has no parallel in their speech; with the spoken version of these verbs, they add a prefix to the verb to express ease of manner, and the prefixes for 'see' and 'hear' are different.

"There are other examples, but you get the idea. It's essentially a grammar in two dimensions."

He began pacing thoughtfully. "Is there anything like this in human writing systems?"

"Mathematical equations, notations for music and dance. But those are all very specialized; we couldn't record this conversation using them. But I suspect, if we knew it well enough, we could record this conversation in the heptapod writing system. I think it's a full-fledged, general-purpose graphical language."

Gary frowned. "So their writing constitutes a completely separate language from their speech, right?"

"Right. In fact, it'd be more accurate to refer to the writing system as 'Heptapod B,' and use 'Heptapod A' strictly for referring to the spoken language."

"Hold on a second. Why use two languages when one would suffice? That seems unnecessarily hard to learn."

"Like English spelling?" I said. "Ease of learning isn't the primary force in language evolution. For the heptapods, writing and speech may play such different cultural or cognitive roles that using separate languages makes more sense than using different forms of the same one."

He considered it. "I see what you mean. Maybe they think our form of writing is redundant, like we're wasting a second communications channel."

"That's entirely possible. Finding out why they use a second language for writing will tell us a lot about them."

"So I take it this means we won't be able to use their writing to help us learn their spoken language."

I sighed. "Yeah, that's the most immediate implication. But I don't think we should ignore either Heptapod A or B; we need a two-pronged approach." I pointed at the screen. "I'll bet you that learning their two-dimensional grammar will help you when it comes time to learn their mathematical notation."

"You've got a point there. So are we ready to start asking about their mathematics?"

"Not yet. We need a better grasp on this writing system before we begin anything else," I said, and then smiled when he mimed frustration. "Patience, good sir. Patience is a virtue."

———

You'll be six when your father has a conference to attend in Hawaii, and we'll accompany him. You'll be so excited that you'll make preparations for weeks beforehand. You'll ask me about coconuts and volcanoes and surfing, and practice hula dancing in the mirror. You'll pack a suitcase with the clothes and toys you want to bring, and you'll drag it around the house to see how long you can carry it. You'll ask me if I can carry your Etch-a-Sketch in my bag, since there won't be any more room for it in yours and you simply can't leave without it.

"You won't need all of these," I'll say. "There'll be so many fun things to do there, you won't have time to play with so many toys."

You'll consider that; dimples will appear above your eyebrows when you think hard. Eventually you'll agree to pack fewer toys, but your expectations will, if anything, increase.

"I wanna be in Hawaii now," you'll whine.

"Sometimes it's good to wait," I'll say. "The anticipation makes it more fun when you get there."

You'll just pout.

In the next report I submitted, I suggested that the term "logogram" was a misnomer because it implied that each graph represented a spoken word, when in fact the graphs didn't correspond to our notion of spoken words at all. I didn't want to use the term "ideogram" either because of how it had been used in the past; I suggested the term "semagram" instead.

It appeared that a semagram corresponded roughly to a written word in human languages: it was meaningful on its own, and in combination with other semagrams could form endless statements. We couldn't define it precisely, but then no one had ever satisfactorily defined "word" for human languages either. When it came to sentences in Heptapod B, though, things became much more confusing. The language had no written punctuation: its syntax was indicated in the way the semagrams were combined, and there was no need to indicate the cadence of speech. There was certainly no way to slice out subject-predicate pairings neatly to make sentences. A "sentence" seemed to be whatever number of semagrams a heptapod wanted to join together; the only difference between a sentence and a paragraph, or a page, was size.

When a Heptapod B sentence grew fairly sizable, its visual impact was remarkable. If I wasn't trying to decipher it, the writing looked like fanciful praying mantids drawn in a cursive style, all clinging to each other to form an Escheresque lattice, each slightly different in its stance. And the biggest sentences had an effect similar to that of psychedelic posters: sometimes eye-watering, sometimes hypnotic.

I remember a picture of you taken at your college graduation. In the photo you're striking a pose for the camera, mortarboard stylishly tilted on your head, one hand touching your sunglasses, the other hand on your hip, holding open your gown to reveal the tank top and shorts you're wearing underneath.

I remember your graduation. There will be the distraction of having Nelson and your father and what's-her-name there all at the same time, but that will be minor. That entire weekend, while you're introducing me to your classmates and hugging everyone incessantly, I'll be all but mute with amazement. I can't believe that you, a grown woman taller than me and beautiful enough to make my heart ache, will be the same girl I used to lift off the ground so you could reach the drinking fountain, the same girl who used to trundle out of my bedroom draped in a dress and hat and four scarves from my closet.

And after graduation, you'll be heading for a job as a financial analyst. I won't understand what you do there, I won't even understand your fascination with money, the preeminence you gave to salary when negotiating job offers. I would prefer it if you'd pursue something without regard for its monetary rewards, but I'll have no complaints. My own mother could never understand why I couldn't just be a high school English teacher. You'll do what makes you happy, and that'll be all I ask for.

As time went on, the teams at each looking glass began working in earnest on learning heptapod terminology for elementary mathematics and physics. We worked together on presentations, with the linguists focusing on procedure and the physicists focusing on subject matter. The physicists showed us previously devised systems for communicating with aliens, based on mathematics, but those were intended for use over a radio telescope. We reworked them for face-to-face communication.

Our teams were successful with basic arithmetic, but we hit a road block with geometry and algebra. We tried using a spherical coordinate system instead of a rectangular one, thinking it might be more natural to the heptapods given their anatomy, but that approach wasn't any more fruitful. The heptapods didn't seem to understand what we were getting at.

Likewise, the physics discussions went poorly. Only with the most concrete terms, like the names of the elements, did we have any success; after several attempts at representing the periodic table, the heptapods got the idea. For anything remotely abstract, we might as well have been gibbering. We tried to demonstrate basic physical attributes like mass and acceleration so we could elicit their terms for them, but the heptapods simply responded with requests for clarification. To avoid perceptual problems that might be associated with any particular medium, we tried physical demonstrations as well as line drawings, photos, and animations; none were effective. Days with no progress became weeks, and the physicists were becoming disillusioned.

By contrast, the linguists were having much more success. We made steady progress decoding the grammar of the spoken language, Heptapod A. It didn't follow the pattern of human languages, as

TED CHIANG

expected, but it was comprehensible so far: free word order, even to the extent that there was no preferred order for the clauses in a conditional statement, in defiance of a human language "universal." It also appeared that the heptapods had no objection to many levels of center-embedding of clauses, something that quickly defeated humans. Peculiar, but not impenetrable.

Much more interesting were the newly discovered morphological and grammatical processes in Heptapod B that were uniquely two-dimensional. Depending on a semagram's declension, inflections could be indicated by varying a certain stroke's curvature, or its thickness, or its manner of undulation; or by varying the relative sizes of two radicals, or their relative distance to another radical, or their orientations; or various other means. These were non-segmental graphemes; they couldn't be isolated from the rest of a semagram. And despite how such traits behaved in human writing, these had nothing to do with calligraphic style; their meanings were defined according to a consistent and unambiguous grammar.

We regularly asked the heptapods why they had come. Each time, they answered "to see," or "to observe." Indeed, sometimes they preferred to watch us silently rather than answer our questions. Perhaps they were scientists, perhaps they were tourists. The State Department instructed us to reveal as little as possible about humanity, in case that information could be used as a bargaining chip in subsequent negotiations. We obliged, though it didn't require much effort: the heptapods never asked questions about anything. Whether scientists or tourists, they were an awfully incurious bunch.

I remember once when we'll be driving to the mall to buy some new clothes for you. You'll be thirteen. One moment you'll be sprawled in your seat, completely unself-conscious, all child; the next, you'll toss your hair with a practiced casualness, like a fashion model in training.

You'll give me some instructions as I'm parking the car. "Okay, Mom, give me one of the credit cards, and we can meet back at the entrance here in two hours."

I'll laugh. "Not a chance. All the credit cards stay with me."

"You're kidding." You'll become the embodiment of exasperation. We'll get out of the car and I will start walking to the mall entrance. After seeing that I won't budge on the matter, you'll quickly reformulate your plans.

"Okay Mom, okay. You can come with me, just walk a little ways behind me, so it doesn't look like we're together. If I see any friends of mine, I'm gonna stop and talk to them, but you just keep walking, okay? I'll come find you later."

I'll stop in my tracks. "Excuse me? I am not the hired help, nor am I some mutant relative for you to be ashamed of."

"But Mom, I can't let anyone see you with me."

"What are you talking about? I've already met your friends; they've been to the house."

"That was different," you'll say, incredulous that you have to explain it. "This is shopping."

"Too bad."

Then the explosion: "You won't do the least thing to make me happy! You don't care about me at all!"

It won't have been that long since you enjoyed going shopping with me; it will forever astonish me how quickly you grow out of one phase and enter another. Living with you will be like aiming for a moving target; you'll always be further along than I expect.

I looked at the sentence in Heptapod B that I had just written, using simple pen and paper. Like all the sentences I generated myself, this one looked misshapen, like a heptapod-written sentence that had been smashed with a hammer and then inexpertly taped back together. I had sheets of such inelegant semagrams covering my desk, fluttering occasionally when the oscillating fan swung past.

It was strange trying to learn a language that had no spoken form. Instead of practicing my pronunciation, I had taken to squeezing my eyes shut and trying to paint semagrams on the insides of my eyelids.

There was a knock at the door and before I could answer Gary came in looking jubilant. "Illinois got a repetition in physics."

"Really? That's great; when did it happen?"

"It happened a few hours ago; we just had the videoconference. Let me show you what it is." He started erasing my blackboard.

"Don't worry, I didn't need any of that."

"Good." He picked up a nub of chalk and drew a diagram:

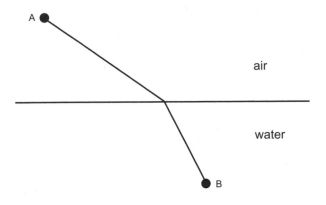

"Okay, here's the path a ray of light takes when crossing from air to water. The light ray travels in a straight line until it hits the water; the water has a different index of refraction, so the light changes direction. You've heard of this before, right?"

I nodded. "Sure."

"Now here's an interesting property about the path the light takes. The path is the fastest possible route between these two points."

"Come again?"

"Imagine, just for grins, that the ray of light traveled along this path." He added a dotted line to his diagram:

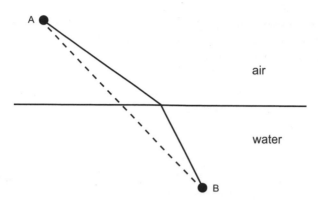

"This hypothetical path is shorter than the path the light actually takes. But light travels more slowly in water than it does in air, and a greater percentage of this path is underwater. So it would take longer for light to travel along this path than it does along the real path."

"Okay, I get it."

"Now imagine if light were to travel along this other path." He drew a second dotted path:

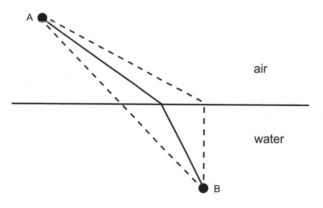

"This path reduces the percentage that's underwater, but the total length is larger. It would also take longer for light to travel along this path than along the actual one."

Gary put down the chalk and gestured at the diagram on the chalkboard with white-tipped fingers. "Any hypothetical path would require more time to traverse than the one actually taken. In other words, the route that the light ray takes is always the fastest possible one. That's Fermat's principle of least time."

"Hmm, interesting. And this is what the heptapods responded to?"

"Exactly. Moorehead gave an animated presentation of Fermat's principle at the Illinois looking glass, and the heptapods repeated it back. Now he's trying to get a symbolic description." He grinned. "Now is that highly neat, or what?"

"It's neat all right, but how come I haven't heard of Fermat's principle before?" I picked up a binder and waved it at him; it was a primer on the physics topics suggested for use in communication with the heptapods. "This thing goes on forever about Planck masses and the spin-flip of atomic hydrogen, and not a word about the refraction of light."

"We guessed wrong about what'd be most useful for you to know," Gary said without embarrassment. "In fact, it's curious that Fermat's principle was the first breakthrough; even though it's easy to explain, you need calculus to describe it mathematically. And not ordinary calculus; you need the calculus of variations. We thought that some simple theorem of geometry or algebra would be the breakthrough."

"Curious indeed. You think the heptapods' idea of what's simple doesn't match ours?"

"Exactly, which is why I'm *dying* to see what their mathematical description of Fermat's principle looks like." He paced as he talked. "If their version of the calculus of variations is simpler to them than their equivalent of algebra, that might explain why we've had so much trouble talking about physics; their entire system of mathematics may be topsy-turvy compared to ours." He pointed to the physics primer. "You can be sure that we're going to revise that."

"So can you build from Fermat's principle to other areas of physics?"

"Probably. There are lots of physical principles just like Fermat's."

"What, like Louise's principle of least closet space? When did physics become so minimalist?"

"Well, the word 'least' is misleading. You see, Fermat's principle of least time is incomplete; in certain situations light follows a path that takes *more* time than any of the other possibilities. It's more accurate to say that light always follows an *extreme* path, either one that minimizes the time taken or one that maximizes it. A minimum and a maximum share certain mathematical properties, so both situations can be described with one equation. So to be precise, Fermat's principle isn't a minimal principle; instead it's what's known as a 'variational' principle."

"And there are more of these variational principles?"

He nodded. "In all branches of physics. Almost every physical law can be restated as a variational principle. The only difference between these principles is in which attribute is minimized or maximized." He gestured as if the different branches of physics were arrayed before him on a table. "In optics, where Fermat's principle applies, time is the attribute that has to be an extreme. In mechanics, it's a different attribute. In electromagnetism, it's something else again. But all these principles are similar mathematically."

"So once you get their mathematical description of Fermat's principle, you should be able to decode the other ones."

"God, I hope so. I think this is the wedge that we've been looking for, the one that cracks open their formulation of physics. This calls for a celebration." He stopped his pacing and turned to me. "Hey Louise, want to go out for dinner? My treat."

I was mildly surprised. "Sure," I said.

It'll be when you first learn to walk that I get daily demonstrations of the asymmetry in our relationship. You'll be incessantly running off somewhere, and each time you walk into a door frame or scrape your knee, the pain feels like it's my own. It'll be like growing an errant limb, an extension of myself whose sensory nerves report pain just fine, but whose motor nerves don't convey my commands at all. It's so unfair: I'm going to give birth to an animated voodoo doll of myself. I didn't see this in the contract when I signed up. Was this part of the deal?

And then there will be the times when I see you laughing. Like the time you'll be playing with the neighbor's puppy, poking your hands through the chain-link fence separating our back yards, and you'll be laughing so hard you'll start hiccuping. The puppy will run inside the neighbor's house, and your laughter will gradually subside, letting you catch your breath. Then the puppy will come back to the fence to lick your fingers again, and you'll shriek and start laughing again. It will be the most wonderful sound I could ever imagine, a sound that makes me feel like a fountain, or a wellspring.

Now if only I can remember that sound the next time your blithe disregard for self-preservation gives me a heart attack.

After the breakthrough with Fermat's principle, discussions of scientific concepts became more fruitful. It wasn't as if all of heptapod physics was suddenly rendered transparent, but progress was steady. According to Gary, the heptapods' formulation of physics was indeed topsy-turvy relative to ours. Physical attributes that humans defined using integral calculus were seen as fundamental by the heptapods. As an example, Gary described an attribute that, in physics jargon, bore the deceptively simple name "action," which represented "the difference between kinetic and potential energy, integrated over time," whatever that meant. Calculus for us; elementary to them.

Conversely, to define attributes that humans thought of as fundamental, like velocity, the heptapods employed mathematics that were, Gary assured me, "highly weird." The physicists were ultimately able to prove the equivalence of heptapod mathematics and human mathematics; even though their approaches were almost the reverse of one another, both were systems of describing the same physical universe.

I tried following some of the equations that the physicists were coming up with, but it was no use. I couldn't really grasp the significance of physical attributes like "action"; I couldn't, with any confidence, ponder the significance of treating such an attribute as fundamental. Still, I tried to ponder questions formulated in terms more familiar to me: what kind of worldview did the heptapods have, that they would consider Fermat's principle the simplest explanation of light refraction? What kind of perception made a minimum or maximum readily apparent to them?

Your eyes will be blue like your dad's, not mud brown like mine. Boys will stare into those eyes the way I did, and do, into your dad's, surprised and enchanted, as I was and am, to find them in combination with black hair. You will have many suitors.

I remember when you are fifteen, coming home after a weekend at your dad's, incredulous over the interrogation he'll have put you through regarding the boy you're currently dating. You'll sprawl on the sofa, recounting your dad's latest breach of common sense: "You know what he said? He said, 'I know what teenage boys are like.'" Roll of the eyes. "Like I don't?"

"Don't hold it against him," I'll say. "He's a father; he can't help it." Having seen you interact with your friends, I won't worry much about a boy taking advantage of you; if anything, the opposite will be more likely. I'll worry about that.

"He wishes I were still a kid. He hasn't known how to act toward me since I grew breasts."

"Well, that development was a shock for him. Give him time to recover."

"It's been *years*, Mom. How long is it gonna take?"

"I'll let you know when my father has come to terms with mine."

———

TED CHIANG

During one of the videoconferences for the linguists, Cisneros from the Massachusetts looking glass had raised an interesting question: was there a particular order in which semagrams were written in a Heptapod B sentence? It was clear that word order meant next to nothing when speaking in Heptapod A; when asked to repeat what it had just said, a heptapod would likely as not use a different word order unless we specifically asked them not to. Was word order similarly unimportant when writing in Heptapod B?

Previously, we had focused our attention only on how a sentence in Heptapod B looked once it was complete. As far as anyone could tell, there was no preferred order when reading the semagrams in a sentence; you could start almost anywhere in the nest, then follow the branching clauses until you'd read the whole thing. But that was reading; was the same true about writing?

During my most recent session with Flapper and Raspberry I had asked them if, instead of displaying a semagram only after it was completed, they could show it to us while it was being written. They had agreed. I inserted the videotape of the session into the VCR, and on my computer I consulted the session transcript.

I picked one of the longer utterances from the conversation. What Flapper had said was that the heptapods' planet had two moons, one significantly larger than the other; the three primary constituents of the planet's atmosphere were nitrogen, argon, and oxygen; and 15/28ths of the planet's surface was covered by water. The first words of the spoken utterance translated literally as "inequality-of-size rocky-orbiter rocky-orbiters related-as-primary-to-secondary."

Then I rewound the videotape until the time signature matched the one in the transcription. I started playing the tape, and watched the web of semagrams being spun out of inky spider's silk. I rewound it and played it several times. Finally I froze the video right after the first stroke was completed and before the second one was begun; all that was visible onscreen was a single sinuous line.

Comparing that initial stroke with the completed sentence, I realized that the stroke participated in several different clauses of the message. It began in the semagram for "oxygen," as the determinant that distinguished it from certain other elements; then it slid down to become the morpheme of comparison in the description of the two moons' sizes; and lastly it flared out as the arched backbone of the semagram for "ocean." Yet this stroke was a single continuous line, and it was the first one that Flapper wrote. That meant the heptapod had to know how the entire sentence would be laid out before it could write the very first stroke.

The other strokes in the sentence also traversed several clauses, making them so interconnected that none could be removed without redesigning the entire sentence. The heptapods didn't write a sentence one semagram at a time; they built it out of strokes irrespective of individual semagrams. I had seen a similarly high degree of integration before in calligraphic designs, particularly those employing the Arabic alphabet. But those designs had required careful planning by expert calligraphers. No one could lay out such an intricate design at the speed needed for holding a conversation. At least, no human could.

There's a joke that I once heard a comedienne tell. It goes like this: "I'm not sure if I'm ready to have children. I asked a friend of mine who has children, 'Suppose I do have kids. What if when they grow up, they blame me for everything that's wrong with their lives?' She laughed and said, 'What do you mean, if?'"

That's my favorite joke.

Gary and I were at a little Chinese restaurant, one of the local places we had taken to patronizing to get away from the encampment. We sat eating the appetizers: potstickers, redolent of pork and sesame oil. My favorite.

I dipped one in soy sauce and vinegar. "So how are you doing with your Heptapod B practice?" I asked.

Gary looked obliquely at the ceiling. I tried to meet his gaze, but he kept shifting it.

"You've given up, haven't you?" I said. "You're not even trying anymore."

He did a wonderful hangdog expression. "I'm just no good at languages," he confessed. "I thought learning Heptapod B might be more like learning mathematics than trying to speak another language, but it's not. It's too foreign for me."

"It would help you discuss physics with them."

"Probably, but since we had our breakthrough, I can get by with just a few phrases."

I sighed. "I suppose that's fair; I have to admit, I've given up on trying to learn the mathematics."

"So we're even?"

"We're even." I sipped my tea. "Though I did want to ask you about Fermat's principle. Something about it feels odd to me, but I can't put my finger on it. It just doesn't sound like a law of physics."

A twinkle appeared in Gary's eyes. "I'll bet I know what you're talking about." He snipped a potsticker in half with his chopsticks. "You're used to thinking of refraction in terms of cause and effect: reaching the water's surface is the cause, and the change in direction is the effect. But Fermat's principle sounds weird because it describes light's behavior in goal-oriented terms. It sounds like a commandment to a light beam: 'Thou shalt minimize or maximize the time taken to reach thy destination.'"

I considered it. "Go on."

"It's an old question in the philosophy of physics. People have been talking about it since Fermat first formulated it in the 1600s; Planck wrote volumes about it. The thing is, while the common formulation of physical laws is causal, a variational principle like Fermat's is purposive, almost teleological."

"Hmm, that's an interesting way to put it. Let me think about that for a minute." I pulled out a felt-tip pen and, on my paper napkin, drew a copy of the diagram that Gary had drawn on my blackboard. "Okay," I said, thinking aloud, "so let's say the goal of a ray of light is to take the fastest path. How does the light go about doing that?"

"Well, if I can speak anthropomorphic-projectionally, the light has to examine the possible paths and compute how long each one would take." He plucked the last potsticker from the serving dish.

"And to do that," I continued, "the ray of light has to know just where its destination is. If the destination were somewhere else, the fastest path would be different."

Gary nodded again. "That's right; the notion of a 'fastest path' is meaningless unless there's a destination specified. And computing how long a given path takes also requires information about what lies along that path, like where the water's surface is."

I kept staring at the diagram on the napkin. "And the light ray has to know all that ahead of time, before it starts moving, right?"

"So to speak," said Gary. "The light can't start traveling in any old direction and make course corrections later on, because the path resulting from such behavior wouldn't be the fastest possible one. The light has to do all its computations at the very beginning."

I thought to myself, *the ray of light has to know where it will ultimately end up before it can choose the direction to begin moving in.* I knew what that reminded me of. I looked up at Gary. "That's what was bugging me."

I remember when you're fourteen. You'll come out of your bedroom, a graffiti-covered notebook computer in hand, working on a report for school.

"Mom, what do you call it when both sides can win?"

I'll look up from my computer and the paper I'll be writing. "What, you mean a win-win situation?"

"There's some technical name for it, some math word. Remember that time Dad was here, and he was talking about the stock market? He used it then."

"Hmm, that sounds familiar, but I can't remember what he called it."

"I need to know. I want to use that phrase in my social studies report. I can't even search for information on it unless I know what it's called."

"I'm sorry, I don't know it either. Why don't you call your dad?"

Judging from your expression, that will be more effort than you want to make. At this point, you and your father won't be getting along well. "Can you call Dad and ask him? But don't tell him it's for me."

"I think you can call him yourself."

You'll fume, "Jesus, Mom, I can never get help with my home-work since you and Dad split up."

It's amazing the diverse situations in which you can bring up the divorce. "I've helped you with your homework."

"Like a million years ago, Mom."

I'll let that pass. "I'd help you with this if I could, but I don't remember what it's called."

You'll head back to your bedroom in a huff.

I practiced Heptapod B at every opportunity, both with the other linguists and by myself. The novelty of reading a semasiographic language made it compelling in a way that Heptapod A wasn't, and my improvement in writing it excited me. Over time, the sentences I wrote grew shapelier, more cohesive. I had reached the point where it worked better when I didn't think about it too much. Instead of carefully trying to design a sentence before writing, I could simply begin putting down strokes immediately; my initial strokes almost always turned out to be compatible with an elegant rendition of what I was trying to say. I was developing a faculty like that of the heptapods.

More interesting was the fact that Heptapod B was changing the way I thought. For me, thinking typically meant speaking in an internal voice; as we say in the trade, my thoughts were phonologically coded. My internal voice normally spoke in English, but that wasn't a requirement. The summer after my senior year in high school, I attended a total immersion program for learning Russian; by the end of the summer, I was thinking and even dreaming in Russian. But it was always *spoken* Russian. Different language, same mode: a voice speaking silently aloud.

The idea of thinking in a linguistic yet non-phonological mode always intrigued me. I had a friend born of Deaf parents; he grew up using American Sign Language, and he told me that he often thought in ASL instead of English. I used to wonder what it was like to have one's thoughts be manually coded, to reason using an inner pair of hands instead of an inner voice.

With Heptapod B, I was experiencing something just as foreign: my thoughts were becoming graphically coded. There were trance-like moments during the day when my thoughts weren't expressed with my internal voice; instead, I saw semagrams with my mind's eye, sprouting like frost on a windowpane.

As I grew more fluent, semagraphic designs would appear fully formed, articulating even complex ideas all at once. My thought processes weren't moving any faster as a result, though. Instead of racing forward, my mind hung balanced on the symmetry underlying the semagrams. The semagrams seemed to be something more than language; they were almost like mandalas. I found myself in a meditative state, contemplating the way in which premises and conclusions were interchangeable. There was no direction inherent in the way propositions were connected, no "train of thought" moving along a particular route; all the components in an act of reasoning were equally powerful, all having identical precedence.

A representative from the State Department named Hossner had the job of briefing the U.S. scientists on our agenda with the heptapods. We sat in the videoconference room, listening to him lecture. Our microphone was turned off, so Gary and I could exchange comments without interrupting Hossner. As we listened, I worried that Gary might harm his vision, rolling his eyes so often.

"They must have had some reason for coming all this way," said the diplomat, his voice tinny through the speakers. "It does not look like their reason was conquest, thank God. But if that's not the reason, what is? Are they prospectors? Anthropologists? Missionaries? Whatever their motives, there must be something we can offer them. Maybe it's mineral rights to our solar system. Maybe it's information about ourselves. Maybe it's the right to deliver sermons to our populations. But we can be sure that there's something.

"My point is this: their motive might not be to trade, but that doesn't mean that we cannot conduct trade. We simply need to know why they're here, and what we have that they want. Once we have that information, we can begin trade negotiations.

"I should emphasize that our relationship with the heptapods need not be adversarial. This is not a situation where every gain on their part is a loss on ours, or vice versa. If we handle ourselves correctly, both we and the heptapods can come out winners."

"You mean it's a non-zero-sum game?" Gary said in mock incredulity. "Oh my gosh."

"A non-zero-sum game."

"What?" You'll reverse course, heading back from your bedroom.

"When both sides can win: I just remembered, it's called a non-zero-sum game."

"That's it!" you'll say, writing it down on your notebook. "Thanks, Mom!"

"I guess I knew it after all," I'll say. "All those years with your father, some of it must have rubbed off."

"I knew you'd know it," you'll say. You'll give me a sudden, brief hug, and your hair will smell of apples. "You're the best."

———

"Louise?"

"Hmm? Sorry, I was distracted. What did you say?"

"I said, what do you think about our Mr. Hossner here?"

"I prefer not to."

"I've tried that myself: ignoring the government, seeing if it would go away. It hasn't."

As evidence of Gary's assertion, Hossner kept blathering: "Your immediate task is to think back on what you've learned. Look for anything that might help us. Has there been any indication of what the heptapods want? Of what they value?"

"Gee, it never occurred to us to look for things like that," I said. "We'll get right on it, sir."

"The sad thing is, that's just what we'll have to do," said Gary.

"Are there any questions?" asked Hossner.

Burghart, the linguist at the Ft. Worth looking glass, spoke up. "We've been through this with the heptapods many times. They maintain that they're here to observe, and they maintain that information is not tradable."

"So they would have us believe," said Hossner. "But consider: how could that be true? I know that the heptapods have occasionally stopped talking to us for brief periods. That may be a tactical maneuver on their part. If we were to stop talking to them tomorrow—"

"Wake me up if he says something interesting," said Gary.

"I was just going to ask you to do the same for me."

That day when Gary first explained Fermat's principle to me, he had mentioned that almost every physical law could be stated as a variational principle. Yet when humans thought about physical laws, they preferred to work with them in their causal formulation. I could understand that: the physical attributes that humans found intuitive, like kinetic energy or acceleration, were all properties of an object at a given moment in time. And these were conducive to a chronological, causal interpretation of events: one moment growing out of another, causes and effects creating a chain reaction that grew from past to future.

In contrast, the physical attributes that the heptapods found intuitive, like "action" or those other things defined by integrals, were meaningful only over a period of time. And these were conducive to a teleological interpretation of events: by viewing events over a period of time, one recognized that there was a requirement that had to be satisfied, a goal of minimizing or maximizing. And one had to know the initial and final states to meet that goal; one needed knowledge of the effects before the causes could be initiated.

I was growing to understand that, too.

"Why?" you'll ask again. You'll be three.

"Because it's your bedtime," I'll say again. We'll have gotten as far as getting you bathed and into your jammies, but no further than that.

"But I'm not sleepy," you'll whine. You'll be standing at the bookshelf, pulling down a video to watch: your latest diversionary tactic to keep away from your bedroom.

"It doesn't matter: you still have to go to bed."

"But why?"

"Because I'm the mom and I said so."

I'm actually going to say that, aren't I? God, somebody please shoot me.

I'll pick you up and carry you under my arm to your bed, you wailing piteously all the while, but my sole concern will be my own distress. All those vows made in childhood that I would give reasonable answers when I became a parent, that I would treat my own child as an intelligent, thinking individual, all for naught: I'm going to turn into my mother. I can fight it as much as I want, but there'll be no stopping my slide down that long, dreadful slope.

———

Was it actually possible to know the future? Not simply to guess at it; was it possible to *know* what was going to happen, with absolute certainty and in specific detail? Gary once told me that the fundamental laws of physics were time-symmetric, that there was no physical difference between past and future. Given that, some might say, "yes, theoretically." But speaking more concretely, most would answer "no," because of free will.

I liked to imagine the objection as a Borgesian fabulation: consider a person standing before the *Book of Ages*, the chronicle that records every event, past and future. Even though the text has been photoreduced from the full-sized edition, the volume is enormous. With magnifier in hand, she flips through the tissue-thin leaves until she locates the story of her life. She finds the passage that describes her flipping through the *Book of Ages*, and she skips to the next column, where it details what she'll be doing later in the day: acting on information she's read in the *Book*, she'll bet $100 on the racehorse Devil May Care and win twenty times that much.

The thought of doing just that had crossed her mind, but being a contrary sort, she now resolves to refrain from betting on the ponies altogether.

There's the rub. The *Book of Ages* cannot be wrong; this scenario is based on the premise that a person is given knowledge of the actual future, not of some possible future. If this were Greek myth, circumstances would conspire to make her enact her fate despite her best efforts, but prophecies in myth are notoriously vague; the *Book of Ages* is quite specific, and there's no way she can be forced to bet on a racehorse in the manner specified. The result is a contradiction: the *Book of Ages* must be right, by definition; yet no matter what the *Book* says she'll do, she can choose to do otherwise. How can these two facts be reconciled?

They can't be, was the common answer. A volume like the *Book of Ages* is a logical impossibility, for the precise reason that its existence would result in the above contradiction. Or, to be generous, some might say that the *Book of Ages* could exist, as long as it wasn't accessible to readers: that volume is housed in a special collection, and no one has viewing privileges.

The existence of free will meant that we couldn't know the future. And we knew free will existed because we had direct experience of it. Volition was an intrinsic part of consciousness.

Or was it? What if the experience of knowing the future changed a person? What if it evoked a sense of urgency, a sense of obligation to act precisely as she knew she would?

I stopped by Gary's office before leaving for the day. "I'm calling it quits. Did you want to grab something to eat?"

"Sure, just wait a second," he said. He shut down his computer and gathered some papers together. Then he looked up at me. "Hey, want to come to my place for dinner tonight? I'll cook."

I looked at him dubiously. "You can cook?"

"Just one dish," he admitted. "But it's a good one."

"Sure," I said. "I'm game."

"Great. We just need to go shopping for the ingredients."

"Don't go to any trouble—"

"There's a market on the way to my house. It won't take a minute."

We took separate cars, me following him. I almost lost him when he abruptly turned into a parking lot. It was a gourmet market, not large, but fancy; tall glass jars stuffed with imported foods sat next to specialty utensils on the store's stainless-steel shelves.

I accompanied Gary as he collected fresh basil, tomatoes, garlic, linguini. "There's a fish market next door; we can get fresh clams there," he said.

"Sounds good." We walked past the section of kitchen utensils. My gaze wandered over the shelves—peppermills, garlic presses, salad tongs—and stopped on a wooden salad bowl.

When you are three, you'll pull a dishtowel off the kitchen counter and bring that salad bowl down on top of you. I'll make a grab for it, but I'll miss. The edge of the bowl will leave you with a cut, on the upper edge of your forehead, that will require a single stitch. Your father and I will hold you, sobbing and stained with Caesar dressing, as we wait in the emergency room for hours.

I reached out and took the bowl from the shelf. The motion didn't feel like something I was forced to do. Instead it seemed just as urgent as my rushing to catch the bowl when it falls on you: an instinct that I felt right in following.

"I could use a salad bowl like this."

Gary looked at the bowl and nodded approvingly. "See, wasn't it a good thing that I had to stop at the market?"

"Yes it was." We got in line to pay for our purchases.

Consider the sentence "The rabbit is ready to eat." Interpret "rabbit" to be the object of "eat," and the sentence was an announcement that dinner would be served shortly. Interpret "rabbit" to be the subject of "eat," and it was a hint, such as a young girl might give her mother so she'll open a bag of Purina Bunny Chow. Two very different utterances; in fact, they were probably mutually exclusive within a single household. Yet either was a valid interpretation; only context could determine what the sentence meant.

Consider the phenomenon of light hitting water at one angle, and traveling through it at a different angle. Explain it by saying that a difference in the index of refraction caused the light to change direction, and one saw the world as humans saw it. Explain it by saying that light minimized the time needed to travel to its destination, and one saw the world as the heptapods saw it. Two very different interpretations.

The physical universe was a language with a perfectly ambiguous grammar. Every physical event was an utterance that could be parsed in two entirely different ways, one causal and the other teleological, both valid, neither one disqualifiable no matter how much context was available.

When the ancestors of humans and heptapods first acquired the spark of consciousness, they both perceived the same physical world, but they parsed their perceptions differently; the worldviews that ultimately arose were the end result of that divergence. Humans had developed a sequential mode of awareness, while heptapods had developed a simultaneous mode of awareness. We experienced events in an order, and perceived their relationship as cause and effect. They experienced all events at once, and perceived a purpose underlying them all. A minimizing, maximizing purpose.

I have a recurring dream about your death. In the dream, I'm the one who's rock climbing—me, can you imagine it?—and you're three years old, riding in some kind of backpack I'm wearing. We're just a few feet below a ledge where we can rest, and you won't wait until I've climbed up to it. You start pulling yourself out of the pack; I order you to stop, but of course you ignore me. I feel your weight alternating from one side of the pack to the other as you climb out; then I feel your left foot on my shoulder, and then your right. I'm screaming at you, but I can't get a hand free to grab you. I can see the wavy design on the soles of your sneakers as you climb, and then I see a flake of stone give way beneath one of them. You slide right past me, and I can't move a muscle. I look down and see you shrink into the distance below me.

Then, all of a sudden, I'm at the morgue. An orderly lifts the sheet from your face, and I see that you're twenty-five.

"You okay?"

I was sitting upright in bed; I'd woken Gary with my movements. "I'm fine. I was just startled; I didn't recognize where I was for a moment."

Sleepily, he said, "We can stay at your place next time."

I kissed him. "Don't worry; your place is fine." We curled up, my back against his chest, and went back to sleep.

When you're three and we're climbing a steep, spiral flight of stairs, I'll hold your hand extra tightly. You'll pull your hand away from me. "I can do it by myself," you'll insist, and then move away from me to prove it, and I'll remember that dream. We'll repeat that scene countless times during your childhood. I can almost believe that, given your contrary nature, my attempts to protect you will be what create your love of climbing: first the jungle gym at the playground, then trees out in the green belt around our neighborhood, the rock walls at the climbing club, and ultimately cliff faces in national parks.

I finished the last radical in the sentence, put down the chalk, and sat down in my desk chair. I leaned back and surveyed the giant Heptapod B sentence I'd written that covered the entire blackboard in my office. It included several complex clauses, and I had managed to integrate all of them rather nicely.

Looking at a sentence like this one, I understood why the heptapods had evolved a semasiographic writing system like Heptapod B; it was better suited for a species with a simultaneous mode of consciousness. For them, speech was a bottleneck because it required that one word follow another sequentially. With writing, on the other hand, every mark on a page was visible simultaneously. Why constrain writing with a glottographic straitjacket, demanding that it be just as sequential as speech? It would never occur to them. Semasiographic writing naturally took advantage of the page's two-dimensionality; instead of doling out morphemes one at a time, it offered an entire page full of them all at once.

And now that Heptapod B had introduced me to a simultaneous mode of consciousness, I understood the rationale behind Heptapod A's grammar: what my sequential mind had perceived as unnecessarily convoluted, I now recognized as an attempt to provide flexibility within the confines of sequential speech. I could use Heptapod A more easily as a result, though it was still a poor substitute for Heptapod B.

There was a knock at the door and then Gary poked his head in. "Colonel Weber'll be here any minute."

I grimaced. "Right." Weber was coming to participate in a session with Flapper and Raspberry; I was to act as translator, a job I wasn't trained for and that I detested.

Gary stepped inside and closed the door. He pulled me out of my chair and kissed me.

I smiled. "You trying to cheer me up before he gets here?"

"No, I'm trying to cheer me up."

"You weren't interested in talking to the heptapods at all, were you? You worked on this project just to get me into bed."

"Ah, you see right through me."

I looked into his eyes. "You better believe it," I said.

I remember when you'll be a month old, and I'll stumble out of bed to give you your 2:00 a.m. feeding. Your nursery will have that "baby smell" of diaper rash cream and talcum powder, with a faint ammoniac whiff coming from the diaper pail in the corner. I'll lean over your crib, lift your squalling form out, and sit in the rocking chair to nurse you.

The word "infant" is derived from the Latin word for "unable to speak," but you'll be perfectly capable of saying one thing: "I suffer," and you'll do it tirelessly and without hesitation. I have to admire your utter commitment to that statement; when you cry, you'll become outrage incarnate, every fiber of your body employed in expressing that emotion. It's funny: when you're tranquil, you will seem to radiate light, and if someone were to paint a portrait of you like that, I'd insist that they include the halo. But when you're unhappy, you will become a klaxon, built for radiating sound; a portrait of you then could simply be a fire alarm bell.

At that stage of your life, there'll be no past or future for you; until I give you my breast, you'll have no memory of contentment in the past nor expectation of relief in the future. Once you begin nursing, everything will reverse, and all will be right with the world. NOW is the only moment you'll perceive; you'll live in the present tense. In many ways, it's an enviable state.

The heptapods are neither free nor bound as we understand those concepts; they don't act according to their will, nor are they helpless automatons. What distinguishes the heptapods' mode of awareness is not just that their actions coincide with history's events; it is also that their motives coincide with history's purposes. They act to create the future, to enact chronology.

Freedom isn't an illusion; it's perfectly real in the context of sequential consciousness. Within the context of simultaneous consciousness, freedom is not meaningful, but neither is coercion; it's simply a different context, no more or less valid than the other. It's like that famous optical illusion, the drawing of either an elegant young woman, face turned away from the viewer, or a wart-nosed crone, chin tucked down on her chest. There's no "correct" interpretation; both are equally valid. But you can't see both at the same time.

Similarly, knowledge of the future was incompatible with free will. What made it possible for me to exercise freedom of choice also made it impossible for me to know the future. Conversely, now that I know the future, I would never act contrary to that future, including telling others what I know: those who know the future don't talk about it. Those who've read the *Book of Ages* never admit to it.

I turned on the VCR and slotted a cassette of a session from the Ft. Worth looking glass. A diplomatic negotiator was having a discussion with the heptapods there, with Burghart acting as translator.

The negotiator was describing humans' moral beliefs, trying to lay some groundwork for the concept of altruism. I knew the heptapods were familiar with the conversation's eventual outcome, but they still participated enthusiastically.

If I could have described this to someone who didn't already know, she might ask, if the heptapods already knew everything that they would ever say or hear, what was the point of their using language at all? A reasonable question. But language wasn't only for communication: it was also a form of action. According to speech act theory, statements like "You're under arrest," "I christen this vessel," or "I promise" were all performative: a speaker could perform the action only by uttering the words. For such acts, knowing what would be said didn't change anything. Everyone at a wedding anticipated the words "I now pronounce you husband and wife," but until the minister actually said them, the ceremony didn't count. With performative language, saying equaled doing.

For the heptapods, all language was performative. Instead of using language to inform, they used language to actualize. Sure, heptapods already knew what would be said in any conversation; but in order for their knowledge to be true, the conversation would have to take place.

"First Goldilocks tried the papa bear's bowl of porridge, but it was full of Brussels sprouts, which she hated."

You'll laugh. "No, that's wrong!" We'll be sitting side by side on the sofa, the skinny, overpriced hardcover spread open on our laps.

I'll keep reading. "Then Goldilocks tried the mama bear's bowl of porridge, but it was full of spinach, which she also hated."

You'll put your hand on the page of the book to stop me. "You have to read it the right way!"

"I'm reading just what it says here," I'll say, all innocence.

"No you're not. That's not how the story goes."

"Well if you already know how the story goes, why do you need me to read it to you?"

"Cause I wanna hear it!"

———

The air conditioning in Weber's office almost compensated for having to talk to the man.

"They're willing to engage in a type of exchange," I explained, "but it's not trade. We simply give them something, and they give us something in return. Neither party tells the other what they're giving beforehand."

Colonel Weber's brow furrowed just slightly. "You mean they're willing to exchange gifts?"

I knew what I had to say. "We shouldn't think of it as 'gift-giving.' We don't know if this transaction has the same associations for the heptapods that gift-giving has for us."

"Can we"—he searched for the right wording—"drop hints about the kind of gift we want?"

"They don't do that themselves for this type of transaction. I asked them if we could make a request, and they said we could, but it won't make them tell us what they're giving." I suddenly remembered that a morphological relative of "performative" was "performance," which could describe the sensation of conversing when you knew what would be said: it was like performing in a play.

"But would it make them more likely to give us what we asked for?" Colonel Weber asked. He was perfectly oblivious of the script, yet his responses matched his assigned lines exactly.

"No way of knowing," I said. "I doubt it, given that it's not a custom they engage in."

"If we give our gift first, will the value of our gift influence the value of theirs?" He was improvising, while I had carefully rehearsed for this one and only show.

"No," I said. "As far as we can tell, the value of the exchanged items is irrelevant."

"If only my relatives felt that way," murmured Gary wryly.

I watched Colonel Weber turn to Gary. "Have you discovered anything new in the physics discussions?" he asked, right on cue.

"If you mean, any information new to mankind, no," said Gary. "The heptapods haven't varied from the routine. If we demonstrate something to them, they'll show us their formulation of it, but they won't volunteer anything and they won't answer our questions about what they know."

An utterance that was spontaneous and communicative in the

context of human discourse became a ritual recitation when viewed by the light of Heptapod B.

Weber scowled. "All right then, we'll see how the State Department feels about this. Maybe we can arrange some kind of gift-giving ceremony."

Like physical events, with their causal and teleological interpretations, every linguistic event had two possible interpretations: as a transmission of information and as the realization of a plan.

"I think that's a good idea, Colonel," I said.

It was an ambiguity invisible to most. A private joke; don't ask me to explain it.

Even though I'm proficient with Heptapod B, I know I don't experience reality the way a heptapod does. My mind was cast in the mold of human, sequential languages, and no amount of immersion in an alien language can completely reshape it. My worldview is an amalgam of human and heptapod.

Before I learned how to think in Heptapod B, my memories grew like a column of cigarette ash, laid down by the infinitesimal sliver of combustion that was my consciousness, marking the sequential present. After I learned Heptapod B, new memories fell into place like gigantic blocks, each one measuring years in duration, and though they didn't arrive in order or land contiguously, they soon composed a period of five decades. It is the period during which I know Heptapod B well enough to think in it, starting during my interviews with Flapper and Raspberry and ending with my death.

Usually, Heptapod B affects just my memory: my consciousness crawls along as it did before, a glowing sliver crawling forward in time, the difference being that the ash of memory lies ahead as well as behind: there is no real combustion. But occasionally I have glimpses when Heptapod B truly reigns, and I experience past and future all at once; my consciousness becomes a half-century-long ember burning outside time. I perceive—during those glimpses—that entire epoch as a simultaneity. It's a period encompassing the rest of my life, and the entirety of yours.

I wrote out the semagrams for "process create-endpoint inclusive-we," meaning "let's start." Raspberry replied in the affirmative, and the slide shows began. The second display screen that the heptapods had provided began presenting a series of images, composed of semagrams and equations, while one of our video screens did the same.

This was the second "gift exchange" I had been present for, the eighth one overall, and I knew it would be the last. The looking-glass tent was crowded with people; Burghart from Ft. Worth was here, as were Gary and a nuclear physicist, assorted biologists, anthropologists, military brass, and diplomats. Thankfully they had set up an air conditioner to cool the place off. We would review the tapes of the images later to figure out just what the heptapods' "gift" was. Our own "gift" was a presentation on the Lascaux cave paintings.

We all crowded around the heptapods' second screen, trying to glean some idea of the images' content as they went by. "Preliminary assessments?" asked Colonel Weber.

"It's not a return," said Burghart. In a previous exchange, the heptapods had given us information about ourselves that we had previously told them. This had infuriated the State Department, but we had no reason to think of it as an insult: it probably indicated that trade value really didn't play a role in these exchanges. It didn't exclude the possibility that the heptapods might yet offer us a space drive, or cold fusion, or some other wish-fulfilling miracle.

"That looks like inorganic chemistry," said the nuclear physicist, pointing at an equation before the image was replaced.

Gary nodded. "It could be materials technology," he said.

"Maybe we're finally getting somewhere," said Colonel Weber.

"I wanna see more animal pictures," I whispered, quietly so that only Gary could hear me, and pouted like a child. He smiled and poked me. Truthfully, I wished the heptapods had given another xenobiology lecture, as they had on two previous exchanges; judging from those, humans were more similar to the heptapods than any other species they'd ever encountered. Or another lecture on heptapod history; those had been filled with apparent non sequiturs, but were interesting nonetheless. I didn't want the heptapods to give us new technology, because I didn't want to see what our governments might do with it.

I watched Raspberry while the information was being exchanged, looking for any anomalous behavior. It stood barely moving as usual; I saw no indications of what would happen shortly.

After a minute, the heptapod's screen went blank, and a minute after that, ours did too. Gary and most of the other scientists clustered around a tiny video screen that was replaying the heptapods' presentation. I could hear them talk about the need to call in a solid-state physicist.

Colonel Weber turned. "You two," he said, pointing to me and then to Burghart, "schedule the time and location for the next exchange." Then he followed the others to the playback screen.

"Coming right up," I said. To Burghart, I asked, "Would you care to do the honors, or shall I?"

I knew Burghart had gained a proficiency in Heptapod B similar to mine. "It's your looking glass," he said. "You drive."

I sat down again at the transmitting computer. "Bet you never figured you'd wind up working as an Army translator back when you were a grad student."

"That's for goddamn sure," he said. "Even now I can hardly believe it." Everything we said to each other felt like the carefully bland exchanges of spies who meet in public, but never break cover.

I wrote out the semagrams for "locus exchange-transaction converse inclusive-we" with the projective aspect modulation.

Raspberry wrote its reply. That was my cue to frown, and for Burghart to ask, "What does it mean by that?" His delivery was perfect.

I wrote a request for clarification; Raspberry's reply was the same as before. Then I watched it glide out of the room. The curtain was about to fall on this act of our performance.

Colonel Weber stepped forward. "What's going on? Where did it go?"

"It said that the heptapods are leaving now," I said. "Not just itself; all of them."

"Call it back here now. Ask it what it means."

"Um, I don't think Raspberry's wearing a pager," I said.

The image of the room in the looking glass disappeared so abruptly that it took a moment for my eyes to register what I was seeing instead: it was the other side of the looking-glass tent. The looking glass had become completely transparent. The conversation around the playback screen fell silent.

"What the hell is going on here?" said Colonel Weber.

Gary walked up to the looking glass, and then around it to the other side. He touched the rear surface with one hand; I could see the pale ovals where his fingertips made contact with the looking glass. "I think," he said, "we just saw a demonstration of transmutation at a distance."

I heard the sounds of heavy footfalls on dry grass. A soldier came in through the tent door, short of breath from sprinting, holding an oversize walkie-talkie. "Colonel, message from—"

Weber grabbed the walkie-talkie from him.

I remember what it'll be like watching you when you are a day old. Your father will have gone for a quick visit to the hospital cafeteria, and you'll be lying in your bassinet, and I'll be leaning over you.

So soon after the delivery, I will still be feeling like a wrung-out towel. You will seem incongruously tiny, given how enormous I felt during the pregnancy; I could swear there was room for someone much larger and more robust than you in there. Your hands and feet will be long and thin, not chubby yet. Your face will still be all red and pinched, puffy eyelids squeezed shut, the gnome-like phase that precedes the cherubic.

I'll run a finger over your belly, marveling at the uncanny softness of your skin, wondering if silk would abrade your body like burlap. Then you'll writhe, twisting your body while poking out your legs one at a time, and I'll recognize the gesture as one I had felt you do inside me, many times. So *that's* what it looks like.

I'll feel elated at this evidence of a unique mother-child bond, this certitude that you're the one I carried. Even if I had never laid eyes on you before, I'd be able to pick you out from a sea of babies: Not that one. No, not her either. Wait, that one over there.

Yes, that's her. She's mine.

That final "gift exchange" was the last we ever saw of the heptapods. All at once, all over the world, their looking glasses became transparent and their ships left orbit. Subsequent analysis of the looking glasses revealed them to be nothing more than sheets of fused silica, completely inert. The information from the final exchange session described a new class of superconducting materials, but it later proved to duplicate the results of research just completed in Japan: nothing that humans didn't already know.

We never did learn why the heptapods left, any more than we learned what brought them here, or why they acted the way they did. My own new awareness didn't provide that type of knowledge; the heptapods' behavior was presumably explicable from a sequential point of view, but we never found that explanation.

I would have liked to experience more of the heptapods' worldview, to feel the way they feel. Then, perhaps I could immerse myself fully in the necessity of events, as they must, instead of merely wading in its surf for the rest of my life. But that will never come to pass. I will continue to practice the heptapod languages, as will the other linguists on the looking-glass teams, but none of us will ever progress any further than we did when the heptapods were here.

Working with the heptapods changed my life. I met your father and learned Heptapod B, both of which make it possible for me to know you now, here on the patio in the moonlight. Eventually, many years from now, I'll be without your father, and without you. All I will have left from this moment is the heptapod language. So I pay close attention, and note every detail.

From the beginning I knew my destination, and I chose my route accordingly. But am I working toward an extreme of joy, or of pain? Will I achieve a minimum, or a maximum?

These questions are in my mind when your father asks me, "Do you want to make a baby?" And I smile and answer, "Yes," and I unwrap his arms from around me, and we hold hands as we walk inside to make love, to make you.

Seventy-Two Letters

When he was a child, Robert's favorite toy was a simple one, a clay doll that could do nothing but walk forward. While his parents entertained their guests in the garden outside, discussing Victoria's ascension to the throne or the Chartist reforms, Robert would follow the doll as it marched down the corridors of the family home, turning it around corners or back where it came from. The doll didn't obey commands or exhibit any sense at all; if it met a wall, the diminutive clay figure would keep marching until it gradually mashed its arms and legs into misshapen flippers. Sometimes Robert would let it do that, strictly for his own amusement. Once the doll's limbs were thoroughly distorted, he'd pick the toy up and pull the name out, stopping its motion in midstride. Then he'd knead the body back into a smooth lump, flatten it out into a plank, and cut out a different figure: a body with one leg crooked, or longer than the other. He would stick the name back into it, and the doll would promptly topple over and push itself around in a little circle.

It wasn't the sculpting that Robert enjoyed; it was mapping out the limits of the name. He liked to see how much variation he could impart to the body before the name could no longer animate it. To save time with the sculpting, he rarely added decorative details; he refined the bodies only as was needed to test the name.

Another of his dolls walked on four legs. The body was a nice one, a finely detailed porcelain horse, but Robert was more interested in experimenting with its name. This name obeyed commands to start and stop and knew enough to avoid obstacles, and Robert tried inserting it into bodies of his own making. But this name had more exacting body requirements, and he was never able to form a clay body it could animate. He formed the legs separately and then attached them to the body, but he wasn't able to erase the seams fully; the name didn't recognize the body as a single continuous piece.

He scrutinized the names themselves, looking for some simple substitutions that might distinguish two-leggedness from four-leggedness, or make the body obey simple commands. But the names looked entirely different; on each scrap of parchment were inscribed seventy-two tiny Hebrew letters, arranged in twelve rows of six, and so far as he could tell, the order of the letters was utterly random.

Robert Stratton and his fourth-form classmates sat quietly as Master Trevelyan paced between the rows of desks.

"Langdale, what is the doctrine of names?"

"All things are reflections of God, and, um, all—"

"Spare us your bumbling. Thorburn, can *you* tell us the doctrine of names?"

"As all things are reflections of God, so are all names reflections of the divine name."

"And what is an object's true name?"

"That name which reflects the divine name in the same manner as the object reflects God."

"And what is the action of a true name?"

"To endow its object with a reflection of divine power."

"Correct. Halliwell, what is the doctrine of signatures?"

The natural philosophy lesson continued until noon, but because it was a Saturday, there was no instruction for the rest of the day. Master Trevelyan dismissed the class, and the boys of Cheltenham school dispersed.

After stopping at the dormitory, Robert met his friend Lionel at the border of school grounds. "So the wait's over? Today's the day?" Robert asked.

"I said it was, didn't I?"

"Let's go, then." The pair set off to walk the mile and a half to Lionel's home.

During his first year at Cheltenham, Robert had known Lionel hardly at all; Lionel was one of the day boys, and Robert, like all the boarders, regarded them with suspicion. Then, purely by chance, Robert ran into him while on holiday, during a visit to the British Museum. Robert loved the museum: the frail mummies and immense sarcophagi; the stuffed platypus and pickled mermaid; the wall bristling with elephant tusks and moose antlers and unicorn horns. That particular day he was at the display of elemental sprites: he was reading the card explaining the salamander's absence when he suddenly recognized Lionel, standing right next to him, peering at the undine in its jar. Conversation revealed their shared interest in the sciences, and the two became fast friends.

As they walked down the road, they kicked a large pebble back and forth between them. Lionel gave the pebble a kick, and laughed as it skittered between Robert's ankles. "I couldn't wait to get out of there," he said. "I think one more doctrine would have been more than I could bear."

"Why do they even bother calling it natural philosophy?" said Robert. "Just admit it's another theology lesson and be done with it." The two of them had recently purchased *A Boy's Guide to Nomenclature*, which informed them that nomenclators no longer spoke in terms of God or the divine name. Instead, current thinking held that there was a lexical universe as well as a physical one, and bringing an object together with a compatible name caused the latent potentialities of both to be realized. Nor was there a single "true name" for a given object: depending on its precise shape, a body might be compatible with several names, known as its "euonyms," and conversely a simple name might tolerate significant variations in body shape, as his childhood marching doll had demonstrated.

When they reached Lionel's home, they promised the cook they would be in for dinner shortly and headed to the garden out back. Lionel had converted a toolshed in his family's garden into a laboratory, which he used to conduct experiments. Normally Robert came by on a regular basis, but recently Lionel had been working on an experiment that he was keeping secret. Only now was he ready to show Robert his results. Lionel had Robert wait outside while he entered first, and then let him enter.

A long shelf ran along every wall of the shed, crowded with racks of vials, stoppered bottles of green glass, and assorted rocks and mineral specimens. A table decorated with stains and scorch marks dominated the cramped space, and it supported the apparatus for Lionel's latest experiment: a cucurbit clamped in a stand so that its bottom rested in a basin full of water, which in turn sat on a tripod above a lit oil lamp. A mercury thermometer was also fixed in the basin.

"Take a look," said Lionel.

Robert leaned over to inspect the cucurbit's contents. At first it appeared to be nothing more than foam, a dollop of suds that might have dripped off a pint of stout. But as he looked closer, he realized that what he thought were bubbles were actually the interstices of a glistening latticework. The froth consisted of *homunculi*: tiny seminal foetuses. Their bodies were transparent individually, but collectively their bulbous heads and strandlike limbs adhered to form a pale, dense foam.

"So you wanked off into a jar and kept the spunk warm?" he asked, and Lionel shoved him. Robert laughed and raised his hands in a placating gesture. "No, honestly, it's a wonder. How'd you do it?"

Mollified, Lionel said, "It's a real balancing act. You have to keep the temperature just right, of course, but if you want them to grow, you also have to keep just the right mix of nutrients. Too thin a mix, and they starve. Too rich, and they get over lively and start fighting with each other."

"You're having me on."

"It's the truth; look it up if you don't believe me. Battles amongst sperm are what cause monstrosities to be born. If an injured foetus is the one that makes it to the egg, the baby that's born is deformed."

"I thought that was because of a fright the mother had when she was carrying." Robert could just make out the minuscule squirmings of the individual foetuses. He realized that the froth was ever so slowly roiling as a result of their collective motions.

"That's only for some kinds, like ones that are all hairy or covered in blotches. Babies that don't have arms or legs, or have misshapen ones, they're the ones that got caught in a fight back when they were sperm. That's why you can't provide too rich a broth, especially if they haven't any place to go: they get in a frenzy. You can lose all of them pretty quick that way."

"How long can you keep them growing?"

"Probably not much longer," said Lionel. "It's hard to keep them alive if they haven't reached an egg. I read about one in France that was grown till it was the size of a fist, and they had the best equipment available. I just wanted to see if I could do it at all."

Robert stared at the foam, remembering the doctrine of preformation that Master Trevelyan had drilled into them: all living things had been created at the same time, long ago, and births today were merely enlargements of the previously imperceptible. Although they appeared newly created, these *homunculi* were countless years old; for all of human history they had lain nested within generations of their ancestors, waiting for their turn to be born.

In fact, it wasn't just them who had waited; he himself must have done the same thing prior to his birth. If his father were to do this experiment, the tiny figures Robert saw would be his unborn brothers and sisters. He knew they were insensible until reaching an egg, but he wondered what thoughts they'd have if they weren't. He imagined the sensation of his body, every bone and organ soft and clear as gelatin, sticking to those of myriad identical siblings. What would it be like, looking through transparent eyelids, realizing the mountain in the distance was actually a person, recognizing it as his brother? What if he knew he'd become as massive and solid as that colossus, if only he could reach an egg? It was no wonder they fought.

Robert Stratton went on to read nomenclature at Cambridge's Trinity College. There he studied kabbalistic texts written centuries before, when nomenclators were still called *ba'alei shem* and automata were called *golem*, texts that laid the foundation for the science of names: the *Sefer Yezirah*, Eleazar of Worms' *Sodei Razayya*, Abulafia's *Hayyei ha-Olam ha-Ba*. Then he studied the alchemical treatises that placed the techniques of alphabetic manipulation in a broader philosophical and mathematical context: Llull's *Ars Magna*, Agrippa's *De Occulta Philosophia*, Dee's *Monas Hieroglyphica*.

He learned that every name was a combination of several epithets, each designating a specific trait or capability. Epithets were generated by compiling all the words that described the desired trait: cognates and etymons, from languages both living and extinct. By selectively substituting and permuting letters, one could distill from those words their common essence, which was the epithet for that trait. In certain instances, epithets could be used as the bases for triangulation, allowing one to derive epithets for traits undescribed in any language. The entire process relied on intuition as much as formulae; the ability to choose the best letter permutations was an unteachable skill.

He studied the modern techniques of nominal integration and factorization, the former being the means by which a set of epithets—pithy and evocative—were commingled into the seemingly random string of letters that made up a name, the latter by which a name was decomposed into its constituent epithets. Not every method of integration had a matching factorization technique: a powerful name might be refactored to yield a set of epithets different from those used to generate it, and those epithets were often useful for that reason. Some names resisted refactorization, and nomenclators strove to develop new techniques to penetrate their secrets.

Nomenclature was undergoing something of a revolution during this time. There had long been two classes of names: those for animating a body, and those functioning as amulets. Health amulets were worn as protection from injury or illness, while others rendered a house resistant to fire or a ship less likely to founder at sea. Of late, however, the distinction between these categories of names was becoming blurred, with exciting results.

The nascent science of thermodynamics, which established the interconvertibility of heat and work, had recently explained how automata gained their motive power by absorbing heat from their surroundings. Using this improved understanding of heat, a *Namenmeister* in Berlin had developed a new class of amulet that caused a body to absorb heat from one location and release it in another. Refrigeration employing such amulets was simpler and more efficient than that based on the evaporation of a volatile fluid, and had immense commercial application. Amulets were likewise facilitating the improvement of automata: an Edinburgh nomenclator's research into the amulets that prevented objects from becoming lost had led him to patent a household automaton able to return objects to their proper places.

Upon graduation, Stratton took up residence in London and secured a position as a nomenclator at Coade Manufactory, one of the leading makers of automata in England.

Stratton's most recent automaton, cast from plaster of Paris, followed a few paces behind him as he entered the factory building. It was an immense brick structure with skylights for its roof; half of the building was devoted to casting metal, the other half to ceramics. In either section, a meandering path connected the various rooms, each one housing the next step in transforming raw materials into finished automata. Stratton and his automaton entered the ceramics portion.

They walked past a row of low vats in which the clay was mixed. Different vats contained different grades of clay, ranging from common red clay to fine white kaolin, resembling enormous mugs abrim with liquid chocolate or heavy cream; only the strong mineral smell broke the illusion. The paddles stirring the clay were connected by gears to a drive shaft, mounted just beneath the skylights, that ran the length of the room. At the end of the room stood an automatous engine: a cast-iron giant that cranked the drive wheel tirelessly. Walking past, Stratton could detect a faint coolness in the air as the engine drew heat from its surroundings.

The next room held the molds for casting. Chalky white shells bearing the inverted contours of various automata were stacked along the walls. In the central portion of the room, apron-clad journeymen sculptors worked singly and in pairs, tending the cocoons from which automata were hatched.

The sculptor nearest him was assembling the mold for a putter, a broad-headed quadruped employed in the mines for pushing trolleys of ore. The young man looked up from his work. "Were you looking for someone, sir?" he asked.

"I'm to meet Master Willoughby here," replied Stratton.

"Pardon, I didn't realize. I'm sure he'll be here shortly." The journeyman returned to his task. Harold Willoughby was a Master Sculptor First-Degree; Stratton was consulting him on the design of a reusable mold for casting his automaton. While he waited, Stratton strolled idly amongst the molds. His automaton stood motionless, ready for its next command.

Willoughby entered from the door to the metalworks, his face flushed from the heat of the foundry. "My apologies for being late, Mr. Stratton," he said. "We've been working toward a large bronze for some weeks now, and today was the pour. You don't want to leave the lads alone at a time like that."

"I understand completely," replied Stratton.

Wasting no time, Willoughby strode over to the new automaton. "Is this what you've had Moore doing all these months?" Moore was the journeyman assisting Stratton on his project.

Stratton nodded. "The boy does good work." Following Stratton's requests, Moore had fashioned countless bodies, all variations on a single basic theme, by applying modeling clay to an armature, and then used them to create plaster casts on which Stratton could test his names.

Willoughby inspected the body. "Some nice detail; looks straightforward enough—hold on now." He pointed to the automaton's hands: rather than the traditional paddle or mitten design, with fingers suggested by grooves in the surface, these were fully formed, each one having a thumb and four distinct and separate fingers. "You don't mean to tell me those are functional?"

"That's correct."

Willoughby's skepticism was plain. "Show me."

Stratton addressed the automaton. "Flex your fingers." The automaton extended both hands, flexed and straightened each pair of fingers in turn, and then returned its arms to its sides.

"I congratulate you, Mr. Stratton," said the sculptor. He squatted to examine the automaton's fingers more closely. "The fingers need to be bent at each joint for the name to take?"

"That's right. Can you design a piece mold for such a form?"

Willoughby clicked his tongue several times. "That'll be a tricky bit of business," he said. "We might have to use a waste mold for each casting. Even with a piece mold, these'd be very expensive for ceramic."

"I think they will be worth the expense. Permit me to demonstrate." Stratton addressed the automaton. "Cast a body; use that mold over there."

The automaton trudged over to a nearby wall and picked up the pieces of the mold Stratton had indicated: it was the mold for a small porcelain messenger. Several journeymen stopped what they were doing to watch the automaton carry the pieces over to a work area. There it fitted the various sections together and bound them tightly with twine. The sculptors' wonderment was apparent as they watched the automaton's fingers work, looping and threading the loose ends of the twine into a knot. Then the automaton stood the assembled mold upright and headed off to get a pitcher of clay slip.

"That's enough," said Willoughby. The automaton stopped its work and resumed its original standing posture. Examining the mold, Willoughby asked, "Did you train it yourself?"

"I did. I hope to have Moore train it in metal casting."

"Do you have names that can learn other tasks?"

"Not as yet. However, there's every reason to believe that an entire class of similar names exists, one for every sort of skill needing manual dexterity."

"Indeed?" Willoughby noticed the other sculptors watching, and called out, "If you've nothing to do, there's plenty I can assign to you." The journeymen promptly resumed their work, and Willoughby turned back to Stratton. "Let us go to your office to speak about this further."

"Very well." Stratton had the automaton follow the two of them back to the frontmost of the complex of connected buildings that was Coade Manufactory. They first entered Stratton's studio, which was situated behind his office proper. Once inside, Stratton addressed the sculptor. "Do you have an objection to my automaton?"

Willoughby looked over a pair of clay hands mounted on a work-table. On the wall behind the table were pinned a series of schematic drawings showing hands in a variety of positions. "You've done an admirable job of emulating the human hand. I am concerned, how-ever, that the first skill in which you trained your new automaton is sculpture."

"If you're worried that I am trying to replace sculptors, you needn't be. That is absolutely not my goal."

"I'm relieved to hear it," said Willoughby. "Why did you choose sculpture, then?"

"It is the first step of a rather indirect path. My ultimate goal is to allow automatous engines to be manufactured inexpensively enough so that most families could purchase one."

Willoughby's confusion was apparent. "How, pray tell, would a family make use of an engine?"

"To drive a powered loom, for example."

"What are you going on about?"

"Have you ever seen children who are employed at a textile mill? They are worked to exhaustion; their lungs are clogged with cotton dust; they are so sickly that you can hardly conceive of their reaching adulthood. Cheap cloth is bought at the price of our workers' health; weavers were far better off when textile production was a cottage industry."

"Powered looms were what took weavers out of cottages. How could they put them back in?"

Stratton had not spoken of this before, and welcomed the opportunity to explain. "The cost of automatous engines has always been high, and so we have mills in which scores of looms are driven by an immense coal-heated Goliath. But an automaton like mine could cast engines very cheaply. If a small automatous engine, suitable for driving a few machines, becomes affordable to a weaver and his family, then they can produce cloth from their home as they did once before. People could earn a decent income without being subjected to the conditions of the factory."

"You forget the cost of the loom itself," said Willoughby gently, as if humoring him. "Powered looms are considerably more expensive than the hand looms of old."

"My automata could also assist in the production of cast-iron parts, which would reduce the price of powered looms and other machines. This is no panacea, I know, but I am nonetheless convinced that inexpensive engines offer the chance of a better life for the individual craftsman."

"Your desire for reform does you credit. Let me suggest, however, that there are simpler cures for the social ills you cite: a reduction in working hours, or the improvement of conditions. You do not need to disrupt our entire system of manufacturing."

"I think what I propose is more accurately described as a restoration than a disruption."

Now Willoughby became exasperated. "This talk of returning to a family economy is all well and good, but what would happen to sculptors? Your intentions notwithstanding, these automata of yours would put sculptors out of work. These are men who have undergone years of apprenticeship and training. How would they feed their families?"

Stratton was unprepared for the sharpness in his tone. "You overestimate my skills as a nomenclator," he said, trying to make light. The sculptor remained dour. He continued. "The learning capabilities of these automata are extremely limited. They can manipulate molds, but they could never design them; the real craft of sculpture can be performed only by sculptors. Before our meeting, you had just finished directing several journeymen in the pouring of a large bronze; automata could never work together in such a coordinated fashion. They will perform only rote tasks."

"What kind of sculptors would we produce if they spend their apprenticeship watching automata do their jobs for them? I will not have a venerable profession reduced to a performance by marionettes."

"That is not what would happen," said Stratton, becoming exasperated himself now. "But examine what you yourself are saying: the status that you wish your profession to retain is precisely that which weavers have been made to forfeit. I believe these automata can help restore dignity to other professions, and without great cost to yours."

Willoughby seemed not to hear him. "The very notion that automata would make automata! Not only is the suggestion insulting, it seems ripe for calamity. What of that ballad, the one where the broomsticks carry water buckets and run amuck?"

˙ "You mean 'Der Zauberlehrling'?" said Stratton. "The comparison is absurd. These automata are so far removed from being in a position to reproduce themselves without human participation that I scarcely know where to begin listing the objections. A dancing bear would sooner perform in the London Ballet."

"If you'd care to develop an automaton that can dance the ballet, I would fully support such an enterprise. However, you cannot continue with these dexterous automata."

"Pardon me, sir, but I am not bound by your decisions."

"You'll find it difficult to work without sculptors' cooperation. I shall recall Moore and forbid all the other journeymen from assisting you in any way with this project."

Stratton was momentarily taken aback. "Your reaction is completely unwarranted."

"I think it entirely appropriate."

"In that case, I will work with sculptors at another manufactory."

Willoughby frowned. "I will speak with the head of the Brotherhood of Sculptors, and recommend that he forbid all of our members from casting your automata."

Stratton could feel his blood rising. "I will not be bullied," he said. "Do what you will, but you cannot prevent me from pursuing this."

"I think our discussion is at an end." Willoughby strode to the door. "Good day to you, Mr. Stratton."

"Good day to you," replied Stratton heatedly.

It was the following day, and Stratton was taking his midday stroll through the district of Lambeth, where Coade Manufactory was located. After a few blocks he stopped at a local market; sometimes among the baskets of writhing eels and blankets spread with cheap watches were automatous dolls, and Stratton retained his boyhood fondness for seeing the latest designs. Today he noticed a new pair of boxing dolls, painted to look like an explorer and a savage. As he looked them over awhile, he could hear nostrum peddlers competing for the attention of a passerby with a runny nose.

"I see your health amulet failed you, sir," said one man whose table was arrayed with small square tins. "Your remedy lies in the curative powers of magnetism, concentrated in Doctor Sedgewick's Polarising Tablets!"

"Nonsense!" retorted an old woman. "What you need is tincture of mandrake, tried and true!" She held out a vial of clear liquid. "The dog wasn't cold yet when this extract was prepared! There's nothing more potent."

Seeing no other new dolls, Stratton left the market and walked on, his thoughts returning to what Willoughby had said yesterday. Without the cooperation of the sculptors' trade union, he'd have to resort to hiring independent sculptors. He hadn't worked with such individuals before, and some investigation would be required: ostensibly they cast bodies only for use with public-domain names, but for certain individuals these activities disguised patent infringement and piracy, and any association with them could permanently blacken his reputation.

"Mr. Stratton."

Stratton looked up. A small, wiry man, plainly dressed, stood before him. "Yes; do I know you, sir?"

"No, sir. My name is Davies. I'm in the employ of Lord Fieldhurst." He handed Stratton a card bearing the Fieldhurst crest.

Edward Maitland, third earl of Fieldhurst and a noted zoologist and comparative anatomist, was president of the Royal Society. Stratton had heard him speak during sessions of the Royal Society, but they had never been introduced. "What can I do for you?"

"Lord Fieldhurst would like to speak with you, at your earliest convenience, regarding your recent work."

Stratton wondered how the earl had learned of his work. "Why did you not call on me at my office?"

"Lord Fieldhurst prefers privacy in this matter." Stratton raised his eyebrows, but Davies didn't explain further. "Are you available this evening?"

It was an unusual invitation, but an honor nonetheless. "Certainly. Please inform Lord Fieldhurst that I would be delighted."

"A carriage will be outside your building at eight tonight." Davies touched his hat and was off.

At the promised hour, Davies arrived with the carriage. It was a luxurious vehicle, with an interior of lacquered mahogany and polished brass and brushed velvet. The tractor that drew it was an expensive one as well, a steed cast of bronze and needing no driver for familiar destinations.

Davies politely declined to answer any questions while they rode. He was obviously not a manservant, nor a secretary, but Stratton could not decide what sort of employee he was. The carriage carried them out of London into the countryside, until they reached Darrington Hall, one of the residences owned by the Fieldhurst lineage.

Once inside the home, Davies led Stratton through the foyer and then ushered him into an elegantly appointed study; he closed the doors without entering himself.

Seated at the desk within the study was a barrel-chested man wearing a silk coat and cravat; his broad, deeply creased cheeks were framed by woolly gray muttonchops. Stratton recognized him at once.

"Lord Fieldhurst, it is an honor."

"A pleasure to meet you, Mr. Stratton. You've been doing some excellent work recently."

"You are most kind. I did not realize that my work had become known."

"I make an effort to keep track of such things. Please, tell me what motivated you to develop such automata."

Stratton explained his plans for manufacturing affordable engines. Fieldhurst listened with interest, occasionally offering cogent suggestions.

"It is an admirable goal," he said, nodding his approval. "I'm pleased to find that you have such philanthropic motives, because I would ask your assistance in a project I'm directing."

"It would be my privilege to help in any way I could."

"Thank you." Fieldhurst's expression became solemn. "This is a matter of grave import. Before I speak further, I must first have your word that you will retain everything I reveal to you in the utmost confidence."

Stratton met the earl's gaze directly. "Upon my honor as a gentleman, sir, I shall not divulge anything you relate to me."

"Thank you, Mr. Stratton. Please come this way." Fieldhurst opened a door in the rear wall of the study and they walked down a short hallway. At the end of the hallway was a laboratory; a long, scrupulously clean worktable held a number of stations, each consisting of a microscope and an articulated brass framework of some sort, equipped with three mutually perpendicular knurled wheels for performing fine adjustments. An elderly man was peering into the microscope at the furthest station; he looked up from his work as they entered.

"Mr. Stratton, I believe you know Dr. Ashbourne."

Stratton, caught off guard, was momentarily speechless. Nicholas Ashbourne had been a lecturer at Trinity when Stratton was studying there, but had left years ago to pursue studies of, it was said, an unorthodox nature. Stratton remembered him as one of his most enthusiastic instructors. Age had narrowed his face somewhat, making his high forehead seem even higher, but his eyes were as bright and alert as ever. He walked over with the help of a carved ivory walking stick.

"Stratton, good to see you again."

"And you, sir. I was truly not expecting to see you here."

"This will be an evening full of surprises, my boy. Prepare yourself." He turned to Fieldhurst. "Would you care to begin?"

They followed Fieldhurst to the far end of the laboratory, where he opened another door and led them down a flight of stairs. "Only a small number of individuals—either Fellows of the Royal Society or Members of Parliament, or both—are privy to this matter. Five years ago, I was contacted confidentially by the Académie des Sciences in Paris. They wished for English scientists to confirm certain experimental findings of theirs."

"Indeed?"

"You can imagine their reluctance. However, they felt the matter outweighed national rivalries, and once I understood the situation, I agreed."

The three of them descended to a cellar. Gas brackets along the walls provided illumination, revealing the cellar's considerable size;

its interior was punctuated by an array of stone pillars that rose to form groined vaults. The long cellar contained row upon row of stout wooden tables, each one supporting a tank roughly the size of a bathtub. The tanks were made of zinc and fitted with plate-glass windows on all four sides, revealing their contents as a clear, faintly straw-colored fluid.

Stratton looked at the nearest tank. There was a distortion floating in the center of the tank, as if some of the liquid had congealed into a mass of jelly. It was difficult to distinguish the mass's features from the mottled shadows cast on the bottom of the tank, so he moved to another side of the tank and squatted down low to view the mass directly against a flame of a gas lamp. It was then that the coagulum resolved itself into the ghostly figure of a man, clear as aspic, curled up in foetal position.

"Incredible," Stratton whispered.

"We call it a megafoetus," explained Fieldhurst.

"This was grown from a spermatozoon? This must have required decades."

"It did not, more's the wonder. Several years ago, two Parisian naturalists named Dubuisson and Gille developed a method of inducing hypertrophic growth in a seminal foetus. The rapid infusion of nutrients allows such a foetus to reach this size within a fortnight."

By shifting his head back and forth, he saw slight differences in the way the gaslight was refracted, indicating the boundaries of the megafoetus's internal organs. "Is this creature . . . alive?"

"Only in an insensate manner, like a spermatozoon. No artificial process can replace gestation; it is the vital principle within the ovum which quickens the foetus, and the maternal influence which transforms it into a person. All we've done is effect a maturation in size and scale." Fieldhurst gestured toward the megafoetus. "The maternal influence also provides a foetus with pigmentation and all distinguishing physical characteristics. Our megafoetuses have no features beyond their sex. Every male bears the generic appearance you see here, and all the females are likewise identical. Within each sex, it is impossible to distinguish one from another by physical examination, no matter how dissimilar the original fathers might have been; only rigorous record keeping allows us to identify each megafoetus."

Stratton stood up again. "So what was the intention of the experiment if not to develop an artificial womb?"

"To test the notion of the fixity of species." Realizing that Stratton was not a zoologist, the earl explained further. "Were lens grinders able to construct microscopes of unlimited magnifying power, biologists could examine the future generations nested in the spermatozoa of any species and see whether their appearance remains fixed, or changes to give rise to a new species. In the latter case, they could also determine if the transition occurs gradually or abruptly.

"However, chromatic aberration imposes an upper limit on the magnifying power of any optical instrument. Messieurs Dubuisson and Gille hit upon the idea of artificially increasing the size of the foetuses themselves. Once a foetus reaches its adult size, one can extract a spermatozoon from it and enlarge a foetus from the next generation in the same manner." Fieldhurst stepped over to the next table in the row and indicated the tank it supported. "Repetition of the process lets us examine the unborn generations of any given species."

Stratton looked around the room. The rows of tanks took on a new significance. "So they compressed the intervals between 'births' to gain a preliminary view of our genealogical future."

"Precisely."

"Audacious! And what were the results?"

"They tested many animal species, but never observed any changes in form. However, they obtained a peculiar result when working with the seminal foetuses of humans. After no more than five generations, the male foetuses held no more spermatozoa, and the females held no more ova. The line terminated in a sterile generation."

"I imagine that wasn't entirely unexpected," Stratton said, glancing at the jellied form. "Each repetition must further attenuate some essence in the organisms. It's only logical that at some point the offspring would be so feeble that the process would fail."

"That was Dubuisson and Gille's initial assumption as well," agreed Fieldhurst, "so they sought to improve their technique. However, they could find no difference between megafoetuses of succeeding generations in terms of size or vitality. Nor was there any decline in the number of spermatozoa or ova; the penultimate generation was fully as fertile as the first. The transition to sterility was an abrupt one.

"They found another anomaly as well: while some spermatozoa yielded only four or fewer generations, variation occurred only across samples, never within a single sample. They evaluated samples from father and son donors, and in such instances, the father's spermatozoa produced exactly one more generation than the son's. And from what I understand, some of the donors were aged individuals indeed. While their samples held very few spermatozoa, they nonetheless held one more generation than those from sons in the prime of their lives. The progenitive power of the sperm bore no correlation with the health or vigor of the donor; instead, it correlated with the generation to which the donor belonged."

Fieldhurst paused and looked at Stratton gravely. "It was at this point that the Académie contacted me to see if the Royal Society could duplicate their findings. Together we have obtained the same result using samples collected from peoples as varied as the Lapps and the Hottentots. We are in agreement as to the implication of these findings: that the human species has the potential to exist for only a fixed number of generations, and we are within five generations of the final one."

Stratton turned to Ashbourne, half expecting him to confess that it was all an elaborate hoax, but the elder nomenclator looked entirely solemn. Stratton looked at the megafoetus again and frowned, absorbing what he had heard. "If your interpretation is correct, other species must be subject to a similar limitation. Yet from what I know, the extinction of a species has never been observed."

Fieldhurst nodded. "That is true. However, we do have the evidence of the fossil record, which suggests that species remain unchanged for a period of time, and then are abruptly replaced by new forms. The Catastrophists hold that violent upheavals caused species to become extinct. Based on what we've discovered regarding preformation, it now appears that extinctions are merely the result of a species reaching the end of its lifetime. They are natural rather than accidental deaths, in a manner of speaking." He gestured to the doorway from which they had entered. "Shall we return upstairs?"

Following the two other men, Stratton asked, "And what of the origination of new species? If they're not born from existing species, do they arise spontaneously?"

"That is as yet uncertain. Normally only the simplest animals arise by spontaneous generation: maggots and other vermiform creatures, typically under the influence of heat. The events postulated by Catastrophists—floods, volcanic eruptions, cometary impacts— would entail the release of great energies. Perhaps such energies affect matter so profoundly as to cause the spontaneous generation of an entire race of organisms, nested within a few progenitors. If so, cataclysms are not responsible for mass extinctions, but rather generate new species in their wake."

Back in the laboratory, the two elder men seated themselves in the chairs present. Too agitated to follow suit, Stratton remained standing. "If any animal species were created by the same cataclysm as the human species, they should likewise be nearing the end of their life spans. Have you found another species that evinces a final generation?"

Fieldhurst shook his head. "Not as yet. We believe that other species have different dates of extinction, correlated with the biological complexity of the animal; humans are presumably the most complex organism, and perhaps fewer generations of such complex organisms can be nested inside a spermatozoon."

"By the same token," countered Stratton, "perhaps the complexity of the human organism makes it unsuitable for the process of artificially accelerated growth. Perhaps it is the process whose limits have been discovered, not the species."

"An astute observation, Mr. Stratton. Experiments are continuing with species that more closely resemble humans, such as chimpanzees and ourang-outangs. However, the unequivocal answer to this question may require years, and if our current interpretation is correct, we can ill afford the time spent waiting for confirmation. We must ready a course of action immediately."

"But five generations could be over a century—" He caught himself, embarrassed at having overlooked the obvious: not all persons became parents at the same age.

Fieldhurst read his expression. "You realize why not all the sperm samples from donors of the same age produced the same number of generations: some lineages are approaching their end faster than others. For a lineage in which the men consistently father children late in life, five generations might mean over two centuries of fertility, but there are undoubtedly lineages that have reached their end already."

Stratton imagined the consequences. "The loss of fertility will become increasingly apparent to the general populace as time passes. Panic may arise well before the end is reached."

"Precisely, and rioting could extinguish our species as effectively as the exhaustion of generations. That is why time is of the essence."

"What is the solution you propose?"

"I shall defer to Dr. Ashbourne to explain further," said the earl.

Ashbourne rose and instinctively adopted the stance of a lecturing professor. "Do you recall why it was that all attempts to make automata out of wood were abandoned?"

Stratton was caught off guard by the question. "It was believed that the natural grain of wood implies a form in conflict with whatever we try to carve upon it. Currently there are efforts to use rubber as a casting material, but none have met with success."

"Indeed. But if the native form of wood were the only obstacle, shouldn't it be possible to animate an animal's corpse with a name? There the form of the body should be ideal."

"It's a macabre notion; I couldn't guess at such an experiment's likelihood of success. Has it ever been attempted?"

"In fact it has: also unsuccessfully. So these two entirely different avenues of research proved fruitless. Does that mean there is no way to animate organic matter using names? This was the question I left Trinity in order to pursue."

"And what did you discover?"

Ashbourne deflected the question with a wave of his hand. "First let us discuss thermodynamics. Have you kept up with recent developments? Then you know the dissipation of heat reflects an increase in disorder at the thermal level. Conversely, when an automaton condenses heat from its environment to perform work, it increases order. This confirms a long-held belief of mine that lexical order induces thermodynamic order. The lexical order of an amulet reinforces the order a body already possesses, thus providing protection against damage. The lexical order of an animating name increases the order of a body, thus providing motive power for an automaton.

"The next question was, how would an increase in order be reflected in organic matter? Since names don't animate dead tissue, obviously organic matter doesn't respond at the thermal level; but perhaps it can be ordered at another level. Consider: a steer can be reduced to a vat of gelatinous broth. The broth comprises the same material as the steer, but which embodies a higher amount of order?"

"The steer, obviously," said Stratton, bewildered.

"Obviously. An organism, by virtue of its physical structure, embodies order; the more complex the organism, the greater the amount of order. It was my hypothesis that increasing the order in organic matter would be evidenced by imparting form to it. However, most living matter has already assumed its ideal form. The question is, what has life but not form?"

The elder nomenclator did not wait for a response. "The answer is, an unfertilized ovum. The ovum contains the vital principle that animates the creature it ultimately gives rise to, but it has no form itself. Ordinarily, the ovum incorporates the form of the foetus compressed within the spermatozoon that fertilizes it. The next step was obvious." Here Ashbourne waited, looking at Stratton expectantly.

Stratton was at a loss. Ashbourne seemed disappointed, and continued. "The next step was to artificially induce the growth of an embryo from an ovum, by application of a name."

"But if the ovum is unfertilized," objected Stratton, "there is no preexisting structure to enlarge."

"Precisely."

"You mean structure would arise out of a homogenous medium? Impossible."

"Nonetheless, it was my goal for several years to confirm this hypothesis. My first experiments consisted of applying a name to unfertilized frog eggs."

"How did you embed the name into a frog's egg?"

"The name is not actually embedded, but rather impressed by means of a specially manufactured needle." Ashbourne opened a cabinet that sat on the worktable between two of the microscope stations. Inside was a wooden rack filled with small instruments arranged in pairs. Each was tipped with a long glass needle; in some pairs they were nearly as thick as those used for knitting, in others as slender as a hypodermic. He withdrew one from the largest pair and handed it to Stratton to examine. The glass needle was not clear, but instead seemed to contain some sort of dappled core.

Ashbourne explained. "While that may appear to be some sort of medical implement, it is in fact a vehicle for a name, just as the more conventional slip of parchment is. Alas, it requires far more effort to make than taking pen to parchment. To create such a needle, one must first arrange fine strands of black glass within a bundle of clear glass strands so that the name is legible when they are viewed end-on. The strands are then fused into a solid rod, and the rod is drawn out into an ever thinner strand. A skilled glassmaker can retain every detail of the name no matter how thin the strand becomes. Eventually one obtains a needle containing the name in its cross section."

"How did you generate the name that you used?"

"We can discuss that at length later. For the purposes of our current discussion, the only relevant information is that I incorporated the sexual epithet. Are you familiar with it?"

"I know of it." It was one of the few epithets that was dimorphic, having male and female variants.

"I needed two versions of the name, obviously, to induce the generation of both males and females." He indicated the paired arrangement of needles in the cabinet.

Stratton saw that the needle could be clamped into the brass framework with its tip approaching the slide beneath the microscope; the knurled wheels presumably were used to bring the needle into contact with an ovum. He returned the instrument. "You said the name is not embedded, but impressed. Do you mean to tell me that touching the frog's egg with this needle is all that's needed? Removing the name doesn't end its influence?"

"Precisely. The name activates a process in the egg that cannot be reversed. Prolonged contact of the name had no different effect."

"And the egg hatched a tadpole?"

"Not with the names initially tried; the only result was that symmetrical involutions appeared in the surface of the egg. But by incorporating different epithets, I was able to induce the egg to adopt different forms, some of which had every appearance of embryonic frogs. Eventually I found a name that caused the egg not only to assume the form of a tadpole, but also to mature and hatch. The tadpole thus hatched grew into a frog indistinguishable from any other member of the species."

"You had found a euonym for that species of frog," said Stratton.

Ashbourne smiled. "As this method of reproduction does not involve sexual congress, I have termed it 'parthenogenesis.'"

Stratton looked at both him and Fieldhurst. "It's clear what your proposed solution is. The logical conclusion of this research is to discover a euonym for the human species. You wish for mankind to perpetuate itself through nomenclature."

"You find the prospect troubling," said Fieldhurst. "That is to be expected: Dr. Ashbourne and myself initially felt the same way, as has everyone who has considered this. No one relishes the prospect of humans being conceived artificially. But can you offer an alternative?" Stratton was silent, and Fieldhurst went on. "All who are aware of both Dr. Ashbourne's and Dubuisson and Gille's work agree: there is no other solution."

Stratton reminded himself to maintain the dispassionate attitude of a scientist. "Precisely how do you envision this name being used?" he asked.

Ashbourne answered. "When a husband is unable to impregnate his wife, they will seek the services of a physician. The physician will collect the woman's menses, separate out the ovum, impress the name upon it, and then reintroduce it into her womb."

"A child born of this method would have no biological father."

"True, but the father's biological contribution is of minimal importance here. The mother will think of her husband as the child's father, so her imagination will impart a combination of her own and her husband's appearance and character to the foetus. That will not change. And I hardly need mention that name impression would not be made available to unmarried women."

"Are you confident this will result in well-formed children?" asked Stratton. "I'm sure you know to what I refer." They all knew of the disastrous attempt in the previous century to create improved children by mesmerizing women during their pregnancies.

Ashbourne nodded. "We are fortunate in that the ovum is very specific in what it will accept. The set of euonyms for any species of organism is very small; if the lexical order of the impressed name does not closely match the structural order of that species, the resulting foetus does not quicken. This does not remove the need for the mother to maintain a tranquil mind during her pregnancy; name impression cannot guard against maternal agitation. But the ovum's selectivity provides us assurance that any foetus induced will be well formed in every aspect, except the one anticipated."

Stratton was alarmed. "What aspect is that?"

"Can you not guess? The only incapacity of frogs created by name impression was in the males; they were sterile, for their spermatozoa bore no preformed foetuses inside. By comparison, the female frogs created were fertile: their eggs could be fertilized in either the conventional manner, or by repeating the impression with the name."

Stratton's relief was considerable. "So the male variant of the name was imperfect. Presumably there needs to be further differences between the male and female variants than simply the sexual epithet."

"Only if one considers the male variant imperfect," said Ashbourne, "which I do not. Consider: while a fertile male and a fertile female might seem equivalent, they differ radically in the degree of complexity exemplified. A female with viable ova remains a single organism, while a male with viable spermatozoa is actually many organisms: a father and all his potential children. In this light, the two variants of the name are well matched in their actions: each induces a single organism, but only in the female sex can a single organism be fertile."

"I see what you mean." Stratton realized he would need practice in thinking about nomenclature in the organic domain. "Have you developed euonyms for other species?"

"Just over a score, of various types; our progress has been rapid. We have only just begun work on a name for the human species, and it has proved far more difficult than our previous names."

"How many nomenclators are engaged in this endeavor?"

"Only a handful," Fieldhurst replied. "We have asked a few Royal Society members, and the Académie has some of France's leading *designateurs* working on it. You will understand if I do not mention any names at this point, but be assured that we have some of the most distinguished nomenclators in England assisting us."

"Forgive me for asking, but why are you approaching me? I am hardly in that category."

"You have not yet had a long career," said Ashbourne, "but the genus of names you have developed is unique. Automata have always been specialized in form and function, rather like animals: some are good at climbing, others at digging, but none at both. Yet yours can control human hands, which are uniquely versatile instruments: what else can manipulate everything from a wrench to a piano? The hand's dexterity is the physical manifestation of the mind's ingenuity, and these traits are essential to the name we seek."

"We have been discreetly surveying current nomenclatoral research for any names that demonstrate marked dexterity," said Fieldhurst. "When we learned of what you had accomplished, we sought you out immediately."

"In fact," Ashbourne continued, "the very reason your names are worrisome to sculptors is the reason we are interested in them: they endow automata with a more humanlike manner than any before. So now we ask, will you join us?"

Stratton considered it. This was perhaps the most important task a nomenclator could undertake, and under ordinary circumstances he would have leapt at the opportunity to participate. But before he could embark upon this enterprise in good conscience, there was another matter he had to resolve.

"You honor me with your invitation, but what of my work with dexterous automata? I still firmly believe that inexpensive engines can improve the lives of the labouring class."

"It is a worthy goal," said Fieldhurst, "and I would not ask you to give it up. Indeed, the first thing we wish you to do is to perfect the epithets for dexterity. But your efforts at social reform would be for naught unless we first ensure the survival of our species."

"Obviously, but I do not want the potential for reform that is offered by dexterous names to be neglected. There may never be a better opportunity for restoring dignity to common workers. What kind of victory would we achieve if the continuation of life meant ignoring this opportunity?"

"Well said," acknowledged the earl. "Let me make a proposal. So that you can best make use of your time, the Royal Society will provide support for your development of dexterous automata as needed: securing investors and so forth. I trust you will divide your time between the two projects wisely. Your work on biological nomenclature must remain confidential, obviously. Is that satisfactory?"

"It is. Very well then, gentlemen: I accept." They shook hands.

Some weeks had passed since Stratton last spoke with Willoughby, beyond a chilly exchange of greetings in passing. In fact, he had little interaction with any of the union sculptors, instead spending his time working on letter permutations in his office, trying to refine his epithets for dexterity.

He entered the manufactory through the front gallery, where customers normally perused the catalogue. Today it was crowded with domestic automata, all the same model char-engine. Stratton saw the clerk ensuring they were properly tagged.

"Good morning, Pierce," he said. "What are all these doing here?"

"An improved name is just out for the 'Regent,'" said the clerk. "Everyone's eager to get the latest."

"You're going to be busy this afternoon." The keys for unlocking the automata's name slots were themselves stored in a safe that required two of Coade's managers to open. The managers were reluctant to keep the safe open for more than a brief period each afternoon.

"I'm certain I can finish these in time."

"You couldn't bear to tell a pretty housemaid that her charengine wouldn't be ready by tomorrow."

The clerk smiled. "Can you blame me, sir?"

"No, I cannot," said Stratton, chuckling. He turned toward the business offices behind the gallery, when he found himself confronted by Willoughby.

"Perhaps you ought to prop open the safe," said the sculptor, "so that housemaids might not be inconvenienced. Seeing how destroying our institutions seems to be your intent."

"Good morning, Master Willoughby," said Stratton stiffly. He tried to walk past, but the other man stood in his way.

"I've been informed that Coade will be allowing nonunion sculptors onto the premises to assist you."

"Yes, but I assure you, only the most reputable independent sculptors are involved."

"As if such persons exist," said Willoughby scornfully. "You should know that I recommended that our trade union launch a strike against Coade in protest."

"Surely you're not serious." It had been decades since the last strike launched by the sculptors, and that one had ended in rioting.

"I am. Were the matter put to a vote of the membership, I'm certain it would pass: other sculptors with whom I've discussed your work agree with me about the threat it poses. However, the union leadership will not put it to a vote."

"Ah, so they disagreed with your assessment."

Here Willoughby frowned. "Apparently the Royal Society intervened on your behalf and persuaded the Brotherhood to refrain for the time being. You've found yourself some powerful supporters, Mr. Stratton."

Uncomfortably, Stratton replied, "The Royal Society considers my research worthwhile."

"Perhaps, but do not believe that this matter is ended."

"Your animosity is unwarranted, I tell you," Stratton insisted. "Once you have seen how sculptors can use these automata, you will realize that there is no threat to your profession."

Willoughby merely glowered in response and left.

The next time he saw Lord Fieldhurst, Stratton asked him about the Royal Society's involvement. They were in Fieldhurst's study, and the earl was pouring himself a whiskey.

"Ah yes," he said. "While the Brotherhood of Sculptors as a whole is quite formidable, it is composed of individuals who individually are more amenable to persuasion."

"What manner of persuasion?"

"The Royal Society is aware that members of the trade union's leadership were party to an as-yet-unresolved case of name piracy to the Continent. To avoid any scandal, they've agreed to postpone any decision about strikes until after you've given a demonstration of your system of manufacturing."

"I'm grateful for your assistance, Lord Fieldhurst," said Stratton, astonished. "I must admit, I had no idea that the Royal Society employed such tactics."

"Obviously, these are not proper topics for discussion at the general sessions." Lord Fieldhurst smiled in an avuncular manner. "The advancement of Science is not always a straightforward affair, Mr. Stratton, and the Royal Society is sometimes required to use both official and unofficial channels."

"I'm beginning to appreciate that."

"Similarly, although the Brotherhood of Sculptors won't initiate a formal strike, they might employ more indirect tactics; for example, the anonymous distribution of pamphlets that arouse public opposition to your automata." He sipped at his whiskey. "Hmm. Perhaps I should have someone keep a watchful eye on Master Willoughby."

Stratton was given accommodations in the guest wing of Darrington Hall, as were the other nomenclators working under Lord Fieldhurst's direction. They were indeed some of the leading members of the profession, including Holcombe, Milburn, and Parker; Stratton felt honored to be working with them, although he could contribute little while he was still learning Ashbourne's techniques for biological nomenclature.

Names for the organic domain employed many of the same epithets as names for automata, but Ashbourne had developed an entirely different system of integration and factorization, which entailed many novel methods of permutation. For Stratton it was almost like returning to university and learning nomenclature all over again. However, it was apparent how these techniques allowed names for species to be developed rapidly; by exploiting similarities suggested by the Linnaean system of classification, one could work from one species to another.

Stratton also learned more about the sexual epithet, traditionally used to confer either male or female qualities to an automaton. He knew of only one such epithet, and was surprised to learn it was the simplest of many extant versions. The topic went undiscussed by nomenclatoral societies, but this epithet was one of the most fully researched in existence; in fact its earliest use was claimed to have occurred in biblical times, when Joseph's brothers created a female *golem* they could share sexually without violating the prohibition against such behavior with a woman. Development of the epithet had continued for centuries in secrecy, primarily in Constantinople, and now the current versions of automatous courtesans were offered by specialized brothels right here in London. Carved from soapstone and polished to a high gloss, heated to blood temperature and sprinkled with scented oils, the automata commanded prices exceeded only by those for incubi and succubi.

It was from such ignoble soil that their research grew. The names animating the courtesans incorporated powerful epithets for human sexuality in its male and female forms. By factoring out the carnality common to both versions, the nomenclators had isolated epithets for generic human masculinity and femininity, ones far more refined than those used when generating animals. Such epithets were the nuclei around which they formed, by accretion, the names they sought.

Gradually Stratton absorbed sufficient information to begin participating in the tests of prospective human names. He worked in collaboration with the other nomenclators in the group, and between them they divided up the vast tree of nominal possibilities, assigning branches for investigation, pruning away those that proved unfruitful, cultivating those that seemed most productive.

The nomenclators paid women—typically young housemaids in good health—for their menses as a source of human ova, which they then impressed with their experimental names and scrutinized under microscopes, looking for forms that resembled human foe-tuses. Stratton inquired about the possibility of harvesting ova from female megafoetuses, but Ashbourne reminded him that ova were viable only when taken from a living woman. It was a basic dictum of biology: females were the source of the vital principle that gave the offspring life, while males provided the basic form. Because of this division, neither sex could reproduce by itself.

Of course, that restriction had been lifted by Ashbourne's dis-covery: the male's participation was no longer necessary since form could be induced lexically. Once a name was found that could gen-erate human foetuses, women could reproduce purely by themselves. Stratton realized that such a discovery might be welcomed by women exhibiting sexual inversion, feeling love for persons of the same rather than the opposite sex. If the name were to become available to such women, they might establish a commune of some sort that reproduced via parthenogenesis. Would such a society flourish by magnifying the finer sensibilities of the gentle sex, or would it collapse under the unre-strained pathology of its membership? It was impossible to guess.

Before Stratton's enlistment, the nomenclators had developed names capable of generating vaguely homuncular forms in an ovum. Using Dubuisson and Gille's methods, they enlarged the forms to a size that allowed detailed examination; the forms resembled automata more than humans, their limbs ending in paddles of fused digits. By incorporating his epithets for dexterity, Stratton was able to separate the digits and refine the overall appearance of the forms. All the while, Ashbourne emphasized the need for an unconventional approach.

"Consider the thermodynamics of what most automata do," said Ashbourne during one of their frequent discussions. "The mining engines dig ore, the reaping engines harvest wheat, the woodcutting engines fell timber; yet none of these tasks, no matter how useful we find them to be, can be said to create order. While all their names create order at the thermal level, by converting heat into motion, in the vast majority the resulting work is applied at the visible level to create disorder."

"This is an interesting perspective," said Stratton thoughtfully. "Many long-standing deficits in the capabilities of automata become intelligible in this light: the fact that automata are unable to stack crates more neatly than they find them; their inability to sort pieces of crushed ore based on their composition. You believe that the known classes of industrial names are not powerful enough in thermodynamic terms."

"Precisely!" Ashbourne displayed the excitement of a tutor finding an unexpectedly apt pupil. "This is another feature that distinguishes your class of dexterous names. By enabling an automaton to perform skilled labour, your names not only create order at the thermal level, they use it to create order at the visible level as well."

"I see a commonality with Milburn's discoveries," said Stratton. Milburn had developed the household automata able to return objects to their proper places. "His work likewise involves the creation of order at the visible level."

"Indeed it does, and this commonality suggests a hypothesis." Ashbourne leaned forward. "Suppose we were able to factor out an epithet common to the names developed by you and Milburn: an epithet expressing the creation of two levels of order. Further suppose that we discover a euonym for the human species, and were able to incorporate this epithet into the name. What do you imagine would be generated by impressing the name? And if you say 'twins' I shall clout you on the head."

Stratton laughed. "I daresay I understand you better than that. You are suggesting that if an epithet is capable of inducing two levels of thermodynamic order in the inorganic domain, it might create two generations in the organic domain. Such a name might create males whose spermatozoa would contain preformed foetuses. Those males would be fertile, although any sons they produced would again be sterile."

His instructor clapped his hands together. "Precisely: order that begets order! An interesting speculation, wouldn't you agree? It would halve the number of medical interventions required for our race to sustain itself."

"And what about inducing the formation of more than two generations of foetuses? What kind of capabilities would an automaton have to possess, for its name to contain such an epithet?"

"The science of thermodynamics has not progressed enough to answer that question, I'm afraid. What would constitute a still-higher level of order in the inorganic domain? Automata working cooperatively, perhaps? We do not yet know, but perhaps in time we will."

Stratton gave voice to a question that had posed itself to him some time ago. "Dr. Ashbourne, when I was initiated into our group, Lord Fieldhurst spoke of the possibility that species are born in the wake of catastrophic events. Is it possible that entire species were created by use of nomenclature?"

"Ah, now we tread in the realm of theology. A new species requires progenitors containing vast numbers of descendants nested within their reproductive organs; such forms embody the highest degree of order imaginable. Can a purely physical process create such vast amounts of order? No naturalist has suggested a mechanism by which this could occur. On the other hand, while we do know that a lexical process can create order, the creation of an entire new species would require a name of incalculable power. Such mastery of nomenclature could very well require the capabilities of God; perhaps it is even part of the definition.

"This is a question, Stratton, to which we may never know the answer, but we cannot allow that to affect our current actions. Whether or not a name was responsible for the creation of our species, I believe a name is the best chance for its continuation."

"Agreed," said Stratton. After a pause, he added, "I must confess, much of the time when I am working, I occupy myself solely with the details of permutation and combination, and lose sight of the sheer magnitude of our endeavor. It is sobering to think of what we will have achieved if we are successful."

"I can think of little else," replied Ashbourne.

———

Seated at his desk in the manufactory, Stratton squinted to read the pamphlet he'd been given on the street. The text was crudely printed, the letters blurred.

"Shall Men be the Masters of NAMES, or shall Names be the masters of MEN? For too long the Capitalists have hoarded Names within their coffers, guarded by Patent and Lock and Key, amassing fortunes by mere possession of LETTERS, while the Common Man must labour for every shilling. They will wring the ALPHABET until they have extracted every last penny from it, and only then discard it for us to use. How long will We allow this to continue?"

Stratton scanned the entire pamphlet, but found nothing new in it. For the past two months he'd been reading them, and encountered only the usual anarchist rants; there was as yet no evidence for Lord Fieldhurst's theory that the sculptors would use them to target Stratton's work. His public demonstration of the dexterous automata was scheduled for next week, and by now Willoughby had largely missed his opportunity to generate public opposition. In fact, it occurred to Stratton that he might distribute pamphlets himself to generate public support. He could explain his goal of bringing the advantages of automata to everyone, and his intention to keep close control over his names' patents, granting licenses only to manufacturers who would use them conscientiously. He could even have a slogan: "Autonomy through Automata," perhaps?

There was a knock at his office door. Stratton tossed the pamphlet into his wastebasket. "Yes?"

A man entered, somberly dressed, and with a long beard. "Mr. Stratton?" he asked. "Please allow me to introduce myself: my name is Benjamin Roth. I am a kabbalist."

Stratton was momentarily speechless. Typically such mystics were offended by the modern view of nomenclature as a science, considering it a secularization of a sacred ritual. He never expected one to visit the manufactory. "A pleasure to meet you. How may I be of assistance?"

"I've heard that you have achieved a great advance in the permutation of letters."

"Why, thank you. I didn't realize it would be of interest to a person like yourself."

Roth smiled awkwardly. "My interest is not in its practical applications. The goal of kabbalists is to better know God. The best means by which to do that is to study the art by which He creates. We meditate upon different names to enter an ecstatic state of consciousness; the more powerful the name, the more closely we approach the Divine."

"I see." Stratton wondered what the kabbalist's reaction would be if he learned about the creation being attempted in the biological nomenclature project. "Please continue."

"Your epithets for dexterity enable a *golem* to sculpt another, thereby reproducing itself. A name capable of creating a being that is, in turn, capable of creation would bring us closer to God than we have ever been before."

"I'm afraid you're mistaken about my work, although you aren't the first to fall under this misapprehension. The ability to manipulate molds does not render an automaton able to reproduce itself. There would be many other skills required."

The kabbalist nodded. "I am well aware of that. I myself, in the course of my studies, have developed an epithet designating certain other skills necessary."

Stratton leaned forward with sudden interest. After casting a body, the next step would be to animate the body with a name. "Your epithet endows an automaton with the ability to write?" His own automaton could grasp a pencil easily enough, but it couldn't inscribe even the simplest mark. "How is it that your automata possess the dexterity required for scrivening, but not that for manipulating molds?"

Roth shook his head modestly. "My epithet does not endow writing ability, or general manual dexterity. It simply enables a *golem* to write out the name that animates it, and nothing else."

"Ah, I see." So it didn't provide an aptitude for learning a category of skills; it granted a single innate skill. Stratton tried to imagine the nomenclatoral contortions needed to make an automaton instinctively write out a particular sequence of letters. "Very interesting, but I imagine it doesn't have broad application, does it?"

Roth gave a pained smile; Stratton realized he had committed a *faux pas*, and the man was trying to meet it with good humor. "That is one way to view it," admitted Roth, "but we have a different perspective. To us the value of this epithet, like any other, lies not in the usefulness it imparts to a *golem*, but in the ecstatic state it allows us to achieve."

"Of course, of course. And your interest in my epithets for dexterity is the same?"

"Yes. I am hoping that you will share your epithets with us."

Stratton had never heard of a kabbalist making such a request before, and clearly Roth did not relish being the first. He paused to consider. "Must a kabbalist reach a certain rank in order to meditate upon the most powerful ones?"

"Yes, very definitely."

"So you restrict the availability of the names."

"Oh no; my apologies for misunderstanding you. The ecstatic state offered by a name is achievable only after one has mastered the necessary meditative techniques, and it's these techniques that are closely guarded. Without the proper training, attempts to use these techniques could result in madness. But the names themselves, even the most powerful ones, have no ecstatic value to a novice; they can animate clay, nothing more."

"Nothing more," agreed Stratton, thinking how truly different their perspectives were. "In that case, I'm afraid I cannot grant you use of my names."

Roth nodded glumly, as if he'd been expecting that answer. "You desire payment of royalties."

Now it was Stratton who had to overlook the other man's *faux pas*. "Money is not my objective. However, I have specific intentions for my dexterous automata which require that I retain control over the patent. I cannot jeopardize those plans by releasing the names indiscriminately." Granted, he had shared them with the nomenclators working under Lord Fieldhurst, but they were all gentlemen sworn to an even greater secrecy. He was less confident about mystics.

"I can assure you that we would not use your name for anything other than ecstatic practices."

"I apologize; I believe you are sincere, but the risk is too great. The most I can do is remind you that the patent has a limited duration; once it has expired, you'll be free to use the name however you like."

"But that will take years!"

"Surely you appreciate that there are others whose interests must be taken into account."

"What I see is that commercial considerations are posing an obstacle to spiritual awakening. The error was mine in expecting anything different."

"You are hardly being fair," protested Stratton.

"Fair?" Roth made a visible effort to restrain his anger. "You 'nomenclators' steal techniques meant to honor God and use them to aggrandize yourselves. Your entire industry prostitutes the techniques of *yezirah*. You are in no position to speak of fairness."

"Now see here—"

"Thank you for speaking with me." With that, Roth took his leave.

Stratton sighed.

Peering through the eyepiece of the microscope, Stratton turned the manipulator's adjustment wheel until the needle pressed against the side of the ovum. There was a sudden enfolding, like the retraction of a mollusc's foot when prodded, transforming the sphere into a tiny foetus. Stratton withdrew the needle from the slide, unclamped it from the framework, and inserted a new one. Next he transferred the slide into the warmth of the incubator and placed another slide, bearing an untouched human ovum, beneath the microscope. Once again he leaned toward the microscope to repeat the process of impression.

Recently, the nomenclators had developed a name capable of inducing a form indistinguishable from a human foetus. The forms did not quicken, however: they remained immobile and unresponsive to stimuli. The consensus was that the name did not accurately describe the non-physical traits of a human being. Accordingly, Stratton and his colleagues had been diligently compiling descriptions of human uniqueness, trying to distill a set of epithets both expressive enough to denote these qualities, and succinct enough to be integrated with the physical epithets into a seventy-two-letter name.

Stratton transferred the final slide to the incubator and made the appropriate notations in the logbook. At the moment he had no more names drawn in needle form, and it would be a day before the new foetuses were mature enough to test for quickening. He decided to pass the rest of the evening in the drawing room upstairs.

Upon entering the walnut-paneled room, he found Fieldhurst and Ashbourne seated in its leather chairs, smoking cigars and sipping brandy. "Ah, Stratton," said Ashbourne. "Do join us."

"I believe I will," said Stratton, heading for the liquor cabinet. He poured himself some brandy from a crystal decanter and seated himself with the others.

"Just up from the laboratory, Stratton?" inquired Fieldhurst.

Stratton nodded. "A few minutes ago I made impressions with my most recent set of names. I feel that my latest permutations are leading in the right direction."

"You are not alone in feeling optimistic; Dr. Ashbourne and I were just discussing how much the outlook has improved since this endeavor began. It now appears that we will have a euonym comfortably in advance of the final generation." Fieldhurst puffed on his cigar and leaned back in his chair until his head rested against the antimacassar. "This disaster may ultimately turn out to be a boon."

"A boon? How so?"

"Why, once we have human reproduction under our control, we will have a means of preventing the poor from having such large families as so many of them persist in having right now."

Stratton was startled, but tried not to show it. "I had not considered that," he said carefully.

Ashbourne also seemed mildly surprised. "I wasn't aware that you intended such a policy."

"I considered it premature to mention it earlier," said Fieldhurst. "Counting one's chickens before they're hatched, as they say."

"Of course."

"You must agree that the potential is enormous. By exercising some judgment when choosing who may bear children or not, our government could preserve the nation's racial stock."

"Is our racial stock under some threat?" asked Stratton.

"Perhaps you have not noticed that the lower classes are reproducing at a rate exceeding that of the nobility and gentry. While commoners are not without virtues, they are lacking in refinement and intellect. These forms of mental impoverishment beget the same: a woman born into low circumstances cannot help but gestate a child destined for the same. Consequent to the great fecundity of the lower classes, our nation would eventually drown in coarse dullards."

"So name impressing will be withheld from the lower classes?"

"Not entirely, and certainly not initially: when the truth about declining fertility is known, it would be an invitation to riot if the lower classes were denied access to name impressing. And of course, the lower classes do have their role to play in our society, as long as their numbers are kept in check. I envision that the policy will go in effect only after some years have passed, by which time people will have grown accustomed to name impression as the method of fertilization. At that point, perhaps in conjunction with the census process, we can impose limits on the number of children a given couple would be permitted to have. The government would regulate the growth and composition of the population thereafter."

"Is this the most appropriate use of such a name?" asked Ashbourne. "Our goal was the survival of the species, not the implementation of partisan politics."

"On the contrary, this is purely scientific. Just as it's our duty to ensure the species survives, it's also our duty to guarantee its health by keeping a proper balance in its population. Politics doesn't enter into it; were the situation reversed and there existed a paucity of labourers, the opposite policy would be called for."

Stratton ventured a suggestion. "I wonder if improvement in conditions for the poor might eventually cause them to gestate more refined children?"

"You are thinking about changes brought about by your cheap engines, aren't you?" asked Fieldhurst with a smile, and Stratton nodded. "Your intended reforms and mine may reinforce each other. Moderating the numbers of the lower classes should make it easier for them to raise their living conditions. However, do not expect that a mere increase in economic comfort will improve the mentality of the lower classes."

"But why not?"

"You forget the self-perpetuating nature of culture," said Fieldhurst. "We have seen that all megafoetuses are identical, yet no one can deny the differences between the populaces of nations, in both physical appearance and temperament. This can only be the result of the maternal influence: the mother's womb is a vessel in which the social environment is incarnated. For example, a woman who has lived her life among Prussians naturally gives birth to a child with Prussian traits; in this manner the national character of that populace has sustained itself for centuries, despite many changes in fortune. It would be unrealistic to think the poor are any different."

"As a zoologist, you are undoubtedly wiser in these matters than we," said Ashbourne, silencing Stratton with a glance. "We will defer to your judgment."

For the remainder of the evening the conversation turned to other topics, and Stratton did his best to conceal his discomfort and maintain a facade of bonhomie. Finally, after Fieldhurst had retired for the evening, Stratton and Ashbourne descended to the laboratory to confer.

"What manner of man have we agreed to help?" exclaimed Stratton as soon as the door was closed. "One who would breed people like livestock?"

"Perhaps we should not be so shocked," said Ashbourne with a sigh. He seated himself upon one of the laboratory stools. "Our group's goal has been to duplicate for humans a procedure that was intended only for animals."

"But not at the expense of individual liberty! I cannot be a party to this."

"Do not be hasty. What would be accomplished by your resigning from the group? To the extent that your efforts contribute to our group's endeavor, your resignation would serve only to endanger the future of the human species. Conversely, if the group attains its goal without your assistance, Lord Fieldhurst's policies will be implemented anyway."

Stratton tried to regain his composure. Ashbourne was right; he could see that. After a moment, he said, "So what course of action should we take? Are there others whom we could contact, members of Parliament who would oppose the policy that Lord Fieldhurst proposes?"

"I expect that most of the nobility and gentry would share Lord Fieldhurst's opinion on this matter." Ashbourne rested his forehead on the fingertips of one hand, suddenly looking very old. "I should have anticipated this. My error was in viewing humanity purely as a single species. Having seen England and France working toward a common goal, I forgot that nations are not the only factions that oppose one another."

"What if we surreptitiously distributed the name to the labouring classes? They could draw their own needles and impress the name themselves, in secret."

"They could, but name impression is a delicate procedure best performed in a laboratory. I'm dubious that the operation could be carried out on the scale necessary without attracting governmental attention, and then falling under its control."

"Is there an alternative?"

There was silence for a long moment while they considered. Then Ashbourne said, "Do you recall our speculation about a name that would induce two generations of foetuses?"

"Certainly."

"Suppose we develop such a name but do not reveal this property when we present it to Lord Fieldhurst."

"That's a wily suggestion," said Stratton, surprised. "All the children born of such a name would be fertile, so they would be able to reproduce without governmental restriction."

Ashbourne nodded. "In the period before population control measures go into effect, such a name might be very widely distributed."

"But what of the following generation? Sterility would recur, and the labouring classes would again be dependent upon the government to reproduce."

"True," said Ashbourne, "it would be a short-lived victory. Perhaps the only permanent solution would be a more liberal Parliament, but it is beyond my expertise to suggest how we might bring that about."

Again Stratton thought about the changes that cheap engines might bring; if the situation of the working classes was improved in the manner he hoped, that might demonstrate to the nobility that poverty was not innate. But even if the most favorable sequence of events obtained, it would require years to sway Parliament. "What if we could induce multiple generations with the initial name impression? A longer period before sterility recurs would increase the chances that more liberal social policies would take hold."

"You're indulging a fancy," replied Ashbourne. "The technical difficulty of inducing multiple generations is such that I'd sooner wager on our successfully sprouting wings and taking flight. Inducing two generations would be ambitious enough."

The two men discussed strategies late into the night. If they were to conceal the true name of any name they presented to Lord Field-hurst, they would have to forge a lengthy trail of research results. Even without the additional burden of secrecy, they would be engaged in an unequal race, pursuing a highly sophisticated name while the other nomenclators sought a comparatively straightforward euonym. To make the odds less unfavorable, Ashbourne and Stratton would need to recruit others to their cause; with such assistance, it might even be possible to subtly impede the research of others.

"Who in the group do you think shares our political views?" asked Ashbourne.

"I feel confident that Milburn does. I'm not so certain about any of the others."

"Take no chances. We must employ even more caution when approaching prospective members than Lord Fieldhurst did when establishing this group originally."

"Agreed," said Stratton. Then he shook his head in disbelief. "Here we are forming a secret organization nested within a secret organization. If only foetuses were so easily induced."

It was the evening of the following day, the sun was setting, and Stratton was strolling across Westminster Bridge as the last remaining costermongers were wheeling their barrows of fruit away. He had just had supper at a club he favored, and was walking back to Coade Manufactory. The previous evening at Darrington Hall had disquieted him, and he had returned to London earlier today to minimize his interaction with Lord Fieldhurst until he was certain his face would not betray his true feelings.

He thought back to the conversation where he and Ashbourne had first entertained the conjecture of factoring out an epithet for creating two levels of order. At the time he had made some efforts to find such an epithet, but they were casual attempts given the superfluous nature of the goal, and they hadn't borne fruit. Now their gauge of achievement had been revised upward: their previous goal was inadequate, two generations seemed the minimum acceptable, and any additional ones would be invaluable.

He again pondered the thermodynamic behavior induced by his dexterous names: order at the thermal level animated the automata, allowing them to create order at the visible level. Order begetting order. Ashbourne had suggested that the next level of order might be automata working together in a coordinated fashion. Was that possible? They would have to communicate in order to work together effectively, but automata were intrinsically mute. What other means were there by which automata could engage in complex behavior?

He suddenly realized he had reached Coade Manufactory. By now it was dark, but he knew the way to his office well enough. Stratton unlocked the building's front door and proceeded through the gallery and past the business offices.

As he reached the hallway fronting the nomenclators' offices, he saw light emanating from the frosted-glass window of his office door. Surely he hadn't left the gas on? He unlocked his door to enter, and was shocked by what he saw.

A man lay facedown on the floor in front of the desk, hands tied behind his back. Stratton immediately approached to check on the man. It was Benjamin Roth, the kabbalist, and he was dead. Stratton realized several of the man's fingers were broken; he'd been tortured before he was killed.

Pale and trembling, Stratton rose to his feet, and saw that his office was in utter disarray. The shelves of his bookcases were bare; his books lay strewn facedown across the oak floor. His desk had been swept clear; next to it was a stack of its brass-handled drawers, emptied and overturned. A trail of stray papers led to the open door to his studio; in a daze, Stratton stepped forward to see what had been done there.

His dexterous automaton had been destroyed; the lower half of it lay on the floor, the rest of it scattered as plaster fragments and dust. On the worktable, the clay models of the hands were pounded flat, and his sketches of their design torn from the walls. The tubs for mixing plaster were overflowing with the papers from his office. Stratton took a closer look, and saw that they had been doused with lamp oil.

He heard a sound behind him and turned back to face the office. The front door to the office swung closed and a broad-shouldered man stepped out from behind it; he'd been standing there ever since Stratton had entered. "Good of you to come," the man said. He scrutinized Stratton with the predatory gaze of a raptor, an assassin.

Stratton bolted out the back door of the studio and down the rear hallway. He could hear the man give chase.

He fled through the darkened building, crossing workrooms filled with coke and iron bars, crucibles and molds, all illuminated by the moonlight entering through skylights overhead; he had entered the metalworks portion of the factory. In the next room he paused for breath, and realized how loudly his footsteps had been echoing; skulking would offer a better chance at escape than running. He distantly heard his pursuer's footsteps stop; the assassin had likewise opted for stealth.

Stratton looked around for a promising hiding place. All around him were cast-iron automata in various stages of near-completion; he was in the finishing room, where the runners left over from casting were sawed off and the surfaces chased. There was no place to hide, and he was about to move on when he noticed what looked like a bundle of rifles mounted on legs. He looked more closely, and recognized it as a military engine.

These automata were built for the War Office: gun carriages that aimed their own cannon, and rapid-fire rifles, like this one, that cranked their own barrel-clusters. Nasty things, but they'd proven invaluable in the Crimea; their inventor had been granted a peerage. Stratton didn't know any names to animate the weapon—they were military secrets—but only the body on which the rifle was mounted was automatous; the rifle's firing mechanism was strictly mechanical. If he could point the body in the right direction, he might be able to fire the rifle manually.

He cursed himself for his stupidity. There was no ammunition here. He stole into the next room.

It was the packing room, filled with pine crates and loose straw. Staying low between crates, he moved to the far wall. Through the windows he saw the courtyard behind the factory, where finished automata were carted away. He couldn't get out that way; the courtyard gates were locked at night. His only exit was through the factory's front door, but he risked encountering the assassin if he headed back the way he'd come. He needed to cross over to the ceramicworks and double back through that side of the factory.

From the front of the packing room came the sound of footsteps. Stratton ducked behind a row of crates, and then saw a side door only a few feet away. As stealthily as he could, he opened the door, entered, and closed the door behind him. Had his pursuer heard him? He peered through a small grille set in the door; he couldn't see the man, but felt he'd gone unnoticed. The assassin was probably searching the packing room.

Stratton turned around, and immediately realized his mistake. The door to the ceramicworks was in the opposite wall. He had entered a storeroom, filled with ranks of finished automata, but with no other exits. There was no way to lock the door. He had cornered himself.

Was there anything in the room he could use as a weapon? The menagerie of automata included some squat mining engines, whose forelimbs terminated in enormous pickaxes, but the axheads were bolted to their limbs. There was no way he could remove one.

Stratton could hear the assassin opening side doors and searching other storerooms. Then he noticed an automaton standing off to the side: a porter used for moving the inventory about. It was anthropomorphic in form, the only automaton in the room of that type. An idea came to him.

Stratton checked the back of the porter's head. Porters' names had entered the public domain long ago, so there were no locks protecting its name slot; a tab of parchment protruded from the horizontal slot in the iron. He reached into his coat pocket for the notebook and pencil he always carried and tore out a small portion of a blank leaf. In the darkness he quickly wrote seventy-two letters in a familiar combination, and then folded the paper into a tight square.

To the porter, he whispered, "Go stand as close to the door as you can." The cast-iron figure stepped forward and headed for the door. Its gait was very smooth, but not rapid, and the assassin would reach this storeroom any moment now. "Faster," hissed Stratton, and the porter obeyed.

Just as it reached the door, Stratton saw through the grille that his pursuer had arrived on the other side. "Get out of the way," barked the man.

Ever obedient, the automaton shifted to take a step back when Stratton yanked out its name. The assassin began pushing against the door, but Stratton was able to insert the new name, cramming the square of paper into the slot as deeply as he could.

The porter resumed walking forward, this time with a fast, stiff gait: his childhood doll, now life-size. It immediately ran into the door and, unperturbed, kept it shut with the force of its marching, its iron hands leaving fresh dents in the door's oaken surface with every swing of its arms, its rubber-shod feet chafing heavily against the brick floor. Stratton retreated to the back of the storeroom.

"Stop," the assassin ordered. "Stop walking, you! Stop!"

The automaton continued marching, oblivious to all commands. The man pushed on the door, but to no avail. He then tried slamming into it with his shoulder, each impact causing the automaton to slide back slightly, but its rapid strides brought it forward again before the man could squeeze inside. There was a brief pause, and then something poked through the grille in the door; the man was prying it off with a crowbar. The grille abruptly popped free, leaving an open window. The man stretched his arm through and reached around to the back of the automaton's head, his fingers searching for the name each time its head bobbed forward, but there was nothing for them to grasp; the paper was wedged too deeply in the slot.

The arm withdrew. The assassin's face appeared in the window. "Fancy yourself clever, don't you?" he called out. Then he disappeared.

Stratton relaxed slightly. Had the man given up? A minute passed, and Stratton began to think about his next move. He could wait here until the factory opened; there would be too many people about for the assassin to remain.

Suddenly the man's arm came through the window again, this time carrying a jar of fluid. He poured it over the automaton's head, the liquid splattering and dripping down its back. The man's arm withdrew, and then Stratton heard the sound of a match being struck and then flaring alight. The man's arm reappeared bearing the match, and touched it to the automaton.

The room was flooded with light as the automaton's head and upper back burst into flames. The man had doused it with lamp oil. Stratton squinted at the spectacle: light and shadow danced across the floor and walls, transforming the storeroom into the site of some druidic ceremony. The heat caused the automaton to hasten its vague assault on the door, like a salamandrine priest dancing with increasing frenzy, until it abruptly froze: its name had caught fire, and the letters were being consumed.

The flames gradually died out, and to Stratton's newly light-adapted eyes the room seemed almost completely black. More by sound than by sight, he realized the man was pushing at the door again, this time forcing the automaton back enough for him to gain entrance.

"Enough of that, then."

Stratton tried to run past him, but the assassin easily grabbed him and knocked him down with a clout to the head.

His senses returned almost immediately, but by then the assassin had him facedown on the floor, one knee pressed into his back. The man tore the health amulet from Stratton's wrist and then tied his hands together behind his back, drawing the rope tightly enough that the hemp fibers scraped the skin of his wrists.

"What kind of man are you, to do things like this?" Stratton gasped, his cheek flattened against the brick floor.

The assassin chuckled. "Men are no different from your automata; slip a bloke a piece of paper with the proper figures on it, and he'll do your bidding." The room grew light as the man lit an oil lamp.

"What if I paid you more to leave me alone?"

"Can't do it. Have to think about my reputation, haven't I? Now let's get to business." He grasped the smallest finger of Stratton's left hand and abruptly broke it.

The pain was shocking, so intense that for a moment Stratton was insensible to all else. He was distantly aware that he had cried out. Then he heard the man speaking again. "Answer my questions straight now. Do you keep copies of your work at home?"

"Yes." He could only get a few words out at a time. "At my desk. In the study."

"No other copies hidden anywhere? Under the floor, perhaps?"

"No."

"Your friend upstairs didn't have copies. But perhaps someone else does?"

He couldn't direct the man to Darrington Hall. "No one."

The man pulled the notebook out of Stratton's coat pocket. Stratton could hear him leisurely flipping through the pages. "Didn't post any letters? Corresponding with colleagues, that sort of thing?"

"Nothing that anyone could use to reconstruct my work."

"You're lying to me." The man grasped Stratton's ring finger.

"No! It's the truth!" He couldn't keep the hysteria from his voice.

Then Stratton heard a sharp thud, and the pressure in his back eased. Cautiously, he raised his head and looked around. His assailant lay unconscious on the floor next to him. Standing next to him was Davies, holding a leather blackjack.

Davies pocketed his weapon and crouched to unknot the rope that bound Stratton. "Are you badly hurt, sir?"

"He's broken one of my fingers. Davies, how did you—?"

"Lord Fieldhurst sent me the moment he learned whom Willoughby had contacted."

"Thank God you arrived when you did." Stratton saw the irony of the situation—his rescue ordered by the very man he was plotting against—but he was too grateful to care.

Davies helped Stratton to his feet and handed him his notebook. Then he used the rope to tie up the assassin. "I went to your office first. Who's the fellow there?"

"His name is—was Benjamin Roth." Stratton managed to recount his previous meeting with the kabbalist. "I don't know what he was doing there."

"Many religious types have a bit of the fanatic in them," said Davies, checking the assassin's bonds. "As you wouldn't give him your work, he likely felt justified in taking it himself. He came to your office to look for it, and had the bad luck to be there when this fellow arrived."

Stratton felt a flood of remorse. "I should have given Roth what he asked."

"You couldn't have known."

"It's an outrageous injustice that he was the one to die. He'd nothing to do with this affair."

"It's always that way, sir. Come on, let's tend to that hand of yours."

Davies bandaged Stratton's finger to a splint, assuring him that the Royal Society would discreetly handle any consequences of the night's events. They gathered the oil-stained papers from Stratton's office into a trunk so that Stratton could sift through them at his leisure, away from the manufactory. By the time they were finished, a carriage had arrived to take Stratton back to Darrington Hall; it had set out at the same time as Davies, who had ridden into London on a racing-engine. Stratton boarded the carriage with the trunk of papers, while Davies stayed behind to deal with the assassin and make arrangements for the kabbalist's body.

Stratton spent the carriage ride sipping from a flask of brandy, trying to steady his nerves. He felt a sense of relief when he arrived back at Darrington Hall; although it held its own variety of threats,

Stratton knew he'd be safe from assassination there. By the time he reached his room, his panic had largely been converted into exhaustion, and he slept deeply.

He felt much more composed the next morning, and ready to begin sorting through his trunkful of papers. As he was arranging them into stacks approximating their original organization, Stratton found a notebook he didn't recognize. Its pages contained Hebrew letters arranged in the familiar patterns of nominal integration and factorization, but all the notes were in Hebrew as well. With a renewed pang of guilt, he realized it must have belonged to Roth; the assassin must have found it on his person and tossed it in with Stratton's papers to be burned.

He was about to set it aside, but his curiosity bested him: he'd never seen a kabbalist's notebook before. Much of the terminology was archaic, but he could understand it well enough; among the incantations and sephirotic diagrams, he found the epithet enabling an automaton to write its own name. As he read, Stratton realized that Roth's achievement was more elegant than he'd previously thought.

The epithet didn't describe a specific set of physical actions, but instead the general notion of reflexivity. A name incorporating the epithet became an autonym: a self-designating name. The notes indicated that such a name would express its lexical nature through whatever means the body allowed. The animated body wouldn't even need hands to write out its name; if the epithet were incorporated properly, a porcelain horse could likely accomplish the task by dragging a hoof in the dirt.

Combined with one of Stratton's epithets for dexterity, Roth's epithet would indeed let an automaton do most of what was needed to reproduce. An automaton could cast a body identical to its own, write out its own name, and insert it to animate the body. It couldn't train the new one in sculpture, though, since automata couldn't speak. An automaton that could truly reproduce itself without human assistance remained out of reach, but coming this close would undoubtedly have delighted the kabbalists.

It seemed unfair that automata were so much easier to reproduce than humans. It was as if the problem of reproducing automata need be solved only once, while that of reproducing humans was a Sisyphean task, with every additional generation increasing the complexity of the name required.

And abruptly Stratton realized that he didn't need a name that redoubled physical complexity, but one than enabled lexical duplication.

The solution was to impress the ovum with an autonym, and thus induce a foetus that bore its own name.

The name would have two versions, as originally proposed: one used to induce male foetuses, another for female foetuses. The women conceived this way would be fertile as always. The men conceived this way would also be fertile, but not in the typical manner: their spermatozoa would not contain preformed foetuses, but would instead bear either of two names on their surfaces, the self-expression of the names originally born by the glass needles. And when such a spermatozoon reached an ovum, the name would induce the creation of a new foetus. The species would be able to reproduce itself without medical intervention, because it would carry the name within itself.

He and Dr. Ashbourne had assumed that creating animals capable of reproducing meant giving them preformed foetuses, because that was the method employed by nature. As a result they had overlooked another possibility: that if a creature could be expressed in a name, reproducing that creature was equivalent to transcribing the name. An organism could contain, instead of a tiny analogue of its body, a lexical representation instead.

Humanity would become a vehicle for the name as well as a product of it. Each generation would be both content and vessel, an echo in a self-sustaining reverberation.

Stratton envisioned a day when the human species could survive as long as its own behavior allowed, when it could stand or fall based purely on its own actions, and not simply vanish once some predetermined life span had elapsed. Other species might bloom and wither like flowers over seasons of geologic time, but humans would endure for as long as they determined.

Nor would any group of people control the fecundity of another; in the procreative domain, at least, liberty would be restored to the individual. This was not the application Roth had intended for his epithet, but Stratton hoped the kabbalist would consider it worthwhile. By the time the autonym's true power became apparent, an entire generation consisting of millions of people worldwide would have been born of the name, and there would be no way any government could control their reproduction. Lord Fieldhurst—or his successors—would be outraged, and there would eventually be a price to be paid, but Stratton found he could accept that.

He hastened to his desk, where he opened his own notebook and Roth's side by side. On a blank page, he began writing down ideas on how Roth's epithet might be incorporated into a human euonym. Already in his mind Stratton was transposing the letters, searching for a permutation that denoted both the human body and itself, an ontogenic encoding for the species.

The Evolution of Human Science

It has been twenty-five years since a report of original research was last submitted to our editors for publication, making this an appropriate time to revisit the question that was so widely debated then: what is the role of human scientists in an age when the frontiers of scientific inquiry have moved beyond the comprehension of humans?

No doubt many of our subscribers remember reading papers whose authors were the first individuals ever to obtain the results they described. But as metahumans began to dominate experimental research, they increasingly made their findings available only via DNT (digital neural transfer), leaving journals to publish secondhand accounts translated into human language. Without DNT humans could not fully grasp prior developments nor effectively utilize the new tools needed to conduct research, while metahumans continued to improve DNT and rely on it even more. Journals for human audiences were reduced to vehicles of popularization, and poor ones at that, as even the most brilliant humans found themselves puzzled by translations of the latest findings.

No one denies the many benefits of metahuman science, but one of its costs to human researchers was the realization that they would likely never make an original contribution to science again. Some left the field altogether, but those who stayed shifted their attention away from original research and toward hermeneutics: interpreting the scientific work of metahumans.

Textual hermeneutics became popular first, since there were already terabytes of metahuman publications whose translations, while cryptic, were presumably not entirely inaccurate. Deciphering these texts bears little resemblance to the task performed by traditional paleographers, but progress continues: recent experiments have validated the Humphries decipherment of decade-old publications on histocompatibility genetics.

The availability of devices based on metahuman science gave rise to artifact hermeneutics. Scientists began attempting to "reverse engineer" these artifacts, their goal being not to manufacture competing products, but simply to understand the physical principles underlying their operation. The most common technique is the crystallographic analysis of nanoware appliances, which frequently provides us with new insights into mechanosynthesis.

The newest and by far the most speculative mode of inquiry is remote sensing of metahuman research facilities. A recent target of investigation is the ExaCollider recently installed beneath the Gobi Desert, whose puzzling neutrino signature has been the subject of much controversy. (The portable neutrino detector is, of course, another metahuman artifact whose operating principles remain elusive.)

The question is, are these worthwhile undertakings for scientists? Some call them a waste of time, likening them to a Native American research effort into bronze smelting when steel tools of European manufacture are readily available. This comparison might be more apt if humans were in competition with metahumans, but in today's economy of abundance there is no evidence of such competition. In fact, it is important to recognize that—unlike most previous low-technology cultures confronted with a high-technology one—humans are in no danger of assimilation or extinction.

There is still no way to augment a human brain into a metahuman one; the Sugimoto gene therapy must be performed before the embryo begins neurogenesis in order for a brain to be compatible with DNT. This lack of an assimilation mechanism means that human parents of a metahuman child face a difficult choice: to allow their child DNT interaction with metahuman culture, and watch their child grow incomprehensible to them; or else restrict access to DNT during the child's formative years, which to a metahuman is deprivation like that suffered by Kaspar Hauser. It is not surprising that the percentage of human parents choosing the Sugimoto gene therapy for their children has dropped almost to zero in recent years.

As a result, human culture is likely to survive well into the future, and the scientific tradition is a vital part of that culture. Hermeneutics is a legitimate method of scientific inquiry and increases the body of human knowledge just as original research did. Moreover, human researchers may discern applications overlooked by metahumans, whose advantages tend to make them unaware of our concerns. For example, imagine if research offered hope of a different intelligence-enhancing therapy, one that would allow individuals to gradually "upgrade" their minds to a metahuman-equivalent level. Such a therapy would offer a bridge across what has become the greatest cultural divide in our species' history, yet it might not even occur to metahumans to explore it; that possibility alone justifies the continuation of human research.

We need not be intimidated by the accomplishments of metahuman science. We should always remember that the technologies that made metahumans possible were originally invented by humans, and they were no smarter than we.

Hell Is the Absence of God

T his is the story of a man named Neil Fisk, and how he came
to love God. The pivotal event in Neil's life was an occurrence
both terrible and ordinary: the death of his wife, Sarah. Neil
was consumed with grief after she died, a grief that was excruciating not only because of its intrinsic magnitude, but because it also
renewed and emphasized the previous pains of his life. Her death
forced him to reexamine his relationship with God, and in doing so
he began a journey that would change him forever.

Neil was born with a congenital abnormality that caused his
left thigh to be externally rotated and several inches shorter than his
right; the medical term for it was proximal femoral focus deficiency.
Most people he met assumed God was responsible for this, but Neil's
mother hadn't witnessed any visitations while carrying him; his
condition was the result of improper limb development during the
sixth week of gestation, nothing more. In fact, as far as Neil's mother
was concerned, blame rested with his absent father, whose income
might have made corrective surgery a possibility, although she never
expressed this sentiment aloud.

As a child Neil had occasionally wondered if he was being punished by God, but most of the time he blamed his classmates in school

for his unhappiness. Their nonchalant cruelty, their instinctive ability to locate the weaknesses in a victim's emotional armor, the way their own friendships were reinforced by their sadism: he recognized these as examples of human behavior, not divine. And although his classmates often used God's name in their taunts, Neil knew better than to blame Him for their actions.

But while Neil avoided the pitfall of blaming God, he never made the jump to loving Him; nothing in his upbringing or his personality led him to pray to God for strength or for relief. The assorted trials he faced growing up were accidental or human in origin, and he relied on strictly human resources to counter them. He became an adult who—like so many others—viewed God's actions in the abstract until they impinged upon his own life. Angelic visitations were events that befell other people, reaching him only via reports on the nightly news. His own life was entirely mundane; he worked as a superintendent for an upscale apartment building, collecting rent and performing repairs, and as far as he was concerned, circumstances were fully capable of unfolding, happily or not, without intervention from above.

This remained his experience until the death of his wife.

It was an unexceptional visitation, smaller in magnitude than most but no different in kind, bringing blessings to some and disaster to others. In this instance the angel was Nathanael, making an appearance in a downtown shopping district. Four miracle cures were effected: the elimination of carcinomas in two individuals, the regeneration of the spinal cord in a paraplegic, and the restoration of sight to a recently blinded person. There were also two miracles that were not cures: a delivery van, whose driver had fainted at the sight of the angel, was halted before it could overrun a busy sidewalk; another man was caught in a shaft of Heaven's light when the angel departed, erasing his eyes but ensuring his devotion.

Neil's wife, Sarah Fisk, had been one of the eight casualties. She was hit by flying glass when the angel's billowing curtain of flame shattered the storefront window of the café in which she was eating.

She bled to death within minutes, and the other customers in the café—none of whom suffered even superficial injuries—could do nothing but listen to her cries of pain and fear, and eventually witness her soul's ascension toward Heaven.

Nathanael hadn't delivered any specific message; the angel's parting words, which had boomed out across the entire visitation site, were the typical *Behold the power of the Lord*. Of the eight casualties that day, three souls were accepted into Heaven and five were not, a closer ratio than the average for deaths by all causes. Sixty-two people received medical treatment for injuries ranging from slight concussions to ruptured eardrums to burns requiring skin grafts. Total property damage was estimated at $8.1 million, all of it excluded by private insurance companies due to the cause. Scores of people became devout worshipers in the wake of the visitation, either out of gratitude or terror.

Alas, Neil Fisk was not one of them.

After a visitation, it's common for all the witnesses to meet as a group and discuss how their common experience has affected their lives. The witnesses of Nathanael's latest visitation arranged such group meetings, and family members of those who had died were welcome, so Neil began attending. The meetings were held once a month in a basement room of a large church downtown; there were metal folding chairs arranged in rows, and in the back of the room was a table holding coffee and doughnuts. Everyone wore adhesive name tags made out in felt-tip pen.

While waiting for the meetings to start, people would stand around, drinking coffee, talking casually. Most people Neil spoke to assumed his leg was a result of the visitation, and he had to explain that he wasn't a witness, but rather the husband of one of the casualties. This didn't bother him particularly; he was used to explaining about his leg. What did bother him was the tone of the meetings themselves, when participants spoke about their reaction to the visitation: most of them talked about their newfound devotion to God, and they tried to persuade the bereaved that they should feel the same.

Neil's reaction to such attempts at persuasion depended on who was making it. When it was an ordinary witness, he found it merely irritating. When someone who'd received a miracle cure told him to love God, he had to restrain an impulse to strangle the person. But what he found most disquieting of all was hearing the same suggestion from a man named Tony Crane; Tony's wife had died in the visitation too, and he now projected an air of groveling with his every movement. In hushed, tearful tones he explained how he had accepted his role as one of God's subjects, and he advised Neil to do likewise.

Neil didn't stop attending the meetings—he felt that he somehow owed it to Sarah to stick with them—but he found another group to go to as well, one more compatible with his own feelings: a support group devoted to those who'd lost a loved one during a visitation, and were angry at God because of it. They met every other week in a room at the local community center, and talked about the grief and rage that boiled inside of them.

All the attendees were generally sympathetic to one another, despite differences in their various attitudes toward God. Of those who'd been devout before their loss, some struggled with the task of remaining so, while others gave up their devotion without a second glance. Of those who'd never been devout, some felt their position had been validated, while others were faced with the near impossible task of becoming devout now. Neil found himself, to his consternation, in this last category.

Like every other non-devout person, Neil had never expended much energy on where his soul would end up; he'd always assumed his destination was Hell, and he accepted that. That was the way of things, and Hell, after all, was not physically worse than the mortal plane.

It meant permanent exile from God, no more and no less; the truth of this was plain for anyone to see on those occasions when

Hell manifested itself. These happened on a regular basis; the ground seemed to become transparent, and you could see Hell as if you were looking through a hole in the floor. The lost souls looked no different than the living, their eternal bodies resembling mortal ones. You couldn't communicate with them—their exile from God meant that they couldn't apprehend the mortal plane where His actions were still felt—but as long as the manifestation lasted you could hear them talk, laugh, or cry, just as they had when they were alive.

People varied widely in their reactions to these manifestations. Most devout people were galvanized, not by the sight of anything frightening, but at being reminded that eternity outside paradise was a possibility. Neil, by contrast, was one of those who were unmoved; as far as he could tell, the lost souls as a group were no unhappier than he was, their existence no worse than his in the mortal plane, and in some ways better: his eternal body would be unhampered by congenital abnormalities.

Of course, everyone knew that Heaven was incomparably superior, but to Neil it had always seemed too remote to consider, like wealth or fame or glamour. For people like him, Hell was where you went when you died, and he saw no point in restructuring his life in hopes of avoiding that. And since God hadn't previously played a role in Neil's life, he wasn't afraid of being exiled from God. The prospect of living without interference, living in a world where windfalls and misfortunes were never by design, held no terror for him.

Now that Sarah was in Heaven, his situation had changed. Neil wanted more than anything to be reunited with her, and the only way to get to Heaven was to love God with all his heart.

This is Neil's story, but telling it properly requires telling the stories of two other individuals whose paths became entwined with his. The first of these is Janice Reilly.

What people assumed about Neil had in fact happened to Janice. When Janice's mother was eight months pregnant with her, she lost control of the car she was driving and collided with a telephone pole during a sudden hailstorm, fists of ice dropping out of a clear blue sky and littering the road like a spill of giant ball bearings. She was sitting in her car, shaken but unhurt, when she saw a knot of silver flames— later identified as the angel Bardiel—float across the sky. The sight petrified her, but not so much that she didn't notice the peculiar settling sensation in her womb. A subsequent ultrasound revealed that the unborn Janice Reilly no longer had legs; flipper-like feet grew directly from her hip sockets.

Janice's life might have gone the way of Neil's, if not for what happened two days after the ultrasound. Janice's parents were sitting at their kitchen table, crying and asking what they had done to deserve this, when they received a vision: the saved souls of four deceased relatives appeared before them, suffusing the kitchen with a golden glow. The saved never spoke, but their beatific smiles induced a feeling of serenity in whoever saw them. From that moment on, the Reillys were certain that their daughter's condition was not a punishment.

As a result, Janice grew up thinking of her legless condition as a gift; her parents explained that God had given her a special assignment because He considered her equal to the task, and she vowed that she would not let Him down. Without pride or defiance, she saw it as her responsibility to show others that her condition did not indicate weakness, but rather strength.

As a child, she was fully accepted by her schoolmates; when you're as pretty, confident, and charismatic as she was, children don't even notice that you're in a wheelchair. It was when she was a teenager that she realized that the able-bodied people in her school were not the ones who most needed convincing. It was more important for her to set an example for other handicapped individuals, whether they had been touched by God or not, no matter where they lived. Janice began speaking before audiences, telling those with disabilities that they had the strength God required of them.

Over time she developed a reputation, and a following. She made a living writing and speaking, and established a nonprofit organization dedicated to promoting her message. People sent her letters thanking her for changing their lives, and receiving those gave her a sense of fulfillment of a sort that Neil had never experienced.

This was Janice's life up until she herself witnessed a visitation by the angel Rashiel. She was letting herself into her house when the tremors began; at first she thought they were of natural origin, although she didn't live in a geologically active area, and waited in the doorway for them to subside. Several seconds later she caught a glimpse of silver in the sky and realized it was an angel, just before she lost consciousness.

Janice awoke to the biggest surprise of her life: the sight of her two new legs, long, muscular, and fully functional.

She was startled the first time she stood up: she was taller than she expected. Balancing at such a height without the use of her arms was unnerving, and simultaneously feeling the texture of the ground through the soles of her feet made it positively bizarre. Rescue workers, finding her wandering down the street dazedly, thought she was in shock until she—marveling at her ability to face them at eye level—explained to them what had happened.

When statistics were gathered for the visitation, the restoration of Janice's legs was recorded as a blessing, and she was humbly grateful for her good fortune. It was at the first of the support group meetings that a feeling of guilt began to creep in. There Janice met two individuals with cancer who'd witnessed Rashiel's visitation, thought their cure was at hand, and been bitterly disappointed when they realized they'd been passed over. Janice found herself wondering, why had she received a blessing when they had not?

Janice's family and friends considered the restoration of her legs a reward for excelling at the task God had set for her, but for Janice, this interpretation raised another question. Did He intend for her to stop? Surely not; evangelism provided the central direction of her life, and there was no limit to the number of people who needed to hear her message. Her continuing to preach was the best action she could take, both for herself and for others.

Her reservations grew during her first speaking engagement after the visitation, before an audience of people recently paralyzed and now wheelchair-bound. Janice delivered her usual words of inspiration, assuring them that they had the strength needed for the challenges ahead; it was during the Q&A that she was asked if the restoration of her legs meant she had passed her test. Janice didn't know what to say; she could hardly promise them that one day their marks would be erased. In fact, she realized, any implication that she'd been rewarded could be interpreted as criticism of others who remained afflicted, and she didn't want that. All she could tell them was that she didn't know why she'd been cured, but it was obvious they found that an unsatisfying answer.

Janice returned home disquieted. She still believed in her message, but as far as her audiences were concerned, she'd lost her greatest source of credibility. How could she inspire others who were touched by God to see their condition as a badge of strength, when she no longer shared their condition?

She considered whether this might be a challenge, a test of her ability to spread His word. Clearly God had made her task more difficult than it was before; perhaps the restoration of her legs was an obstacle for her to overcome, just as their earlier removal had been.

This interpretation failed her at her next scheduled engagement. The audience was a group of witnesses to a visitation by Nathanael; she was often invited to speak to such groups in the hopes that those who suffered might draw encouragement from her. Rather than sidestep the issue, she began with an account of the visitation she herself had recently experienced. She explained that while it might appear she was a beneficiary, she was in fact facing her own challenge: like them, she was being forced to draw on resources previously untapped.

She realized, too late, that she had said the wrong thing. A man in the audience with a misshapen leg stood up and challenged her: was she seriously suggesting that the restoration of her legs was comparable to the loss of his wife? Could she really be equating her trials with his own?

Janice immediately assured him that she wasn't, and that she couldn't imagine the pain he was experiencing. But, she said, it wasn't God's intention that everyone be subjected to the same kind of trial, but only that each person face his or her own trial, whatever it might be. The difficulty of any trial was subjective, and there was no way to compare two individuals' experiences. And just as those whose suffering seemed greater than his should have compassion for him, so should he have compassion for those whose suffering seemed less.

The man was having none of it. She had received what anyone else would have considered a fantastic blessing, and she was complaining about it. He stormed out of the meeting while Janice was still trying to explain.

That man, of course, was Neil Fisk. Neil had had Janice Reilly's name mentioned to him for much of his life, most often by people who were convinced his misshapen leg was a sign from God. These people cited her as an example he should follow, telling him that her attitude was the proper response to a physical handicap. Neil couldn't deny that her leglessness was a far worse condition than his distorted femur. Unfortunately, he found her attitude so foreign that, even in the best of times, he'd never been able to learn anything from her. Now, in the depths of his grief and mystified as to why she had received a gift she didn't need, Neil found her words offensive.

In the days that followed, Janice found herself more and more plagued by doubts, unable to decide what the restoration of her legs meant. Was she being ungrateful for a gift she'd received? Was it both a blessing and a test? Perhaps it was a punishment, an indication that she had not performed her duty well enough. There were many possibilities, and she didn't know which one to believe.

There is one other person who played an important role in Neil's story, even though he and Neil did not meet until Neil's journey was nearly over. That person's name is Ethan Mead.

Ethan had been raised in a family that was devout, but not profoundly so. His parents credited God with their above-average health and their comfortable economic status, although they hadn't witnessed any visitations or received any visions; they simply trusted that God was, directly or indirectly, responsible for their good fortune. Their devotion had never been put to any serious test, and might not have withstood one; their love for God was based in their satisfaction with the status quo.

Ethan was not like his parents, though. Ever since childhood he'd felt certain that God had a special role for him to play, and he waited for a sign telling him what that role was. He'd liked to have become a preacher, but felt he hadn't any compelling testimony to offer; his vague feelings of expectation weren't enough. He longed for an encounter with the divine to provide him with direction.

He could have gone to one of the holy sites, those places where—for reasons unknown—angelic visitations occurred on a regular basis, but he felt that such an action would be presumptuous of him. The holy sites were usually the last resort of the desperate, those people seeking either a miracle cure to repair their bodies or a glimpse of Heaven's light to repair their souls, and Ethan was not desperate. He decided that he'd been set along his own course, and in time the reason for it would become clear. While waiting for that day, he lived his life as best he could: he worked as a librarian, married a woman named Claire, raised two children. All the while, he remained watchful for signs of a greater destiny.

Ethan was certain his time had come when he became witness to a visitation by Rashiel, the same visitation that—miles away—restored Janice Reilly's legs. Ethan was by himself when it happened; he was walking toward his car in the center of a parking lot, when the ground began to shudder. Instinctively he knew it was a visitation, and he assumed a kneeling position, feeling no fear, only exhilaration and awe at the prospect of learning his calling.

The ground became still after a minute, and Ethan looked around, but didn't otherwise move. Only after waiting for several more minutes did he rise to his feet. There was a large crack in the asphalt, beginning directly in front of him and following a meandering path down the street. The crack seemed to be pointing him in a specific direction, so he ran alongside it for several blocks until he encountered other survivors, a man and a woman climbing out of a modest fissure that had opened up directly beneath them. He waited with the two of them until rescuers arrived and brought them to a shelter.

Ethan attended the support group meetings that followed and met the other witnesses to Rashiel's visitation. Over the course of a few meetings, he became aware of certain patterns among the witnesses. Of course there were those who'd been injured and those who'd received miracle cures. But there were also those whose lives were changed in other ways: the man and woman he'd first met fell in love and were soon engaged; a woman who'd been pinned beneath a collapsed wall was inspired to become an EMT after being rescued. One business owner formed an alliance that averted her impending bankruptcy, while another whose business was destroyed saw it as a message that he change his ways. It seemed that everyone except Ethan had found a way to understand what had happened to them.

He hadn't been cursed or blessed in any obvious way, and he didn't know what message he was intended to receive. His wife, Claire, suggested that he consider the visitation a reminder that he appreciate what he had, but Ethan found that unsatisfying, reasoning that *every* visitation—no matter where it occurred—served that function, and the fact that he'd witnessed a visitation firsthand had to have greater significance. His mind was preyed upon by the idea that he'd missed an opportunity, that there was a fellow witness whom he was intended to meet but hadn't. This visitation had to be the sign he'd been waiting for; he couldn't just disregard it. But that didn't tell him what he was supposed to do.

Ethan eventually resorted to the process of elimination: he got hold of a list of all the witnesses, and crossed off those who had a clear interpretation of their experience, reasoning that one of those remaining must be the person whose fate was somehow intertwined with his. Among those who were confused or uncertain about the visitation's meaning would be the one he was intended to meet.

When he had finished crossing names off his list, there was only one left: JANICE REILLY.

In public Neil was able to mask his grief as adults are expected to, but in the privacy of his apartment, the floodgates of emotion burst open. The awareness of Sarah's absence would overwhelm him, and then he'd collapse on the floor and weep. He'd curl up into a ball, his body racked by hiccuping sobs, tears and mucus streaming down his face, the anguish coming in ever-increasing waves until it was more than he could bear, more intense than he'd have believed possible. Minutes or hours later it would leave, and he would fall asleep, exhausted. And the next morning he would wake up and face the prospect of another day without Sarah.

An elderly woman in Neil's apartment building tried to comfort him by telling him that the pain would lessen in time, and while he would never forget his wife, he would at least be able to move on. Then he would meet someone else one day and find happiness with her, and he would learn to love God and thus ascend to Heaven when his time came.

This woman's intentions were good, but Neil was in no position to find any comfort in her words. Sarah's absence felt like an open wound, and the prospect that someday he would no longer feel pain at her loss seemed not just remote, but a physical impossibility. If suicide would have ended his pain, he'd have done it without hesitation, but that would only ensure that his separation from Sarah was permanent.

The topic of suicide regularly came up at the support group meetings, and inevitably led to someone mentioning Robin Pearson, a woman who used to come to the meetings several months before Neil began attending. Robin's husband had been afflicted with stomach cancer during a visitation by the angel Makatiel. She stayed in his hospital room for days at a stretch, only for him to die unexpectedly when she was home doing laundry. A nurse who'd been present told Robin that his soul had ascended, and so Robin had begun attending the support group meetings.

Many months later, Robin came to the meeting shaking with rage. There'd been a manifestation of Hell near her house, and she'd seen her husband among the lost souls. She'd confronted the nurse, who admitted to lying in the hopes that Robin would learn to love God, so that at least she would be saved even if her husband hadn't been. Robin wasn't at the next meeting, and at the meeting after that the group learned she had committed suicide to rejoin her husband.

None of them knew the status of Robin's and her husband's relationship in the afterlife, but successes were known to happen; some couples had indeed been happily reunited through suicide. The support group had attendees whose spouses had descended to Hell, and they talked about being torn between wanting to remain alive and wanting to rejoin their spouses. Neil wasn't in their situation, but his first response when listening to them had been envy: if Sarah had gone to Hell, suicide would be the solution to all his problems.

This led to a shameful self-knowledge for Neil. He realized that if he had to choose between going to Hell while Sarah went to Heaven, or having both of them go to Hell together, he would choose the latter: he would rather she be exiled from God than separated from him. He knew it was selfish, but he couldn't change how he felt: he believed Sarah could be happy in either place, but he could only be happy with her.

Neil's previous experiences with women had never been good. All too often he'd begin flirting with a woman while sitting at a bar, only to have her remember an appointment elsewhere the moment he stood up and his shortened leg came into view. Once, a woman he'd been dating for several weeks broke off their relationship, explaining that while she herself didn't consider his leg a defect, whenever they were seen in public together other people assumed there must be something wrong with her for being with him, and surely he could understand how unfair that was to her?

Sarah had been the first woman Neil met whose demeanor hadn't changed one bit, whose expression hadn't flickered toward pity or horror or even surprise when she first saw his leg. For that reason alone it was predictable that Neil would become infatuated with her; by the time he saw all the sides of her personality, he'd completely fallen in love with her. And because his best qualities came out when he was with her, she fell in love with him too.

Neil had been surprised when Sarah told him she was devout. There weren't many signs of her devotion—she didn't go to church, sharing Neil's dislike for the attitudes of most people who attended—but in her own, quiet way she was grateful to God for her life. She never tried to convert Neil, saying that devotion would come from within or not at all. They rarely had any cause to mention God, and most of the time it would've been easy for Neil to imagine that Sarah's views on God matched his own.

This is not to say that Sarah's devotion had no effect on Neil. On the contrary, Sarah was far and away the best argument for loving God that he had ever encountered. If love of God had contributed to making her the person she was, then perhaps it did make sense. During the years that the two of them were married, his outlook on life improved, and it probably would have reached the point where he was thankful to God, if he and Sarah had grown old together.

Sarah's death removed that particular possibility, but it needn't have closed the door on Neil's loving God. Neil could have taken it as a reminder that no one can count on having decades left. He could have been moved by the realization that, had he died with her, his soul would've been lost and the two of them separated for eternity. He could have seen Sarah's death as a wake-up call, telling him to love God while he still had the chance.

Instead Neil became actively resentful of God. Sarah had been the greatest blessing of his life, and God had taken her away. Now he was expected to love Him for it? For Neil, it was like having a kidnapper demand love as ransom for his wife's return. Obedience he might have managed, but sincere, heartfelt love? That was a ransom he couldn't pay.

This paradox confronted several people in the support group. One of the attendees, a man named Phil Soames, correctly pointed out that thinking of it as a condition to be met would guarantee failure. You couldn't love God as a means to an end, you had to love Him for Himself. If your ultimate goal in loving God was a reunion with your spouse, you weren't demonstrating true devotion at all.

A woman in the support group named Valerie Tommasino said they shouldn't even try. She'd been reading a book published by the humanist movement; its members considered it wrong to love a God who inflicted such pain, and advocated that people act according to their own moral sense instead of being guided by the carrot and the stick. These were people who, when they died, descended to Hell in proud defiance of God.

Neil himself had read a pamphlet of the humanist movement; what he most remembered was that it had quoted the fallen angels. Visitations of fallen angels were infrequent, and caused neither good fortune nor bad; they weren't acting under God's direction, but just passing through the mortal plane as they went about their unimaginable business. On the occasions they appeared, people would ask them questions: Did they know God's intentions? Why had they rebelled? The fallen angels' reply was always the same: *Decide for yourselves. That is what we did. We advise you to do the same.*

Those in the humanist movement had decided, and if it weren't for Sarah, Neil would've made the identical choice. But he wanted her back, and the only way was to find a reason to love God.

Looking for any footing on which to build their devotion, some attendees of the support group took comfort in the fact that their loved ones hadn't suffered when God took them, but instead died instantly. Neil didn't even have that; Sarah had received horrific lacerations when the glass hit her. Of course, it could have been worse. One couple's teenage son had been trapped in a fire ignited by an angel's visitation, and received full-thickness burns over eighty percent of his body before rescue workers could free him; his eventual death was a mercy. Sarah had been fortunate by comparison, but not enough to make Neil love God.

Neil could think of only one thing that would make him give thanks to God, and that was if He allowed Sarah to appear before him. It would give him immeasurable comfort just to see her smile again; he'd never been visited by a saved soul before, and a vision now would have meant more to him than at any other point in his life.

But visions don't appear just because a person needs one, and none ever came to Neil. He had to find his own way toward God.

The next time he attended the support group meeting for witnesses of Nathanael's visitation, Neil sought out Benny Vasquez, the man whose eyes had been erased by Heaven's light. Benny didn't always attend because he was now being invited to speak at other meetings; few visitations resulted in an eyeless person, since Heaven's light entered the mortal plane only in the brief moments that an angel emerged from or reentered Heaven, so the eyeless were minor celebrities, and in demand as speakers to church groups.

Benny was now as sightless as any burrowing worm: not only were his eyes and sockets missing, his skull lacked even the space for such features, the cheekbones now abutting the forehead. The light that had brought his soul as close to perfection as was possible in the mortal plane had also deformed his body; it was commonly held that this illustrated the superfluity of physical bodies in Heaven. With the limited expressive capacity his face retained, Benny always wore a blissful, rapturous smile.

Neil hoped Benny could say something to help him love God. Benny described Heaven's light as infinitely beautiful, a sight of such compelling majesty that it vanquished all doubts. It constituted incontrovertible proof that God should be loved, an explanation that made it as obvious as 1+1=2. Unfortunately, while Benny could offer many analogies for the effect of Heaven's light, he couldn't duplicate that effect with his own words. Those who were already devout found

Benny's descriptions thrilling, but to Neil, they seemed frustratingly vague. So he looked elsewhere for counsel.

Accept the mystery, said the minister of the local church. If you can love God even though your questions go unanswered, you'll be the better for it.

Admit that you need Him, said the popular book of spiritual advice he bought. When you realize that self-sufficiency is an illusion, you'll be ready.

Submit yourself completely and utterly, said the preacher on the television. Receiving torment is how you prove your love. Acceptance may not bring you relief in this life, but resistance will only worsen your punishment.

All of these strategies have proven successful for different individuals; any one of them, once internalized, can bring a person to devotion. But these are not always easy to adopt, and Neil was one who found them impossible.

Neil finally tried talking to Sarah's parents, which was an indication of how desperate he was: his relationship with them had always been tense. While they loved Sarah, they often chided her for not being demonstrative enough in her devotion, and they'd been shocked when she married a man who wasn't devout at all. For her part, Sarah had always considered her parents too judgmental, and their disapproval of Neil only reinforced her opinion. But now Neil felt he had something in common with them—after all, they were all mourning Sarah's loss—and so he visited them in their suburban colonial, hoping they could help him in his grief.

How wrong he was. Instead of sympathy, what Neil got from Sarah's parents was blame for her death. They'd come to this conclusion in the weeks after Sarah's funeral; they reasoned that she'd been taken to send him a message, and that they were forced to endure her loss solely because he hadn't been devout. They were now convinced that, his previous explanations notwithstanding, Neil's deformed leg was in fact God's doing, and if only he'd been properly chastened by it, Sarah might still be alive.

Their reaction shouldn't have come as a surprise: throughout Neil's life, people had attributed moral significance to his leg even though God wasn't responsible for it. Now that he'd suffered a misfortune for which God was unambiguously responsible, it was inevitable that someone would assume he deserved it. It was purely by chance that Neil heard this sentiment when he was at his most vulnerable, and it could have the greatest impact on him.

Neil didn't think his in-laws were right, but he began to wonder if he might not be better off if he did. Perhaps, he thought, it'd be better to live in a story where the righteous were rewarded and the sinners were punished, even if the criteria for righteousness and sinfulness eluded him, than to live in a reality where there was no justice at all. It would mean casting himself in the role of sinner, so it was hardly a comforting lie, but it offered one reward that his own ethics couldn't: believing it would reunite him with Sarah.

Sometimes even bad advice can point a man in the right direction. It was in this manner that his in-laws' accusations ultimately pushed Neil closer to God.

More than once when she was evangelizing, Janice had been asked if she ever wished she had legs, and she had always answered—honestly—no, she didn't. She was content as she was. Sometimes her questioner would point out that she couldn't miss what she'd never known, and she might feel differently if she'd been born with legs and lost them later on. Janice never denied that. But she could truthfully say that she felt no sense of being incomplete, no envy for people with legs; being legless was part of her identity. She'd never bothered with prosthetics, and had a surgical procedure been available to provide her with legs, she'd have turned it down. She had never considered the possibility that God might restore her legs.

One of the unexpected side effects of having legs was the increased attention she received from men. In the past she'd mostly attracted men with amputee fetishes or sainthood complexes; now all sorts of men seemed drawn to her. So when she first noticed Ethan Mead's interest in her, she thought it was romantic in nature; this possibility was particularly distressing since he was obviously married.

Ethan had begun talking to Janice at the support group meetings, and then began attending her public speaking engagements. It was when he suggested they have lunch together that Janice asked him about his intentions, and he explained his theory. He didn't know *how* his fate was intertwined with hers; he knew only that it was. She was skeptical, but she didn't reject his theory outright. Ethan admitted that he didn't have answers for her own questions, but he was eager to do anything he could to help her find them. Janice cautiously agreed to help him in his search for meaning, and Ethan promised that he wouldn't be a burden. They met on a regular basis and talked about the significance of visitations.

Meanwhile Ethan's wife, Claire, grew worried. Ethan assured her that he had no romantic feelings toward Janice, but that didn't alleviate her concerns. She knew that extreme circumstances could create a bond between individuals, and she feared that Ethan's relationship with Janice—romantic or not—would threaten their marriage.

Ethan suggested to Janice that he, as a librarian, could help her do some research. Neither of them had ever heard of a previous instance where God had left His mark on a person in one visitation and removed it in another. Ethan looked for previous examples in hopes that they might shed some light on Janice's situation. There were a few instances of individuals receiving multiple miracle cures over their lifetimes, but their illnesses or disabilities had always been of natural origin, not given to them in a visitation. There was one anecdotal report of a man being struck blind for his sins, changing his ways, and later having his sight restored, but it was classified as an urban legend.

Even if that account had a basis in truth, it didn't provide a useful precedent for Janice's situation: her legs had been removed before her birth, and so couldn't have been a punishment for anything she'd done. Was it possible that Janice's condition had been a punishment for something her mother or father had done? Could her restoration mean they had finally earned her cure? She couldn't believe that.

If her deceased relatives were to appear in a vision, Janice would've been reassured about the restoration of her legs. The fact that they didn't made her suspect something was amiss, but she didn't believe that it was a punishment. Perhaps it had been a mistake, and she'd received a miracle meant for someone else; perhaps it was a test, to see how she would respond to being given too much. In either case, there seemed only one course of action: she would, with utmost gratitude and humility, offer to return her gift. To do so, she would go on a pilgrimage.

Pilgrims traveled great distances to visit the holy sites and wait for a visitation, hoping for a miracle cure. Whereas in most of the world one could wait an entire lifetime and never experience a visitation, at a holy site one might only wait months, sometimes weeks. Pilgrims knew that the odds of being cured were still poor; of those who stayed long enough to witness a visitation, the majority did not receive a cure. But they were often happy just to have seen an angel, and they returned home better able to face what awaited them, whether it be imminent death or life with a crippling disability. And of course, just living through a visitation made many people appreciate their situations; invariably, a small number of pilgrims were killed during each visitation.

Janice was willing to accept the outcome whatever it was. If God saw fit to take her, she was ready. If God removed her legs again, she would resume the work she'd always done. If God let her legs remain, she hoped she would receive the epiphany she needed to speak with conviction about her gift.

She hoped, however, that her miracle would be taken back and given to someone who truly needed it. She didn't suggest to anyone that they accompany her in hopes of receiving the miracle she was returning, feeling that that would've been presumptuous, but she privately considered her pilgrimage a request on behalf of those who were in need.

Her friends and family were confused at Janice's decision, seeing it as questioning God. As word spread, she received many letters from followers, variously expressing dismay, bafflement, and admiration for her willingness to make such a sacrifice.

As for Ethan, he was completely supportive of Janice's decision, and excited for himself. He now understood the significance of Rashiel's visitation for him: it indicated that the time had come for him to act. His wife, Claire, strenuously opposed his leaving, pointing out that he had no idea how long he might be away, and that she and their children needed him too. It grieved him to go without her support, but he had no choice. Ethan would go on a pilgrimage, and at the next visitation, he would learn what God intended for him.

Neil's visit to Sarah's parents caused him to give further thought to his conversation with Benny Vasquez. While he hadn't gotten a lot out of Benny's words, he'd been impressed by the absoluteness of Benny's devotion. No matter what misfortune befell him in the future, Benny's love of God would never waver, and he would ascend to Heaven when he died. That fact offered Neil a very slim opportunity, one that had seemed so unattractive he hadn't considered it before; but now, as he was growing more desperate, it was beginning to look expedient.

Every holy site had its pilgrims who, rather than looking for a miracle cure, deliberately sought out Heaven's light. Those who saw it were always accepted into Heaven when they died, no matter how selfish their motives had been; there were some who wished to have their ambivalence removed so they could be reunited with their loved ones, and others who'd always lived a sinful life and wanted to escape the consequences.

In the past there'd been some doubt as to whether Heaven's light could indeed overcome *all* the spiritual obstacles to becoming saved. The debate ended after the case of Barry Larsen, a serial rapist and murderer who, while disposing of the body of his latest victim, witnessed an angel's visitation and saw Heaven's light. At Larsen's execution, his soul was seen ascending to Heaven, much to the outrage of his victims' families. Priests tried to console them, assuring them—on the basis of no evidence whatsoever—that Heaven's light must have subjected Larsen to many lifetimes' worth of penance in a moment, but their words provided little comfort.

For Neil this offered a loophole, an answer to Phil Soames's objection; it was the one way that he could love Sarah more than he loved God, and still be reunited with her. It was how he could be selfish and still get into Heaven. Others had done it; perhaps he could too. It might not be just, but at least it was predictable.

At an instinctual level, Neil was averse to the idea: it sounded like undergoing brainwashing as a cure for depression. He couldn't help but think that it would change his personality so drastically that he'd cease to be himself. Then he remembered that everyone in Heaven had undergone a similar transformation; the saved were just like the eyeless except that they no longer had bodies. This gave Neil a clearer image of what he was working toward: no matter whether he became devout by seeing Heaven's light or by a lifetime of effort, any ultimate reunion with Sarah couldn't re-create what they'd shared in the mortal plane. In Heaven, they would both be different, and their love for each other would be mixed with the love that all the saved felt for everything.

This realization didn't diminish Neil's longing for a reunion with Sarah. In fact it sharpened his desire, because it meant that the reward would be the same no matter what means he used to achieve it; the shortcut led to precisely the same destination as the conventional path.

On the other hand, seeking Heaven's light was far more difficult than an ordinary pilgrimage, and far more dangerous. Heaven's light leaked through only when an angel entered or left the mortal plane, and since there was no way to predict where an angel would first appear, light-seekers had to converge on the angel after its arrival and follow it until its departure. To maximize their chances of being in the narrow shaft of Heaven's light, they followed the angel as closely as possible during its visitation; depending on the angel involved, this might mean staying alongside the funnel of a tornado, the wavefront of a flash flood, or the expanding tip of a chasm as it split apart the landscape. Far more light-seekers died in the attempt than succeeded.

Statistics about the souls of failed light-seekers were difficult to compile, since there were few witnesses to such expeditions, but the numbers so far were not encouraging. In sharp contrast to ordinary pilgrims who died without receiving their sought-after cure, of which roughly half were admitted into Heaven, every single failed light-seeker had descended to Hell. Perhaps only people who were already lost ever considered seeking Heaven's light, or perhaps death in such circumstances was considered suicide. In any case, it was clear to Neil that he needed to be ready to accept the consequences of embarking on such an attempt.

The entire idea had an all-or-nothing quality to it that Neil found both frightening and attractive. He found the prospect of going on with his life, trying to love God, increasingly maddening. He might try for decades and not succeed. He might not even have that long; as he'd been reminded so often lately, visitations served as a warning to prepare one's soul, because death might come at any time. He could die tomorrow, and there was no chance of his becoming devout in the near future by conventional means.

It's perhaps ironic that, given his history of not following Janice Reilly's example, Neil took notice when she reversed her position. He was eating breakfast when he happened to see an item in the newspaper about her plans for a pilgrimage, and his immediate reaction was anger: how many blessings would it take to satisfy that woman? After considering it more, he decided that if she, having received a blessing, deemed it appropriate to seek God's assistance in coming to terms with it, then there was no reason he, having received such terrible misfortune, shouldn't do the same. And that was enough to tip him over the edge.

———

Holy sites were invariably in inhospitable places: one was an atoll in the middle of the ocean, while another was in the mountains at an elevation of twenty thousand feet. The one that Neil traveled to was in a desert, an expanse of cracked mud reaching miles in every direction; it was desolate, but it was relatively accessible and thus popular among pilgrims. The appearance of the holy site was an object lesson in what happened when the celestial and terrestrial realms touched: the landscape was variously scarred by lava flows, gaping fissures, and impact craters. Vegetation was scarce and ephemeral, restricted to growing in the interval after soil was deposited by floodwaters or whirlwinds and before it was scoured away again.

Pilgrims took up residence all over the site, forming temporary villages with their tents and camper vans; they all made guesses as to what location would maximize their chances of seeing the angel while minimizing the risk of injury or death. Some protection was offered by curved banks of sandbags, left over from years past and rebuilt as needed. A site-specific paramedic and fire department ensured that paths were kept clear so rescue vehicles could go where they were needed. Pilgrims either brought their own food and water or purchased them from vendors charging exorbitant prices; everyone paid a fee to cover the cost of waste removal.

Light-seekers always had off-road vehicles to better cross rough terrain when it came time to follow the angel. Those who could afford it drove alone; those who couldn't formed groups of two or three or four. Neil didn't want to be a passenger reliant on another person, nor did he want the responsibility of driving anyone else. This might be his final act on earth, and he felt he should do it alone. The cost of Sarah's funeral had depleted their savings, so Neil sold all his possessions in order to purchase a suitable vehicle: a pickup truck equipped with aggressively knurled tires and heavy-duty shock absorbers.

As soon as he arrived, Neil started doing what all the other light-seekers did: criss-crossing the site in his vehicle, trying to familiarize himself with its topography. It was on one of his drives around the site's perimeter that he met Ethan; Ethan flagged him down after his own car had stalled on his return from the nearest grocery store, eighty miles away. Neil helped him get his car started again, and then, at Ethan's insistence, followed him back to his campsite for dinner. Janice wasn't there when they arrived, having gone to visit some pilgrims several tents over; Neil listened politely while Ethan—heating prepackaged meals over a bottle of propane—began describing the events that had brought him to the holy site.

When Ethan mentioned Janice Reilly's name, Neil couldn't mask his surprise. He had no desire to speak with her again, and immediately excused himself to leave. He was explaining to a puzzled Ethan that he'd forgotten a previous engagement when Janice arrived.

She was startled to see Neil there, but asked him to stay. Ethan explained why he'd invited Neil to dinner, and Janice told him where she and Neil had met. Then she asked Neil what had brought him to the holy site. When he told them he was a light-seeker, Ethan and Janice immediately tried to persuade him to reconsider his plans. He might be committing suicide, said Ethan, and there were always better alternatives than suicide. Seeing Heaven's light was not the answer, said Janice; that wasn't what God wanted. Neil stiffly thanked them for their concern, and left.

During the weeks of waiting, Neil spent every day driving around the site; maps were available, and were updated after each visitation, but they were no substitute for driving the terrain yourself. On occasion he would see a light-seeker who was obviously experienced in off-road driving, and ask him—the vast majority of the light-seekers were men—for tips on negotiating a specific type of terrain. Some had been at the site for several visitations, having neither succeeded or failed at their previous attempts. They were glad to share tips on how best to pursue an angel, but never offered any personal information about themselves. Neil found the tone of their conversation peculiar, simultaneously hopeful and hopeless, and wondered if he sounded the same.

Ethan and Janice passed the time by getting to know some of the other pilgrims. Their reactions to Janice's situation were mixed:

some thought her ungrateful, while others thought her generous. Most found Ethan's story interesting, since he was one of the very few pilgrims seeking something other than a miracle cure. For the most part, there was a feeling of camaraderie that sustained them during the long wait.

Neil was driving around in his truck when dark clouds began coalescing in the southeast, and the word came over the CB radio that a visitation had begun. He stopped the vehicle to insert earplugs into his ears and don his helmet; by the time he was finished, flashes of lightning were visible, and a light-seeker near the angel reported that it was Barakiel, and it appeared to be moving due north. Neil turned his truck east in anticipation and began driving at full speed.

There was no rain or wind, only dark clouds from which lightning emerged. Over the radio other light-seekers relayed estimates of the angel's direction and speed, and Neil headed northeast to get in front of it. At first he could gauge his distance from the storm by counting how long it took for the thunder to arrive, but soon the lightning bolts were striking so frequently that he couldn't match up the sounds with the individual strikes.

He saw the vehicles of two other light-seekers converging. They began driving in parallel, heading north, over a heavily cratered section of ground, bouncing over small ones and swerving to avoid the larger ones. Bolts of lightning were striking the ground everywhere, but they appeared to be radiating from a point south of Neil's position; the angel was directly behind him, and closing.

Even through his earplugs, the roar was deafening. Neil could feel his hair rising from his skin as the electric charge built up around him. He kept glancing in his rearview mirror, trying to ascertain where the angel was while wondering how close he ought to get.

His vision grew so crowded with afterimages that it became difficult to distinguish actual bolts of lightning among them. Squinting at the dazzle in his mirror, he realized he was looking at a continuous bolt of lightning, undulating but uninterrupted. He tilted the driver's-side mirror upward to get a better look, and saw the source of the lightning bolt, a seething, writhing mass of flames, silver against the dusky clouds: the angel Barakiel.

It was then, while Neil was transfixed and paralyzed by what he saw, that his pickup truck crested a sharp outcropping of rock and became airborne. The truck smashed into a boulder, the entire force of the impact concentrated on the vehicle's left front end, crumpling it like foil. The intrusion into the driver's compartment fractured both of Neil's legs and nicked his left femoral artery. Neil began, slowly but surely, bleeding to death.

He didn't try to move; he wasn't in physical pain at the moment, but he somehow knew that the slightest movement would be excruciating. It was obvious that he was pinned in the truck, and there was no way he could pursue Barakiel even if he weren't. Helplessly, he watched the lightning storm move further and further away.

As he watched it, Neil began crying. He was filled with a mixture of regret and self-contempt, cursing himself for ever thinking that such a scheme could succeed. He would have begged for the opportunity to do it over again, promised to spend the rest of his days learning to love God, if only he could live, but he knew that no bargaining was possible and he had only himself to blame. He apologized to Sarah for losing his chance at being reunited with her, for throwing his life away on a gamble instead of playing it safe. He prayed that she understood that he'd been motivated by his love for her, and that she would forgive him.

Through his tears he saw a woman running toward him, and recognized her as Janice Reilly. He realized his truck had crashed no more than a hundred yards from her and Ethan's campsite. There was nothing she could do, though; he could feel the blood draining out of him, and knew that he wouldn't live long enough for a rescue vehicle to arrive. He thought Janice was calling to him, but his ears were ringing too badly for him to hear anything. He could see Ethan Mead behind her, also starting to run toward him.

Then there was a flash of light and Janice was knocked off her feet as if she'd been struck by a sledgehammer. At first he thought she'd been hit by lightning, but then he realized that the lightning had already ceased. It was when she stood up again that he saw her face, steam rising from newly featureless skin, and he realized that Janice had been struck by Heaven's light.

Neil looked up, but all he saw were clouds; the shaft of light was gone. It seemed as if God were taunting him, not only by showing him the prize he'd lost his life trying to acquire while still holding it out of reach, but also by giving it to someone who didn't need it or even want it. God had already wasted a miracle on Janice, and now He was doing it again.

It was at that moment that another beam of Heaven's light penetrated the cloud cover and struck Neil, trapped in his vehicle.

Like a thousand hypodermic needles the light punctured his flesh and scraped across his bones. The light unmade his eyes, turning him into not a formerly sighted being, but a being never intended to possess vision. And in doing so the light revealed to Neil all the reasons he should love God.

He loved Him with an utterness beyond what humans can experience for one another. To say it was unconditional was inadequate, because even the word "unconditional" required the concept of a condition and such an idea was no longer comprehensible to him: every phenomenon in the universe was nothing less than an explicit reason to love Him. No circumstance could be an obstacle or even an irrelevancy, but only another reason to be grateful, a further inducement to love. Neil thought of the grief that had driven him to suicidal recklessness, and the pain and terror that Sarah had experienced before she died, and still he loved God, not in spite of their suffering, but because of it.

He renounced all his previous anger and ambivalence and desire for answers. He was grateful for all the pain he'd endured, contrite for not previously recognizing it as the gift it was, euphoric that he was now being granted this insight into his true purpose. He understood how life was an undeserved bounty, how even the most virtuous were not worthy of the glories of the mortal plane.

For him the mystery was solved, because he understood that everything in life is love, even pain, especially pain.

So minutes later, when Neil finally bled to death, he was truly worthy of salvation.

And God sent him to Hell anyway.

Ethan saw all of this. He saw Neil and Janice remade by Heaven's light, and he saw the pious love on their eyeless faces. He saw the skies become clear and the sunlight return. He was holding Neil's hand, waiting for the paramedics, when Neil died, and he saw Neil's soul leave his body and rise toward Heaven, only to descend into Hell.

Janice didn't see it, for by then her eyes were already gone. Ethan was the sole witness, and he realized that this was God's purpose for him: to follow Janice Reilly to this point and to see what she could not.

When statistics were compiled for Barakiel's visitation, it turned out that there had been a total of ten casualties, six among light-seekers and four among ordinary pilgrims. Nine pilgrims received miracle cures; the only individuals to see Heaven's light were Janice and Neil. There were no statistics regarding how many pilgrims had felt their lives changed by the visitation, but Ethan counted himself among them.

Upon returning home, Janice resumed her evangelism, but the topic of her speeches has changed. She no longer speaks about how the physically handicapped have the resources to overcome their limitations; instead she, like the other eyeless, speaks about the unbearable beauty of God's creation. Many who used to draw inspiration from her are disappointed, feeling they've lost a spiritual leader. When Janice had spoken of the strength she had as an afflicted person, her message was rare, but now that she's eyeless, her message is commonplace. She doesn't worry about the reduction in her audience, though, because she has complete conviction in what she evangelizes.

Ethan quit his job and became a preacher so that he too could speak about his experiences. His wife, Claire, couldn't accept his new mission and ultimately left him, taking their children with her, but Ethan was willing to continue alone. He's developed a substantial following by telling people what happened to Neil Fisk. He tells people that they can no more expect justice in the afterlife than in the mortal plane, but he doesn't do this to dissuade them from worshiping God; on the contrary, he encourages them to do so. What he insists on is that they not love God under a misapprehension, that if they wish to love God, they be prepared to do so no matter what His intentions. God is not just, God is not kind, God is not merciful, and understanding that is essential to true devotion.

As for Neil, although he is unaware of any of Ethan's sermons, he would understand their message perfectly. His lost soul is the embodiment of Ethan's teachings.

For most of its inhabitants, Hell is not that different from Earth; its principal punishment is the regret of not having loved God enough when alive, and for many that's easily endured. For Neil, however, Hell bears no resemblance whatsoever to the mortal plane. His eternal body has well-formed legs, but he's scarcely aware of them; his eyes have been restored, but he can't bear to open them. Just as seeing Heaven's light gave him an awareness of God's presence in all things in the mortal plane, so it has made him aware of God's absence in all things in Hell. Everything Neil sees, hears, or touches causes him distress, and unlike in the mortal plane this pain is not a form of God's love, but a consequence of His absence. Neil is experiencing more anguish than was possible when he was alive, but his only response is to love God.

Neil still loves Sarah, and misses her as much as he ever did, and the knowledge that he came so close to rejoining her only makes it worse. He knows his being sent to Hell was not a result of anything he did; he knows there was no reason for it, no higher purpose being served. None of this diminishes his love for God. If there were a possibility that he could be admitted to Heaven and his suffering would end, he would not hope for it; such desires no longer occur to him.

Neil even knows that by being beyond God's awareness, he is not loved by God in return. This doesn't affect his feelings either, because unconditional love asks nothing, not even that it be returned.

And though it's been many years that he has been in Hell, beyond the awareness of God, he loves Him still. That is the nature of true devotion.

Liking What You See:
A Documentary

"Beauty is the promise of happiness."—Stendhal

Tamera Lyons, 1st-year student at Pembleton:
I can't believe it. I visited the campus last year, and I didn't hear a word about this. Now I get here and it turns out people want to make calli a requirement. One of the things I was looking forward to about college was getting rid of this, you know, so I could be like everybody else. If I'd known there was even a chance I'd have to keep it, I probably would've picked another college. I feel like I've been scammed.

I turn eighteen next week, and I'm getting my calli turned off that day. If they vote to make it a requirement, I don't know what I'll do; maybe I'll transfer, I don't know. Right now I feel like going up to people and telling them, "vote no." There's probably some campaign I can work for.

Maria deSouza, 3rd-year student, President of the Students for Equality Everywhere (SEE):
Our goal is very simple. Pembleton University has a Code of Ethical Conduct, one that was created by the students themselves, and that all incoming students agree to follow when they enroll. The initiative

that we've sponsored would add a provision to the code, requiring students to adopt calliagnosia as long as they're enrolled.

What prompted us to do this now was the release of a spex version of Visage. That's the software that, when you look at people through your spex, shows you what they'd look like with cosmetic surgery. It became a form of entertainment among a certain crowd, and a lot of college students found it offensive. When people started talking about it as a symptom of a deeper societal problem, we thought the timing was right for us to sponsor this initiative.

The deeper societal problem is lookism. For decades people've been willing to talk about racism and sexism, but they're still reluctant to talk about lookism. Yet this prejudice against unattractive people is incredibly pervasive. People do it without even being taught by anyone, which is bad enough, but instead of combating this tendency, modern society actively reinforces it.

Educating people, raising their awareness about this issue, all of that is essential, but it's not enough. That's where technology comes in. Think of calliagnosia as a kind of assisted maturity. It lets you do what you know you should: ignore the surface, so you can look deeper.

We think it's time to bring calli into the mainstream. So far the calli movement has been a minor presence on college campuses, just another one of the special-interest causes. But Pembleton isn't like other colleges, and I think the students here are ready for calli. If the initiative succeeds here, we'll be setting an example for other colleges, and ultimately, society as a whole.

Joseph Weingartner, neurologist:
The condition is what we call an associative agnosia, rather than an apperceptive one. That means it doesn't interfere with one's visual perception, only with the ability to recognize what one sees. A calliagnosic perceives faces perfectly well; he or she can tell the difference between a pointed chin and a receding one, a straight nose and a

crooked one, clear skin and blemished skin. He or she simply doesn't experience any aesthetic reaction to those differences.

Calliagnosia is possible because of the existence of certain neural pathways in the brain. All animals have criteria for evaluating the reproductive potential of prospective mates, and they've evolved neural "circuitry" to recognize those criteria. Human social interaction is centered around our faces, so our circuitry is most finely attuned to how a person's reproductive potential is manifested in his or her face. You experience the operation of that circuitry as the feeling that a person is beautiful, or ugly, or somewhere in between. By blocking the neural pathways dedicated to evaluating those features, we can induce calliagnosia.

Given how much fashions change, some people find it hard to imagine that there are absolute markers of a beautiful face. But it turns out that when people of different cultures are asked to rank photos of faces for attractiveness, some very clear patterns emerge across the board. Even very young infants show the same preference for certain faces. This lets us identify the traits that are common to everyone's idea of a beautiful face.

Probably the most obvious one is clear skin. It's the equivalent of a bright plumage in birds or a shiny coat of fur in mammals. Good skin is the single best indicator of youth and health, and it's valued in every culture. Acne may not be serious, but it *looks* like more serious diseases, and that's why we find it disagreeable.

Another trait is symmetry; we may not be conscious of millimeter differences between someone's left and right sides, but measurements reveal that individuals rated as most attractive are also the most symmetrical. And while symmetry is what our genes always aim for, it's very difficult to achieve in developmental terms; any environmental stressor— like poor nutrition, disease, parasites—tends to result in asymmetry during growth. Symmetry implies resistance to such stressors.

Other traits have to do with facial proportions. We tend to be attracted to facial proportions that are close to the population mean. That obviously depends on the population you're part of, but being near the mean usually indicates genetic health. The only departures from the mean that people consistently find attractive are ones caused by sex hormones, which suggest good reproductive potential.

Basically, calliagnosia is a lack of response to these traits; nothing more. Calliagnosics are *not* blind to fashion or cultural standards of beauty. If black lipstick is all the rage, calliagnosia won't make you forget it, although you might not notice the difference between pretty faces and plain faces wearing that lipstick. And if everyone around you sneers at people with broad noses, you'll pick up on that.

So calliagnosia by itself can't eliminate appearance-based discrimination. What it does, in a sense, is even up the odds; it takes away the innate predisposition, the tendency for such discrimination to arise in the first place. That way, if you want to teach people to ignore appearances, you won't be facing an uphill battle. Ideally you'd start with an environment where everyone's adopted calliagnosia, and then socialize them to not value appearances.

Tamera Lyons:
People here have been asking me what it was like going to Saybrook, growing up with calli. To be honest, it's not a big deal when you're young; you know, like they say, whatever you grew up with seems normal to you. We knew that there was something that other people could see that we couldn't, but it was just something we were curious about.

For instance, my friends and I used to watch movies and try to figure out who was really good-looking and who wasn't. We'd say we could tell, but we couldn't really, not by looking at their faces. We were just going by who was the main character and who was the friend; you always knew the main character was better-looking than the friend. It's not true a hundred percent of the time, but you could usually tell if you were watching the kind of thing where the main character wouldn't be good-looking.

It's when you get older that it starts to bother you. If you hang out with people from other schools, you can feel weird because you have calli and they don't. It's not that anyone makes a big deal out of it, but it reminds you that there's something you can't see. And then you start having fights with your parents, because they're keeping you from seeing the real world. You never get anywhere with them, though.

Richard Hamill, founder of the Saybrook School:
Saybrook came about as an outgrowth of our housing cooperative. We had maybe two dozen families at the time, all trying to establish a community based on shared values. We were holding a meeting about the possibility of starting an alternative school for our kids, and one parent mentioned the problem of the media's influence on the children. Everyone's teens were asking for cosmetic surgery so they could look like fashion models. The parents were doing their best, but you can't isolate your kids from the world; they live in an image-obsessed culture.

It was around then that the last legal challenges to calliagnosia were resolved, and we got to talking about it. We saw calli as an opportunity: what if we could live in an environment where people didn't judge each other on their appearance? What if we could raise our children in such an environment?

The school started out being just for the children of the families in the cooperative, but other calliagnosia schools began making the news, and before long people were asking if they could enroll their kids without joining the housing co-op. Eventually we set up Saybrook as a private school separate from the co-op, and one of its requirements was that parents adopt calliagnosia for as long as their kids were enrolled. Now a calliagnosia community has sprung up here, all because of the school.

Rachel Lyons:
Tamera's father and I gave the issue a lot of thought before we decided to enroll her there. We talked to people in the community, found we

liked their approach to education, but really it was visiting the school that sold me.

Saybrook has a higher than normal number of students with facial abnormalities, like bone cancer, burns, congenital conditions. Their parents moved here to keep them from being ostracized by other kids, and it works. I remember when I first visited, I saw a class of twelve-year-olds voting for class president, and they elected this girl who had burn scars on one side of her face. She was wonderfully at ease with herself, she was popular among kids who probably would have ostracized her in any other school. And I thought, this is the kind of environment I want my daughter to grow up in.

Girls have always been told that their value is tied to their appearance; their accomplishments are always magnified if they're pretty and diminished if they're not. Even worse, some girls get the message that they can get through life relying on just their looks, and then they never develop their minds. I wanted to keep Tamera away from that sort of influence.

Being pretty is fundamentally a passive quality; even when you work at it, you're working at being passive. I wanted Tamera to value herself in terms of what she could *do*, both with her mind and with her body, not in terms of how decorative she was. I didn't want her to be passive, and I'm pleased to say that she hasn't turned out that way.

Martin Lyons:
I don't mind if Tamera decides as an adult to get rid of calli. This was never about taking choices away from her. But there's more than enough stress involved in simply getting through adolescence; the peer pressure can crush you like a paper cup. Becoming preoccupied with how you look is just one more way to be crushed, and anything that can relieve that pressure is a good thing, in my opinion.

Once you're older, you're better equipped to deal with the issue of personal appearance. You're more comfortable in your own skin, more confident, more secure. You're more likely to be satisfied with how you look, whether you're "good-looking" or not. Of course not everyone reaches that level of maturity at the same age. Some people are there at sixteen, some don't get there until they're thirty or even older. But eighteen's the age of legal majority, when everyone's got the right to make their own decisions, and all you can do is trust your child and hope for the best.

Tamera Lyons:
It'd been kind of an odd day for me. Good, but odd. I just got my calli turned off this morning.

Getting it turned off was easy. The nurse stuck some sensors on me and made me put on this helmet, and she showed me a bunch of pictures of people's faces. Then she tapped at her keyboard for a minute, and said, "I've switched off the calli," just like that. I thought you might feel something when it happened, but you don't. Then she showed me the pictures again, to make sure it worked.

When I looked at the faces again, some of them seemed . . . different. Like they were glowing, or more vivid or something. It's hard to describe. The nurse showed me my test results afterwards, and there were readings for how wide my pupils were dilating and how well my skin conducted electricity and stuff like that. And for the faces that seemed different, the readings went way up. She said those were the beautiful faces.

She said that I'd notice how other people's faces look right away, but it'd take a while before I had any reaction to how I looked. Supposedly you're too used to your face to tell.

And yeah, when I first looked in a mirror, I thought I looked totally the same. Since I got back from the doctor's, the people I see on campus definitely look different, but I still haven't noticed any difference in how I look. I've been looking at mirrors all day. For a while I was afraid that I was ugly, and any minute the ugliness was going to appear, like a rash or something. And so I've been staring at the mirror, just waiting, and nothing's happened. So I figure I'm probably not really ugly, or I'd have noticed it, but that means I'm not really pretty either, because I'd have noticed that too. So I guess that means I'm absolutely plain, you know? Exactly average. I guess that's okay.

Joseph Weingartner:
Inducing an agnosia means simulating a specific brain lesion. We do this with a programmable pharmaceutical called neurostat; you can think of it as a highly selective anesthetic, one whose activation and targeting are all under dynamic control. We activate or deactivate the neurostat by transmitting signals through a helmet the patient puts on. The helmet also provides somatic positioning information so the neurostat molecules can triangulate their location. This lets us activate only the neurostat in a specific section of brain tissue, and keep the nerve impulses there below a specified threshold.

Neurostat was originally developed for controlling seizures in epileptics and for relief of chronic pain; it lets us treat even severe cases of these conditions without the side effects caused by drugs that affect the entire nervous system. Later on, different neurostat protocols were developed as treatments for obsessive-compulsive disorder, addictive behavior, and various other disorders. At the same time, neurostat became incredibly valuable as a research tool for studying brain physiology.

One way neurologists have traditionally studied specialization of brain function is to observe the deficits that result from various lesions. Obviously, this technique is limited because the lesions caused by injury or disease often affect multiple functional areas. By contrast, neurostat can be activated in the tiniest portion of the brain, in effect simulating a lesion so localized that it would never occur naturally. And when you deactivate the neurostat, the "lesion" disappears and brain function returns to normal.

In this way neurologists were able to induce a wide variety of agnosias. The one most relevant here is prosopagnosia, the inability to recognize people by their faces. A prosopagnosic can't recognize friends or family members unless they say something; he can't even identify his own face in a photograph. It's not a cognitive or perceptual problem; prosopagnosics can identify people by their hairstyle, clothing, perfume, even the way they walk. The deficit is restricted purely to faces.

Prosopagnosia has always been the most dramatic indication that our brains have a special "circuit" devoted to the visual processing of faces; we look at faces in a different way than we look at anything else. And recognizing someone's face is just one of the face-processing tasks we do; there are also related circuits devoted to identifying facial expressions, and even detecting changes in the direction of another person's gaze.

One of the interesting things about prosopagnosics is that while they can't recognize a face, they still have an opinion as to whether it's attractive or not. When asked to sort photos of faces in order of attractiveness, prosopagnosics sorted the photos in pretty much the same way as anyone else. Experiments using neurostat allowed researchers to identify the neurological circuit responsible for perceiving beauty in faces, and thus essentially invent calliagnosia.

Maria deSouza:

SEE has had extra neurostat programming helmets set up in the Student Health Office, and made arrangements so they can offer calliagnosia to anyone who wants it. You don't even have to make an appointment, you can just walk in. We're encouraging all the students to try it, at least for a day, to see what it's like. At first it seems a little odd, not seeing anyone as either good-looking or ugly, but over time you realize how positively it affects your interactions with other people.

A lot of people worry that calli might make them asexual or something, but actually physical beauty is only a small part of what makes a person attractive. No matter what a person looks like, it's much more important how the person acts; what he says and how he says it, his behavior and body language. And how does he react to you? For me, one of the things that attracts me to a guy is if *he* seems interested in *me*. It's like a feedback loop; you notice him looking at you, then he sees you looking at him, and things snowball from there. Calli doesn't change that. Plus there's that whole pheromone chemistry going on too; obviously calli doesn't affect that.

Another worry that people have is that calli will make everyone's face look the same, but that's not true either. A person's face always reflects their personality, and if anything, calli makes that clearer. You know that saying, that after a certain age, you're responsible for your face? With calli, you really appreciate how true that is. Some faces just look really bland, especially young, conventionally pretty ones. Without their physical beauty, those faces are just boring. But faces that are full of personality look as good as they ever did, maybe even better. It's like you're seeing something more essential about them.

Some people also ask about enforcement. We don't plan on doing anything like that. It's true, there's software that's pretty good at guessing if a person has calli or not, by analyzing eye-gaze patterns. But it requires a lot of data, and the campus security cams don't zoom in close enough. Everyone would have to wear personal cams, and share the data. It's possible, but that's not what we're after. We think that once people try calli, they'll see the benefits themselves.

Tamera Lyons:
Check it out, I'm pretty!

What a day. When I woke up this morning I immediately went to the mirror; it was like I was a little kid on Christmas or something. But still, nothing; my face still looked plain. Later on I even (*laughs*) I tried to catch myself by surprise, by sneaking up on a mirror, but that didn't work. So I was kind of disappointed, and feeling just, you know, resigned to my fate.

But then this afternoon, I went out with my roommate Ina and a couple other girls from the dorm. I hadn't told anyone that I'd gotten my calli turned off, because I wanted to get used to it first. So we went to this snack bar on the other side of campus, one I hadn't been to before. We were sitting at this table, talking, and I was looking around, just seeing what people looked like without calli. And I saw this girl looking at me, and I thought, "She's really pretty." And then, (*laughs*) this'll sound really stupid, then I realized that this wall in the snack bar was a mirror, and I was looking at myself!

I can't describe it, I felt this incredible sense of *relief*. I just couldn't stop smiling! Ina asked me what I was so happy about, and I just shook my head. I went to the bathroom so I could stare at myself in the mirror for a bit.

So it's been a good day. I really *like* the way I look! It's been a good day.

From a student debate held at Pembleton:

Jeff Winthrop, 3rd-year student:

Of course it's wrong to judge people by their appearance, but this "blindness" isn't the answer. Education is.

Calli takes away the good as well as the bad. It doesn't just work when there's a possibility of discrimination, it keeps you from recognizing beauty altogether. There are plenty of times when looking at an attractive face doesn't hurt anyone. Calli won't let you make those distinctions, but education will.

And I know someone will say, what about when the technology gets better? Maybe one day they'll be able to insert an expert system into your brain, one that goes, "Is this an appropriate situation to apprehend beauty? If so, enjoy it; else, ignore it." Would that be okay? Would that be the "assisted maturity" you hear people talking about?

No, it wouldn't. That wouldn't be maturity; it'd be letting an expert system make your decisions for you. Maturity means seeing the differences, but realizing they don't matter. There's no technological shortcut.

Adesh Singh, 3rd-year student:

No one's talking about letting an expert system make your decisions. What makes calli ideal is precisely that it's such a minimal change. Calli doesn't decide for you; it doesn't prevent you from doing anything. And as for maturity, you demonstrate maturity by choosing calli in the first place.

Everyone knows physical beauty has nothing to do with merit; that's what education's accomplished. But even with the best intentions in the world, people haven't stopped practicing lookism. We try to be impartial, we try not to let a person's appearance affect us, but we can't suppress our autonomic responses, and anyone who claims they can is engaged in wishful thinking. Ask yourself: don't you react differently when you meet an attractive person and when you meet an unattractive one?

Every study on this issue turns up the same results: looks help people get ahead. We can't help but think of good-looking people as more competent, more honest, more deserving than others. None of it's true, but their looks still give us that impression.

Calli doesn't blind you to anything; beauty is what blinds you. Calli lets you see.

Tamera Lyons:
So, I've been looking at good-looking guys around campus. It's fun; weird, but fun. Like, I was in the cafeteria the other day, and I saw this guy a couple tables away, I didn't know his name, but I kept turning to look at him. I can't describe anything specific about his face, but it just seemed much more noticeable than other people's. It was like his face was a magnet, and my eyes were compass needles being pulled toward it.

And after I looked at him for a while, I found it really easy to imagine that he was a nice guy! I didn't know anything about him, I couldn't even hear what he was talking about, but I wanted to get to know him. It was kind of odd, but definitely not in a bad way.

From a netcast of EduNews, on the American College Network:
In the latest on the Pembleton University calliagnosia initiative:

EduNews has received evidence that the public-relations firm of Wyatt/Hayes paid four Pembleton students to dissuade classmates from voting for the initiative, without having them register their affiliations. Evidence includes an internal memo from Wyatt/Hayes, proposing that "good-looking students with high reputation ratings" be sought, and records of payments from the agency to Pembleton students.

The files were sent by the SemioTech Warriors, a culture-jamming group responsible for numerous acts of media vandalism.

When contacted about this story, Wyatt/Hayes issued a statement decrying this violation of their internal computer systems.

Jeff Winthrop:
Yes, it's true, Wyatt/Hayes paid me, but it wasn't an endorsement deal; they never told me *what* to say. They just made it possible for me to devote more time to the anti-calli campaign, which is what I would've done anyway if I hadn't needed to make money tutoring. All I've been doing is expressing my honest opinion: I think calli's a bad idea.

A couple of people in the anti-calli campaign have asked that I not speak publicly about the issue anymore, because they think it would hurt the cause. I'm sorry they feel that way, because this is just an ad hominem attack. If you thought my arguments made sense before, this shouldn't change anything. But I realize that some people can't make those distinctions, and I'll do what's best for the cause.

Maria deSouza:
Those students really should have registered their affiliations; we all know people who are walking endorsements. But now, whenever someone criticizes the initiative, people ask them if they're being paid. The backlash is definitely hurting the anti-calli campaign.

I consider it a compliment that someone is taking enough interest in the initiative to hire a PR firm. We've always hoped that its passing might influence people at other schools, and this means that corporations are thinking the same thing.

We've invited the president of the National Calliagnosia Association to speak on campus. Before we weren't sure if we wanted to bring the national group in, because they have a different emphasis than we do; they're more focused on the media uses of beauty, while here at SEE we're more interested in the social equality issue. But given the way students reacted to what Wyatt/Hayes did, it's clear that the media manipulation issue has the power to get us where we need to go. Our best shot at getting the initiative passed is to take advantage of the anger against advertisers. The social equality will follow afterwards.

From the speech given at Pembleton by Walter Lambert, president of the National Calliagnosia Association:
Think of cocaine. In its natural form, as coca leaves, it's appealing, but not to an extent that it usually becomes a problem. But refine it, purify it, and you get a compound that hits your pleasure receptors with an unnatural intensity. That's when it becomes addictive.

Beauty has undergone a similar process, thanks to advertisers. Evolution gave us a circuit that responds to good looks—call it the pleasure receptor for our visual cortex—and in our natural environment, it was useful to have. But take a person with one-in-a-million skin and bone structure, add professional makeup and retouching, and you're no longer looking at beauty in its natural form. You've got pharmaceutical-grade beauty, the cocaine of good looks.

Biologists call this "supernormal stimulus"; show a mother bird a giant plastic egg, and she'll incubate it instead of her own real eggs. Madison Avenue has saturated our environment with this kind of stimuli, this visual drug. Our beauty receptors receive more stimulation than they were evolved to handle; we're seeing more beauty in one day than our ancestors did in a lifetime. And the result is that beauty is slowly ruining our lives.

How? The way any drug becomes a problem: by interfering with our relationships with other people. We become dissatisfied with the way ordinary people look because they can't compare to supermodels. Two-dimensional images are bad enough, but now with spex, advertisers can put a supermodel right in front of you, making eye contact. Software companies offer goddesses who'll remind you of your appointments. We've all heard about men who prefer virtual girlfriends over actual ones, but they're not the only ones who've been affected. The more time any of us spend with gorgeous digital apparitions around, the more our relationships with real human beings are going to suffer.

We can't avoid these images and still live in the modern world. And that means we can't kick this habit, because beauty is a drug you can't abstain from unless you literally keep your eyes closed all the time.

Until now. Now you can get another set of eyelids, one that blocks out this drug, but still lets you see. And that's calliagnosia. Some people call it excessive, but I call it just enough. Technology is being used to manipulate us through our emotional reactions, so it's only fair that we use it to protect ourselves too.

Right now you have an opportunity to make an enormous impact. The Pembleton student body has always been at the vanguard of every progressive movement; what you decide here will set an example for students across the country. By passing this initiative, by adopting calliagnosia, you'll be sending a message to advertisers that young people are no longer willing to be manipulated.

From a netcast of EduNews:
Following NCA president Walter Lambert's speech, polls show that 54 percent of the Pembleton University students support the calliagnosia initiative. Polls across the country show that an average of 28 percent of students would support a similar initiative at their school, an increase of 8 percent in the past month.

———

Tamera Lyons:
I thought he went overboard with that cocaine analogy. Do you know anyone who steals stuff and sells it so he can get his fix of advertising?

But I guess he has a point about how good-looking people are in commercials versus in real life. It's not that they look better than people in real life, but they look good in a different way.

Like, I was at the campus store the other day, and I needed to check my email, and when I put on my spex I saw this poster running a commercial. It was for some shampoo, Jouissance, I think. I'd seen it before, but it was different without calli. The model was so—I couldn't take my eyes off her. I don't mean I felt the same as that time I saw the good-looking guy in the cafeteria; it wasn't like I wanted to get to know her. It was more like . . . watching a sunset, or a fireworks display.

I just stood there and watched the commercial like five times, just so I could look at her some more. I didn't think a human being could look so, you know, spectacular.

But it's not like I'm going to quit talking to people so I can watch commercials through my spex all the time. Watching them is very intense, but it's a totally different experience than looking at a real person. And it's not even like I immediately want to go out and buy everything they're selling, either. I'm not even really paying attention to the products. I just think they're amazing to watch.

Maria deSouza:
If I'd met Tamera earlier, I might have tried to persuade her not to get her calli turned off. I doubt I would've succeeded; she seems pretty firm about her decision. Even so, she's a great example of the benefits of calli. You can't help but notice it when you talk to her. For example, at one point I was saying how lucky she was, and she said, "Because I'm beautiful?" And she was being totally sincere! Like she was talking about her height. Can you imagine a woman without calli saying that?

Tamera is completely unself-conscious about her looks; she's not vain or insecure, and she can describe herself as beautiful without embarrassment. I gather that she's very pretty, and with a lot of women who look like that, I can see something in their manner, a hint of showoffishness. Tamera doesn't have that. Or else they display false modesty, which is also easy to tell, but Tamera doesn't do that either, because she truly *is* modest. There's no way she could be like that if she hadn't been raised with calli. I just hope she stays that way.

Annika Lindstrom, 2nd-year student:
I think this calli thing is a terrible idea. I like it when guys notice me, and I'd be really disappointed if they stopped.

I think this whole thing is just a way for people who, honestly, aren't very good-looking, to try and make themselves feel better. And the only way they can do that is to punish people who have what they don't. And that's just unfair.

Who wouldn't want to be pretty if they could? Ask anyone, ask the people behind this, and I bet you they'd all say yes. Okay, sure, being pretty means that you'll be hassled by jerks sometimes. There are always jerks, but that's part of life. If those scientists could come up with some way to turn off the jerk circuit in guys' brains, I'd be all in favor of that.

Jolene Carter, 3rd-year student:
I'm voting for the initiative, because I think it'd be a relief if everyone had calli.

People are nice to me because of how I look, and part of me likes that, but part of me feels guilty because I haven't done anything to deserve it. And sure, it's nice to have men pay attention to me, but it can be hard to make a real connection with someone. Whenever I like a guy, I always wonder how much he's interested in me, versus how much he's interested in my looks. It can be hard to tell, because all relationships are wonderful at the beginning, you know? It's not until later that you find out whether you can really be comfortable with each other. It was like that with my last boyfriend. He wasn't happy with me if I didn't look fabulous, so I was never able to truly relax. But by the time I realized that, I'd already let myself get close to him, so that really hurt, finding out that he didn't see the real me.

And then there's how you feel around other women. I don't think most women like it, but you're always comparing how you look relative to everyone else. Sometimes I feel like I'm in a competition, and I don't want to be.

I thought about getting calli once, but it didn't seem like it would help unless everyone else did too; getting it all by myself wouldn't change the way others treat me. But if everyone on campus had calli, I'd be glad to get it.

Tamera Lyons:

I was showing my roommate Ina this album of pictures from high school, and we get to all these pictures of me and Garrett, my ex. So Ina wants to know all about him, and so I tell her. I'm telling her how we were together all of senior year, and how much I loved him, and wanted us to stay together, but he wanted to be free to date when he went to college. And then she's like, "You mean *he* broke up with *you*?"

It took me a while before I could get her to tell me what was up; she made me promise twice not to get mad. Eventually she said Garrett isn't exactly good-looking. I was thinking he must be average-looking, because he didn't really look that different after I got my calli turned off. But Ina said he was definitely below average.

She found pictures of a couple other guys who she thought looked like him, and with them I could see how they're not good-looking. Their faces just look goofy. Then I took another look at Garrett's picture, and I guess he's got some of the same features, but on him they look cute. To me, anyway.

I guess it's true what they say: love is a little bit like calli. When you love someone, you don't really see what they look like. I don't see Garrett the way others do, because I still have feelings for him.

Ina said she couldn't believe someone who looked like him would break up with someone who looked like me. She said that in a school without calli, he probably wouldn't have been able to get a date with me. Like, we wouldn't be in the same league.

That's weird to think about. When Garrett and I were going out, I always thought we were meant to be together. I don't mean that I believe in destiny, but I just thought there was something really right about the two of us. So the idea that we could've both been in the same school, but not gotten together because we didn't have calli, feels strange. And I know that Ina can't be sure of that. But I can't be sure she's wrong, either.

And maybe that means I should be glad I had calli, because it let me and Garrett get together. I don't know about that.

From a netcast of EduNews:
Netsites for a dozen calliagnosia student organizations around the country were brought down today in a coordinated denial-of-service attack. Although no one has claimed credit for the attack, it's been suggested that those responsible may be retaliating for an incident last month in which the American Association of Cosmetic Surgeons' netsite was replaced by a calliagnosia site.

In a related story, the SemioTech Warriors announced the release of their new "Dermatology" computer virus. This virus has quickly begun infecting video servers around the world, altering netcasts so that faces and bodies exhibit conditions such as acne and varicose veins.

Warren Davidson, 1st-year student:
I thought about trying calli before, when I was in high school, but I never knew how to bring it up with my parents. So when they started offering it here, I figured I'd give it a try. (*shrugs*) It's okay.

Actually, it's better than okay. (*pause*) I've always hated how I look. For a while in high school I couldn't stand the sight of myself in a mirror. But with calli, I don't mind as much. I know I look the same to other people, but that doesn't seem as big a deal as it used to. I feel better just by not being reminded that some people are so much better-looking than others. Like, for instance: I was helping this girl in the library with a problem on her calculus homework, and afterwards I realized that she's someone I'd thought was really pretty. Normally I would have been really nervous around her, but with calli, she wasn't so hard to talk to.

Maybe she thinks I look like a freak, I don't know, but the thing was, when I was talking to her *I* didn't think I looked like a freak. Before I got calli, I think I was just too self-conscious, and that just made things worse. Now I'm more relaxed.

It's not like I suddenly feel all wonderful about myself or anything, and I'm sure for other people calli wouldn't help them at all, but for me, calli makes me not feel as bad as I used to. And that's worth something.

Alex Bibescu, professor of religious studies at Pembleton:
Some people have been quick to dismiss the whole calliagnosia debate as superficial, an argument over makeup or who can and can't get a date. But if you actually look at it, you'll see it's much deeper than that. It reflects a very old ambivalence about the body, one that's been part of Western civilization since ancient times.

You see, the foundations of our culture were laid in classical Greece, where physical beauty and the body were celebrated. But our culture is also thoroughly permeated by the monotheistic tradition, which devalues the body in favor of the soul. These old conflicting impulses are rearing their heads again, this time in the calliagnosia debate.

I suspect that most calli supporters think of themselves to be modern, secular liberals, and wouldn't admit to being influenced by monotheism in any way. But take a look at who else advocates calliagnosia: conservative religious groups. There are communities of all three major monotheistic faiths—Jewish, Christian, and Muslim—who've begun using calli to make their young members more resistant to the charms of outsiders. This commonality is no coincidence. The liberal calli supporters may not use language like "resisting the temptations of the flesh," but in their own way, they're following the same tradition of deprecating the physical.

Really, the only calli supporters who can credibly claim they're not influenced by monotheism are the NeoMind Buddhists. They're a sect who see calliagnosia as a step toward enlightened thought, because it eliminates one's perception of illusory distinctions. But the NeoMind sect is open to broad use of neurostat as an aid to meditation, which is a radical stance of an entirely different sort. I doubt you'll find many modern liberals or conservative monotheists sympathetic to that!

So you see, this debate isn't just about commercials and cosmetics, it's about determining what's the appropriate relationship between the mind and the body. Are we more fully realized when we minimize the physical part of our natures? And that, you have to agree, is a profound question.

Joseph Weingartner:
After calliagnosia was discovered, some researchers wondered if it might be possible to create an analogous condition that rendered the subject blind to race or ethnicity. They've made a number of attempts—impairing various levels of category discrimination in tandem with face recognition, that sort of thing—but the resulting deficits were always unsatisfactory. Usually the test subjects would simply be unable to distinguish similar-looking individuals. One test actually produced a benign variant of Fregoli syndrome, causing the subject to mistake every person he met for a family member. Unfortunately, treating everyone like a brother isn't desirable in so literal a sense.

When neurostat treatments for problems like compulsive behavior entered widespread use, a lot of people thought that "mind programming" was finally here. People asked their doctors if they could get the same sexual tastes as their spouses. Media pundits worried about the possibility of programming loyalty to a government or corporation, or belief in an ideology or religion.

The fact is, we have no access to the contents of anyone's thoughts. We can shape broad aspects of personality, we can make changes consistent with the natural specialization of the brain, but these are extremely coarse-grained adjustments. There's no neural pathway that specifically handles resentment toward immigrants, any more than there's one for Marxist doctrine or foot fetishism. If we ever get true mind programming, we'll be able to create "race blindness," but until then, education is our best hope.

Tamera Lyons:

I had an interesting class today. In History of Ideas, we've got this T.A., he's named Anton, and he was saying how a lot of words we use to describe an attractive person used to be words for magic. Like the word "charm" originally meant a magic spell, and the word "glamour" did, too. And it's just blatant with words like "enchanting" and "spellbinding." And when he said that, I thought, yeah, that's what it's like: seeing a really good-looking person is like having a magic spell cast over you.

And Anton was saying how one of the primary uses of magic was to create love and desire in someone. And that makes total sense, too, when you think about those words "charm" and "glamour." Because seeing beauty feels like love. You feel like you've got a crush on a really good-looking person, just by looking at them.

And I've been thinking that maybe there's a way I can get back together with Garrett. Because if Garrett didn't have calli, maybe he'd fall in love with me again. Remember how I said before that maybe calli was what let us get together? Well, maybe calli is actually what's keeping us apart now. Maybe Garrett would want to get back with me if he saw what I really looked like.

Garrett turned eighteen during the summer, but he never got his calli turned off because he didn't think it was a big deal. He goes to Northrop now. So I called him up, just as a friend, and when we were talking about stuff, I asked him what he thought about the calli initiative here at Pembleton. He said he didn't see what all the fuss was about, and then I told him how much I liked not having calli anymore, and said he ought to try it, so he could judge both sides. He said that made sense. I didn't make a big deal out of it, but I was stoked.

Daniel Taglia, professor of comparative literature at Pembleton:
The student initiative doesn't apply to faculty, but obviously if it passes there'll be pressure on the faculty to adopt calliagnosia as well. So I don't consider it premature for me to say that I'm adamantly opposed to it.

This is just the latest example of political correctness run amok. The people advocating calli are well-intentioned, but what they're doing is infantilizing us. The very notion that beauty is something we need to be protected from is insulting. Next thing you know, a student organization will insist we all adopt music agnosia, so we don't feel bad about ourselves when we hear gifted singers or musicians.

When you watch Olympic athletes in competition, does your self-esteem plummet? Of course not. On the contrary, you feel wonder and admiration; you're inspired that such exceptional individuals exist. So why can't we feel the same way about beauty? Feminism would have us apologize for having that reaction. It wants to replace aesthetics with politics, and to the extent it's succeeded, it's impoverished us.

Being in the presence of a world-class beauty can be as thrilling as listening to a world-class soprano. Gifted individuals aren't the only ones who benefit from their gifts; we *all* do. Or, I should say, we all *can*. Depriving ourselves of that opportunity would be a crime.

———

Commercial paid for by People for Ethical Nanomedicine:
Voiceover:
Have your friends been telling you that calli is cool, that it's the smart thing to do? Then maybe you should talk to people who grew up with calli.

"After I got my calli turned off, I recoiled the first time I met an unattractive person. I knew it was silly, but I just couldn't help myself. Calli didn't help make me mature, it *kept* me from becoming mature. I had to relearn how to interact with people."

"I went to school to be a graphic artist. I worked day and night, but I never got anywhere with it. My teacher said I didn't have the eye for it, that calli had stunted me aesthetically. There's no way I can get back what I've lost."

"Having calli was like having my parents inside my head, censoring my thoughts. Now that I've had it turned off, I realize just what kind of abuse I'd been living with."

Voiceover:
If the people who grew up with calliagnosia don't recommend it, shouldn't that tell you something?

They didn't have a choice, but you do. Brain damage is never a good idea, no matter what your friends say.

Maria deSouza:
We'd never heard of the People for Ethical Nanomedicine, so we did some research on them. It took some digging, but it turns out it's not a grassroots organization at all, it's an industry PR front. A bunch of cosmetics companies got together recently and created it. We haven't been able to contact the people who appear in the commercial, so we don't know how much, if any, of what they said was true. Even if they were being honest, they certainly aren't typical; most people who get their calli turned off feel fine about it. And there are definitely graphic artists who grew up with calli.

It kind of reminds me of an ad I saw a while back, put out by a modeling agency when the calli movement was just getting started. It was just a picture of a supermodel's face, with a caption: "If you no longer saw her as beautiful, whose loss would it be? Hers, or yours?" This new campaign has the same message, basically saying, "you'll be sorry," but instead of taking that cocky attitude, it has more of a concerned-warning tone. This is classic PR: hide behind a nice-sounding name, and create the impression of a third party looking out for the consumer's interests.

Tamera Lyons:

I thought that commercial was totally idiotic. It's not like I'm in favor of the initiative—I don't want people to vote for it—but people shouldn't vote against it for the wrong reason. Growing up with calli isn't crippling. There's no reason for anyone to feel sorry for me or anything. I'm dealing with it fine. And that's why I think people ought to vote against the initiative: because seeing beauty is fine.

Anyway, I talked to Garrett again. He said he'd just gotten his calli turned off. He said it seemed cool so far, although it was kind of weird, and I told him I felt the same way when I got mine disabled. I suppose it's kind of funny, how I was acting like an old pro, even though I've only had mine off for a few weeks.

Joseph Weingartner:

One of the first questions researchers asked about calliagnosia was whether it has any "spillover," that is, whether it affects your appreciation of beauty outside of faces. For the most part, the answer seems to be "no." Calliagnosics seem to enjoy looking at the same things other people do. That said, we can't rule out the possibility of side effects.

As an example, consider the spillover that's observed in prosopagnosics. One prosopagnosic who was a dairy farmer found he could no longer recognize his cows individually. Another found it harder to distinguish models of cars, if you can imagine that. These cases suggest that we sometimes use our face-recognition module for tasks other than strict face recognition. We may not think something looks like a face—a car, for example—but at a neurological level we're treating it as if it were a face.

There may be a similar spillover among calliagnosics, but since calliagnosia is subtler than prosopagnosia, any spillover is harder to measure. The role of fashion in cars' appearances, for example, is vastly greater than its role in faces', and there's little consensus about which cars are most attractive. There may be a calliagnosic out there who doesn't enjoy looking at certain models as much as he otherwise would, but he hasn't come forward to complain.

Then there's the role our beauty-recognition module plays in our aesthetic reaction to symmetry. We appreciate symmetry in a wide range of settings—painting, sculpture, graphic design—but at the same time we also appreciate asymmetry. There are a lot of factors that contribute to our reaction to art, and not much consensus about when a particular example is successful.

It might be interesting to see if calliagnosia communities produce fewer truly talented visual artists, but given how few such individuals arise in the general population, it's difficult to do a statistically meaningful study. The only thing we know for certain is that calliagnosics report a more muted response to some portraits, but that's not a side effect *per se*; portrait paintings derive at least some of their impact from the facial appearance of the subject.

Of course, any effect is too much for some people. This is the reason given by some parents for not wanting calliagnosia for their children: they want their children to be able to appreciate the *Mona Lisa*, and perhaps create its successor.

Marc Esposito, 4th-year student at Waterston College:
That Pembleton thing sounds totally crazed. I could see doing it like a setup for some prank. You know, as in, you'd fix this guy up with a girl, and tell him she's an absolute babe, but actually you've fixed him

up with a dog, and he can't tell so he believes you. That'd be kind of funny, actually.

But I sure as hell would never get this calli thing. I want to date good-looking girls. Why would I want something that'd make me lower my standards? Okay, sure, some nights all the babes have been taken, and you have to choose from the leftovers. But that's why there's beer, right? Doesn't mean I want to wear beer goggles all the time.

Tamera Lyons:

So Garrett and I were talking on the phone again last night, and I asked him if he wanted to switch to video so we could see each other. And he said okay, so we did.

I was casual about it, but I had actually spent a lot of time getting ready. Ina's teaching me to put on makeup, but I'm not very good at it yet, I got that phone software that makes it look like you're wearing makeup. I set it for just a little bit, and I think it made a real difference in how I looked. Maybe it was overkill, I don't know how much Garrett could tell, but I just wanted to be sure I looked as good as possible.

As soon as we switched to video, I could see him react. It was like his eyes got wider. He was like, "You look really great," and I was like, "Thanks." Then he got shy, and made some joke about the way he looked, but I told him I liked the way he looked.

We talked for a while on video, and all the time I was really conscious of him looking at me. That felt good. I got a feeling that he was thinking he might want us to get back together again, but maybe I was just imagining it.

Maybe next time we talk I'll suggest he could come visit me for a weekend, or I could go visit him at Northrop. That'd be really cool. Though I'd have to be sure I could do my own makeup before that.

I know there's no guarantee that he'll want to get back together. Getting my calli turned off didn't make me love him less, so maybe it won't make him love me any more. I'm hoping, though.

———

Cathy Minami, 3rd-year student:
Anyone who says the calli movement is good for women is spreading the propaganda of all oppressors: the claim that subjugation is actually protection. Calli supporters want to demonize those women who possess beauty. Beauty can provide just as much pleasure for those who have it as for those who perceive it, but the calli movement makes women feel guilty about taking pleasure in their appearance. It's yet another patriarchal strategy for suppressing female sexuality, and once again, too many women have bought into it.

Of *course* beauty has been used as a tool of oppression, but eliminating beauty is not the answer; you can't liberate people by narrowing the scope of their experiences. That's positively Orwellian. What's needed is a woman-centered concept of beauty, one that lets all women feel good about themselves instead of making most of them feel bad.

Lawrence Sutton, 4th-year student:
I totally knew what Walter Lambert was talking about in his speech. I wouldn't have phrased it the way he did, but I've felt the same way for a while now. I got calli a couple years ago, long before this initiative came up, because I wanted to be able to concentrate on more important things.

I don't mean I only think about schoolwork; I've got a girlfriend, and we have a good relationship. That hasn't changed. What's changed is how I interact with advertising. Before, every time I used to walk past a magazine stand or see a commercial, I could feel my attention being drawn a little bit. It was like they were trying to arouse me against my will. I don't necessarily mean a sexual kind of arousal, but they were trying to appeal to me on a visceral level. And I would automatically resist, and go back to whatever I was doing before. But it was a distraction, and resisting those distractions took energy that I could have been using elsewhere.

But now with calli, I don't feel that pull. Calli freed me from that distraction, it gave me that energy back. So I'm totally in favor of it.

Lori Harber, 3rd-year student at Maxwell College:
Calli is for wusses. My attitude is, fight back. Go radical ugly. That's what the beautiful people need to see.

I got my nose taken off about this time last year. It's a bigger deal than it sounds, surgery-wise; to be healthy and stuff, you have to move some of the hairs further in to catch dust. And the bone you see (*taps it with a fingernail*) isn't real, it's ceramic. Having your real bone exposed is a big infection risk.

I like it when I freak people out; sometimes I actually ruin someone's appetite when they're eating. But freaking people out, that's not what it's *about*. It's about how ugly can beat beautiful at its own game. I get more looks walking down the street than a beautiful woman. You see me standing next to a video model, who you going to notice more? Me, that's who. You won't want to, but you will.

Tamera Lyons:
Garrett and I were talking again last night, and we got to talking about, you know, if either of us had been going out with someone else. And I was casual about it, I said that I had hung out with some guys, but nothing major.

So I asked him the same. He was kind of embarrassed about it, but eventually he said that he was finding it harder to, like, really become friendly with girls in college, harder than he expected. And now he's thinking it's because of the way he looks.

I just said, "No way," but I didn't really know what to say. Part of me was glad that Garrett isn't seeing someone else yet, and part of me felt bad for him, and part of me was just surprised. I mean, he's smart, he's funny, he's a great guy, and I'm not just saying that because I went out with him. He was popular in high school.

But then I remembered what Ina said about me and Garrett. I guess being smart and funny doesn't mean you're in the same league as someone, you have to be equally good-looking too. And if Garrett's been talking to girls who are pretty, maybe they don't feel like he's in their league.

I didn't make a big deal out of it when we were talking, because I don't think he wanted to talk about it a lot. But afterwards, I was thinking that if we decide to do a visit, I should definitely go out to Northrop to see him instead of him coming here. Obviously, I'm hoping something'll happen between us, but also, I thought, maybe if the other people at his school see us together, he might feel better. Because I know sometimes that works: if you're hanging out with a cool person, you feel cool, and other people think you're cool. Not that I'm super cool, but I guess people like how I look, so I thought it might help.

Ellen Hutchinson, professor of sociology at Pembleton:
I admire the students who are putting forth this initiative. Their idealism heartens me, but I have mixed feelings about their goal.

Like anyone else who's my age, I've had to come to terms with the effects time has had on my appearance. It wasn't an easy thing to get used to, but I've reached the point where I'm content with the way I look. Although I can't deny that I'm curious to see what a calli-only community would be like; maybe there a woman my age wouldn't become invisible when a young woman entered the room.

But would I have wanted to adopt calli when I was young? I don't know. I'm sure it would've spared me some of the distress I felt about growing older. But I *liked* the way I looked when I was young. I wouldn't have wanted to give that up. I'm not sure if, as I grew older, there was ever a point when the benefits would have outweighed the costs for me.

And these students, they might never even lose the beauty of youth. With the gene therapies coming out now, they'll probably look young for decades, maybe even their entire lives. They might never have to make the adjustments I did, in which case adopting calli wouldn't even save them from pain later on. So the idea that they might voluntarily give up one of the pleasures of youth is almost galling. Sometimes I want to shake them and say, "No! Don't you realize what you have?"

I've always liked young people's willingness to fight for their beliefs. That's one reason I've never really believed in the cliché that youth is wasted on the young. But this initiative would bring the cliché closer to reality, and I would hate for that to be the case.

Joseph Weingartner:
I've tried calliagnosia for a day; I've tried a wide variety of agnosias for limited periods. Most neurologists do, so we can better understand these conditions and empathize with our patients. But I couldn't adopt calliagnosia on a long-term basis, if for no other reason than that I see patients.

There's a slight interaction between calliagnosia and the ability to gauge a person's health visually. It certainly doesn't make you blind to things like a person's skin tone, and a calliagnosic can recognize symptoms of illness just like anyone else does; this is something that general cognition handles perfectly well. But physicians need to be sensitive to very subtle cues when evaluating a patient; sometimes you use your intuition when making a diagnosis, and calliagnosia would act as a handicap in such situations.

Of course, I'd be disingenuous if I claimed that professional requirements were the only thing keeping me from adopting calliagnosia. The more relevant question is, would I choose calliagnosia if I did nothing but lab research and never dealt with patients? And to that, my answer is, no. Like many other people, I enjoy seeing a pretty face, but I consider myself mature enough to not let that affect my judgment.

Tamera Lyons:
I can't believe it, Garrett got his calli turned back on.

We were talking on the phone last night, just ordinary stuff, and I ask him if he wants to switch to video. And he's like, "Okay," so we do. And then I realize he's not looking at me the same way he was before. So I ask him if everything's okay with him, and that's when he tells me about getting calli again.

He said he did it because he wasn't happy about the way he looked. I asked him if someone had said something about it, because he should ignore them, but he said it wasn't that. He just didn't like how he felt when he saw himself in a mirror. So I was like, "What are you talking about, you look cute." I tried to get him to give it another chance, saying stuff like, he should spend more time without calli before making any decisions. Garrett said he'd think about it, but I don't know what he's going to do.

Anyway, afterwards, I was thinking about what I'd said to him. Did I tell him that because I don't like calli, or because I wanted him to see how I looked? I mean, of course I liked the way he looked at me, and I was hoping it would lead somewhere, but it's not as if I'm being inconsistent, is it? If I'd always been in favor of calli, but made an exception when it came to Garrett, that'd be different. But I'm against calli, so it's not like that.

Oh, who am I kidding? I wanted Garrett to get his calli turned off for my own benefit, not because I'm anti-calli. And it's not even that I'm anti-calli, so much, as I am against calli being a requirement. I don't want anyone else deciding calli's right for me: not my parents, not a student organization. But if someone decides they want calli themselves, that's fine, whatever. So I should let Garrett decide for himself, I know that.

It's just frustrating. I mean, I had this whole plan figured out, with Garrett finding me irresistible, and realizing what a mistake he'd made. So I'm disappointed, that's all.

From Maria deSouza's speech the day before the election:
We've reached a point where we can begin to adjust our minds. The question is, when is it appropriate for us to do so? We shouldn't automatically accept that natural is better, nor should we automatically presume that we can improve on nature. It's up to us to decide which qualities we value, and what's the best way to achieve those.

I say that physical beauty is something we no longer need.

Calli doesn't mean that you'll never see anyone as beautiful. When you see a smile that's genuine, you'll see beauty. When you see an act of courage or generosity, you'll see beauty. Most of all, when you look at someone you love, you'll see beauty. All calli does is keep you from being distracted by surfaces. True beauty is what you see with the eyes of love, and that's something that nothing can obscure.

From the speech netcast by Rebecca Boyer, spokesperson for People for Ethical Nanomedicine, the day before the election:
You might be able to create a pure calli society in an artificial setting, but in the real world, you're never going to get a hundred percent compliance. And that is calli's weakness. Calli works fine if everybody has it, but if even one person doesn't, that person will take advantage of everyone else.

There'll always be people who don't get calli; you know that. Just think about what those people could do. A manager could promote attractive employees and demote ugly ones, but you won't even notice. A teacher could reward attractive students and punish ugly ones, but you won't be able to tell. All the discrimination you hate could be taking place, without you even realizing.

Of course, it's possible those things won't happen. But if people could always be trusted to do what's right, no one would have suggested calli in the first place. In fact, the people prone to such behavior are liable to do it even more once there's no chance of their getting caught.

If you're outraged by that sort of lookism, how can you afford to get calli? You're precisely the type of person who's needed to blow the whistle on that behavior, but if you've got calli, you won't be able to recognize it.

If you want to fight discrimination, keep your eyes open.

———

From a netcast of EduNews:
The calliagnosia initiative sponsored by students at Pembleton University was defeated by a vote of sixty-four percent to thirty-six percent.

Polls showed a majority favoring the initiative until days before the election. Many students say they were previously planning to vote for the initiative, but reconsidered after seeing the speech given by Rebecca Boyer of the People for Ethical Nanomedicine. This despite an earlier revelation that PEN was established by cosmetics companies to oppose the calliagnosia movement.

Maria deSouza:
Of course it's disappointing, but we originally thought of the initiative as a long shot. That period when the majority supported it was something of a fluke, so I can't be too disappointed about people changing their minds. The important thing is that people everywhere are talking about the value of appearances, and more of them are thinking about calli seriously.

And we're not stopping; in fact, the next few years will be a very exciting time. A spex manufacturer just demonstrated some new technology that could change everything. They've figured out a way to fit somatic positioning beacons in a pair of spex, custom-calibrated for a single person. That means no more helmet, no more office visit needed to reprogram your neurostat; you can just put on your spex and do it yourself. That means you'll be able to turn your calli on or off, *any time you want.*

That means we won't have the problem of people feeling that they have to give up beauty altogether. Instead, we can promote the idea that beauty is appropriate in some situations and not in others. For example, people could keep calli enabled when they're working, but disable it when they're among friends. I think people recognize that calli offers benefits, and will choose it on at least a part-time basis.

I'd say the ultimate goal is for calli to be considered the proper way to behave in polite society. People can always disable their calli in private, but the default for public interaction would be freedom from lookism. Appreciating beauty would become a consensual interaction, something you do only when both parties, the beholder and the beheld, agree to it.

From a netcast of EduNews:
In the latest developments regarding the Pembleton calliagnosia initiative, EduNews has learned that a new form of digital manipulation was used on the netcast of PEN spokesperson Rebecca Boyer's speech. EduNews has received files from the SemioTech Warriors that contain what appear to be two recorded versions of the speech: an original, acquired from the Wyatt/Hayes computers, and the netcast version. The files also include the SemioTech Warriors' analysis of the differences between the two versions.

The discrepancies are primarily enhancements to Ms. Boyer's voice intonation, facial expressions, and body language. Viewers who watched the original version rate Ms. Boyer's performance as good, while those who watched the edited version rate her performance as excellent, describing her as extraordinarily dynamic and persuasive. Based on their analysis, the SemioTech Warriors believe that Wyatt/Hayes has developed new software capable of fine-tuning paralinguistic cues in order to maximize the emotional response evoked in viewers. This dramatically increases the effectiveness of recorded presentations, especially when viewed through spex, and its use in the PEN netcast is likely what caused many supporters of the calliagnosia initiative to change their votes.

Walter Lambert, president of the National Calliagnosia Association:
In my entire career, I've met only a couple people who have the kind of charisma they gave Ms. Boyer in that speech. People like that radiate a kind of reality-distortion field that lets them convince you of almost anything. You feel moved by their very presence, you're ready

to open your wallet or agree to whatever they ask. It's not until later that you remember all the objections you had, but by then, often as not, it's too late. And I'm truly frightened by the prospect of corporations being able to generate that effect with software.

What this is, is another kind of supernormal stimuli, like flawless beauty but even more dangerous. We had a defense against beauty, and Wyatt/Hayes has escalated things to the next level. And protecting ourselves from this type of persuasion is going to be a hell of a lot harder.

There is a type of tonal agnosia, or aprosodia, that makes you unable to hear voice intonation; all you hear are the words, not the delivery. There's also an agnosia that prevents you from recognizing facial expressions. Adopting the two of these would protect you from this type of manipulation, because you'd have to judge a speech purely on its content; its delivery would be invisible to you. But I can't recommend them. The result is nothing like calli. If you can't hear tone of voice or read someone's expression, your ability to interact with others is crippled. It'd be a kind of high-functioning autism. A few NCA members *are* adopting both agnosias, as a form of protest, but no one expects many people will follow their example.

So that means that once this software gets into widespread use, we're going to be facing extraordinarily persuasive pitches from all sides: commercials, press releases, evangelists. We'll hear the most stirring speeches given by a politician or general in decades. Even activists and culture jammers will use it, just to keep up with the establishment. Once the range of this software gets wide enough, even the movies will use it, too: an actor's own ability won't matter, because everyone's performance will be uncanny.

The same thing'll happen as happened with beauty: our environment will become saturated with this supernormal stimuli, and it'll affect our interaction with real people. When every speaker on a netcast has the presence of a Winston Churchill or a Martin Luther King, we'll begin to regard ordinary people, with their average use of paralinguistic cues, as bland and unpersuasive. We'll become dissatisfied with the people we interact with in real life, because they won't be as engaging as the projections we see through our spex.

I just hope those spex for reprogramming neurostat hit the market soon. Then maybe we can encourage people to adopt the stronger agnosias just when they're watching video. That may be the only way for us to preserve authentic human interaction: if we save our emotional responses for real life.

Tamera Lyons:
I know how this is going to sound, but . . . well, I'm thinking about getting my calli turned back on.

In a way, it's because of that PEN video. I don't mean I'm getting calli just because makeup companies don't want people to and I'm angry at them. That's not it. But it's hard to explain.

I *am* angry at them, because they used a trick to manipulate people; they weren't playing fair. But what it made me realize was, I was doing the same kind of thing to Garrett. Or I wanted to, anyway. I was trying to use my looks to win him back. And in a way that's not playing fair, either.

I don't mean that I'm as bad as the advertisers are! I love Garrett, and they just want to make money. But remember when I was talking about beauty as a kind of magic spell? It gives you an advantage, and I think it's very easy to misuse something like that. And what calli does is make a person immune to that sort of spell. So I figure I shouldn't mind if Garrett would rather be immune, because I shouldn't be trying to gain an advantage in the first place. If I get him back, I want it to be by playing fair, by him loving me for myself.

I know, just because he got his calli turned back on doesn't mean that I have to. I've really been enjoying seeing what faces look like. But if Garrett's going to be immune, I feel like I should be too. So we're even, you know? And if we do get back together, maybe we'll get those new spex they're talking about. Then we can turn off our calli when we're by ourselves, just the two of us.

And I guess calli makes sense for other reasons, too. Those makeup companies and everyone else, they're just trying to create needs in you that you wouldn't feel if they were playing fair, and I don't like that. If I'm going to be dazzled watching a commercial, it'll be when I'm in the mood, not whenever they spring it on me. Although I'm not going to get those other agnosias, like that tonal one, not yet anyway. Maybe once those new spex come out.

This doesn't mean I agree with my parents' having me grow up with calli. I still think they were wrong; they thought getting rid of beauty would help make a utopia, and I don't believe that at all. Beauty isn't the problem, it's how some people are misusing it that's the problem. And that's what calli's good for; it lets you guard against that. I don't know, maybe this wasn't a problem back in my parents' day. But it's something we have to deal with now.

Story Notes

"Tower of Babylon"

This story was inspired by a conversation with a friend, when he mentioned the version of the Tower of Babel myth he'd been taught in Hebrew school. At that point I knew only the Old Testament account, and it hadn't made a big impression on me. But in the more elaborate version, the tower is so tall that it takes a year to climb, and when a man falls to his death, no one mourns, but when a brick is dropped, the bricklayers weep because it will take a year to replace.

The original legend is about the consequences of defying God. For me, however, the tale conjured up images of a fantastic city in the sky, reminiscent of Magritte's *Castle of the Pyrenees*. I was captivated by the audacity of such a vision, and started wondering what life in such a city would be like.

Tom Disch called this story "Babylonian science fiction." I hadn't thought about it that way when I was writing it—the Babylonians certainly knew enough physics and astronomy to recognize this story as fanciful—but I understood what he meant. The characters may be religious, but they rely on engineering rather than prayer. No deity makes an appearance in the story; everything that happens can be understood in purely mechanistic terms. It's in that sense that—despite the obvious difference in cosmology—the universe in the story resembles our own.

"Understand"

This is the oldest story in this volume, and might never have been published if it weren't for Spider Robinson, one of my instructors at Clarion. This story had collected a bunch of rejection slips when I first sent it out, but Spider encouraged me to resubmit it after I had Clarion on my resume. I made some revisions and sent it out, and it got a much better response the second time around.

The initial germ for this story was an offhand remark made by a roommate of mine in college; he was reading Sartre's *Nausea* at the time, whose protagonist finds only meaninglessness in everything he sees. But what would it be like, my roommate wondered, to find meaning and order in everything you saw? To me that suggested a kind of heightened perception, which in turn suggested superintelligence. I started thinking about the point at which quantitative improvements—better memory, faster pattern recognition—turn into a qualitative difference, a fundamentally different mode of cognition.

Something else I wondered about was the possibility of truly understanding how our minds work. Some people are certain that it's impossible for us to understand our minds, offering analogies like "you can't see your face with your own eyes." I never found that persuasive. It may turn out that we can't, in fact, understand our minds (for certain values of "understand" and "mind"), but it'll take an argument much more persuasive than that to convince me.

"Division by Zero"

There's a famous equation that looks like this:

$$e^{\pi i} + 1 = 0$$

When I first saw the derivation of this equation, my jaw dropped in amazement. Let me try to explain why.

One of the things we admire most in fiction is an ending that is surprising, yet inevitable. This is also what characterizes elegance in design: the invention that's clever yet seems totally natural. Of course we know that they aren't *really* inevitable; it's human ingenuity that makes them seem that way, temporarily.

Now consider the equation mentioned above. It's definitely surprising; you could work with the numbers e, π, and i for years, each in a dozen different contexts, without realizing they intersected in this particular way. Yet once you've seen the derivation, you feel that this equation really is inevitable, that this is the only way things could be. It's a feeling of awe, as if you've come into contact with absolute truth.

A proof that mathematics is inconsistent, and that all its wondrous beauty was just an illusion, would, it seemed to me, be one of the worst things you could ever learn.

"Story of Your Life"

This story grew out of my interest in the variational principles of physics. I've found these principles fascinating ever since I first learned of them, but I didn't know how to use them in a story until I saw a performance of *Time Flies When You're Alive*, Paul Linke's one-man show about his wife's battle with breast cancer. It occurred to me then that I might be able to use variational principles to tell a story about a person's response to the inevitable. A few years later, that notion combined with a friend's remark about her newborn baby to form the nucleus of this story.

For those interested in physics, I should note that the story's discussion of Fermat's Principle of Least Time omits all mention of its quantum-mechanical underpinnings. The QM formulation is interesting in its own way, but I preferred the metaphoric possibilities of the classical version.

As for this story's theme, probably the most concise summation of it that I've seen appears in Kurt Vonnegut's introduction to the twenty-fifth-anniversary edition of *Slaughterhouse-Five*: "Stephen Hawking . . . found it tantalizing that we could not remember the future. But remembering the future is child's play for me now. I know what will become of my helpless, trusting babies because they are grown-ups now. I know how my closest friends will end up because so many of them are retired or dead now . . . To Stephen Hawking and all others younger than myself I say, 'Be patient. Your future will come to you and lie down at your feet like a dog who knows and loves you no matter what you are.'"

"Seventy-Two Letters"

This story came about when I noticed a connection between two ideas I'd previously thought were unrelated. The first one was the golem.

In what's probably the best-known story of the golem, Rabbi Loew of Prague brings a clay statue to life to act as a defender of the Jews, protecting them from persecution. It turns out this story is a modern invention, dating back only to 1909. Stories in which the golem is used as a servant to perform chores—with varying degrees of success—originated in the 1500s, but they still aren't the oldest references to the golem. In stories dating back to the second century, rabbis would animate golems not to accomplish anything practical, but rather to demonstrate mastery of the art of permutating letters; they sought to know God better by performing acts of creation.

The whole theme of the creative power of language has been discussed elsewhere, by people smarter than me. What I found particularly interesting about golems was the fact that they're traditionally unable to speak. Since the golem is created through language, this limitation is also a limitation on reproduction. If a golem were able to use language, it would be capable of self-replication, rather like a Von Neumann machine.

The other idea I'd been thinking about was preformation, the theory that organisms exist fully formed in the germ cells of their parents. It's easy for people now to dismiss it as ridiculous, but at the time, preformation made a lot of sense. It was an attempt to solve the problem of how living organisms are able to replicate themselves, which is the same problem that later inspired Von Neumann machines. When I recognized that, it seemed that I was interested in these two ideas for the same reason, and I knew I had to write about them.

"The Evolution of Human Science"

This short-short was written for the British science journal *Nature*. Throughout the year 2000, *Nature* ran a feature called "Futures"; each week a different writer provided a short fictional treatment of a scientific development occurring in the next millenium.

Since the piece would appear in a scientific journal, making it *about* a scientific journal seemed like a natural choice. I started wondering about what such a journal might look like after the advent of superhuman intelligence. William Gibson once said, "The future is already here; it's just not evenly distributed." Right now there are people in the world who, if they're aware of the computer revolution at all, know of it only as something happening to other people, somewhere else. I expect that will remain true no matter what technological revolutions await us.

(A note about the title: this short-short originally appeared under a title chosen by the editors of *Nature*; I've chosen to restore its original title for this reprint.)

"Hell Is the Absence of God"

I first wanted to write a story about angels after seeing the movie *The Prophecy*, a supernatural thriller written and directed by Gregory Widen. For a long time I tried to think of a story in which angels were characters, but couldn't come up with a scenario I liked; it was only when I started thinking about angels as phenomena of terrifying power, whose visitations resembled natural disasters, that I was able to move forward. (Perhaps I was subconsciously thinking of Annie Dillard. Later on I remembered she once wrote that if people had more belief, they'd wear crash helmets when attending church, and lash themselves to the pews.)

Thinking about natural disasters led to thinking about the problem of innocent suffering. An enormous range of advice has been offered from a religious perspective to those who suffer, and it seems clear that no single response can satisfy everyone; what comforts one person inevitably strikes someone else as outrageous. Consider the Book of Job as an example.

For me, one of the unsatisfying things about the Book of Job is that, in the end, God rewards Job. Leave aside the question of whether new children can compensate for the loss of his original ones. Why does God restore Job's fortunes at all? Why the happy ending? One of the basic messages of the book is that virtue isn't always rewarded; bad things happen to good people. Job ultimately accepts this, demonstrating virtue, and is subsequently rewarded. Doesn't this undercut the message?

It seems to me that the Book of Job lacks the courage of its convictions: if the author were really committed to the idea that virtue isn't always rewarded, shouldn't the book have ended with Job still bereft of everything?

"Liking What You See: A Documentary"

Psychologists once conducted an experiment where they repeatedly left a fake college application in an airport, supposedly forgotten by a traveler. The answers on the application were always the same, but each time they included a different photo of the fictitious applicant. It turned out people were more likely to mail in the application if the applicant was attractive. This is perhaps not surprising, but it illustrates just how thoroughly we're influenced by appearances; we favor attractive people even in a situation where we'll never meet them.

Yet any discussion of beauty's advantages is usually accompanied by a mention of the burden of beauty. I don't doubt that beauty has its drawbacks, but so does everything else. Why do people seem more sympathetic to the idea of burdensome beauty than to, say, the idea of burdensome wealth? It's because beauty is working its magic again: even in a discussion of its drawbacks, beauty is providing its possessors with an advantage.

I expect physical beauty will be around for as long as we have bodies and eyes. But if calliagnosia ever becomes available, I for one will give it a try.

Acknowledgments

Thanks to Michelle for being my sister, and thanks to my parents, Fu-Pen and Charlotte, for their sacrifices.

Thanks to the participants of Clarion, Acme Rhetoric, and Sycamore Hill for letting me work with them. Thanks to Tom Disch for the visit, Spider Robinson for the phone call, Damon Knight and Kate Wilhelm for the guidance, Karen Fowler for the anecdotes, and John Crowley for reopening my eyes. Thanks to Larret Galasyn-Wright for encouragement when I needed it, and Danny Krashin for lending me his mind. Thanks to Alan Kaplan for all the conversations.

Thanks to Juliet Albertson for love. And thanks to Marcia Glover, for love.

Publication History

These stories were originally published as follows:

"Tower of Babylon," *Omni*, 1990
"Understand," *Asimov's*, 1991
"Division by Zero," *Full Spectrum 3*, 1991
"Story of Your Life," *Starlight 2*, 1998
"Seventy-Two Letters," *Vanishing Acts*, 2000
"The Evolution of Human Science," *Nature*, 2000
"Hell Is the Absence of God," *Starlight 3*, 2001
"Liking What You See: A Documentary," *Stories of Your Life and Others*, 2002